Pocket Full of Teeth

An Aimee Hardy Novel

Pocket Full of Teeth, A Novel

text copyright © 2024 Reserved by Aimee Hardy

Edited by Lisa Diane Kastner

Published in North America and Europe by Running Wild Press. Visit Running

Wild Press at www.runningwildpress.com, Educators, librarians, book clubs

(as well as the eternally curious), go to www.runningwildpress.com.

Paperback ISBN: 978-1-960018-53-3

eBook ISBN: 978-1-960018-55-7

Transcript

Just to be clear, this isn't my story, and I'm still not sure what is real and what isn't. You enjoying your tea?

It's a family recipe. It's no problem to make more if you want. I can just —

Well, just let me know. It's no trouble to make it for the two of ya. I've been working in the garage this morning, going through my mom's things, so I apologize for my appearance.

Okay. Can I adjust this mic first?

Ya sure it's workin right? Will it be able to hear everything?

Just me? Well, that's a little intimidating, but I guess that makes sense. I just hope I don't sound like I'm talking to myself.

There's tea in the pot, if you want it.

You sure?

Okay.

Yeah. I know why you're here. It was the necklace, wasn't it? The locket? That's how you tracked me down.

See, it's not that simple. To tell you about the body, we need to start with Cat's story.

She grew up in the town just like my mom. Her story's in that manuscript. Here, I brought it with me. The mayor sent it to my mom a few years ago. I didn't know why then. I guessed he thought she'd be able to check on what was real and what wasn't, and I'm sure he figured out her connection to the story early on, but I think I'm still tryna come to terms with it all. Yeah, make a note of that and be sure to ask Mr. Mayor what he was thinking, sending that story out like that.

No, I don't mean he's the murderer you're looking for. I just mean that it seems irresponsible to send it out, knowin full well what happened to the others.

1

Just look. Right there at the page on top. The mayor wrote about how it was cursed right from the beginning.

Well, hogwash or not, I'm a believer, and I'm happy to let you take it off my hands.

I guess he sent it because he thought Mom should hear Cat's story. I didn't even know she was from there. Not at first. I grew up in Atlanta. It's where Mom went to school and became the History Department Chair at Georgia State University at the time, so I never even thought about her bein' from somewhere else.

My mom? She died last year. No, it's fine now. I mean, I still get a little sad, but it's not like it was when she first passed away. You get these thoughts running through your head, you know? All the things that you could have said and should have done, only it's too late, and that makes it even worse because you can't go back. You can't just rewrite things and give them a happy ending. They're just done. Over with. And you have to move on.

Yeah, she got this manuscript during the summer of 2020. We were in the middle of the pandemic, and she desperately needed something to do besides watching the news.

No, she never talked to me about it. She didn't even finish her research before she died, and I didn't know about it until I found it buried in the back of her desk drawer.

Sure. We were close when I was little. I grew up with my mom and dad in this house. My mom was strict, and she worked a lot. She got a position at Georgia State when I was still in diapers, and I always saw her with some kind of book or journal in her hands. You should have seen our house before I cleaned out a bunch of her things. If we'd ever had a fire, the place would have burned for months with so many books inside.

After my father passed away, our

relationship became even more strained — so strained, in fact, that we didn't speak for almost a decade. My father? Sure, he worked for Atlanta Gas and managed the night shift, but he was coming home one morning and fell asleep. No, it was a long time ago. I'm fine now. Well, there's not much to say about me. I was studying History, thanks to my mom, and was married to Stephen James, head of the History Department, again, thanks to my mom, but we'll get into that later.

I came back home after the divorce. The pandemic was just getting started, and I had no idea what was in store.

Home. That's a funny word, isn't it? It was the only place that felt safe, and coming home allowed me to make amends, but home feels different when you've gone away and then come back, doesn't it?

I always knew Mom was holding things back. She'd get quiet when I'd ask her about her childhood — if she had any siblings, what were her Christmas traditions, did she go on any family trips — that kinda thing.

So, when she passed away last year, I found this manuscript in her things. It was nearly complete and edited, yet it was hidden in a drawer. Was she unhappy with the story? Was it too tragic? Did she just not have the time to finish it and send it back?

I found answers as I read, as will you, no doubt, but I know I'll need to fill in some holes. Mom provided tons of research, and I've left her footnotes in so you can read through them. She was able to confirm most of the facts from her resources at Georgia State and her connections to the University of Alabama at Birmingham, Alabama state archives, the National Register of Historic Places. There's research from books about Alabama history, local newspapers, tax records, marriage licenses, birth certificates, death certificates, and property records. She was thorough.

I guess it all starts with the Saunders Estate built in 1821, but there's stories about the place from centuries before. It's interesting, isn't it, how stories sometimes can't be separated from the land they're on.

From what Mom found, the town was established in 1807 by a guy named Thomas Saunders. He was a wealthy landowner who ran several steel and coal mines in the early 1800s. The mines brought lots of money, all that coal and iron, and Saunders wanted to establish a sort of dream community for himself and his friends in the mountains, so he split the land into twenty plots and sold most of them to his friends.

He built a grocery store, post office, pharmacy, church, even a recreation hall that would show movies and host dinners. They even had a newspaper — The Daily Tribune — although it was published weekly, and get this, they published their first issue on April Fool's Day. I'm not joking.

I'm gettin to it. I promise. To me, this story is a circle. A year in the life of a girl who was lost and wanted to come back home. At least it started that way. There are a lot of parallels between the two of us, and to tell my story — and the story about the body — I have to tell her's as well. Stories are like that, aren't they? My story affects your story which affects someone else's. You could go home after this and forget this whole thing, but one day, when you least expect it, you'll turn to someone and say, "Hey, remember that body they found out at the old Saunders' well? Shoot, do I have a story for you…"

And the truth is, this story changed me. It's nice to see my mom living on in some way, even if it's just in Cat's footnotes. Truth be told, this story was a way to finally get to know her and to see my mom as a person all her own because even though it's not my story, it became a part of me. And I think it will change you, too.

As a warning, Cat talks about sensitive topics — such as abuse (both physical, verbal, and sexual), addiction, and mental health issues — all the things that can be sensitive to readers but are sadly a reality for many of us. And there are a few scary moments, so don't say I didn't warn ya.

So with that, I guess I'll just start readin, and we'll see how it all unfolds. Sounds good?

June 28th, 2020

Georgia State University
ATTN: History Department
35 Broad St NW
Atlanta, GA 30303

Dear Beatrix Sparrow,

We are writing in response to the historical items requested for a new display on the history of █████, and your name was sent to us as a specialist on this subject. This may be a little out of the ordinary. We usually send old tools, photographs, and antique furniture — but we came across this manuscript. It came to us from an estate sale in 2018 after the estate's owner passed away. Without any living relatives, the house and all its possessions went to the town in order to establish a park to honor Muscogee Creek land. The park covers 400 square acres on Blood Mountain, and we hope to establish it as a family recreational destination, complete with an activity center, hiking trails, and nature preserve. This manuscript was found in a canister buried in the backyard garden of the abandoned Saunders' estate. The memoir is estimated to have been written between the 1990s and the mid-2000s based on references to local businesses.

With the advent of the COVID-19 pandemic, the town looked to catalog and exhibit the artifacts themselves for an online virtual tour, yet mystery has surrounded this piece. The manuscript was first read by a construction worker by the name of Thomas Fredericks and then shared with the foreman, William Lovejoy. Two months later, Fredericks and Lovejoy were tragically struck by lightning as they worked on leveling the estate during a spring thunderstorm. The manuscript passed to Lovejoy's widow, who read it that summer. By the fall, she was diagnosed with stage IV pancreatic cancer. Friends and family members shared that the three said they noticed strange things after reading, but when pressed for specifics, they were not able to offer additional details. Since then, rumors have surrounded the manuscript as being haunted or cursed, but I read the manuscript, as did my secretary Gina Hall, and have not experienced any adverse effects. Although several members of our town expressed reservations about submitting it, the majority voted in favor with the hope that it might add to your exhibit and present a different viewpoint of local legends from our town.

I thought that this manuscript might interest you as you will see when you read. We've followed your writings on the historic Trussville and Springville communities, and we know that you have more resources and connections than we do and would like to pass along this mystery to someone who is more equipped to handle it. Even if this mystery is just an act of the imagination, hopefully, it will find a home in your hands. Feel free to contact us if you have further questions.

Sincerely,
John Dawes
Mayor of █████

JANUARY 2001

Mama always told me that secrets come out after sundown. She said that when the darkness of night crept into the corners of my room oily shadows would unfurl themselves from under my bed, while the crows sleeping in the tree outside my window would flutter to the pane's sharp edge to tap at the cracks in the casement, and the monster in my closet would sigh, opening its eyes before it scratched at the closet door. I'd only have to be quiet and listen.

I heard Mama's words in my head as I gripped the rusted trashcan of the dingy gas station[1]. Bile burned my throat until my stomach heaved again, and I heard hot liquid meet the cool plastic garbage bag. I stared at the fries from earlier, the only thing I had been able to eat in days as they settled in steaming chunks in the bottom of the trash bag. I was left spitting and trying to catch my breath.

"Card reader's not workin," I heard my quasi step-father, Ray, bark over my shoulder. His face drew up into a sour wince as he eyed the trash can.

I wiped my mouth with the back of my sleeve and shivered in the cold.

---

1 Marathon, established in 1986, is still in operation off Cartwright Rd. off Interstate 59.

"Here," Ray said as he pulled a crisp bill from his wallet. "Pay, and I'll pump."

I took the money and cringed, careful not to touch his fingers. Crossing the parking lot, the artificial lights overhead buzzed, and I couldn't help but notice the thick layer of dirt and grime that blanketed the gas station. *We're sick*, I thought. *Me. The gas station. Ray. We're all rotting from the inside.* I shook the thoughts from my head as I pushed my way into the gas station, thankful to get out of the chill.

"Help you?" I heard a sharp voice to my right. I jumped, and the voice cackled. "Didn't mean to startle ya, sweetheart."

I turned around to face an older woman at the counter. She was gray-haired and thin, with wrinkles that cut their way down her leathered cheeks. She wore a threadbare University of Alabama[2] t-shirt under a thick blue flannel and eyed me suspiciously. Her watchful eyes judged my every movement, making my skin feel like it crawled with insects.

"I need gas," I squeaked. My voice sounded slight and willowy. "We tried the card reader, but I don't think it-"

"Hasn't worked in years," the woman interrupted.

I nodded and held out a twenty-dollar bill.

The woman accepted the money with a jagged smile. "We don't get many pretty ladies like you in town. What brings ya here?"

"I'm headed home," I said and snuck a look at her face. Her narrowed eyes and missing teeth made my stomach tighten.

"Home?" She mimicked my voice and laughed again. "Anywhere around here?"

---

2 UAB, the University of Alabama at Birmingham, was founded June 16th, 1969, when it was established as a fully autonomous university through the University of Alabama System. It is a public research university offering over 140 programs of study and 12 academic divisions. It began as an academic extension center in 1936, became a four-year university in 1966, and is currently one of the largest academic medical centers in the United States.

"The Saunders Estate[3]," I muttered, half-hoping she wouldn't hear me so that I could move on.

"You live up there?" The woman asked with her eyebrows raised. The O of her mouth revealed even more missing teeth.

"Yeah," I gestured to my car outside. "I haven't been back in about a year, but-"

"Isn't that where that woman died? What was her name?" The woman interrupted. She stood with her mouth open. A trap for flies, my mother would have said.

"I'm on pump three." I slid the money on the counter closer to her.

"No one goes to the old Saunders house. Not even kids. Been rumors before I was born, but especially since that woman —"

"Is that it?" I asked, edging away from the counter.

The woman closed her mouth and picked up the money, sliding it into the register while keeping her eyes on me. I turned and headed back to the front of the store still feeling her eyes on me. The door dinged as I opened it and let the cold air inside.

"Her name was Sarah," I said over my shoulder, "and she was my mom."

I tightened my scarf against the incessant wind and jogged back to Ray's truck. He unscrewed the gas cap and watched as the gas pump's numbers ticked in a soft mechanical metronome. I shivered and opened the truck's heavy passenger door, sliding inside and pulling the door closed behind me.

I sat back, thankful for the quiet and the warmth inside the truck. Exhaling, I sat back and put a hand to my head as I closed my eyes. Everything faded away. The gas station. The nosy clerk. The truck around me. Even Ray.

---

3 This is the first mention of the Saunders Estate. Property records show that the town of ▮▮▮ was established in 1807 by Thomas Sauders. According to The Hidden History of Birmingham's Mines by Robert McClintock, Saunders was a wealthy land-owner who established several steel and coal mines in the early 1800s. The mines brought soaring profits, and Saunders wanted to establish a respite for himself and his friends in the mountains away from industry and larger cities.

A loud *BOOM* sounded outside the truck, and I jumped. My eyes snapped open when I heard another loud explosion.

Leaning forward in the cab and peering out the front windshield, I saw the red and blue crackle of fireworks that exploded over the tops of the bare trees. The air overhead shook with colorful thunder until the glittering explosions faded to nothing. Pulses of color and dark punctuated the night sky until I heard Ray replace the gas nozzle and open the driver's side door.

"Rednecks," he rolled his eyes before turning the keys in the ignition. "Too much time and ammo."

"It *is* New Year's," I shrugged, and Ray turned to look at me.

Ray chuffed and put the truck in first gear, pulling out of the parking lot. As we turned the corner, I saw more bright fireworks.

"Mama would make wishes on fireworks," I said in a voice that was just above a whisper. "She said she always -"

"Your mama's dead, Cat," Ray returned in a flat voice.

My eyes stung from his words, and I silently wished for Mama. I wished that she could come back, take me away, tuck me in, warm and safe and sound, and tell me one of her stories. I wanted to be anywhere else, anywhere else in the world but in that truck with Ray. My stomach churned, and my hands tightened into fists as a soundless rage burned in my chest.

As if reading my thoughts, Ray sighed. "It's only a year, Cat. That's what the courts said." He shifted gears as he drove through the old, deserted buildings of our small downtown.

I blinked away the tears and turned to look at his face. Illuminated by the streetlights, he was thinner than usual and looked like he had aged years in the past few months alone. Dark circles lined his eyes, and I could see new worry lines on his forehead, on his cheeks, circling his mouth. His Carhartt jacket was worn and dirty as were his jeans and work boots.

I didn't know how he tricked the judge into giving him custody of me. I knew he couldn't hold a steady job and that he must have exaggerated his financial records, but I was happy (if not a little nervous) to go back home.

I felt the familiar turn as Ray steered the truck onto our street that took us up Blood Mountain[4]. We followed the winding dirt drive up the mountain until it ended at the front of an old house, dark and solid in the January cold. I had thought about this house every day since I left and was struck by the permanence of it. Its brick met solid brick. Stone stacked onto stone. The walls stretched up three stories, and its dark windows held my gaze.

I couldn't stand being in that truck with Ray for one more second. I grabbed my bag from the floorboard and ran up the steps, wrapping my scarf around my neck as the cold wind bit at my heels. Fog clung to the top of the mountain, and a stinging, persistent rain made my hair damp and icy. I hopped from foot to foot, trying to stay warm until Ray mounted the steps and unlocked the front door.

Inside, the house smelled stale and unlived in. The wind outside began to howl between rough, bare tree trunks and skirted around the eaves before tumbling down the mountain. Tiny ice crystals pinged against the windows in a soft hiss, and gasps of frigid air slipped between the door seals and window frames. I could almost hear whispers in the next room as shadows poked their heads out of darkened closets and left oily marks along the walls.

"Heat's still busted, so I stacked some firewood in your room," Ray said as he hung up his jacket in the front hall. "Everything's pretty much the same."

---

4 Blood Mountain is in the north part of town. It was named in 1821 and sold to Saheter Sarubian, a Northerner who specialized in foreign trade (see property records for 1820). Sarubian built the house for his wife, Olivia Saunders, presumed to be Thomas Saunders's only daughter, as a wedding gift since it was built just after their marriage in the spring of 1820. The Daily Tribune (issues were released weekly, not daily as the title implies) published an article about the wedding in the town square. Olivia wore an imported lace dress from Paris. Her flowers were orchids shipped in from New York, and the cake was from a specialty pastry shop in Atlanta. A small reception was held in the recreation hall with music and dance lasting well into the night. A month after the wedding the two honeymooned in several cities across Europe and Asia before returning home six months later.

I looked around the front hall. Mama's flowers sat dry and preserved in the vase on the entryway table. Her jacket hung on its hook next to Ray's. Her boots pointed to the wall by the front door. My throat squeezed tight, and I opened my mouth to respond, but nothing came out.

I nodded instead and headed up the front steps.

"Welcome home, Cat," Ray called after me. "And happy birthday."

I paused, and one foot hovered mid-step. I took a breath, not daring to look at him, not daring to let him see my face; hot tears stung my eyes. The only thing that would hurt worse than losing Mama would be to fall apart in front of Ray, the man who ate her from the inside until there was nothing left.

I barely slept that first night. The rain turned to ice as soon as it fell, coating the trees and rooftop. The mountain echoed with the weight of the trees' frozen burden as branches cracked and popped in the harsh wind.[5]

I padded downstairs and made a fresh cup of tea from Mama's dried herbs. I sat at the kitchen table and watched the eastern horizon take on the purple hue of a deep bruise then ease to pink, then orange, then the yellow of sunrise.

As the sun rose, I could see downed tree limbs on the lawn. The sun filtered through the dirty window over the sink, falling

---

5 Winter ice storms were common in this region, particularly at higher elevations. A particularly bad ice storm struck in March of 1821, delaying construction of the Saunders Estate. There were reports of several accidents during the ice storm. The house was finished in 1821, in spite of strange accidents delaying the construction. A construction worker fell off the roof while installing the framing, breaking his back. Another three workers were injured; two were killed from a rare late-January tornado. The Daily Tribune covered the completion and "Welcome Home" party a little over a year after Saheter Sarubian and Olivia Saunders were first married, boasting the house's five bedrooms, three bathrooms, a formal dining room, library, sunroom, and gardens. Land at the back of the house featured a well that tapped into a local spring, a rose garden filled with white roses, waterfall, and a small orchard. Sarubian shipped in orange trees from Florida for his orchard, obviously unaware of the harsh winters in northern Alabama.

on the dirty dishes in the sink, the layers of grime that had been hidden in the darkness from the night before. The house, frozen as it was on the mountaintop, was also frozen in disuse and neglect.

"Cat." I jumped as Ray walked into the kitchen. "What are you doing in here?"

I turned around and lifted my mug. "Tea. Want some?" I offered. He shook his head, a look of disgust hung at the corners of his mouth.

"Stay outta here," he grumbled and made his way to the cabinet next to the stove. He was dressed in his customary flannel, worn jeans, and wool socks. A thin spot at the crown of his head shone in the light. He reached up and opened the kitchen cabinet, and the door cracked, ripping clean off its hinges.

"Jesus," Ray exhaled. "This whole house is falling apart."

He rubbed his head and set the cabinet door on the tiled floor before pulling out a mug from the shelf.

"We're out of food," I ventured, shifting on my feet as hope threaded its way into my voice. "I could pick some up if you need."

I was eager to get out of the house, to get away from Ray. He made a sound that wasn't a yes or a no but rather a groan of annoyance. He busied himself with the coffee instead until he turned and grunted over his shoulder, "Pick up some more coffee grounds while you're out. Milk. Eggs. But don't open anything. And stop lurking about."

His voice sharpened to a point, and I jumped. I headed to my room to change and grab my coat, then bounded down the stairs and grabbed and grabbed the wad of cash that Ray had left on the entryway table.

"Get the cheap stuff," he called from the kitchen. "Money's tight, so none of that name-brand business."

"Be back soon," I shouted and burst out the front door and into the cold morning air. As I walked down the long driveway, the ice melted slowly, and my walk into town was a cadence of color and receding ice.

The trees crowded the asphalt, and the small two-lane road wound through the mountains. Clotheslines held together each front lawn, and old cars sat rusting on rotted tires. Houses sighed as I passed, sagging gently in the middle, but their lazy slope didn't stop the welcoming feel of each front door.

The town appeared suddenly as if cut into the forest by a giant's hand making space for its toys. The buildings were made of rough brick that slanted at strange angles around the curving main street. There was an old-fashioned barbershop with Christmas lights in the window, a soda fountain featuring huge silver foil presents in the doorway, and a general store sign sprayed with fake snow. Even the lampposts were decorated with lighted snowflakes to celebrate the new year.[6]

At the town center, a group of sour-faced men sat outside the general store's fake-frosted sign. Their eyes turned toward me, and their frowns hardened, deepening the wrinkles that lined their eyes and the corners of their mouths. I hurried past them, concentrated on my steps, and avoided their glares. I could feel their breaths on my neck, jackals salivating as if I were prey. Panicked, I glanced around and found the first door to my left, yanked it open, and ducked inside.

The door closed behind me, and I was met with the warm smell of fresh coffee and maple muffins. Cozy chairs were well-worn, and soft jazz music played in waves from hidden speakers. Soft light streamed in from the front window where

---

6 The cafe seems to be a prominent part of downtown. After the nearby mines closed in 1950, several towns in the area struggled. Without a steady flow of mine workers, infrastructure crumbled, businesses moved closer to the Birmingham area, and only a few towns remained. ▮▮▮ is one of the few that survived by providing incentives for new businesses, including a few chain businesses, such as Starbucks, Chipotle, Yogurt Mountain, and Target. There has been a recent push to preserve the historic downtown buildings with the installation of historic markers and a small museum dedicated to the history of mining in the area.

condensation crept up the glass, obscuring the cold outside world from the toasty inside of the cafe[7].

"Good morning," a voice sang from behind the counter.

I turned around and spotted her.

She was a petite woman, thin and graceful, and she refilled the coffee mugs of a young couple crouched nose to nose. Her hair was pulled back into a low bun, but a few strands had escaped her rubber band. Her powder blue shirt shone bright like an aching and empty sky, and when she opened her mouth, her smile reached all the way to her eyes. I didn't need to see her nametag to know that it was Liz.

"'Mornin', what can I get ya?" She asked without looking up.

I sat down at the counter and ran my hand through my windswept hair. I could feel the weight of dark circles in the space just under my eyes from not sleeping. Slipping off my coat, I felt self-conscious about my old tee shirt.

"I'll have tea and a muffin if you still have them," I said as I tried to catch her eye.

Liz wiped the glittering Formica countertop and tossed her rag on the workspace behind her. Then she gestured to a list of entrees on a chalkboard menu above the counter. Without looking up, she said, "I have blueberry and banana muffins. I also have sandwiches if you'd like a melt or some soup. Perfect for this chilly weather."

Finally, she turned and looked at me and stopped short. Her mouth opened, and I held my breath for what she might say, but she smiled instead and put her hands on her hips.

"Soup sounds great," I started. "And maybe a turkey melt?"

She nodded. "And a tea, you said?"

---

7 Front Paige News was established in 1978 by Paige Livingston. The shop changed various owners over the years and ended up being purchased by the Johns family, who frequently bought struggling shops and plots of land. By 1992, the Johnss diversified their business model and developed the land into subdivisions, bringing in more business and more profits. Currently, the Johns family owns all of the shopping plazas which are rented by local business and supported by the influx of families living in their subdivisions.

"English Breakfast, if you have it."

I sat back in my chair and noticed the couple next to me grab their coats. They wove through the tables on the way to the door. Their skin seemed to be made of magnets, and every time they separated, their hands found one another. I could feel the aching in their palms even as they walked out the door and into the cold.

I turned my attention back to Liz. Her fingers twitched as if she were playing a symphony that crescendoed as the sandwich sizzled in the press. She was different from when I last saw her. Taller. Her braces were gone. But she still had that same friendliness about her that put me at ease when I was around her.

She wiped her forehead with the back of her forearm and reached across the counter for a square of butcher paper when her arm grazed the grill. *Hssssss*, her skin sizzled at the touch.

"Ouch," she said, snatching her arm away from the heat. She inhaled as she looked down at her arm. An angry red mark was already showing.

"Do you have any vinegar or honey?" I asked as I reached for her arm, a gesture that caught us both off guard. "They can help," I said as I gestured to see her arm. She looked down at the quickly-swelling burn as I continued. "Vinegar will help it heal faster, and honey will stop the blistering."

"Really?" She asked, looking up at me, still unsure.

"Yeah, I can show you," I said.[8]

Liz hesitated, taking me in as her eyes moved over my face before she bent down to gather the vinegar and honey from behind the counter.

"So, you're back?" She asked as she put the jars on the counter.

"I just got back last night," I said as I dabbed vinegar onto a paper napkin and softly blew on her arm. The crease in her brow softened as the sting eased. "We were frozen in until a few hours

---

8 Vinegar is acetic and can relieve pain, itching, and inflammation. It has been used to pull the heat away from burns and relieve pain naturally. Honey is an anti-inflammatory and an antibacterial and acts to heal the burn. Other natural remedies for burns include cold water compress, aloe vera, and coconut oil.

ago."

She raised her eyebrows, and I uncapped the honey.

"How's Ray?" She asked without meeting my gaze.

I shrugged but didn't reply. Instead, I dabbed the honey on her burn carefully.

"Where did you learn all this?" She gestured to her arm as she admired my work.

"My mom, actually," I said, pulling back slightly. "She knew all about this kind of stuff."[9]

Liz smiled, and behind her, something popped on the grill.

"Shit, your sandwich," she muttered as she turned around. By the time she pried the burnt remnants off the grill, the cafe was filled with smoke.

"I'm so sorry," she said, redness creeping into her cheeks. "I'm not usually so clumsy. Hold on a minute, and I can make you another."

"Don't worry about it," I reassured her. I glanced outside, and gray clouds were building once again on the horizon. The bare trees outside shook in the cold.

"No, it's fine. I can just —"

"It's okay," I said, standing up and grabbing my jacket. I couldn't afford to be caught unaware in another ice storm. "I need to run by the general store to get some stuff, anyway."

Liz nodded and slid two muffins into a paper bag before pushing it across the counter. "Blueberry. They're Ray's favorite. At least they used to be."

I felt my stomach flop as I thought about Ray, and I stopped buttoning my jacket and looked up, noticing the eagerness in her eyes like she had so much to stay but didn't know where to start. It was a look that I had gotten a lot in the past year. "I'd better head out before we get more ice."

---

9 Many southern remedies were passed down in families and in farmer publications, including the farmer's almanac. Some populations still practice natural medicine, similar to Eastern medicine. Many remedies have been confirmed by science while others have been debunked.

The clouds outside leered over the mountains. "Good idea," she said as she smiled and leaned her elbows on the counter. "Maybe I'll come by sometime, Cat."

I nodded, still not able to meet her eyes, pushed the door open, and made my way past the grumpy men. The wind cut through my jacket as I headed out into the cold afternoon.[10]

In the general store, I loaded up my cart, making a few meals in my head. When I passed a lady and her young son, the woman pulled him to her chest. An older woman on the next aisle dropped her oatmeal and practically ran to the next aisle. At checkout, the young man couldn't take his eyes off me.

"Something wrong?" I asked, cringing under his stare but not wanting to appear weak.

"Sorry," he muttered.

I shook my head and pulled out my wallet.

Did they think it was catching? That death was contagious?[11]

I paid for the groceries and piled the bulging paper bags in my arms, thankful that most of the bags blocked my view of the shoppers around me.

The cold outside cut through my jacket, and I hugged the grocery bags closer to me. I could hear the men whisper as I passed. Just as I rounded the corner, a gust of wind slammed into my chest, and I heard one of the sacks rip as various canned goods fell to the asphalt, rolling in silver flashes onto the road.

"I got it," a deep voice called behind me, and when I turned around, a guy around my age jogged over with a smile.

He was tall and muscular. His eyes were dark and friendly, the color of fresh dirt from the garden, and his orange flannel shirt

---

10 Liz is Elizabeth Greene, born in 1980, daughter of Carrie Greene, sister of Ray, who is Cat's stepfather. Through this interaction, we can assume that although Cat and Liz might have known each other distantly, they were never close growing up.

11 Although death is not considered contagious in southern superstitions, some legends persist, including covering mirrors after a death, painting a porch "haint blue" to scare away evil spirits, and death and tragedy occurring in threes.

flashed in the sun. His hair fell across his forehead in a way that felt both practiced and accidental, like a magazine cover, posed yet candid. I knew that face. Owen.

He scooped up the cans and took a bag from my arms, placing each one carefully inside.

"Uh, thanks," I muttered, taking a step back.

"No problem," Owen returned with a smile. His teeth[12] were perfectly white, and his eyes were gentle and curious. Did he really not recognize me?

"Where are you parked?" He nodded toward the parking lot.

"I walked, actually," I shrugged.

"From where?"

"Blood Mountain," I said, and he stopped in his tracks, his eyes filled with surprise.

"Wait, Cat?" He looked at me, measuring me up from the tips of my toes to the top of my head. I was suddenly more than just a damsel in distress. I was someone of interest.

I nodded and stuffed my hands in my pockets.

"Cat," he repeated, his smile grew impossibly bigger. His surprised expression was replaced by impressed curiosity, and he followed me as I started to walk back through town. "I heard you were back in town. It's a long walk up that mountain, you know."

"I'll be fine," I said, reaching for my overstuffed bag of groceries.

He pulled back playfully. "You know my mama would kill me if I let you walk. Want a ride?" He raised his eyebrows.

"I'm okay." I shook my head, still reaching for the bag, an

---

12 This is the first mention of teeth. Teeth have various symbols throughout literature. In ancient Ireland, wisdom teeth were connected to poetic enlightenment. The Tooth Fairy in Western culture refers to a mythical creature that collects children's teeth. In fact, children's teeth were so valuable in Norse culture that they were collected to protect soldiers on the battlefield and were even traded as currency. In Bram Stroker's Dracula, teeth are a symbol of dangerous sexuality used to intimidate and later penetrate unsuspecting victims. Carrying on the theme of virality, Sigmund Freud famously published The Interpretation of Dreams which likens teeth in dreams to sexuality and a desire for children. Today, if someone is "toothy" or "tasty" (or more recently described as a "snack"), they are described as sexually attractive.

image of Marianne, Mama's best friend growing up, came to mind. Manicured. Polite. Always the social butterfly.

"I'm not doubting you could make it," he winked, "but I'm headed that way anyway."

Was he flirting with me? I wasn't used to guys flirting with me, even before everything happened, so his advances made me uncomfortable.

"It's fine, really." I kept walking and tried to gauge him without staring. His stride easily matched my own, and he nudged me.

"Come on, it's cold. I'm right over here," he changed course and stepped toward a small parking lot where a few cars were parked between long-faded white lines.

I sighed, not having a choice, and followed him and the grocery bags to a battered Jeep the color of week-old snow.

"The Owen-mobile is over here[13]," he said over his shoulder. He unlocked the passenger door and opened it for me before moving to the driver's side. I watched him, still trying to understand his intentions. He slid inside and put the groceries on the seat beside him, cranking the car and warming his hands.

"You coming? It's freezing out," he said as he gestured to the open door, urging me to get inside and close the door so he could get warm.

I sighed one more time. This was definitely a bad idea, but against my better judgment, I slid inside and closed the heavy metal door.

Owen smiled and shifted the Jeep into drive before guiding the car out of the parking lot. He followed the road through town and up the winding road toward Blood Mountain. I felt secure with the bag of groceries beside us and turned my head to look at him.

He was devastatingly handsome. He had grown up since I last

---

13 Owen Smith, born in 1985, would have been sixteen. He was the son of Marianne Johns and the distant relative of Sheriff Smythe, one of the town's first police officers who was sworn into office in 1831.

saw him and had what Mama called a strong jaw. He was muscular but lean. His large hands gripped the steering wheel, and there was something about him that made me feel safe, which made me even leerier because no one made me feel safe except for Mama, and even that had resulted in me being all alone in the end.

I sighed and had to fill the silence.

"So, what *is* this?" I said with a sharpness in my voice.

"What do you mean?" He raised his eyebrows but kept his eyes on the road.

"Giving me a ride home." I gestured to the road and the groceries beside us.

"It's freezing out. I couldn't let you walk all that way. Besides, you know how my mom is." He shook his head as if I had just suggested something completely outrageous, as if my walking home was inconceivable, and with Marianne as his mom, I guess it was.

I shrugged, warming my hands in front of the heater. "I haven't even seen your mom in over a year, and I don't know the last time she and Mama talked. It's strange to think she still cares." I wasn't complaining, but I didn't trust good intentions, especially after everything that had happened in the last year. Good intentions usually ended in people sticking their noses where they didn't belong.

"Well, she's always said that your mom was like a sister to her. You know she's always had a soft spot for you. She even tried to get custody of you until Ray stepped in. Said she knew you'd want to stay in your house and be close to your mom," Owen said as he looked my way, flashing a shy smile, before looking back at the narrow road. My hands were turning red as they warmed, my cuticles silhouetted by raw, bitten nails. That was one habit that had stuck with me since childhood that I could never quite kick.

"What's it like, anyway?" He asked in a genuine but curious voice.

"What's what like?" I put my hands back inside my pockets to hide my ugly nails.

"Living up there. Is it spooky?"

"Why? Because my mom died there?" I could feel anger building, but Owen shook his head.

"No. Sorry. I didn't mean — It's just that people have said that place has been haunted for hundreds, maybe even thousands of years."[14]

"There wasn't even a house up there a few hundred years ago, much less thousands." I rolled my eyes.

"Not a house, but I guess the Native Americans said the land was cursed. Said they wouldn't even go up there." He raised his eyebrows, the smirk still on his face.

"Where did you hear that?" Skepticism crept into my voice.

"I did a stupid history project once on the town. They have books about it in the library. And supposedly, there's a maze made of rose bushes and even an old orchard."

"The rose maze is real, although it's barely a maze anymore, but there's never been an orchard."

"There was when the house was first built. It was abandoned shortly after, though. The idiot owner thought oranges could

---

14 In Doris Gellar's Northern Alabama's Native American Folktales, 1994, she recounts stories passed down by the settlers. A story titled "Spoiled Heaven" seems to refer to the area now called Blood Mountain. In the stories, it is said that a family wandered onto the land and that the man's wife and child were stricken with fevers. They passed away, and the man was full of grief. He cried so loudly that a group of crows circled around him. The man said all he wanted was to be closer to his wife and child, so the crows dug their claws into the earth and raised it high into the sky, forming a mountain that touched the sky. The man cried happy tears because he could touch the sky where his wife and child lived. As the day turned to night, however, the mountain turned dark, and evil things roamed. The darkness lodged itself inside the man, and he was never seen again. Tales warn to take care when visiting "Spoiled Heaven" because although the day is filled with light, night will always come, and its darkness is complete.

survive here?" His voice ended with a question.[15]

"That must have been a long time ago," I exhaled. "And I haven't seen any ghosts."

"Well, that's good news," he smiled. "I don't believe in ghosts, anyway."

I leaned back, still trying to figure him out when I saw my street in the distance.

"It's this turn, here." I pointed.

Owen slowed the Jeep and turned it up the gravel drive. We bumped along in silence the rest of the way. I could feel him trying to think of something to say, trying to ease the chill in the air between us, but as he rounded the next corner, the house came into view.

God, Mama loved that house. She loved the solidness of it. She'd told me so. The permanent bricks, the angles, the rounded tower of the east rooms, the slope of the roof as it met stone. With its imposing nature, who would be able to see the secrets that hid inside?

"So." Owen shifted into park. "I guess we're here."

"Sure are," I exhaled, but when I glanced up at him, at his innocent concern, I faltered. I took a breath and looked down at my hands.

"Look, I —" I started as I turned toward him. "I'm really thankful for the drive up, I am —"

"It's no problem," he said, cutting off my attempt to dissuade

---

15 Sarubian shipped in orange trees from Florida for his orchard in 1821 just before the house was finished, obviously unaware of the harsh winters in northern Alabama. He had an orchard planted at the back of the house, installed a well to tap into the local spring, and planted a rose garden. Blankenship's writing confirmed the existence of the orange orchard. Blood oranges, to be specific – hence the name Blood Mountain. She wrote, "Sarubian purchased 100 orange saplings from Harold Felton in St. Augustine, Florida. The trees were installed in April, but when a cold snap occurred in October 1821, Sarubian quickly realized the complexity of northern Alabama's climate. Sarubian hired extra workers from the mining community, namely the wives of nearby miners looking to make some extra money before the holidays, to make quilts that could be used to shield the trees during cold nights. He hired children to dig small fire pits that would be able to warm the ground and keep it from freezing solid." The oranges successfully survived the first winter through Sarubian's sheer determination.

him from saying anything more. I moved toward the grocery bag between us.

"You know, you've grown up since I last saw you, and you're not like they said," he offered, catching my eye. "You're nice. Maybe a little shy," he laughed, "but not bad at all."

I looked away and picked up the brown paper bag, my other hand already on the door.

"Yeah." I opened the door and got out.

"Maybe, I'll see you around." I heard him yell over my shoulder as I slammed the Jeep's door.

I could feel him watching me. I walked up the front porch steps and unlocked the door, balancing the overfilled grocery bag on my hip. I turned to see him reverse in the yard before pulling back onto the drive that led down the mountain. I took another breath, still not believing that I had been in the truck, still not believing that I was back at the house, still not believing that I was without Mama. The tumble of emotions swirled around inside my head as I fumbled with my keys.

I opened the door and felt Ray's presence even before I entered the kitchen.

"Who was that?" Ray slurred without looking up.

"Some guy," I muttered.

I had been gone for so long that I had almost forgotten how Ray's mood could permeate every inch of the house, every floorboard and cupboard. He sat at the kitchen table reading the paper, a drink in one hand, an unlit cigarette in his other.

"So, you're gettin' rides from 'some guys?'" He tried to laugh but it came out as a cough.

I ignored him and started putting up the groceries.

"Is that really what they're callin' it now?" Ray's voice ran together, lazy with alcohol, and it wasn't even three yet.

"They were out of bananas, so I bought apples," I said over my shoulder. "And I saw Liz. She gave me some muffins. Said they were your favorite or something."

"I thought I taught you better than that," he said in a low

voice, ignoring my words and stepping slowly into the kitchen.

My stomach tightened, and I couldn't look him in the eyes.

"It wasn't like that," I mumbled, feeling shame color my cheeks.

Ray laughed again and shook his head, lighting up a cigarette and exhaling a thick cloud before taking another drink.

Despite Ray and his nauseating insinuations, my stomach grumbled. I put the off-brand box of macaroni and cheese I had just bought on the counter and pulled a pot from the cabinet. I filled the pot halfway and was lighting the burner when Ray snapped to attention.

"What are you doing?" He snapped. His eyes were wide with surprise.

"I'm hungry," I said flatly.

"Jesus," he said, stuffing his cigarette in a small glass and getting up from the table. "Don't. I'll get it."

He shouldered me out of the way.

"I can help out," I protested.

"No. Stop it, Cat." He shook his head. "I'll do it myself." His voice rose.

"I know you can do it yourself, Ray," I muttered, "but look around."

I gestured around the room, at the pile of dirty dishes, the stacks of newspaper strewn across the kitchen table, the trash overflowing in the corner. He looked around as if seeing it, really seeing it, for the first time.

"I'm in this," I started, "whether we both want me here or not. I'm here." I could feel my voice shake. "And dammit, Ray. I may hate you, and you may hate me right back, but this was Mama's house." He looked up at me with surprise. "She wouldn't want you living like this. And she wouldn't want the house in this shape."

He ran his hands through his thinning hair and walked in a slow circle around the kitchen. "Shit," he swore, looking at me again. "I don't know anything about kids, especially teenage girls, and you know it." He made a face and threw his hands in the air, and I had to agree with him. It made no sense.

"I know," I exhaled, "but now, you're stuck with me for the rest of the year, so what are we going to do now?"

He stared at the kitchen wall that was stained from years of neglect. Mama had always wanted to remodel the house, but there wasn't any time. There was never enough time. Or money.

"I don't know," he said, sifting through bills under the help wanted ads. "No one will hire me, and the bills. We're behind on them all."

"I can get a job," I suggested.

"Yeah, right," he snorted. "If they won't hire me, they damn well won't hire you." He gave a sour, pathetic laugh.

"Well, I can at least try. It's better than what you're doing."

He exhaled and looked back at the box on the counter.

"What is this? Mac and cheese?"

"Yep," I confirmed, eager to talk about something lighter.

"What kind of brand is this?" He asked as he lit the burner under the pot, crinkling his nose.

We ate the macaroni in silence. I watched the sky darken into a rich chocolate outside the kitchen window. Mama's chair sat like a black hole, permanent and oppressive in the stillness of twilight.

Ray pushed back his plate and wiped his mouth with the back of his hand. "I'm hittin' the hay," he got up and grabbed his empty cup. No doubt he had a bottle stashed upstairs. I sat at the table, listening to him climb the steps and make his way down the upstairs hall to the master bedroom. The house moaned, groaning with movement as if digesting him, tucking him away in its bowels.

I collected the dirty bowls and glasses and walked over to the sink when I heard water filter through the pipes to the shower. I turned on the kitchen faucet and soaped the sponge, scrubbing the first bowl. Shifting from foot to foot, I listened to the familiar squeak of the loose floorboard. Mama used to stand in that exact spot in front of the kitchen sink, swaying to the bluesy music Ray would play in the afternoons.

I could see my reflection in the dark window. I had grown up so much in the last year. I was taller, and my hair was shorter, darker than it ever had been. I could see Mama's face in there, hiding behind my jawline, my cheekbones, my eyes, my red hair. But I wasn't her, and I never could be.

I closed my eyes, picturing Mama standing right where I stood. I could almost see her, smiling there beside me, putting her arms around me. I felt the soft breeze of her breath in my hair and opened my eyes.

It was Mama.

Her face replaced my own in the window's reflection, her eyes, fierce and frantic in a way that I had only seen once in my entire life.

I screamed, dropping the dish. It crashed in the sink, the white ceramic shattering into fragments that would never be whole again. Blood came from one of my fingers that had been sliced by a ricocheting shard. It cut clean through my skin.

I looked back up at the window and saw nothing but my own stricken face. Was it a trick of the light? I scanned the kitchen, desperate for an explanation, any confirmation that Mama had been there, but the room was silent except for the running water and the muffled sounds of Ray shuffling off to bed.

I wrapped the kitchen towel around my hand and shut off the water, abandoning the dishes in the sink. I would get to it in the morning when it was light, when ghosts didn't creep in and mess with my mind.

Still shaking, I checked my hand again. It had stopped bleeding. I tossed the rag, threadbare and stained, into the trashcan beside the back door. I clicked off the light and walked down the hall toward the front door when my foot stepped in something wet.

I jumped back and looked down at the floor. The hallway was dim, but I could see wet puddles reflected in the soft blue light coming from the front porch. They dotted down the hall, trailing from the kitchen to the front room on the right.

No, not puddles. Footprints. Wet footprints.

The prints dotted the worn wooden floors from the kitchen to where my toes touched water. I recoiled, flattening myself against the wall, and followed their trail where it continued down the hall and entered the front room: the library.[16]

My feet moved by themselves, and I entered the library. The walls were packed edge to edge with cracked spines and curling pages from floor to ceiling. The musty smell of aged paper the texture of moth's wings filled the air. Books towered over me, weaving themselves into a wall that protected me from the world. My fingers ran down their bindings, the velvets, the cloths, and the sewn pages all whispered their mysteries in words that I couldn't quite catch.

In the light that spilled in from the front windows, I pulled a few books from their places on the shelves and thumbed through them. There were books on nature and gardening, on science and astronomy. I could see Mama pacing the floor lost in the book she held in her hands, draped across the chair with her head in her hands, writing notes in her journal, looking out the window as the trees changed color each fall and spring.

Other than the absence of Mama, no one was there. I sighed, missing her more than I could ever miss air, and walked back to the hall. Just as I put my foot on the first step, I heard a loud bang from the library.

I ran into the room, partly to catch whoever had made those footprints, partly to make sure I didn't lose my nerve, but again found it empty. I switched on the library's light and looked

---

16 In literature, libraries have often represented sources of knowledge and insight. Although knowledge is typically good, it can also bring unsettling affects to the protagonist, like knowledge as power in Ray Bradbury's Fahrenheit 451 and self-knowledge leading to insanity in Shirley Jackson's The Haunting of Hill House. In libraries, characters often gain knowledge about themselves that will be useful in the plot and their overall character development while highlighting the dangers of knowledge that could lead to insanity and even death.

behind Mama's chair. Laying face-down on the floor was a book. Bending down to pick it up, I felt fresh tears well in my eyes. It was her journal.

I flipped through the pages, cradling the journal in my hands, barely breathing as my eyes danced over her familiar writing. From the dates, it looked like the journal she started two years ago, the last year of her life.

I looked around the room once more, again finding it empty, in an attempt to explain how the book had dropped there. Shivers ran down my spine, and my scalp prickled. I hugged Mama's journal close and took the stairs two at a time.

Safely inside my room, I locked the door, flopped on my bed, and began to read.[17]

---

17 The following journal entry appears to have been ripped out of an A5 sized lined journal. The writing was in pen and in a style that can be described as half cursive, half print. These sections were included in the original manuscript and have been preserved to maintain their authenticity.

January 2, 1999

I'll never forget the moment I saw him. He wasn't like the others, and I was so young, and so was he, but I didn't fall in love with him until I was eighteen. Catherine was still a baby, and Marianne had talked me into going to that New Year's dance- the Snow Castle Ball.[18]

I kept telling her that I didn't wanna go. I was tired from double shifts at the cafe and Catherine's ear infection. We were living in that apartment, but Marianne said her Mama wanted to watch Catherine. And being as they were the Johnss, I figured I couldn't argue. Marianne even let me borrow a dress and did my hair and makeup. I hated to leave Cat, especially there, but I knew better than to say no. No one says no to a Johns. Especially to Mr. Johns.[19]

We were what Marianne called fashionably late. It took Marianne an hour to get our hair pinned back. I can still smell the hairspray and see the hole in the ozone. I cough just thinking about them. But there we were, walking into the civic center's disco-ball-lit gym. Marianne pushed me toward every single guy she could corner by the punchbowl, and I cringed every time one of them took my hand. Every time I had to explain myself. Yes, I had a daughter. Yes, she's still around. No, I don't know the daddy. No, I'm not looking for another daddy. It made me sick.

Marianne gave me a forced smile that told me I'd better dance, and I'd better have a good time or else. Who needs a mama when you had Marianne forcing you to socialize and whatnot? And little did we both know that we'd end up dancing with someone we'd eventually fall in love with. It's where Marianne first danced with

---

18 The Snow Castle Ball started in 1962 and is still celebrated today.

19 The Johns family is one of the original families who bought land from Thomas Saunders in the early 1800's. Since then, the family has increased their influence on the town through land ownership and prominent titles. Marianne was the daughter of Mr. David Johns and Mrs. Edna Hicks Johns. She had a half-sibling, Raymond Johns, from Mr. Johns' first marriage. Raymond, or Ray, later became Cat's mother's boyfriend who lived with them. He was disowned by the Johns family shortly before his eighteenth birthday and written out of all inheritance records. Marianne married Henry Smith in 1983 and had two sons, Owen and Davis, and is a prominent member of the greater Birmingham area's affluent society.

31

her now-husband, way before she settled into married and had kids. One of the boys pulled me to the dancefloor as a slow song came on. The boy's face generic, average height, scratchy suit. Completely forgettable.

And then I saw him.

Ray.

He had his arms around a tall brunette, but he looked just the way I remembered as a boy only taller. He had that look in his eyes, that intense look he'd always give me as if he had some great secret to tell me. The girl had her slender fingers laced behind his neck. His eyes met mine, and I knew what he was thinking. I could feel him trace my neck, my bare shoulders, my curves so that I had to concentrate on breathing just to keep standing. I'd been looked at like that before, but with Ray, it was different.

Glittery light spun around the room. Dancing couples twirled. A solar system of swaying in strangers' arms while getting sideways looks from across the dancefloor. I was his prey, and he was circling, but I didn't mind.

After an hour of him giving me those looks, he finally approached me. I never could resist those eyes. Ray's date had gone to the bathroom, and he asked me to dance, but I said no. I was young but not that young, so I knew the game.

And besides, there was something about Ray that scared me. Something about the way he looked at me made me feel jittery in a way I never had before. When the dance ended, I got to Marianne's car, but Ray was leaning there on the passenger's side door, waiting on me with a sly smile. He said he'd drive me home, and when I said I had to get home to Cat, he shook his head and insisted that he could give me a ride to Marianne's instead.

Marianne gave him a strange look as if seeing him, really seeing him for the first time and then smiled. It was the first time that I saw someone get the better of her, but it was her older brother, so she just nodded and said that it was fine if I said it was fine.

I remember riding in his truck that night, so scared of what to say. We rode through town, my window cracked to counter the intense heat from the truck's vents, and I remembered not wanting the night to end, so I suggested we go up to the old Saunders place. It had been in my mother's family but sat empty. There were rumors of ghosts, but I had been in love with the place since I spent summers there with my grandmother as a kid.[20]

We sat in the dark silence completely in awe of the house. The night hid the redness that ran to my cheeks. The woods were dark, and when Ray turned to me, he put a finger to his lips and nodded to the house. He got out of the truck and took my hand and led me to the sunken front porch.

I told him about the house, about my great-great-grandfather, the man who built it. Said he built it for his wife. Wanted it to be perfect, and that one day, I'd live there. Ray took my hand and smiled, he said that if I wanted it, then he would get it, he would buy it and fix it up for us, for me and Catherine, and maybe have two or three other kids running around, and I wanted to tell him about his dad, then, but I couldn't find the words.

Instead, I told him I'd believe it when I saw it but couldn't help blushing again in the dark. It was perfect. He was perfect. And after all those years, I still thought about that night. I still thought about my hand in his and him promising me the house and the whole rest of our lives together.

I just didn't know it would end up like this, a failure as a wife, a failure as a mother. We got the house. I got it after all, and I didn't even need Ray. I just feel ashamed about how I got it, about where all the money came from. Thank God no one asked, but I know that Ray had his suspicions. He was disowned at eighteen, thrown out, and told to make something of himself before he ever came back, and I guess it was never good enough, he never met that expectation, because his father never talked to him again, and he was completely written out of the will.

---

20 The Saunders estate was passed down to the descendants of Olivia Saunders until it was sold to the Johnss in 1982. Although the Johnss converted most of their properties into retail and residential income properties, the Saunders estate on Blood Mountain was left untouched and sold back to Sarah Saunders in 1984, a year after Cat's birth.

Things were fine for a while. Me. Ray. Cat. Marianne coming to visit. Even Ray's other sister, Ginny, and her daughter came to visit a few times. But then, I visited my mom's grave, and Ray and I had this big fight about my sister in Atlanta. She's always been too good for me, so I knew better than to take her side over Ray's, but I just hoped things were different after all that time, but they weren't, and it seemed like everything was coming together, like our dreams were coming true.

But nothing lasts.

Especially dreams.

You have to wake up and go back to reality eventually.

Now, I sat with the reality that I chose. I just didn't know it would be like this. The house sighed when no one listened. I could hear it. Almost as if there's someone there, behind the walls, someone creeping and watching and judging. No one ever tells you that there's no happily ever after. When the story on the page ends, reality sets in. No one ever tells you about the silence and the stillness that comes after. The everyday tasks that take over. The absence that can suffocate you. How can I survive in all this nothingness? Where did it all go wrong?

I read Mama's words and stood in the library, hands shaking as the puddles dried. When my bones were stiff, I made my way upstairs. I splashed water over my face and brushed my teeth, then laid out my prescription on the counter, one by one, turning each label toward me before opening the top and doling them out in my palm. They felt like weightless pebbles, like magic seeds that could grow overnight. I pictured them growing in my belly and transporting me to a world far, far away, like Jack and the Beanstalk.[21]

---

21 "Jack and the Beanstalk" is an English fairy tale that first appeared in print as "The Story of Jack Spriggins and the Magic Bean" in Round About our Coal-Fire in 1734, again published as "The History of Jack and the Bean-Stalk" in 1807, Henry Cole's (pen name Felix Summerly) The Home Treasury in 1845, and Joseph Jacob's English Fairy Tales in 1890, but Proto-Indo-European languages suggests the tale dates back to 4500 BC to 2500 BC.

Long after, I laid awake, staring up at the ceiling. I could hear Ray's snores from down the hall. The winter wind shook the windows, and I pulled my comforter even tighter around my neck.

My mind reeled. I didn't know that Mama had met Ray that early. I remembered her dating. Dating a lot. The swirl of phases she went through. Ronnie the drummer. Harry the salesman. Carl the gym man. There was Bill the insurance guy and Larry the... what did he do again? I tried to think back, but I couldn't remember.

Each time my mom dated one of these men, it was like a cloud came over the house. With Ronnie, Mama started wearing ripped jeans and cropped band t-shirts. She switched to pencil skirts when Harry would take her to dinners with clients. She adopted sweatsuits as she took cardio sessions alongside Carl at the gym. Cardigans with Bill as he listed the many ways one could die simply on their way to work. And with Harry, she started to mirror him. Gray sweatpants, oversized sweaters. Mama was the kind of woman to get lost in a guy, but I had no idea she had met Ray before. Was he always there, lurking in the background? Had he watched her go through all those phases, too? Become shadows of these men she belonged to?

And why had Mama called herself a failure? What had happened to her?

I got up, still not able to go to sleep, just as the hall clock struck three. The devil's hour. I unlocked my door and crept back downstairs, brewing a fresh cup of tea, just like Mama had taught me. I sipped it and let myself cry, let all of my tears go until I was shaking and gasping and spent.

The walls swirled around me with the memories of Mama cooking in the kitchen, of her stories told in whispers before bed, of her with dirty hands in the garden, of her smiling over shared tea.

I closed my eyes and thought I heard it, too. The creeping. It started out soft, a tiny step, a barely audible exhale. That was the first time I heard her.

"Mama?" I asked into the darkness. "Is that you?"

But she didn't answer. The silence of the house counted out the clock as it ticked upstairs. The wind whistled through the eaves, an owl made its way through the maze out back as it hunted in the dark. I hugged myself and cried until my lungs were raw and my ribs were sore. Then, I climbed the steps once more and went to sleep.

Transcript
I've gone back and forth about even talking about this, and I'm still not convinced that I can do it. It's a long story, and it's much more complicated than you think.

My mom and I never really had the best relationship — she was always so strict. Uptight, ya know? She could never sit still and just be. She was always reading or writing. Somewhere else, so I did a lot of things just to get her attention.

Yeah, like getting into history. My earliest memory was of a dinner party that she hosted. I remember sitting by the fire and listening to my mom talk while she played with my hair. I have no idea what she was talking about, but her voice was so clear, so sure, and I remember being so happy that her attention was on me, even though she was talking to other people the whole time, and later, when I woke up in my bed, I was struck by how cold and lonely it was in my room.

And as I got older, I kinda got tired of always hanging around, waiting for her to remember she even had a daughter. She tried to bond with me. She even gave me that locket you found — the one with the black and white photo of mom and her sister inside — but since she never wanted to talk about that, I hardly even wore it.

I know, I'm being harsh, but it's how I felt at the time. I remember not being able to wait until I turned eighteen, and when I found out how much college tuition was, I was forced to stay. Okay, forced isn't the right word, but you know what I mean.

My mom always had a hard time differentiating between herself and me. We even had the same eyes — one brown, one blue — and I often found that she assumed I wanted many of the same things as she did. I just remember always trying to make her happy, even if I couldn't stand her at that time, and that's how I became a history major in college. According to my mom, it was only natural that I'd gotten into history. She'd become the youngest department chair at Georgia State. She was making history in the History Department, as she'd say, and it was only logical that I would follow in her footsteps.

But my getting into history was also how we fell out and why it took over a decade for us to even speak again.

The manuscript? Yeah, at first, I had no idea why she was working on it. I mean, Mom would typically write her own materials and had written several books on folk tales and strange stories of the South, and I was confused she even took on this project. She'd only appear in superscript, just an echo under Cat's story, and I knew Mom was so much bigger than an echo.

But as I poured through Mom's notes — and I mean, pages and pages of notes — I could see why she found it interesting. I have a whole pile of extra research here —

Sure, I can give you those, also. Mom had those separated out based on something called "spine limitations."

Yeah, I had the same question. I was like, Who's spine? The reader's? The book couldn't have been heavy, but it refers to the spine. It can only hold so many pages, and that makes more sense, doesn't it?

It'd be something if a book had a spine, wouldn't it? Something strong to hold on to. Then maybe it could have a heart. The lines could be the heartbeat. And it could have lungs. Maybe when you read it out loud or when you turn each page? And if it has all of those, could it also have eyes? What does a book see when it looks back at you? What could it hear?

Smell? And what if it had teeth? Could it bite and —
— Yes, sorry. Back to the story. You sure you don't want that tea first? It's getting cold.
Sure. Well, just let me know. Tea's my specialty.

FEBRUARY 2001

I thought February would sweep in warmer weather. Instead, it was a continuation of the gray chill of January. Fog settled in the valleys and hugged the top of the mountain, blinding me in a colorless coma. It wouldn't matter if the groundhog saw his shadow; winter would never loosen its grip.[22]

I'd been to my therapy sessions but still felt raw. Ray finally agreed that I should get a job when his only job for the month of January barely paid to keep the lights on. I wanted to help out, contribute, make some friends, so I put in applications at the library and general store but never got a call back. Maybe Ray was right. Who would hire me?

I pulled my scarf higher to protect my neck from the biting wind as my feet crunched on the frozen dirt. Birds chirped and jumped from branches shivering with frozen dew. The trees thinned as I neared town, and I joined a narrow, snaking sidewalk.

Hearts and cupids had replaced the Christmas decor that hung there when I first arrived. The pinks and reds clashed, made

---

22 Although January is typically the coldest and snowiest month of the year, with temperatures ranging from 32.7 to 46.7 degrees Fahrenheit and 1.77 inches of average snowfall. February, however, is the cloudiest month of the year with an average of 52% of the days being overcast, causing fog in high elevations.

worse by the shop window displays that carried on the theme: roses, lovebirds, perfectly tied knots. It made me want to gag.

The pavement straightened out, and I measured my steps to avoid the cracks. Head down, I counted. One, two, three, crack. One, two, three, crack. Just as I was passing the library, I saw something flutter in the dead leaves that sat under a dormant shrub. I bent down and picked it up.

A five-dollar bill. A sign of good luck.

I smiled and looked around for its owner, but no one else was on the street. Stuffing it into my pocket, I felt my chest lighten. It would be a good day.

Turning the corner, I walked to the diner. The front window was decorated with champagne flutes and a diamond ring. I shook my head and opened the door.

The diner was much warmer than outside. Plates clinked, and people talked quietly at their tables, but when I unwound my scarf, I could hear the noises soften and then stop altogether. When I looked up, I realized that all eyes were on me.

I took a deep breath and made my way to the counter. An older woman, skinny and nervous, gave me a nod. "Help you?" she asked.

"Yes," I started, my voice wavering. I cleared my throat and continued. "I was wondering if you were hiring."

The woman's mouth opened just slightly, and she reminded me of a fish.

"Do I need an application or..."

I could feel the whole diner's attention on me. The lady behind the counter closed her mouth, took out a rag, and began wiping the already clean counter.

"No positions right now." She was already turning away.

"Please, I can clean or cook or —"

"No," she said a little too loud as she turned back to me, genuine panic in her eyes. She glanced around the room, flashing a tight smile. "We're not hiring," she muttered.

I let out a breath, red shame crept into my face. I could feel tears sting my eyes. I had to get out of there.

I turned and walked out, aware of everyone still looking at me. I crossed the street to get away from them and wrapped my scarf around my neck. I choked back tears but paused mid-step in the street. The old men saton the sidewalk, seemingly salivating, waiting for me to approach them.

A car approached, and I kept walking, my head down once more. The men sat on the bench outside the general store. Their cigarette smoke hung in a cloud over their heads, cigarettes perched at the edges of their cracked mouths.

I choked as I walked into their smoke, but my coughs couldn't drown out their mumbling.

"She's the one —"

"You know her mama —"

"They say that —"

"Dangerous."

I wrapped my scarf tighter and picked up my speed.

"Hey, there, girlie. Won't ya come on over here for a minute?"

The men behind him laughed, and I could hear them jostle one another. I snuck a glance back at them, their sour faces taut with fresh laughter, and before I could turn around again, I slammed into someone.

"Hey," the voice exclaimed. "I got you."

Arms wrapped around me, steadying me, and I looked up to find Owen's face smiling down at me.

"Jesus, you're shaking," he said. "Come on, let's get out of the cold."

Owen pulled me inside the first door, and I let him guide me, thankful to get out of the cold and the angry presence of the old men outside. I breathed a sigh of relief when the doors closed behind us, and when I inhaled again, I was met with the warm smell of cinnamon buns and blueberry muffins. Soft piano music played somewhere in the distance, and I realized that we were in the cafe.

"Mornin'," called Liz, but she stopped short when she saw me.

"Hey," she said in a meek voice, glancing from me to Owen and then back again.

I smiled, and Owen turned to me. "Want a coffee?" He asked.

"Sure," I nodded, still looking at Liz who was busy wiping an already clean counter.

"We'll have two coffees," he said as he approached the register and pulled out his wallet. I walked to a table at the back of the cafe and took a seat. Liz took the money and gave Owen his change.

"For here or to go?" She glanced at me and then back at him.

"Here would be great," he answered.

"I'll bring them right out." She smiled, grabbed two paper cups, and filled them with coffee.

Owen serpentined through the tables and sat across from me with a smile.

"Those guys are always awful." He shook his head.

I nodded and watched Liz work behind the counter. The liquid steamed, and she added cream, sugar, and spices before stirring them and selecting the honey, which turned out to be empty. She rummaged under the counter before finding a new bottle.

"What are you doing in town today?"

"Can't I go to town?" My voice came out more annoyed than I had planned.

"Sorry, I —" He put his hands up, but I caught them in mid-air, stopping them before he could finish.

"No, I'm sorry," I said, noticing the hurt in his eyes. "I didn't mean it. I'm just not used to…" My voice trailed off, and I looked at the shiny green linoleum of the coffee shop floor.

I took a breath and looked back at him. "I'm just not used to someone being nice."

Owen's hurt melted into a sadness that stopped just short of pity.

"I've been to town all week, looking for a job, and everywhere I go, they tell me that they're not hiring, or they tell me to fill out an application and then throw it away, like actually throw it away in the trash before I've even left the building."

"There's no way —"

"The library. The general store. Town hall. The flower shop. The diner," I said in a flat voice.

He raised his eyebrows. "Sorry, I had no idea."

"No, and you shouldn't. It shouldn't be that way, but it is. I just really need a job." I looked down at my hands. Ray and I had taken to layering on blankets and feeding scraps of wood to the fireplaces to keep us warm at night. My bones had almost gotten used to the ache so that they felt stiff in the warmth of the cafe.

"You'll find one," he said in a naive voice. "Don't worry."

I raised my eyebrows and nodded, unconvinced, but it was my problem to worry about.

"Hey, I need to run to the restroom," he said as he slipped off his coat. "I'll be right back."

I gave him a smile and nodded, pulling my coat from my shoulders and unwinding my scarf. I felt all of my tendons release, all of my muscles relax in the comfort of the cafe. The ease felt wonderful and uncomfortable at the same time because I knew the cold walk back and the chilly house would be waiting.

"Here we are," Liz said over my shoulder, jarring me from my thoughts. "I added some cream, cinnamon, nutmeg, clove, and local honey. Do you need anything else?"

She held my gaze, waiting.

"Um, no. That sounds perfect," I said as I reached out for the two cups.

"Careful, they're hot." She sat one down in front of Owen's chair and handed the other one to me. Her hands were small, the color of caramel, and the ends of her fingers were tinged indigo.

I took the cups and nodded toward her fingers.

"Have you been painting lately?"

Liz looked down at her hands, turning them palm up, revealing more blotches of blue.

"Dyes, actually. We got an order of blueberries the other day, and they made the most beautiful stains on the dishrag when they were drying, so I used that as inspiration on a new canvas series."

"You still paint?" I asked as I watched her wipe her hands on her apron. I could remember a few holidays when we'd visited Ray's family. Was it Christmas? New Year's? I remembered that it was cold. Mama told me to go put our jackets in one of the bedrooms, and I guess I'd entered Liz's. It seemed like every surface was covered in art — drawings and paintings, paper mache, and pottery. I stood there, looking around the room until I heard a voice behind me.

"That one was my favorite."

My heart thumped in my chest, and I turned to see Liz, wild-haired, wearing a lavender dress that made no sense in winter. She smiled, a head taller than me, but the panic that I'd felt at being caught snooping slipped away. Instead, she slipped past me and picked up an unfinished sketch.

"I've been working on this one for months," she sighed and tilted her head, examining it as she did so. "It's a self-portrait that I just can't get right."

"I think it's pretty," I offered.

She sighed in response and set the drawing down on her dresser where I had been looking at it before we heard the rest of the family calling us from the kitchen. It was time to eat.

I'd only really spent time with her at those few family dinners, and she'd always been that way — creative, warm, a true individual. But that was before her mother died. Was it cancer? A heart defect? I couldn't remember. After that, she'd moved to live with her aunt in Colorado or California — somewhere out West.

Standing there in the cafe, I could see the years that had passed between us. How much different did I look to her? Could she see all the things that had happened since we'd last seen each other? Or did I still look the same?

"You know, I could come by sometime," she offered. "Ray called and said that —"

"You don't have to do that. He really shouldn't've —" I started, but Owen came around the corner. Liz followed my gaze and nodded, lips tight as she tried to hide her annoyance.

"Let me know if you need anything else," she said and made her way back to the counter.

"Looks like I'm right on time," Owen said as he took a seat.

I picked up my coffee, noticing the delicate cream heart and sprinkles on top, and took a sip. The spices reminded me of Mama, how she would make me fresh cocoa when the weather turned cold. One year, she wanted to watch a meteor shower from the back garden. She made a warm thermos full of hot cocoa and bundled us up in blankets before leading us through the gardens.

The gardens were my mom's favorite thing about the house. Hedgerows of roses twisted and turned into a small labyrinth. In the center was a well, worn smooth, and flat by the elements and was falling down in places and half covered by rotting planks.

We would lay near the well, looking up at the stars while she told me stories and held my hand. She let me point out all the shooting stars and told me to make a wish on each one.

"You know what I think?" Owen said, interrupting my thoughts. "I think you're just in a funk."

"A funk?" I repeated, wiping my mouth free of cream.

"Yeah. You just need to shake off the funk."

"And how would I do that?" I set my mug down in front of me, truly curious.

"You need to get out. Have some fun." His face beamed, and I wondered how many women were secretly in love with him. He was gentle and kind, at least so far, happy-go-lucky and wide-eyed. His innocence was refreshing.

"What are you doing for Valentine's Day? You know there's a dance in town."

"I don't dance," I shook my head.

"Sure, you do." He scrunched up his nose. "Everybody dances."

"Not me," I reiterated.

"Come on. You gotta come with me. I know it would help, and it would help you get to know everyone." His face swelled with pride at the idea.

"See, that's exactly why I don't want to go."

"What do you mean? You're great."

"Sure, but everyone else." I gestured with my hands. "I don't think they'd want me there."

"They would if you were with me." He touched my hand and flashed me his quarterback smile. He started playing football as I was graduating, but everyone whispered about his greatness, even then. He was a Johns, afterall.

"Come on." He squeezed my hand. "Please?"

I looked at him doubtfully.

"If you don't come with me, I'll just have to come to you. Bring the dance to you."

"Bring the dance?" I asked.

"Sure. I'll bring dinner and music, maybe a few friends."

"No," I said, thinking of Ray's reaction.

"It'll be fun. And you wouldn't even need to leave the house."

"I said, no," I shouted louder than I had planned to, and Owen sat back, surprised. "You don't have to come over," I explained. "I'll go. I'll go to the dance with you."

Owen pumped his fist and whooped. "You're gonna have a blast, just wait," he said, still celebrating.

We finished our coffees, and Owen offered to give me a ride home. I waved goodbye to Liz before we left and got into his truck, still feeling awkward but not as uncomfortable as I had the first time.[23]

---

23 Continued research on the Saunders estate on Blood Mountain has revealed that the name Blood Mountain is derived from the color of the blood oranges in the Sarubian orchard but also the series of mishaps that occurred on the land, including the construction of the estate all the way back to rumors of strange occurrences by the original settlers and indigenous people who called it home. It was rumored to be sacred ground, a natural resource of mineral-rich spring water as well as rare minerals, such as coal, iron, and steel.

When I got home, the house was empty and quiet. The floors creaked with all of the lives that had lived there. Inside the door, I paused and listened. I wondered if one of the sounds was Mama giving me a bath when I was little or creeping down the stairs to lay out presents at Christmas.

I leaned against the wall, and my shoulder rested on Mama's old jacket. I pulled it on and inhaled. Mama's scent had faded, and I wrapped the jacket around myself even tighter, desperate to capture the tiniest bit of her, but all that was left was the stale smell of neglect and loneliness.

On Valentine's Day, I awoke to a gray so thick and silent that it felt like water. I didn't dare open the windows and doors. I could almost see the fog rolling in through an open door, invading the house, and it choked my lungs.

I could hear Ray moving around down the hall. He had come in the night before, stumbled upstairs, and started snoring immediately. He slept late and, as he made his way downstairs, I could hear him pause at my door, and I held my breath.

I watched his shadow under my door. It wavered, shifting left, then right, before moving on. He was gone within a few minutes, enough to grab his coat and keys. His truck, banged up as it was, limped down the drive, taillights haloed in red like two angry eyes that faded quickly to the gray nothingness of mid-morning.

With the house to myself, I made my way downstairs to the library. I built a fire and settled into Mama's chair, feeling the warmth from the fire creep up my legs and ease the chill in my bones. In the golden light of the fire, I pulled Mama's journal on my lap and started to read.

Today is Valentine's Day. Money's been a stretch, especially lately with fewer customers coming to the cafe after the holidays, but I've been able to make a little extra money reading tarot and making teas for some of the ladies in town. Ray hates it, of course, calls me an old witch, living up here in this house and meddling in that, but I don't think it's so bad. My grandma used to make her own recipes, after all, and the cafe lets me sell the tea bags at the counter.

The house seems to have a mind of its own lately. I feel like, sometimes, when I come into the room, things are different, like they changed somehow, but I can't quite put my finger on it. Kinda like when someone leaves the room, and you can still smell their perfume, only the feeling doesn't come with a smell. It's just a feeling I get at the back of my neck. Ray says I'm being silly, says all that tarot's gone to my head, but something's going on with this house.

The rose maze out back has started to show its buds. It's way too early. A bad sign that means sickness is on the wind. I've started adding elderberry to our tea, especially with Cat since she's getting older. She's sixteen, and I can't believe how big she's gotten, especially in this last year. She does independent study now, which means that she's ahead of all of her classmates and is taking college classes, and she writes nonstop. She makes up these stories you wouldn't believe.

I don't know how she thinks up this stuff, but sometimes it reminds me of my stories, fairy tales that my own mama told me. I guess she comes by it honestly. Ray scoffs at it, says she is wasting her time making up lies like that, but she says sometimes there's more truth to fiction than real life. Although I don't really know what she means, I almost do.

Ray's been working more now than ever. He says business is good and brings me chocolates from a shop downtown that he's been remodeling. After his dad died, he started his own carpentry business, and he makes the most beautiful things with wood.

Things have been good lately. He even dances with me in the kitchen after Cat goes to bed. That man makes me feel like there's no one else in the world, like I'm the only one he sees.

And the way he kisses me... well, there's nothing like it. Let's just say that.

Cat's been in more moods lately. Says she's working on some story for school, but I don't want her to move too far away. It's been me and her from the beginning, and even though I have Ray, things won't be the same without her. God, she's smart, though. Gonna graduate a whole year and a half early. And she did it all by herself. But maybe she's too smart and can't see things that are right in front of her. That's what Ray says at least.

The other night, we were having dinner. Ray's drink was running low, and he said he was gonna go out to get more after we ate. Well, Cat said she wasn't feeling well and went upstairs. We finished eating, and when Ray tried to leave, his keys weren't on the entryway table where he always leaves them. We looked everywhere for them. All his coat pockets, in the truck, even down the air vent by the hall table just in case they had fallen through. We must have searched for an hour.

Finally, I gave up and headed upstairs to take a shower. I was passing by Cat's room, and you'll never guess what I heard. Giggling. It sounded like she was talking to someone, sharing a laugh, but when I opened the door, no one was there, only her and her notebook. But that smile was still on her face.

When I asked her what was so funny, she just shook her head, and as I went to close the door, I just happened to look down at her trash can, and there, right on top of some crumpled-up papers, was Ray's keys.

I was so mad because we had searched everywhere for them, and they were right there in her room the whole time. I know she heard us looking for them. And it's not the first time that things of his have gone missing. Things have been disappearing for years, basically since Ray had moved in, but I always thought he was just forgetful. I never thought it was Cat.

When I came downstairs with the keys, Ray already knew. He asked me if she'd had them all along. I didn't answer, but I couldn't meet his eyes. He turned red, then, and I knew that if he'd have gone upstairs, he woulda hit her. I blocked the stairs and calmed him down, knowing that Cat was up there hearing everything, hearing all the names he was calling her, but at least he wasn't hitting her. I wouldn't stand for that.

Ray looked at me and said that she was always like a cat, slinking around and plotting, playing the part but never showing her true colors. If he woulda said something like that any other time, I'd of thought he was just angry, just putting on, but then I remembered that giggle before I opened up her door, the way her eyes danced toward the trash can, the heat in her cheeks at getting caught but not at feeling bad. I'd never seen that side of her before. Sure, she'd told white lies before, but I didn't think she was conniving like that. Was she always like that? Maybe I'd been the blind one, not her. Maybe I was the one who couldn't see things right in front of me.[24]

---

24 I found more about the Saunders family. The town newspaper, The Daily Tribune, did not announce the birth of Olivia's child after the article that said she was expecting. Although miscarriage data is not available for the early 1800's, it is estimated that half of all pregnancies ended in a miscarriage. The Daily Tribune does, however, report that Saheter began to travel for work, only coming home every few months with a new gift for Olivia, so it is assumed that the first ended in a miscarriage. Saheter Sarubian was reportedly travelling off and on for the next few years and held lavish parties whenever he was home. Olivia seemed to retreat inside the house only emerging when Saheter hosted parties or required her attendance in town. Pictures of her in the Daily Tribune showed her pale and thin, lips pinched and eyes wearier with every passing year.

Finally, in August 1826, The Daily Tribune reported another pregnancy announcement for Olivia and Saheter just after pregnancy rumors started to swirl. Olivia was reported as being very sick during this time, and the town doctor was called. He gave the pregnancy prognosis, although she was at least five months pregnant at that time. Dr. Adams ordered her to stay inside on bed rest and monitored her every week. Saheter stayed away most of the year, only returning when he received word of a successful birth – a set of twin girls on New Year's Day 1827. Helen Rose and Eleanor "Nellie" Daisy were healthy and seemed to breathe life into Olivia. She was seen in the paper, smiling and interacting at town events, as she showed off her daughters and enjoyed her motherhood.

When the girls were four, Olivia hosted a party for their birthday, inviting members of the town for a lavish evening of food, music, and entertainment. The children were invited to a sleepover in the twin's large play area located in the attic while the parents enjoyed piano music and fresh champagne. Saheter was in attendance as well, although things had seemed icy between Olivia and Saheter in the years since the twin's birth. They were featured in the gossip column more than a handful of times with anonymous sources reporting rumors of affairs and constant disagreements, although nothing more concrete had been confirmed.

During the birthday party, however, in the book *Mysteries of the South*, Sally Devereaux writes "During the party, Olivia complained of a headache, making sure to announce that she was going upstairs to lie down for the night. Shortly before this, however, some of the guests said they saw her arguing heatedly with her husband in the gardens. After she retired upstairs, Saheter seemed to be in good spirits. He visited with the guests and was friendly toward a singer who accompanied the pianist. He even challenged the guests to a race through the maze and awarded the winner, Muriel Jones, a set of silk scarves from Egypt. Later that night, he was seen escorting a young lady, presumably the beautiful, young piano singer, through the gardens." It was rumored that Saheter was a professional philanderer and had been courting lovers across the globe after marrying Olivia.

Yet, the rumors didn't stop there. Saheter's financial records between the years of 1822 and 1831 reflect vast amounts of money being funneled to private accounts in Paris, Dubai, Bombay, and Florence, where he would stay for months at a time. Further research revealed that the families all had young daughters at the time who were looking for marriage and financial stability. Since Saheter could not settle down, as he was already married, he would move on to the next young woman in port in hopes of wooing her to be his new lover.

At the night of the party, however, tragedy struck. Sometime in the early morning, the head servant went out to fetch water from the well. As she lifted the water pail, it got hung on something at the bottom. When she tugged at the obstruction, she heard a splash and called several orchard workers to clear the well. After none of them could clear the obstruction, one of them ventured into the hole.

Devereaux writes, "The man was tied into a makeshift harness and was lowered into the well with a lantern. When he reached the bottom, he screamed a scream that would bury itself into the marrow of any listener. 'A body,' he cried out. 'There's a body down here!' They pulled him up and called the police right away. The police chief, Sheriff Smyth, pulled up the body, bloated with hours of exposure to the cold, wet dregs of the well, was none other than Saheter Sarubian, himself." Saheter had been dead for hours, and when Sheriff Smyth interviewed Olivia (seen in the official police report), he noted that her hair, "was wet as if she had been in the well with him." Although this was not public knowledge, the Daily Tribune did run news of Saheter's death. See news article below:

The Daily Trib

Iss. 172   Sunday, the 5th of February

Stormy Times on Saunders Mountain

William White

It has been most stormy on Saunders Mountain. On Friday, the 2nd of February, Chief of Police Benjamin Smythe was called to the Sarubian Estate, formerly the Saunders Estate, after the Sarubian estate's head servant found the body of Mr. Saheter Sarubian at the bottom of the well.

Members of the town were in attendance at the residence the previous evening for a formal dinner where music and dancing lasted into the early morning hours. The dinner was to celebrate the anniversary of Mr. and Mrs. Saheter Sarubian and to celebrate his homecoming from his worldwide travels in India and the horn of Africa. Mr. Sarubian has become famous in the South as being a leading importer of exotic silks, jewels, and furniture.

He is survived by his wife, Mrs. Olivia Virginia Sarubian and his twin daughters Helen Rose Sarubian and Eleanor Daisy Sarubian. An only child, Sarubian was the only living member of his family.

When asked about Sarubian's death, Chief Benjamin Smythe states "Sarubian must have leaned a little too far back and lost his balance. He tumbled to the bottom, sustained a cranial fracture, and drowned in the water below." No foul play is suspected at this time.

The town is heartbroken and will hold a candlelight vigil at sundown tonight at the town church in Sarubian's honor. Funeral services are to be announced.

53

After Saheter's death, Olivia and the twins retreated to the Sarubian estate, renamed the Saunders's estate on Blood Mountain. Olivia stopped coming to public events and homeschooled her daughters. Sheriff Smyth is quoted in the Tribune as saying, "Saheter must have had too much to drink and wandered out to the well." Townspeople wrote anonymous letters to the paper with accusations about foul play in regard to Saheter's death, yet no formal charges were filed against Olivia or anyone else at the party, as no concrete evidence was found.

Rare respiratory diseases struck workers in the orange orchard particularly in the summer months after Saheter's death, and the local doctor warned of "farmer's lung." Doctors from Birmingham were called in the following spring (1822). Although medical officials never declared an official cause of farmer's lung, it was rumored that the oranges were the source of the mold, and orchard workers were forced to wear face coverings while caring for the oranges.

That winter, a particularly bad ice storm struck, and Olivia let most of the grounds workers and house staff go, realizing the impossibility of keeping the sensitive oranges alive in the mountains of north Alabama.

So, Mom wrote a lot about the Saunders' rose garden. Before the house was demolished, the garden resembled a hedge maze that had these wooden slats you could move so that in one configuration, you could enter straight into the maze. In another, you could block the path so you'd have to turn left. You could also change it so you had to turn right instead, or leave it all open so you could choose which direction you'd go from the very beginning.

Yeah, kinda like that. The slats allowed for sixty-four different designs. And here's the kicker, there's only one combination that is unsolvable.

In the center was a well the Saunders' dug to tap into a fresh spring that existed on the mountain. Mom also found a local superstition surrounding the rose maze, and it turns out that roses were typically planted above graves to protect the dead from evil spirits, and that got me thinking about who or what could be buried up there. There were rumors that bodies were buried up there — Native Americans, construction workers, and even Saheter Sarubian. They were all buried beneath the roses. Mom never found evidence of any of that, though. Either way, it sure makes you think.

A knock at the door interrupted my reading. *Shit,* I thought. *The dance.*

I jumped up and took the stairs two at a time, yelling over my shoulder. "It's open. I'll just be a minute."

I shuffled through my clothes, but all of my dresses were at least two sizes too small. Why hadn't I thought about what to wear earlier? I shook my head.

Easy, I thought. I didn't want to go in the first place. I exhaled and held up the only thing that still fit — a small stack of sweats and a handful of second-hand T-shirts.

I crept into the hall and spotted Owen standing in the foyer. He wore a dark suit with a bright, red rose.

"Shit," I cursed under my breath, and he jerked his head up. I ducked over the side just in time, flattening myself against the wall.

"Cat?" He said, and the floorboard creaked underneath his weight as he shifted forward.

"Almost ready," I called out. With no other options, I tiptoed into Mama and Ray's room. The curtains were drawn, and I could smell Ray's alcohol mixed with sweat and mold. My stomach tightened, so I held my breath and pulled open the closet. Flicking on the light, Mama's clothes were just how she had left them.

Mama loved clothes. She loved patterns and colors. She loved fabrics, textures, and sequins. All of her favorites were in there. The conservative suits, the party dresses, the workout wear, the sweaters, and the flannel shirts. And I could see all the men she associated to each of them.

I used to dress up in her clothes when I was little, strutting around in metallic dresses and feather boas, all bought second-hand but impeccably cared for. Mama would play her records and cheer me on, joining in at my pleading, dancing with me as she stood on the balls of her feet.

I flipped through the back of her closet, the part reserved for special occasions, and found a green velvet dress. I went into Mama's bathroom and stepped into the shower, shampooed my hair, and washed my body, mindful of Owen waiting downstairs. I wiped the mirror, ran a brush through my hair, and slipped on the dress, and when I looked back at the mirror, I gasped. I had only seen Mama wear it once at Christmas, but when I looked at my reflection, I was the mirror image of her. It was like looking at two halves of a face, similar, coming together to form a whole, but dissonant, nonetheless.

I applied a layer of Mama's red lipstick, downed my daily dose of pills from their orange containers, grabbed Mama's fur coat and a pair of heels from her closet, and headed downstairs. Owen waited with his hands in his pockets. He had removed his jacket and looked up as he heard me coming down the stairs.

"Wow," he exhaled. "You are…" His voice trailed off, and I blushed under his gaze. "Amazing. Absolutely stunning."

"Sorry if I kept you waiting," I said as I stuck one arm into the coat.

"Not at all," he said, helping me with the other arm. I pulled the fur coat around me and tasseled my hair, still wet from the shower. "You ready to go?"

"Yep," I said with a shy smile, still feeling uncomfortable at being gushed at.

Owen led me to his Jeep and helped me inside before getting in and turning the keys in the ignition.

"I'm not gonna lie, it was a little creepy in there," Owen said as he reversed the truck. The house loomed over us, its presence dominant. "You sure it isn't haunted in there?"

"Not this again." I shook my head. "If you think about it, all places are a little bit haunted."

"What do you mean?" He asked.

"They all hold memories, stories of lives that had lived long ago."

He shrugged and put the truck into drive. "I guess. You ever see anything?"

"Anything?" I repeated.

"Anything weird. You know."

"Nope," I said, trying to push the wet footsteps and the house's creaking from my mind. "They're just stories."

Owen shrugged again, and we drove the rest of the way listening to the radio. The Rec Hall, as the sign out front read, pulsed with music. The heavy metal doors were propped halfway open, and rainbow streamers shielded its entrance. Inside, silver sparkles of light danced across painted cement walls, tables draped in tablecloths, snacks spread on perimeter tables, bodies moved in sequence to the music.[25]

At the dance, I clung to Owen's arm. He introduced me to person after person, their faces and names blending into one another, and even convinced me to dance a few times. I could feel the curious gazes on us, on me, but when the light dimmed, I could feel myself relax. The music swirled around us like a galaxy of anonymity and connectedness, separate heartbeats that pounded in sync.

Owen grew more and more relaxed and hugged me tighter as the night went on. He nuzzled my hair, an acrid punch of alcohol on his breath when he whispered, "Cat," and pulled me even closer.

"Sorry," I muttered, pushing against his chest. His hands were sticky with sweat "I think I'm a little tired."

"Come on," he pleaded. "Let's dance some more."

"I don't think so," I said a little louder. The couples around us looked but averted their eyes.

"Okay," he said, taking a step back. "We can get out of here."

He led the way off the dancefloor, waving to people as we passed. Our feet crunched on the gritty parking lot as we headed to his truck. He pulled his keys from his pocket and fumbled them. They clinked on the blacktop.

"Shit," Owen swore and bent down to pick them up. He

---

25 These are typically referred to as Civic Centers, or publicly-funded municipal buildings which host events, conventions, and entertainment for the larger community that grew out of Progressive Era ideas about city planning, society, and the role of government in surrporting local communities.

licked his lips and unlocked the passenger side door.

"Are you sure you're okay to drive?" I hesitated.

He laughed and ran his hand through his hair. "I'm always okay to drive."

"I don't know," I said as I stepped away from the truck.

"Come on. You said you wanted to get out of here. Let's go someplace quiet where we can get to know each other a little better." He stepped close to me and put his hand on my neck, lifting my chin with his thumb.

"Stop," I said, knocking his hand away. "I wanted to go home."

"Taking me home already? I didn't know you'd want to take things that fast, Cat," he flirted and grabbed my hand.

"No, not with you. I said I was tired." I snatched my hand away. His smile froze on his lips, curling with understanding.

"What did you think we were doing here, Cat?" He spat.

"What do you mean?"

"I mean the dance, the rides home, everything."

"You said you were just being nice," I said in a small voice.

He let out a breath and laughed. "You know what they say about you, right?"

"So, what?" I felt heat rise in my chest. "You thought you'd just mess with the haunted girl whose mom died?"

"No, Cat." His expression softened. "I didn't mean it like that. It's just-" He opened his mouth, but nothing came out.

"Forget it," I said, backing away. "Just forget it."

I jogged across the parking lot with Owen calling behind me, but I slipped into the shadows and followed the treeline back to the main road.

The town square was empty. Almost everything in town had shut down early, and the storefronts sat dark and jagged in the cold. I heard the clicking sound of a heavy door locking and saw Liz with her keys in hand.

"Hey," I called out, and she turned around. Her curly hair caught in the wind, and she smiled when she saw it was me.

"Hey." Surprise brightened her eyes. "What are you doing?"

"I was at the dance."

"Right. With Owen," she said, her face clouded with disappointment.

"Well, yeah, but it wasn't really my scene," I said with a purposeful understatement.

"Mine either." She grabbed a bike sitting by the cafe's front door and pushed off, and we walked together in silence, listening to the click of the bicycle's wheels as we walked.

"So, how do you know Owen?" She asked, breaking the silence.

"I don't really. He's my mom's best friend's son, but he was younger, so I didn't really get to know him. He was always hanging out with his dad and playing football. When I came back to town, he gave me a ride home a few times and then asked me to the dance."

"You don't really seem like his type." I could feel the irritation in her voice.

"I'm not," I replied defensively.

"I'm not trying to be mean," she explained. "It's just, you're not — well, you know — blonde and tall and thin and... well, you're just different."

She finished in a matter-of-fact voice. I didn't know if it was a compliment or not, but she didn't seem to be insulting me. "Thanks," I said, not knowing what else to say. "How do you know him?"

"He comes in sometimes, usually on a date. He's not really a coffee shop kind of guy but comes in just to show his sensitive side." She crinkled her nose at the word sensitive.

"Anyway," she said, shrugging her shoulders, "wanna ride on my handlebars?"

"Seriously?" I asked.

"Why not? No one's around." She nudged me with her shoulder. "Here," she said as she straddled her bike. "Hop on."

I looked around. The asphalt was bare and cold, slightly damp and twinking with the fractured reflections of streetlights. The town echoed with a breeze that squeezed itself between the buildings. She was right: the streets were empty.

I took a breath and straddled the front wheel, lifting myself onto her bars. "Am I too heavy?" I asked over my shoulder.

"Not at all," she answered and pushed off from the curb. Her bike clicked, and I held my breath, bracing myself for a wobble or tilt that would send me flying headfirst onto the pavement.

"Look out world," Liz shouted and whooped. She picked up speed and laughed. The wind shot through me like lightning spreading across a summer sky. My heart was beating fast, my hands tight on the handlebars next to hers, and I found myself smiling and giggling right along with her.

"That way." I pointed to the narrow driveway that led up Blood Mountain.

Liz turned the bike, the back wheel slid slightly as she maintained control. She pedaled, slowing as the incline increased, her breath puffed out in front of her, until she came to a stop.

"That's all I have," she panted and planted her feet.

I dropped down to the pavement, and she swung her leg back over the bike so she could walk alongside it. I listened to the crunch of our feet walking up the mountain until I couldn't stand the silence.

"Where did you go when you left here?" I ventured. She looked surprised, as if she had forgotten I was walking beside her but smiled when she saw me.

"Everywhere, really. My aunt lived in California, but I moved around a lot when I turned eighteen." She shrugged.

"Why?" I asked, suddenly brave in the dark.

She shrugged. "To see things, you know? I liked the feeling of coming to a new city, of meeting people and making new art."

"You were a traveling artist?"

"Sort of." Her face flushed, and her jaw stiffened. "I guess I hated the feeling of being stagnant, you know?"

"But you ended up here?"

I stiffened, thinking I had offended her, but she laughed in response.

"You always were honest." She shook her head. "After my mom died, I didn't know where I should call home, you know? My house never really felt the same."

"I know that feeling," I said in a low voice.

"Well, after Mom died, the house sold, and Aunt Ginny said I could come live with her."

"How old were you again?"

"Twelve."

I thought back to the girl I knew in the lavender dress.

"I remember she had a beautiful smile," I offered.

"She did," Liz admitted. "But you know what's crazy?"

"What?"

"I can remember she had small hands and brown eyes, but I can't really remember her face. Weird, huh?"

"Not that weird." I shrugged. "Sometimes details get fuzzy when I think of my mom, and it's only been a little over a year."

"I just feel like I'm betraying her in a way, by forgetting her."

"Yeah. And by moving on," I added.

"Hmmmm," she agreed.

"What about the cafe? How'd you start working there?"

"It wasn't my intent when I came back to the South. I'd heard of an artist's collective in Atlanta, but when I got there, I only saw derivatives of the same art. And I stuck out immediately."

"Well, at least you have a unique voice."

"Yeah, but my inability to bend to clients didn't help."

"What do you mean?"

"That's how artists get paid. They commission art for high-end clients to fund their personal projects. And once they get established enough, their passion projects become their bread and butter."

"I never thought of it like that," I said. "I guess I just thought the art drove the art, you know?"

"I do, sis. I definitely do."

Liz spoke in a voice that was quiet, yet strong. Her curly, brown hair swept across her shoulders, and she tossed it out of her face. The air grew thick as a hazy fog drifted down the mountain, stuck between the trees like cotton caught in a brush.

"What about you? You okay being back here?"

"Not really," I answered. "I hate living with Ray."

"My mom did, too. She moved out as soon as she got the chance."

"I don't blame her."

"I always thought she was being dramatic. Is he really that bad?"

I shrugged. "He hasn't been since Mama died. He's actually been surprisingly nice. Well, at least for Ray."

"Has he not always been?"

I shook my head. "Mama said I was too young to remember, but I remember the first time I met Ray."

Liz's bike clicked steadily beside her.

"Mama made him dinner. She's just bought the Saunders house."

"I thought it was a family home," she interrupted.

"It was, but my grandma sold it before she died. She always blamed the house for things going wrong and had nothing to blame but herself when bad things continued after she sold the house.

"Anyway," I continued. "Mama cooked Ray this delicious meal — country-fried steak with mashed potatoes and green beans. I hated it. And I hated him. But that didn't matter. After a few months, Ray moved in.

"Mama was usually happy. She worked as a waitress in the diner and had friends. Marianne was her best friend, but after Ray came into the picture, Mama stopped having fun. She stopped playing and started waiting by the door while Ray was at work. He was all that she could see."

"I'm guessing you didn't feel the same?"

I shrugged. "At first, he was all right. He was handsome and charming. I remember him and Mama dancing after dinner in the kitchen."

I was silent for a moment, imagining Mama and Ray swaying with their bodies pressed up against one another as they found that tender spot in the kitchen that squeaked softly under their weight.

"But that's also when the drinking started," I said, breaking the silence, "and the staying out all night."

Liz watched me carefully, still unsure of what to say.

"Do you want to hear a story that she used to tell me?" I asked, interrupting the silence.

"Of course," she breathed next to me as the road slanted uphill.

"She used to tell it to me in her garden, under the stars. She said it was the only place where she felt safe. This one was her favorite.

"Once upon a time, there was a little girl, a princess. The little girl was all alone in the world. She had no mom, no dad, no siblings, no friends. Each night, she looked down at the town from a tall tower where she was locked away, where she would have one day been crowned queen if the town below hadn't forgotten about her. The girl didn't know how long she had been locked away up there or why she was locked away in the first place, but she dreamed of escape, of adventures and fairy tale endings. The little girl longed to join the rest of the world.

"She watched the town below her with envy. From her window, she could see children as they played with one another in the street. She could see shop owners selling goods from their carts. But the little girl could not leave her tower."

Liz raised her eyebrows, and I continued.

"You see, the girl wasn't alone. A monster lived in the tower with her. It would come out at night and gently stroke her hair. It would lean close and whisper that it would never leave the girl's side. Never. Not in a million years. He said that that was real love."

I licked my lips and continued, "As the little girl grew, so did the monster. She grew flowers on the trellis of the tower and fed the monster late at night. It gobbled her flowers as soon as she could grow them, and it grew fat with gluttony. It swelled and left pieces of itself wherever it touched. Its sticky skin slid against hers every night as its voice croaked in her ear, promising to never leave."

"Okay," Liz said, holding up one of her hands. "That is creepy."

I laughed softly, thinking of Mom. "I know."

"Your mom used to tell you stories like that?"

"Yeah, Mama was an odd one."[26]

I laughed again, and my house came into view, the porch light shone through the misty fog. The house was obscured in a fog so thick it was palpable. Rain glazed the grass like confetti. It sparkled in the dim lights of the front porch. It was a cold, wet drizzle that soaked everything in misery.

"This weather is terrible," I mumbled, not quite wanting to go inside.

"It might freeze. It's been cold enough lately." She held out

---

26 Sarah, Cat's mom, seems to enjoy stories based on fairy tales. Fairy tales are generally folktales that were written down in the seventeenth century for European aristocrats. The first fairy tales published were in 1697 by Charles Perrault's Histoires ou Contes du Temps Passé, or Tales of Mother Goose, which told the stories Sleeping Beauty, Cinderella, Little Red Riding Hood, and Puss in Boots. The Brothers Grimm published stories from 1812-1857 – including Hansel and Gretel, Cinderella, and Rumpelstiltskin. From 1835-1870, Hans Christian Andersen collected folk tales and published 156 stories across nine volumes – including The Little Mermaid, Thumbelina, The Snow Queen, The Red Shoes, and The Emperor's New Clothes.

There are a few defining characteristics of the fairy tale. First, all fairy tales are short narratives designed to be read in a single sitting. The second characteristic is that all fairy tales have a similar plot and often borrow from one another – the mistreated orphan, the wicked step-mother, the evil monster, the princess who needs to be rescued. The way elements come together, and the characters resolve the central conflict, however, makes them unique in their own way. The third characteristic is that all fairy tales include symbols and motifs – the apple, the frog, the mirror – that communicate meaning. The fourth and last characteristic is that all fairy tales have a nugget of wisdom in them. Their stories feel familiar because they are relatable, and the reader is able to apply the theme or message of the tale to their own life.

her hand in front of her.

"What do you mean?" I watched her breath puff out in front of her in the dim porch light.

"It's rare but happens sometimes when it's foggy and the temperature drops. Here," she said, reaching her free hand toward me. Her fingers brushed my cheek and touched a piece of my hair. As she pulled her hand away, something sparkled between her fingers.

"Ice," I whispered involuntarily.

"Ice," she repeated. "Freezing fog leaves everything in sight coated in ice crystals. It won't be enough to mess up the roads, but it's beautiful."

Her words hung in the air.

"They're usually a bad sign, though," she said as she looked down at her bike. "I should get going."

"Okay," I said, and she turned to go. "Actually, I —"

Liz turned around, her face fully illuminated in the light.

"I was wondering if, maybe, I could get a job. At the cafe?"

"You want to work at the cafe?" She asked, her voice coated in skepticism.

"Yeah, I mean, I need the money. Plus, my mom used to sell her teas there. Forever ago, but still."

Liz thought for a moment and looked back up at me.

"Sure," she said. "I could use some help."

"Great. When should I —"

"Tomorrow, if that's okay. Come in tomorrow morning."

"Okay. That sounds good. What time do you open?"

"Eight, but I get there at six. Breakfast won't cook itself, you know."

"Perfect."

She gripped her handlebars and turned down the hill. I watched her shadow disappear down the driveway and into the fog. Beside me, ice crystals covered the front banister and crunched underneath my feet.

The house was drafty, and I shivered and pulled a blanket

around my shoulders and made myself a warm cup of tea in the kitchen as I watched the fog freeze in silent slow motion from the kitchen window. It was the same window where Mama used to stand washing dishes every night. She used to put on an album for dinner and sway to the music, her apron tied around her waist, hands covered in suds, and a smile on her face.

I shuffled to the library and sipped my tea, warming my hands on my mug as the library's fireplace began to warm the room. The front windows fogged with condensation. I let my shoulders settle into the chair and thought about Mama, thought about Ray's accident and his return home, thought about the college acceptance letters that still sat in my desk drawer upstairs. I ran my free hand idly over the cover of Mama's diary.

I was struck by the strangeness of her words, of being caught off guard by someone I thought I knew so well. Every time I started to read through her diary, I felt like someone was watching me, creeping just out of sight. I flipped open the pages and scanned her handwriting. What other secrets hid inside the loops of her o's, the slice of her t's, the pierced dots of her i's?

"What the hell is this?" I jumped at the sound of Ray's voice, cutting through my thoughts. I hadn't heard him come in. Had he been home the whole time?

"Ray, you scared me," I gasped, sliding Mama's diary behind the chair's pillow and covering it with the blanket that had been around my shoulders.

"Sarah?" His voice slurred and sagged into sadness, then hope. "What are you —" He choked as he stifled a sob.

"Ray?" I asked confused. Didn't he recognize me?

"Sarah, I thought you were — I thought —" He stepped forward, but when I stepped back, he hesitated. The space between his eyebrows creased as his eyes took me in. "You're not —"

"Ray, it's me, Cat." I held out my hands.

"What are you doing here? Why are you wearing her things?" Ray's face soured into pure disgust.

"Ray, I —"

"You think you can just come in and take her things?" He spat and stepped forward again. I could smell thick liquor on his breath as he showed his teeth. "You think this is all yours, don't you, Cat? And that you can just come in here and —"

"She was my mom, Ray. We were —"

Ray's arm swung, and the back of his hand caught my cheekbone. I saw white as pain exploded across my face and forced me backward into Mama's chair.

"Take it off," he demanded.

"Ray, I —"

"Take it off, now!" He screamed, bending over me with his hand raised once more.

My shoulders started to shake as sobs threatened to break loose. I swallowed and slipped the dress off one shoulder, then another. The dress dropped to the floor, and I was left shivering in the drafty library.

I bent down and picked up the dress. Ray snatched it out of my hands before I could extend my arm, and I cried out, wincing as I braced for him to hit me again.

Ray zig-zagged to the steps, unsteady on his feet. He climbed the stairs slowly, the world spinning with alcohol, no doubt.

"Stay out of her stuff," he growled over his shoulder.

I was left in the cold dark of the library. I could feel my hot cheek pulse with every heartbeat. Sinking to the floor, I finally allowed the pain in my chest to break loose. Sobs hitched in my chest, and tears stung my eyes and trailed cold streaks down my face that dried in salty outlines like dried riverbeds until there was nothing left.

I sat there, numb to the cold and the pain until a tapping sound rang through the library. I glanced near the window but couldn't see the source of the sound. I shivered, glanced around the room again, and pulled myself to stand. The room was empty, so I pulled back on the blanket. Still shaking, I made a cup of tea and warmed myself as I made my way back to the library. I eased into Mama's chair, sliding the pillow aside to reveal Mama's diary when I heard the tapping sound again.

Pulling myself to my feet, I walked to the windows. They were clouded over with a film of moisture that separated the frigid February wind from the stale, drafty breath of the house. I still didn't see what could have made the noise and turned back to the chair when I spotted a dark spot in the corner of the window.

I bent closer and gasped.

Someone had drawn the outline of a heart on the glass.

The heart was quickly dissipating, fogging over once more as water collected on the surface of the window.

Interview with Eddy Sparrow
2:41 p.m. April 27th, 2021
Case No. HI30823

Yeah, Mom loved researching the myths and Southern stories, and it makes me sorta nostalgic to read Cat's version and Mom's notes.

I remember when this manuscript came in the mail, and I remember it so well because it was scorching hot that day, and the mailbox burned my fingers when I touched it, and I had to touch it to wrestle out this thick package that the mail woman — named Mercedes although she drove a Jeep — had wedged inside. It was in this thick manila envelope, and I remember Mom sitting at her desk with all these papers around her.

The pandemic still had everything shut down, and since I'd only recently come back home, we would sit and talk in the evenings. She would tell me stories like old times, only this time, she wasn't performing for a room. She was just talking to me, and reading this to you now, it's kinda like revisiting the stories from my childhood. I'd sit for hours and trace her skinny pen marks in the margins and on the backs of printed articles. Cat's story's threaded by fairy tales, superstitions, and mythology, and my mom's handwriting is right there along with them.

Mom found that the recreation hall in Cat's manuscript is still open and hosts events, like the school's "North Pole Radio" during Christmas and "The Easter Extravaganza." The cafe where Liz worked went out of business before the pandemic and has been turned into a Starbucks, of all things. I think Liz woulda hated that.

Cat's story supposedly took place in 2001, and there were several ice storms. You know the kind. Rounds of freezing rain for the north Alabama mountains, tons of rain for the south, and a whole lotta mess in the middle. Mom did confirm a rare frozen fog on Valentine's Day, 2001. I found some pictures online.

Mom made notes to keep looking into the Saunders family at this point, and she was particularly interested in the genealogy involved, especially how Cat was related to them all.

She also found an ad in the paper for Ray's Remodel from the nineties, let me see if I can find it...

Here. See? It looks like a small construction company, but the phone number has been disconnected.

I can't imagine the hours of her life Mom poured into this project. And what was I doing while she threw herself into this?

I took a lot of naps back then — depression does that to you, doesn't it? Too tired to cry but too sad to go to sleep the whole night through...

Well, all this happened after I moved back in with her.

Yeah, after the divorce.

I'm gettin' there. Just hold on.

You sure you don't want water or anything? It's no trouble.

Suit yourself, then, because this is where it really gets interesting.

MARCH 2001

The first week of March was unseasonably warm. Mama always said that March was the most temperamental month of the year. I walked down the mountain with my jacket under my arm, letting my hair blow in the wind, smelling the sweet scent of tepid air. The branches relaxed in the sunshine, and I knew that buds were soon to follow.[27]

It was early when I made it to town. The shops were just opening when I walked down Main Street. So early, in fact, that the clump of old men who usually clung to the outside of the general store had not yet congregated.

When I opened the cafe's front door, the lights were on, and the small kitchen was busy with life. Coffee steamed and bacon sizzled. Cinnamon rolls cooled on the counter, waiting for a final glaze of icing. Soft jazz music played overhead.

"Mornin'," Liz said over her shoulder. She was working at the counter with her back toward me. Her hair, slightly wet from a morning shower, was pulled back in her typical bun. She wore jeans and a black t-shirt with her white apron tied around her

---

27 March typically marks the start of the severe weather season in the spring in North and Central Alabama.

Alabama's deadliest weather outbreak was on March 21, 1932, resulting in 38 tornadoes across the Deep South, killing more than 268 people and injuring 1,750 people in Alabama alone.

waist.

"Hey, you're here already," I said, genuinely surprised at how much she had done. I had assumed that she would be just opening the cafe when she asked me to come at six o'clock.

"Yeah, I wanted to get these rolls out before the church ladies stop by." She turned as she squeezed a pastry bag in her hands and rounded the corner of the front counter.

"You'll need an apron." She nodded to the wall by the back room that held a stack of crisp white linens. "They're on the second shelf."

I took the one from the top of the stack and unfolded it. I held it up to my body but made a face when I noticed that its neck strap was not attached.

"Here, let me help," Liz said as she set down the pastry bag.

She came over and placed the apron onto my chest and looped the strap around my neck, fastening it onto the buckle.

"You know, my first job was a waitress. My aunt used to sing in these clubs, and I used to go around pretending that I was a waitress, asking people if they needed anything. I think I was twelve? Maybe thirteen?" She smiled, and a piece of hair fell into her face. She brushed it back with fingers that moved like blades of grass. She folded my apron at the waist and crossed the ties in the back. "They started letting me keep the tips after a while."

Liz leaned back and assessed her work. "Jesus, you're short." She frowned, adjusting the length once more before tying it at the front.

"Not bad, though." She nodded as she appraised me. "I need you over here." She gestured to the display case as she pulled a fresh tray of croissants from the oven. "I'll get these rolls ready if you'll stock the display," she said, already turning back to her work.

I didn't know what I had expected when I took the job. Liz was different from most people in town, that was for sure. She was independent and direct. She didn't prescribe to small talk and southern pleasantries, but she made me feel at ease, and I could tell that she was simply herself, straightforward, if not a little bossy.

When the cafe opened at eight, the doorbell dinged as the church ladies came in. I had just lined up the croissants and muffins Liz pulled from another shelf of the oven. I started to think her oven was limitless, perpetually baking new things by itself as if by magic.[28]

When I looked up, I saw Marianne. She had on a matching skirt suit, high heels, manicured, hair perfectly coiffed. She looked just like Tippi Hedron from The Birds but older. Her eyes sharpened when they spotted me, her face rose in surprise. I looked around for somewhere to hide, but it was too late. I had been spotted.

"Cat," she exclaimed. "Owen said you're back, but just look at you."

I flinched when I heard Owen's name, felt my mouth go dry, and looked at Liz for support.

"I'm tellin' you, it's been so long, and I think about your Mama every day. Lord, I miss her so much, and I can't even imagine how you're feelin'. You know, I offered to take you in, but Ray, he's so stubborn. Said you shouldn't have to leave your home, and well, I..."

The church ladies behind Marianne looked from the floor to the windows to the displays — anywhere but to me — and I could feel Liz's eyes on me.

"You know, you gotta come and see me sometime," Marianne pressed. "I could have you over this Wednesday if you can. We could have one of those big dinners with the whole fam —"

"Here you are, Mrs. Smith," Liz interrupted her and slid the box of cinnamon rolls across the counter.

"Oh, you're such a dear," Marianne beamed. "You know, Liz, here makes the best cinnamon rolls in town. We just have to have

---

28 The cafe has since been turned into a Starbucks, all employee data of the cafe has been lost, and the city did not keep personnel employment records at that time.

'em for our Ladies Through Christ meetings."

I nodded and stepped back.

One of the ladies behind her leaned forward. "She didn't make these, did she?" The lady looked toward me and grimaced like she had eaten something bitter.

"It's all me," Liz said in a curt voice. "Just like always."

The woman licked her lips and took a step back, still eyeing me. "Anything else?" Liz sang in what I knew to be false cheeriness.

"That will be it," Marianne responded. She picked up the box of cinnamon rolls and nodded toward me. "I mean it, Cat. It's real nice to see ya."

She walked to the door, and the women behind her trailed like leaves caught in a spiderweb, mirroring her movements, glued to her trajectory that led them out the door. The sour-faced women took one more look at me before they left and headed onto the sidewalk.

When the door closed, silence took over, and the soft jazz felt out of place, like neon lighting up a sanctuary. I could tell that Liz was avoiding my gaze as she organized an impeccably arranged spice rack.

"Thanks," I said in a voice barely above a whisper.

She didn't respond. Instead, she turned her attention to the fruits, arranging them into containers before opening the fridge and sliding in the baskets of blueberries, strawberries, and raspberries.

"She's always doing that," I said, still trying to break the silence. "Asking me over. She used to be best friends with my mom when they were little. At least that's what she's always telling me."

Liz closed the refrigerator and adjusted her apron before wiping the counter so that the silver top gleamed spotless and clear.

"So, your mom passed away?" She said without looking at me.

"Yeah." I nodded. How had she not heard in this small town?

She had to have picked up some of the gossip in town serving coffee. "She died a little over a year ago."

"Is that why you went away?" She still wasn't looking at me. Instead, she kept wiping the already clean counter.

So maybe she had heard the gossip.

"Kind of." I tried to gauge her, figure out how much she already knew, but her face was blank, unreadable. I sighed, deciding to just be honest. Who cared how much she already knew? She seemed different. Maybe she would understand. "I got sick when she died. I had just graduated in December, so they sent me to this program to recover, but the courts said I had to come back home until I turned eighteen."

"How long is that?"

"This coming New Years. I just have to finish out the year."

"And then?" Her question hung between us. I had been thinking about that a lot recently but figured I had plenty of time. The truth was, I had never been on my own. Even when Ray moved in, it was still mostly Mama and me.

"I'm not quite sure yet," I confessed.

She nodded before continuing. "And you're okay now?" She asked, looking into my eyes.

"Yeah," I breathed, my heart skipping a beat. "I'm fine."

Liz stopped wiping the counter but didn't respond. She looked at me, measuring me up. My chest tightened, and I stepped forward.

"Look, I really need this job," I pleaded. "Things at home aren't the best, and I really need the money."

"For what? Your big escape at the end of the year?" She asked in a pointed voice.

"Maybe," I admitted, "but mostly, it's for the house. We barely have money for basic groceries. No one will hire Ray."

"Well get used to seeing Marianne around." She sighed and looked around her, then turned back to the counter, pulling out a ball of dough from a container where it had been rising. "She's always poppin' in to see if I'm actually working."

"Wait, does she own this place?"

Liz nodded. "Yeah, along with most of the businesses in town. I just run it during the day."

"Figures," I breathed, anger seeping into my voice.

"Anyway, I guess we'll just have to make this work." She looked across the cafe and gestured. "You keep the dining area neat, and I'll handle the food. The bathrooms will need cleaned once an hour. Same thing with the floors. Aside from that, we have leftovers almost every day, and I can pay weekly."

I opened my mouth to say thank you, but she nodded to the corner.

"The broom's in the back closet. Grab that and the mop, and I'll show you have to prep the dining area."

I took a breath and headed to the closet, happy that Liz had taken me in without question. Well, with only a few questions, at least.

The first time I found out my grandmother was a witch was on a night much like this one. Showers rolled in this morning, and the house was stuck in a thick fog. It feels like I'm the only one left in the world. Cat had to stay late at school, and Ray isn't home yet, but tonight reminds me of a stormy March night when I stayed at the house with my grandmother. She was the kind of woman who always wore a dress and did her hair, even if we were staying in the house every day. She put on her rings and a gold watch every day, cooked in an apron, and always had cookies on hand, although Mom said that last part was because Grandmother knew how much I loved cookies.

One night that summer, she had cooked pancakes for breakfast, and we fell asleep reading fairy tales. She told me about a princess who had two different colored eyes (one blue and one green) just like me. She said I was special, said I had the mark of a witch.[29] When I awoke around midnight, I heard voices downstairs.

Grandmother was at the table with a woman. I couldn't hear what they said, so I crept closer. The woman's hands were shaking, and a terrible moan came from somewhere deep in her belly. It was a moan of pure sadness. I had never heard someone make that noise before. It sounded like some sort of animal. Grandmother asked if she was sure. The woman nodded and handed her a wad of money, which Grandmother stashed in a tin she kept by the breadbasket. Then, the woman pushed a small bag across the table. She took the contents out, one by one. A photograph. A strand of hair. A handwritten letter. A pair of cufflinks.

I must have moved or made a noise because Grandmother saw me and took me back to bed. When I asked her about the woman, she said that sometimes people need help. Sometimes they need someone

---

29 Heterochromia is a rare genetic trait that is seen in less than 1% of the world population. This must be referring to complete heterochromia, where two eyes are completely different colors. I have partial heterochromia, so most people don't realize it, but my eyes are slightly different colors as well. Heterochromia is alsoa sign of Horner's syndrome or Sturge-Weber syndrome.

to listen to, to tell them they're all right, that everything's gonna be okay. Other times, they need someone to help. They need someone on their side to make sure it all turns out all right.

Later, I found out a shop owner in town died of a heart attack. He was fine that morning. His wife said he was fine that morning. He went to the shop, opened it like normal, and then two hours later, he dropped dead of a heart attack. The shop assistant found him. Her picture appeared in the paper, and I recognized her instantly. She was the woman who came during the storm. I asked Grandmother about it the next time I visited, but she said that I was asking about the wrong things, nosing into grown folks' business and that I should go play in the garden instead.

I stayed with Grandmother every summer from the age of twelve until the year I turned fourteen while my sister went to an accelerated writing camp (or nerd camp, as I called it). I studied her as she made tinctures and tended to the garden. She taught me about tea leaves and nightshades, ointments and moon cycles. We had tea parties in the garden and would play hide and seek in the roses, but she could be overprotective.

Marianne wanted to hang out, but Grandmother refused. She said they were from new money and shouldn't be entertained. She said we were better than that, better than them, but I was never allowed to go to her house. I asked her if we could get ice cream from the shop in town, maybe meet Marianne there, and she said that we could make our own ice cream.

I tried to tell her that wasn't the point, but she didn't understand. She couldn't see the excitement of going into town, sitting at the soda fountain counter, meeting friends, and ordering a delicious glass of ice cream. All she could see was the end of summer, looming in the distance and the little time she had left.

A few weeks after I asked her if we could meet Marianne for ice cream, Marianne said she was having a birthday party and that everyone would be there, but I knew Grandmother would never let me go. I told her that I would make the tea that night and slipped in a few drops of the nighttime tincture she'd give to her customers. We had our tea in the garden, and I could see Grandmother's eyes get glassy. I told her I was tired and got a bath early, ditching my tea into the roses before we went inside. She brushed my hair lazily, and I pretended to yawn and rub my eyes, and because I had never lied to her before, she believed me.

When the sky turned dark and I was sure she was asleep, I snuck downstairs, tiptoed out the front door, and ran all the way into town. I was late, but I was so excited when I got to the party. Marianne's parents welcomed me, and Marianne hugged me and told me how much she had missed me over the last few weeks. There were games and presents and songs and girls in party dresses. I ate cake and played late until Marianne's dad invited me to stay, and I did.

It wasn't until later, until the next morning when I came down from my bedroom, groggy from lack of sleep, that I knew something was wrong.

Grandmother knew.

I don't know how she knew, but she did. And the funny part was, she wasn't even mad. She said that it was what children did. They loved you and wanted you and needed you until they simply didn't anymore.

It was different after that. Sometimes I would catch Grandmother looking at me as if I were a stranger, as if she didn't even know me. When I asked her what was wrong, she just shook her head. I still feel guilty about lying and sneaking out. I wish she was here still, especially on nights like tonight when the house is so quiet. But she died that fall. It was like she knew her time was running out, and not just with me but with everyone. Mom always said the house was haunted, and after Grandmother died and Cat was born, she was convinced. She sold the house to Mr. Johns, Marianne's dad. He said he'd take care of it. Anyway, I don't have to worry about any of that anymore. The house is mine and so is Cat and Ray. Only…

Ray's been staying out at night lately. Says he's been working a lot, but something doesn't seem right. And last night was awful. I put on an album and was cooking dinner. He came home just at sundown, and I could tell he'd been drinking. He had that hazy look *in his eyes, but I didn't mind because it made him pull me close, right in the middle of cooking. He just took my hand and pulled me onto his lap and kissed me like he used to. God, that man can make the whole world melt away.*

But then his hand tightened on my wrist, and he pulled, making me cry out. He asked me about my watch, Grandmother's watch, and when I told him that I'd had it, his hand hit my cheekbone in a flash of white. Pain spread across my face, and I couldn't see.

Cat must of heard me scream, and when I could see again, Ray was standing over me, and Cat was behind him in the doorway. I told Cat that it was all right, that I had just slipped and hit my face on the chair.

I didn't want to upset her, and I didn't know what else to say. Ray had never hit me before. He'd never do that. At least not normally.

Maybe it's 'cause he'd been working so much. Maybe it's 'cause Marianne's been calling again. I just don't know what to do. Everything seems out of order lately, and I don't know how to make it all right again. I just don't want to end up alone like all the other Saunders women. [30]

---

30 In Small Town Talk: The Hidden History of Alabama's Small Towns by Franklin Walthrop, Olivia Saunders and her twin daughters, Helen and Eleanor, retreated from society from 1831 to 1857. They were not mentioned in any newspaper articles or event details in town and did not host parties during that time. They maintained a skeleton staff of three, a cook, a maid, and a gardener, to maintain the grounds.

On December 21st, 1846, the longest night of the year, it is reported that Olivia made her way through the gardens, wandering deep into the rose maze before she collapsed in front of the well where Saheter died. Her wanderings were not unusual with multiple letters published in the paper about lights moving at the top of the mountain, presumably Olivia, walking the grounds until the early morning hours. That night however, Olivia's light didn't make it back to the house. In fact, it went out forever. Walthrop published a rare quote from Helen about Olivia's death, writing, "As usual, our mother was suffering her sickness by the time we got home- we could hear her coughing from the front porch. Recently, her breathing had gotten difficult- especially at night. She took to the ruined orange orchard to roam under the light of the moon." The cook found her body by the well that morning when she went out to draw water for the kitchen. Doctors said she must have gotten pneumonia due to her late-night walks through the orchard.

Mom found more stuff on "farmer's lung." Here, it's in this pile.

See? She looked up their symptoms and found that it's most likely somethin called Stachybotrys chartarum — or black mold. It's a fungus that works as a complex system, kinda like how ants work as a colony. It reproduces asexually with the help of high moisture or humidity, something we have lots of in the South. And high pulp environments, like rotting trees or even in houses that help it produce something called mycotoxins, which cause respiratory and even neurological diseases. The rotting orchard would have been perfect for black mold and coulda caused the workers and Olivia to have reactions. It coulda caused her to get sick easily, especially if she was exposed to the cold like she woulda been if she was walkin outside at night. Anyway, Cat's part is next.

By the end of March, Liz and I settled into a routine. My therapy sessions were going well, and they were adjusted to once a month instead of once a week. Ray was mostly leaving me alone and even helping out around the house. Liz and I would open the cafe and work until closing. Then, we'd stay late, talking and cleaning up. She taught me how to make a lemon pound cake that melted in your mouth and how to wait until the dough was slow to move as a sign that it was ready to be shaped. I was better at natural remedies, drying herbs, and making teas, but Liz was patient in a way that I'd never seen. Sometimes she'd remind me of Mama, how she sang when she moved around in the kitchen. Other times, she'd remind me that she was nothing like Mama, how she'd get moody and cold sometimes when I thought she'd finally called us friends.

Regardless, she'd ride through town with me on her handlebars as the sun sank beneath the trees. We'd walk up the drive to my house, and Liz would say the air gave her creative ideas. I doubted that the reason she walked all the way up to my house was to get inspiration but didn't say anything. It was nice to have a friend.

One night when we reached the house, Liz turned to me and asked, "You ever see ghosts in there?"

"You listen to too much gossip," I laughed, shaking my head.

"I hired you, though," she shot back, and I couldn't help but feel a stab of pain. She noticed in the thick dusk and continued, "I don't take much stock in gossip, but I do believe in ghosts."

"Sometimes I hear things." I hesitated, not wanting to mention the woman I imagined creeping behind the walls for the last few months.

Liz raised her eyebrows. "Old houses are like that. Anything else?"

Again, I hesitated.

"Kind of. I saw wet footprints once." I held my breath and waited for her reply.

"Like ghostly footprints?"

"I guess so. No one else was downstairs at the time."

"Why were they wet, though? Seems weird."

"Yeah," I agreed. "Very."

"Look," Liz said, pointing at the sky and interrupting my train of thought. "A satellite."

I followed the silver flash of her arm in the dim light to the inky sky above us. What looked like a star trekked its way across the sky, steady and bright. It looked just like a star except that it was moving.

"Is that an airplane?" I asked, not sure about what I was seeing.

"No," she said. "See, airplanes blink." She pointed to a blinking trail on the horizon, beating out the Morse code of untold adventures over cities and suburbs as families washed dishes and got ready for bed. "Satellites look like moving stars, solid and steady, but sometimes, when the light hits them just right- There!" She shouted, pointing at the satellite again.[31]

The satellite brightened into a beacon. Its silver turned to gold, flashing wildly before fading into a barely visible pinpoint. I glanced over at her watching the satellite.

"I've never even heard of watching for satellites before. Stars, sure, but not-"

"What do you think would happen if someone were to wish on one? You think it would come true?"

I shrugged my shoulders, not sure of how to respond. Liz was the only person I'd ever heard talk like that. "Maybe," I said. "Wanna see what happens if we do?"

Liz turned to me and smiled. "Okay. Well, I wish —"

---

31 Although there were significantly less satellites in 2001 versus now, it's possible that she's referring to an iridium flare, or a satellite flare. Although they look like meteors entering the atmosphere, the flares are caused by a satellite crossing the night sky, usually only visible in the absence of ambient light from cities and on clear nights where visibility is optimal. A satellite must cross the night sky at an angle where the sun's light can reflect off its surface. Generally, the satellite will look like a star but will move in a straight line across the night sky. An iridium flare is named after the Iridium satellite constellation of 66 orbiting stations used for satellite, aircraft, and military communications. Originally, the constellation was supposed to launch with 77 satellites, the scientific number for Iridium on the periodic table, but only 66 satellites were necessary. A flare, however, occurs when the sun hits the iridium panels and reflects the light back to earth.

"You're not supposed to say it out loud," I interrupted.

"Then, how will you know if it comes true or not? How will you know I'm not just saying that it came true?"

"You don't seem like a liar to me," I ventured.

"You don't either, but people lie all the time." She shrugged and kept her eyes on the rough driveway under our feet.

I thought about that for a second. Everyone I had ever known had lied to me at some point, had withheld the truth, or disappointed me in some way. Every single person.

"Okay, then let's make a wish together."

"How are we gonna do that?" She asked, doubtful.

"We agree on a wish."

"I wish I could sell some of my art pieces," she exhaled.

"I wish I didn't have to live with Ray," I said under my breath.

"And that I had enough money to buy the cafe," she continued.

"And that I was normal."

"Normal is boring." She nudged my arm with her elbow. I shrugged but didn't answer. I knew she was trying to make me feel better, but it didn't work.

"I wish my mom were still here," I said in a voice so thin that it was like paper crinkling in a fire.

"Mine, too. I wish a lot of things were different."

"I'm glad you're here," I admitted. I could feel Liz turn my words over in her mind, but she didn't say anything for a minute, so kept talking. "My great-grandmother lived in the house, too. She was a witch."

"Really?" Her voice was skeptical.

"Really. My mom used to spend summers with her. My mom wrote in her diary about one of her summers here, and she used to write about Ray." I stopped short and shook my head, but Liz waited, patient and silent.

I took another breath and continued, "It was always different with Ray," I began. With Mama, everything started with Ray. "They met at some cheesy dance. He swept her off her feet and made all these promises. But it was Mama who bought the house and made this life for us. Ray was just, sort of, there." I made a face and looked at Liz, but her expression was blank, open and listening, empty of judgment, so I kept talking.

"Things were fine at first. They were happy enough, but then, he started to bring beer home. First, on special occasions. Then, on the weekends. Then, every night. The bottles would pile up like shiny beetles in the trash can, and when Mama brought it up, he said, 'Fine.' The beer stopped showing up in the fridge."

I could feel Liz study my face.

"But then I noticed his trips to the bathroom after work, during dinner, all hours of the night, his fiery breath, the rage behind his eyes. I knew he was sneaking liquor every time he went to 'go take a leak.' And so did Mama, only she didn't say anything."

Liz shook her head and waited for me to continue, but I couldn't speak at first. Instead, I saw Mama, standing barefoot in the kitchen, cooking at the stove, doing dishes at the sink. Mama's favorite thing to cook was stew. She could grow just about anything and had a huge cookbook filled with delicious meals she'd inherited from my great-grandmother. Sometimes I wondered if she kept some of that nurturing for herself, maybe she wouldn't have been so broken. Maybe she wouldn't have needed Ray to make her whole. Maybe I could have been enough.

But as it was, there was no escape.

Ray had sucked her dry.

He sucked us both dry.

"One night," I started, "everything changed. It was like I could feel it before it happened. Mama was cooking, and Ray came in. He used to do this thing where he would pull her to him and kiss her. It was disgusting, but Mama loved it."

As I pictured them embracing, I could almost smell her, that same scent I had been trying to capture ever since: rosewater shampoo, lavender, rich earth, sunshine, coming rain.

"Ray hugged her, but as they let go, he grabbed her wrist and asked her where she had gotten the watch she was wearing. She tried to explain that it had been her grandmother's, that she had just gotten the latch fixed with her tips from the diner when he —"

I could see it in my head. Ray's clenched jaw. Mama's open mouth, explaining. My breath caught as I tried to think of something — anything — to diffuse the situation when I saw his hand silhouetted against the fading twilight in the kitchen window.

"He hit her," I finished. "He hit her, and I didn't even do anything. I just sat there."

"Cat, you were a child. What could you have done?"

I shrugged and did the only thing I could think to do. I kept talking.

"Ray stalked out of the house. Mama tried to call after him, begging him not to leave her, but he didn't listen. He stayed out all night that night, and Mama stayed there at the kitchen table.

"I tried to get her to eat, drink water, anything, but she refused. Instead, she took my hand and told me that once when she was little, she'd go to the fair with her mother. She had been amazed by all the sights and sounds, by all the lights.

"But her favorite ride by far had been the teacups. She remembered gripping the wheel and spinning the cup faster and faster. The lights of the fair spun into blurs. The smells of funnel cakes swirled around her. Fellow riders cried out in terror and delight.

"And when she got off the ride, she stumbled from side to side trying to find her bearing, but it was impossible. Instead, she sat down on the bench outside until the lights stopped spinning and the people stopped squealing and the world came back to Earth. She looked up at her mother, smiled, and asked to ride one more time.

"Mama used to say it was kinda like that, being with Ray. Sometimes it felt like the fair, and sometimes it felt like the teacups, and you had to sit down and catch your breath so that the world would stop spinning out of control. Before Ray was like a merry-go-round of men, of identities, and after Ray, it was a ride she couldn't get off. But she couldn't get enough of him. She always wanted more."

Liz looked doubtful, and I knew it sounded irrational, but there was something about the pull of another person. I'd felt it too, at times, with Mama. When she was in one of her good moods, we were on top of the world, and with the bad moods, everything turned to teacups. She'd needed me so much in both good and bad times. There's nothing like the feeling of being needed.

"Does he ever hit you?" She asked, narrowing her eyes in concern.

"No," I said quickly, avoiding her eyes, and I couldn't help but think that that's exactly how Mama used to answer that same question. I felt myself blush, but I knew I couldn't tell her — I couldn't tell anyone — about Ray's temper. I'd just end up in foster care, away from home, away from all the memories of Mama. I couldn't let that happen.

I could see Liz nod out of the corner of my eyes, and she took a long breath. "Tell you what," she started, "we can make that wish, but let's focus on this year."

"This year?"

"Yeah, why not? You have until the end of the year here, and I'm savin' up money, so why don't we wish to have an amazing, teacup-free, year."

"I like that," I nodded as we reached the house.

"Cool," she said, turning her bike around. "Tomorrow morning, then?"

"Yeah, I'll be there." I returned and watched her head back

down the mountain, looking up at the stars.[32]

That night, I laid in bed, listening to the house shift beneath me. I could almost hear whispers. Were they from people who had lived there long ago, words that had settled into the wallpaper, imprinted themselves on the wood floors, hiding in the dark corners of closets, or were they from the women, stuck, creeping, just waiting to get out and dance in the sunshine.[33]

---

32 Images of tea as a source of knowledge, specifically knowledge of the future, have been found in cultures across the world. Origins of tea readings come from Asia, the Middle East, and Ancient Greece. In the 17th century, tea first came from China to Britain's aristocratic society. With strict religious and often superstitious structures in place, lower-class individuals often embraced a chance to look into the future where their futures may be improved. In the 18th century, the first book was published on tea leaf symbols for the purpose of divination, called Reading Tea Leaves. In fact, the book outlines a technique where the reader tosses the teacup, spinning it around counter-clockwise three times before interpreting the leaves.

Teacups are also featured in Western literature when referring to upper-class society. Idioms, such as "It's not my cup of tea," typically call to attention to societal norms that prioritize Western of "civility," "wealth," "productivity," "individualism," and strict class, racial, and gender roles. In America, the importance of tea is symbolic in the American Revolution, the Boston Tea Party for example, and the beginning of America's identity as an individual entity separate from the British empire.

33 Research this month has been a little slow. I've had doctor's appointments and my daughter is having a tough time lately, so I've been spending more time with her, showing her how to grow herbs and bake. It seems to help so far, and time is so precious. More research will follow.

It's pretty cool to see her reference me here. It makes me feel special in a way. I guess Mom tried several times to call town hall to access records. You know, archives, property records, deeds, wills — things she wasn't able to access online.

I remember a call that came in the fall. We were still knee-deep in the pandemic. Things were getting better — for the world and for me. I'd made it through the saddest parts of summer, and I was starting to talk more to Mom, although I didn't realize that she already knew her health was failing.

The call was from a clerk at town hall, but Mom was sleeping. I offered to wake her up since it was just about tea time anyway, but the lady on the phone said not to. She was just responding to Mom's many messages — she emphasized   by the way — that most of the records she was requesting had been lost. Confused, I told her I'd pass along the message.

I hung up and went to Mom's room, and she was still asleep. The air was warm. It still had that muggy tinge before October's rain moved through, and she had the window open. The sun slanted through the window, and everything was this golden - yellow color — hey, I never claimed to be a poet, so don't laugh.

Anyway, she looked so peaceful. And I remember being so happy to be back home and to have this second chance with her. I just wish that we could have had more time, ya know?

I'm sorry to hear that. Losin' your mom's hard, and I wouldn't wish it on my worst enemy. But they never talk about after, ya know? They never talk about how a house feels after someone has died. Like the soul has gone right out of the place.

No wonder Cat felt a woman creeping about. There's just an eerie feeling that sets in, and that's when it hits you: the fact that she'll never wear the housecoat she had hangin' on the back of her door or that she'll never pull on her shoes again to go for her morning walks or that she'll never use her recipe cards again to bake cakes, although she had them memorized anyway, but she said she loved to pull them out and remember when her own mom once cooked with her.

Yeah, we'd had a falling out. It was years back when I was an undergrad, and we went for ten years or so of not talking, and I'd give anything to talk to her again.

I do remember that she loved tea, just like Cat's mom. All kinds of tea. Jasmine tea, honeysuckle, chamomile, lavender. And they were always so sweet that more than one glass would give you a tummy ache. Maybe it's a Southern thing, but she was always a lady. She never put her pocket book on the floor, and she never left the house without her face on. And loved her afternoon teas. She grew her herbs on the front porch right out there, and I could tell the season based on the tea we drank in the afternoons. God, I really do miss her. And this house is so quiet. But not now.

Now, I have you to talk to. Want me to keep readin'?

APRIL 2001

"Can you hand me the cups out of the dishwasher?" Liz called over her shoulder.

The cafe was packed that morning. We'd had storms and a cold snap that had lasted two weeks, and it was finally sunny enough for people to venture out of their homes to enjoy a Saturday outside.

I unloaded the clean dishes and began loading dirty ones as Liz filled cups with coffee, creams, and sugars to make drinks called lattes and mochas and espressos. I still couldn't tell the difference, but it didn't matter because I was so busy with clearing tables and managing the floor that I didn't have time to be behind the counter for long.

That morning, however, the line stretched out the door. Liz pushed her hair off her forehead, something I noticed she only did when she was nervous or overwhelmed.

She turned her attention to the cash register and stopped, hand in mid-air as she was about to push a loose curl off her forehead. Her hand faltered, and she tucked a piece of hair behind her ear.

A man a little older than us stood at the counter. He was tall, thin, Asian, and wore glasses and a button-up. He looked like a young professor, only the closest college was more than thirty minutes away.

"Josh," she breathed.

My hands slowed as they loaded cups on the top rack of the dishwasher. For the past month, I'd seen Liz greet customers with a mix of detachment and forced congeniality, but this was different.

"What are you doing here?" She asked.

"I could ask you the same thing," he said in a flat voice.

She snuck a look at me over her shoulder, feeling my gaze, and took another breath before looking back at Josh. I stared, too, unable to look away. I had never seen Liz uneasy before, but with Josh's arrival, I saw the color in her face, the way she licked her lips nervously, the way her breathing became shallow and uneven.

"I'll just have a coffee for now." Josh gave a thin smile and placed a crisp five-dollar bill on the counter.

Liz, still frozen in place, stared, so I did the only thing I could think to do at that moment. I grabbed a mug and filled it with coffee that steamed angrily in the morning light, pushed it carefully across the counter, and continued working the cash register.

"Your change," I said, looking up at him.

Josh straightened himself, realizing that he wasn't the only person in line and headed to the back corner to brood over my interruption, no doubt.

"Next," I called, and the woman behind him hesitated slightly before stepping forward. She looked over at Josh sipping his coffee and decided that in her caffeine-deprived state that I was as good a waitress as any and started her order: a ham and cheese scone with a cup of coffee to go.

I turned to get her order, and Liz still stood there, watching the man across the room.

"Take a quick break," I said as I stuffed a scone into a to-go bag. "I can handle the line for a few minutes."

She nodded, still shaken by Josh's appearance, and headed into the back room.

I handed the woman her food and coffee, and although she hesitated slightly — I mean, who would want to be served by the freaky kid who lived in the haunted house — she took her food with a nod and headed out the door.

The morning and lunch hour passed with me taking orders while Liz worked in the kitchen or took breaks in the back, but Josh never left his corner. After the crowd thinned and the shadows began to grow long again, I sighed and rounded the corner.

"You know we're closing soon," I said, checking over my shoulder to ensure Liz was still in the back.

Josh looked up at me, measuring me up from my old converses to my frazzled hair. I stiffened and held his gaze.

"Another cup of coffee would be great." He nodded, and I rolled my eyes.

"Why are you here?" I asked.

"Oh, is this the part where you tell me I don't belong here? To go back to where I came from?" He raised his eyebrows at me, challenging me back.

"You're clearly here to intimidate Liz, and you've done that. All day, in fact. You can leave now."

"I wish it were that simple, sweetie."

I bristled at his patronizing tone. "I'm not your sweetie," I muttered.

"Clearly," he said under his breath and pulled out a cigarette. "But I'll go when I've gotten what I came here for."

"Which is?" I crossed my arms in front of my chest.

"None of your business," he answered as he flicked his lighter open and lit the cigarette dangling between his lips. "Wait, you're that girl, aren't you?"

He looked at me, measuring me up from toe to crown. I snuck a glance at the front counter when Liz, who rounded the corner from the back room, stopped in her tracks when she saw our close proximity. She lowered her head, slowly removed her apron, and walked over. Josh had a smug look on his face as she approached.

"There's no smoking in here," she muttered. He shrugged, a smile curled around the cigarette. "How'd you find me?" She asked as she dropped into the seat across from him.

"The usual," he said with amusement. "I just followed your trail to Atlanta, and when it went cold in Birmingham, it didn't take long to find you. The Art department at UAB was happy to point me your way. Your work's been impressive lately. I just had to come see about this new collection I've been hearing about. Johansson said they're getting top dollar."[34]

"It's not about the money," she said in a weak voice.

"Clearly not to you, but we have investors…" His voice tailed off, and she stiffened.

Investors? What was he talking about?

Liz sighed and pushed her hair back from her face. They continued as if I wasn't standing right in front of him.

"Do you know how hard it was to explain your disappearance?" He leaned forward.

"Josh, I —"

"Just days before your show."

"I told you it wasn't ready. You saw the work. It was —"

"It's never ready, Liz. There's always just one more thing you want to add or just one more painting that needs tweaking." Josh's voice rose to a caricature of Liz's voice.

"That's not fair, Josh. I —"

"Have the habit of leaving me to explain it all. Well, not this time. This time, I'm taking full advantage of this new collection, so we can finish this goddam show."

"Josh, I — I can't just produce a whole show on a dime. I've been working on some really great ideas, and there's this energy here, not for a show, but for the joy of making art." He rolled his

---

34 Art is typically priced based on the size, materials, techniques used, visual quality, and reputation of the artist.

Larger canvas sizes, rare materials, special techniques, and established artists usually earn higher prices at gallery sales or auctions. Sometimes a well-respected gallery will attract more attention, and competitive pricing. Other factors, such as price to transport and preservation requirements can influence the price.

eyes, and she put her hand on her hip. "Just let me show you what I've been creating."

Josh looked skeptical but didn't respond. He ashed his cigarette in the mug and looked at her over the table.

"I promise. You won't regret it," she said. He took a breath and drummed his fingers on the table, looking out at the dim light that stubbornly held down Main Street. "And think about the opportunities this new work will bring, even if it's not a full show. Limited quantities. Rare pieces. Think of the investors, I bet they'll love it," Liz ventured, and Josh couldn't help himself. He rolled his eyes, stood up, and grabbed his coat. She turned to me. "You up for some moral support?"

I nodded, not knowing how I could offer that when I didn't even know who this guy was or what he wanted, but I knew from the look in her eyes that she needed me. And that was enough.

Transcript

<u>Interview with Eddy Sparrow</u>

4:06 p.m. April 27th, 2021

<u>Case No. HI30823</u>

It's interesting that this Josh guy could track down Liz like that. Birmingham has a tight-knit art community. Mom worked closely with lots of other departments in the South, and she was close with the Art department chair, Anita Graham, at UAB, and she confirmed that UAB's art events are for students as well as artists in the larger community.

Look at this event. Here's a flyer for one of their exhibits which includes students, emerging artists, established artists, local studios, and buyers.

Here's a note where Mom called UAB's Abroms-Engel Institute for the Visual Arts (AEIVA) for a list of past exhibits — maybe Liz's name could be listed as a past exhibitor — but she didn't find anything.

Stephen, my ex-husband, used to go to these and the Art after Dark events all the time.

I know. I'm gettin to him. Just be patient.

After closing the cafe, we walked to Liz's house. It was nothing like I'd imagined and exactly how I'd imagined. It was small and quaint. Every inch of it was decorated in color and texture. The front door was painted with violets and palms, and a bright sun peeked over the top of tall banyan trees on a painted horizon. Inside, my feet were met with beautiful carpets, lush in feel and in color. Various paintings and pictures hung on the walls, covering all but skinny white grids that surrounded the frames. Plants hugged together in the windows, reaching for sunshine. The furniture was vintage, a pink velvet sofa, a high-backed rattan chair that resembled a throne, a mid-century modern reclined chair, a modular 80s-style coffee table. A crystal mobile that threw rainbows over the walls. Various hanging plants and seashell wind chimes hung from the ceiling. I stopped, trying to catch each detail of the room while it breathed us in.

Liz parted Josh and me, and we followed her through a cramped kitchen that was packed with jars of flour and hanging herbs. Other herbs sat on the windowsill behind a small glass cafe table.

She opened the back door and walked to a tiny garden shed that she had converted into a studio. The smell of paint thinner and oil hit my nose, and I was met by the most beautiful swirls of blue, twisting shades of cobalt, cerulean, and lapus, navy, azure, and berry, blending to form faces. Over and over the faces repeated on each canvas. A woman with a knowing smile, as if a delicious secret hung right inside her mouth, turning her head away, always away, her eyes locked on mine.[35]

---

35 Reminiscent of Picasso's Blue Period. Blue is a color that rarely exists in nature. Although Ancient Egyptians created a blue pigment around 2200 B.C., the ancient Greeks and Romans didn't even have a term for the color blue. In fact, Homer described the sea as "wine-red," and it was only later coined the term "true blue" (or lapis lazuli) in the 6th century in a Buddhist painting in Afghanistan. It was later renamed ultramarine (or "beyond the sea") by Italian traders in the 14th century, and it was used by the wealthy during the medieval period as a symbol of status (see The Girl with the Pearl Earring).

"Liz, yes!" Josh exclaimed as he licked his lips. I could see him calculating the value of each canvas, and the thought made me sick. "How many are ready? At least twelve, right?" She paused and looked at the ground. "Fourteen are ready. I probably have another six that can be ready within the month."

"Perfect." His eyes glazed over as he nodded his head, and he excused himself, he was already dialing various buyers and studios.

With a promise to check in next week for updates, Josh left, his vintage roadster growling as he pulled out of the driveway. Liz sighed beside me, picked herself up off the sofa, and headed to the kitchen.

"Wanna drink?" She called over her shoulder, already pulling two glasses from the shelf.

I opened my mouth to tell her no, that I wasn't even eighteen yet, that even the sight of alcohol reminded me of Ray, but the thought died on my lips. I knew I'd sound like an idiot kid.

"Fresh lemonade," she said, pulling a bag of lemons from the fruit bowl and looking over at me.

I smiled, reassured, and nodded.

Liz nodded to the cabinet next to the stove and said, "Grab the sugar?"

I nodded and found the canister, neatly labeled in cursive. "The measuring cup's in the next one over. We'll need about a cup," she said as her knife neatly sliced the lemon into even crescents.

I found the measuring cup and poured the sugar level to the thick red line. She smiled and nudged me, but I couldn't contain

---

Typically, blue paint was harder to make, and more expensive, so blue-tinged art was rare. Michelangelo is rumored to have left his painting The Entombment unfinished because he could not afford to finish it. Eventually, other blue paint pigments emerged, and blue paints became cheaper. Picasso, one of the most famous artists to adopt a "Blue Period," started painting in cool monochromatic hues after the death of his friend. As his mental state worsened, blue paint dominated his art, and was quickly replaced by his "Rose Period" when he finally emerged from his depression and his psychological state improved.

my curiosity. "So, that guy…"

"Josh," she finished.

"Is he —"

"An art dealer. He works for the studio that bought a bunch of my work." She shook her head. "I signed a contract a few years ago, and now I owe them a certain number of pieces per year for the next two years."

"Is that legal?"

"Surprisingly," she chuffed. "I was so young, and they offered me a steady source of income."

"Where did the baking come in?"

"That, I learned as I traveled." She smiled and started juicing lemon halves into a vintage lemonade juicer. "Some diners don't mind if you're just passing through or if you can't provide references, but they have some of the best chefs and pastry chefs you've ever seen."

"Diner apple pies," I said dreamily, thinking about the pies Mama would make at the diner in town and bring home.

"Exactly." She smiled and finished squeezing the lemon halves. She reached for the sugar and brushed my arm, and I must have jumped because she jumped and pulled back suddenly, causing the knife to skitter off the counter. Without thinking, her hand flew out to catch it, forgetting the sharp edge that had cut so cleanly through the lemon hulls.

She inhaled sharply, pulling her hand back, squeezing it as she tried to convince herself that the blade had missed, that she'd grabbed the handle instead, but after a few breaths, red bloomed between her fingers.

"Liz —"

"I'm fine," she said, examining her finger. "I just nicked it."

I grabbed a towel from the sink and wrapped it around her finger.

"Come on, let's get you cleaned up," I said, pulling her out of the kitchen. "Your bathroom?"

She gestured to the narrow hall's first door, and I led her

inside.

"First aid kit?"

Her eyes went to the medicine cabinet, and I pulled down various items that we might need: cotton balls, hydrogen peroxide, Neosporin, bandages. I washed her hand in the sink, noting the small clean cut and the blood continued to pour. Applying pressure, I raised her arm and looked at Liz's face.

Her eyes were wide with panic, and to be fair, the small wound bled like the cut was much bigger than it was. It hadn't looked like she'd need stitches, so I continued to squeeze her hand. Her eyes met mine, and she gave a small smile, her breath still shallow and quick.

As we waited, my eyes took in the bathroom. The blue stained-glass window behind her. The small chandelier over the tub. The turquoise tile behind the sink. It was like being underwater, and I watched as the light shimmered over our hair and shoulders, like confetti fractured into a million specular dimples.

"Here we go," I said, finally releasing her arm. "Come and sit down." I gestured to the tub.

Liz sat on the edge of the bathtub, and I took the place next to her. The porcelain was cold beneath our legs. I carefully unwrapped the towel and began to clean her finger.

She was right. It was just a nick, but it had sliced her skin in such a way that it bled with inflated urgency. The bleeding had mostly stopped as I wiped the wound with a clean cotton ball bubbling with peroxide. She winced just once when I first began to clean the cut and then visibly relaxed. She was safe.

"My mother used to do this thing whenever I had a scraped knee," I started, glancing up at her. "She would clean me up like this, cotton balls, and everything, and then she'd put on a Band-Aid and kiss it for good luck. Then, when she tucked me in that night, she would tell me all about the Band-Aid fairy."

"The Band-Aid fairy?" She asked, skeptically.

"Let me explain," I said, laughing and only slightly

embarrassed by the childhood memory. "My mother loved to tell me fairy tales when I went to sleep. You know the kind, princesses in towers, evil dragons, wicked stepmothers with poisoned apples."

Liz smiled back at me.

"And, one particular night, after I scraped my knee, she told me about the Band-Aid fairy. She said that when I went to sleep that night, the fairy would come and sprinkle a magic healing powder, and I would be better in no time. And when I woke up I found a teeny tiny note, written on teeny tiny paper in writing so small I could barely read it."

"What did the note say?" Liz asked.

"It told me that I was loved and that I would be better in no time, just like Mom said." I swiftly applied the Band-Aid, making sure it was smooth and sealed tight before giving back her hand. "There, you're all done. No need for the Band-Aid fairy after this."

She inspected the Band-Aid carefully, holding it out in front of her and nodding her head.

"I think it stopped bleeding. You must be a professional," she teased.

I blushed at her compliment. "I wouldn't say that, but I am sorry, Liz. I shouldn't have—"

"No, it's not your fault."

"Still," I responded.

"It's just a nick. Really. Now, how about that lemonade?"

I laughed in return, and we went back down the hall to get our drinks and recall old memories about family and dysfunction that only we could understand.[36]

Ray was awake when I got home. He had been drinking for a while and sat at the kitchen table, staring at Mama's spot at the sink that overlooked the backyard. She swore that she could see the center of the rose maze from there if she stood on her tippy toes.

"You're home late," he grumbled as I entered.

"Just helping a friend," I said as I sat my bag on the nearest kitchen chair.

"Dinner's keeping warm in the oven." He nodded to the other side of the room, and as I walked further into the room, I stopped. It smelled... clean. Scanning the room, I could see that he had done the dishes and mopped the floor. I opened my mouth to say something, but closed it again, afraid that my words might puncture what seemed to be Ray's good mood.

Instead, I walked over to the stove and took out a foil-covered casserole dish and scooped a piping-hot spoonful onto my plate. I couldn't make out the exact ingredients, but it smelled good, so I pulled out a chair and joined him at the table. He looked at me as I chewed.

---

36 The Band-Aid Fairy feels reminiscent of the Tooth Fairy, which traces its origin to Europe in the Twelfth Century. In Northern Europe, children's teeth were seen as valuable. Once a child lost a tooth, the parents would leave a "tooth fee." Children's items, including teeth, were also seen as good luck and were often taken to the battlefield. During this period, Norse warriors were often seen wearing necklaces made out of children's teeth as a token of good luck. In the Middle Ages in Europe, these legends morphed into warnings about witches stealing children's teeth for spells and for proper disposal in fire to send the teeth into the spirit realm. If teeth were not properly disposed of, a child could be controlled by an evil witch or could spend eternity searching for their lost teeth in the afterlife.

In other countries, such as in Hispanic, Spanish, French, and Italian countries, the tradition of replacing lost teeth with gifts is typically done by a small mouse, but in 1908, an article in the Chicago Daily Tribune titled "Household Hints" used these "little mouse" stories as the basis for a "tooth fairy" who is a friendly, comforting figure who can reward a child. The Tooth Fairy is often depicted as a small fairy similar to Tinker Bell who collects a child's lost tooth and leaves a gift in its place and is still celebrated in various countries, in various forms (whether fairy or mouse or other) all over the world.

"Any good?" He asked.

I nodded my head, and he scoffed and shook his head. "You're a terrible liar."

"And you're a terrible cook," I countered.

We both laughed. He pulled out a small flask, offering it to me. I shook my head, and he took a drink.

"The house looks good," I said between bites. I hadn't been lying. The casserole was tasteless but edible.

"I figured since I can't work right now, I can at least get this place back in order." I raised my eyebrows. Ray was many things. He was handy. He was tough. He was direct. He was hardworking. But he was not nurturing, and he was not someone who cleaned.

I ate in silence, letting his words settle, before I sat back and looked at him again. "I'm not letting them take the house if that's what you're worried about. And the judge said you have to 'take care' of me. At least until the first of the year. After that, I don't want to see you again."

His jaw worked, and I could feel his anger radiate toward me. "I'm the one who got this house where it is today. I'm the one who rebuilt the front porch. I'm the one who installed the updated septic tank. Goddamn it, I'm the one who paid the mortgage while your mom was flittin' around at the diner."

"You weren't legally married. Besides, she was the one who paid the mortgage. Every cent you got, you drank."

He stood up, then, rounding the side of the table, and slapped me hard on the cheek. I sat there, feeling the heat from where the heel of his hand smacked my face, my own hand felt small against the throbbing handprint.

"I will fight for this house, little girl. You won't take this from me."

I closed my eyes and traced his footsteps as he stomped out of the kitchen, up the stairs, and into the bedroom, his flask sloshed all the way. He slammed the bedroom door, and a few minutes later, I heard the shower start.

I cleaned up the dishes and made my way upstairs, careful to keep quiet so that he wouldn't hear me and slap me again. I shut my bedroom door, locked it, and heaved a sigh of relief. I was safe. For now.

I spread out on my bed and pulled Mama's journal from under the corner of my mattress. God, I missed her more than ever, and I opened the pages, feeling so alone, before I picked up reading where I had left off.

Yeah, I thought the same thing.

Cat and her mom seem to be close, so much closer than Mom and me. It just goes to show you that even when you think you know someone, there could be a whole other side of them that you knew nothin about. Just look at Cat. She's seein' a whole different side of her mom. And look at me. I had no idea she'd even taken on this project.

Mom was older when she had me. My mom struggled for years to get pregnant, and she finally had me at the age of forty-two. My father died when I was little. As I said earlier, he was working as a manager at Atlanta Gas Company when he fell asleep while drivin'. He ran right into a bridge support column. The police said he was still asleep on impact, that it was instant, that he didn't suffer, and after that, it was just my mom and me.

And she was tough to please. To say she was overprotective would be an understatement. My therapist thinks that it was just the fear of even more loss — that she'd already lost so much that she couldn't bear the idea of losing me as well — but at the time, it felt like she was being unreasonable on purpose.

I grew up with every second of the day scheduled — ballet lessons, piano lessons, tutoring, art clubs, drama — and so I retreated into books. Mom would take me to department meetings at the university, and I would sit and listen to them talk about whole lives that had been lost, forgotten in the past, and when I started showing interest in history and in writing stories, Mom was pleased. All the pressure was off me, and the focus was on someone else — something else — the person, the community, the story I was trying to tell. I loved to step back and see how things came to be and how they played out, like tracing a line from start to finish in a race that I didn't need to be inside.

And I told you how Mom would host these big parties for all the experts and the up-and-coming new faces — anyone who was anyone would be there — so that our house was a constant flow of voices and faces. It was exhilarating, yet all I wanted was my mom, and she was always preoccupied.

Like I said, she treated me like I was a child, like I needed protected, when all I wanted was to find my own way in life. That is to say, I only knew the identity she set out for me. So, when I started college and she pulled out my "life plan" as she called it, I just followed in her footsteps.

One night, she hosted yet another dinner party for some young new voice in the South — some guy who had just graduated but was publishing his own book on "the hidden history of bootlegging and underground unionization of Alabama's mines." It all sounded boring to me, but since I was just starting college, I tried to stick around and "network" as much as I could, knowing full well that everyone would remember me as "Dr. Sparrow's daughter" and not Eddy Sparrow with a mind and ambitions of her own.

Anyway, we'll get to all that later. Let's keep readin'.

Today was not one of the best days.

Yesterday, two boys walked into a school and started shooting at the other kids. So many of them died. And why? Why?

It doesn't make sense.

So much death.

And for what reason?

I can't wrap my head around it, and they were Cat's age.

Today, my aunt visited with her five-year-old daughter, and we put flowers on Mother's grave. I kept thinking about Mama's last words to me, about how I was a disappointment, having Cat so young, not getting married, getting the house back even though she told me time and again that the house was cursed.

But the house isn't cursed. It's just an old house that has held tragedy, like so many houses in America, but any house can be cleaned.

I remember Mama telling me about a pair of twins living here. My great-grandmother or great-great-grandmother, I'm not really sure which; she was a twin. Her own mother died of heartbreak, and all they had was each other. Both of their stories ended in tragedy, but what life isn't met with death at the end?[37]

And, no, I'm not married, but that's just because I don't believe

---

[37] This reference refers to Olivia and Eleanor "Nellie" Saunders, the twin daughters of Olivia Saunders. After their mother's death, they attended a finishing school near Atlanta, and upon graduation, worked in Atlanta for a time. In their mid-twenties, however, they moved back to the Saunders's estate where their mother was buried (rumored to be on the other side of the roses as her husband, although I cannot confirm this) after an alleged scandal in Atlanta (their move seemed hurried, but I cannot confirm this either), as reported in the local paper in the spring of 1854. Upon moving back, the Saunders twins brought a maid and a marginally successful chef from Atlanta to live with them.

Several months after their return, the newspaper reported suspected financial issues for the Saunders twins, and the chef departed before the end-of-year holidays. Although they enjoyed a luxurious childhood, their funds grew lower with each year, and Charles, a distant relative by marriage, visited at the suggestion of one of the twin's great-uncles, as it was common for family circles to inter-marry in order to keep their wealth and reputation. Charles brought the wealth while Helen, the outgoing and independent twin, brought the good reputation. That should have been a bad omen – a man with a bad reputation needing a wife – yet one can only be so picky when desperate to care for her sister and her family homestead.

in marriage. I couldn't — and would NEVER — marry Cat's real dad. I couldn't. I know Mother wanted me to be happy and feel love and be loved in return, but that wasn't love. Not at all.

Love is what I have with Ray, and he hates the idea of marriage too. We don't need a piece of paper or rings to show that we belong together. Our love is much deeper than that. And Cat's the biggest blessing that I could have ever imagine.

I just wish Mother could have held Cat before she died. That would have changed her mind about everything. I just know it.

Cat was so small when she was born, just over six pounds, and she was perfect. Auntie Bea was there, so I was excited about her visit, but as the days got closer, Ray seemed to get agitated.

It was like a dark cloud moved in and the air inside the house got thick. It was like that feeling you get before a storm where everything is so still, so electric like we were all waiting for lightning to strike. But it didn't.

Ray disappeared the night before Auntie Bea came. He'd been doing that more and more — going out, not coming home until morning, disappearing when I need him the most. He works hard. I know he does. And I know that he needs to blow off some steam every once in a while, but it's hard. I want him home. I just miss him so much. And money is already tight. I barely make enough money as it is to cover the utilities, and the roof needs replaced.

Anyway, Auntie Bee came, and her daughter was so cute — this teeny, tiny mouse of a girl. I remember when Cat was that little. It made me ache just to be around her. And maybe a little sad, if I'm being honest. It made me miss how much Cat needed me, how she would lay her head in my lap, how I would tuck her in at night. It's like she doesn't need me anymore.

And with Ray staying out, I feel so cut off, even with my shifts at the diner because at the end of the night, everyone goes home to their families, and I go home to a dark house. I came home the other night after a long shift and picked up Cat from the library after school. I guess she was working on a project or something.

That girl is so smart. She's set to graduate in December — a whole year and a half ahead of schedule. She should be driving already, but she doesn't seem interested in cars. Her head is always in a book, and she is so sharp — her head is filled with all kinds of facts and stories and things I've never even thought about.

I remember that night so clearly, though, because we made hamburgers and had the windows open so the spring breeze could air out the smell. Ray wasn't home yet, and I didn't know when to expect him, so we ate at the kitchen table, and I mentioned that she should go to the spring formal. She laughed and shook her head and said she didn't even know how to dance, so I told her that I could teach her. So, we danced in the kitchen with me counting the steps and her mostly following but sometimes stumbling, then Ray came home.

He stood at the door watching us, and I could tell he had already had a few drinks after work, but I was happy to see him standing there. I loved when his attention was on me. But then he shook his head and said that Cat would never learn how to dance like that. He said how could she learn how to follow without a man to lead her and cut right in.

Then, he proceeded to dance with her. I could see her stiffen in his arms, but she avoided my eyes and concentrated on her steps. I couldn't help but feel jealous with his arms around her and not me.

Isn't that crazy?!

He hadn't even said hello, just waltzed in and took Cat.

Is that what the world will do? Have her graduate early and then step in? Sweep her away? Have her not even look at me again?

I guess I've been fearing that since the day she was born — that her father, some boy, the world — would just come in and take her away. I just couldn't articulate it until then. Needless to say, I couldn't sleep that night. I stayed up and made tea and sat at the kitchen table, watching the spot where Ray danced with her, unable to stop my mind from spinning. What is wrong with me?

Transcript
Interview with Eddy Sparrow
4:44 p.m. April 27th, 2021
Case No. HI30823

That's interesting. I thought that too. She has all the signs of a codependent. We might think these feelings are irrational, but they're common in someone with codependency. Living with Mom and trying to get her attention so much as a child, I often felt some of these same things growing up. And even after. But I'm getting ahead of myself.

First, we need to talk about Stephen.

Yes, he's my ex-husband, and as I said earlier, Mom had this big dinner about the young guy that was publishing a "groundbreaking" novel — her words, not mine — and was the youngest something-or-other to do some important thing. Sorry, I sort of tuned out all the details.

It was that point in the semester where exams are over and your brain is toast, and I was questioning my decision to study History, and sure, I admit I'd had a little too much wine that night, but hey, I was bored and young and admittedly dumb, so I swiped a bottle of wine and headed to the den Mom converted into a library.

I remember opening the book   and trying to figure out who was who and if that man really killed his wife or not when I heard a voice behind me.

A man whispered something like,

Yeah, I know. Cheesy, right?

Then, he asked about who this mysterious young guy was. He even questioned why everyone was so excited about him, but I knew exactly who he was. He was the guest of honor.

Outside the library, we heard people toast to him, and he blushed, like a for real blush that ran across his cheeks and down his neck even.

I smiled and held up my bottle of wine and mimicked the others and said,   , before I took a swig.

And then he smiled and said that great minds

must think alike because he'd also swiped a bottle of wine to disappear in the library.

Well, for one, he was gorgeous. He was tall with dark hair and a perpetual five o'clock shadow, but there was something magnetic about him. If you were in a room full of people, you'd somehow find your way to him because that's just the pull he had.

We stayed in there the rest of the night talking about stories and playing chess. I know, it sounds lame, but it was the most fun I'd had at one of Mom's parties since I fell asleep with my head in her lap as a child. I felt like I could finally connect with someone, like I had ideas that were fresh and interesting, like I had found someone who was also interesting. He made me feel like I was special.

I know. I remember reading this for the first time and being so creeped out. I'd only read it during the day, but it still gave me the creeps.

Matter of fact, I got scared one particular night after reading about Cat's house. I guess I'd falled asleep while reading at the table here and was woken up by the phone.

I jumped up to get it, still half asleep, but no one answered. There was this crackling at the other end of the line, and I could hear what sounded like breathing.

Freaked out, I hung up the phone and tried to smooth down all the goosebumps that'd popped up on my arms, and the phone rang again.

More silence. More creepy breathing. So I hung up again. More ringing, so I left the phone off the hook.

No, I never found out who it was, but it still gives me the creeps.

Anyway, let's get back to Cat.

MAY 2001

Mama's favorite month was always May, and it was the first month that I was able to put a dent in some of the house's debt. I was able to buy groceries — real groceries and not simply leftovers at the cafe — and I should have enough money by the end of the month to pay some of last year's property taxes. I was still getting bills from the hospital and the funeral home, but those would have to wait. Therapy was still going well. It hurt to talk about Mama sometimes, but my therapist seemed happy to talk about Liz and the cafe, taking it as a sign that I was moving on... which I was.

Liz opened the cafe on the first day of May with a surprise. I got there just after sunrise and was met with dozens of flowers crowding every surface of the cafe: periwinkle cornflowers, jade ferns, buttery daffodils, tangerine daylilies, pink peonies, burgundy roses.[38]

"What do you think?" Liz asked over the top of a vase of crooked orchids.

"It's…" I trailed off, trying to find the words. "Wow."

"Wow?" she said with eyebrows raised. "That's all you got?"

"Where did you find all these?"

"Mrs. Maisey," she shrugged as she loaded a tray of muffins into the oven behind her. "She loaned these on consignment. Mother's Day and all. I talked her into displaying them here so customers could pick up their Mother's Day treats and some flowers in one stop. Smart, right?"

I had to give it to her, she was always willing to go outside the box and take a chance.

"Wanna give me a hand with these cakes? You get the boxes ready, and I'll ice."

I nodded, got to work, and packaged ten cakes before our doors opened at seven. Because of Liz's big flower idea, we were busy all morning filling coffee and selling flowers. Our usual morning coffee crew camped out between the flowers while other customers stopped by to pick up bakery orders and peek in to see what was going on with all the flowers in the front window.

As foot traffic died down, I heard a familiar voice from the door.

"Look at this," a honey-sweet voice crooned, and I didn't need to turn around to know that it was Marianne. "Just gorgeous," she gasped. I couldn't help but think about birthdays, Mama

---

38 The Victorian use of flowers as language is widely documented. Each flower comes with a meaning so that sending flowers became an art of communication. Cornflowers represented celibacy while ferns meant fascination. Daffodils meant regard, and daylilies signaled flirtation. Peonies symbolized shame or bashfulness, while each color of rose had a wildly different meaning. The passing of these messages through flowers allowed people to communicate to one another under the strict rules of a Victorian society that looked down on passion, candidness, and sexuality – all of which went against Victorian etiquette. Lovers could communicate nonverbally without alerting their chaperones. A flower handed in the right hand would mean "yes" while a flower handed in the left hand would mean "no." Whole conversations and love affairs were conducted with flowers. Although the Victorian era ended in 1901, the influences of the Victorian dictionary of language still lives on today.

lighting candles and Marianne flashing her black Kodak camera, whispering *Just gorgeous.*

"Morning, Mrs. Marianne," I said, turning with a smile. "What can I getcha?"

"Cat, how wonderful to see you!" She gaped, although she must have known I would be there.

"You, too," I returned. "Need a cake for church?"

"You know me." She smiled. I glanced across the room at Liz who was busy prepping sandwiches for our lunch crowd and led Marianne over to the cash register. She pointed to an off-white cake decorated in cream-colored roses. "We're having an art show for the kids at church, and my Davis is going to be in it," she offered in an attempt to make conversation. I smiled in response, nodding as I rang up her cake and coffee, while a vague image of her colic baby came to mind. "And Owen's going to prom. I just can't believe how big they're getting."

I nodded and gave her the total, and she dug in her wallet for the exact change. I reached out to give her the receipt, and she grabbed my hand.

"Also," she hesitated, glancing over her shoulder and leaning in close, "I'd love to buy some flowers for your mother, but I wouldn't want to over-step."

Immediately, I felt heat on my cheeks.

"For Mother's Day. I think it'd be nice," she added. "I know when my parents passed away, I —"

"She was cremated," I said, cutting her off. "I don't think flowers would..."

As I trail off, Marianne squeezed my hand, which was still trapped in hers. "Or maybe I can make a few meals? Have you stop by and have a girl's day. Remember? Like we used to do?"

I thought about the movie nights and shopping sprees, the lake days and sunny picnics with her and Mama leading the way, talking and laughing — but that was before Ray. It seemed like everything stopped when Ray entered the picture.

"S-sure," I stuttered, and Marianne smiled, releasing my hand.

Liz's voice cut between us.

"Cat, can you give me a hand?" she called over her shoulder.

"Sorry," I mumbled and left Marianne with her cake and coffee. As I walked over to Liz, I could see a smirk on her face.

"I saw you needed help," she whispered.

"Thanks," I whispered back and nudged her. "I was about to get roped into dinner at her house."

"With Owen?"

"And his snotty little brother," I added and wrinkled my nose.

"Sounds like I saved the day." She smirked. "You might owe me."

"Oh yeah? And what do I owe you?"

"Since you don't have dinner plans with Marianne, maybe you can come to my house on Friday?" I thought about her house, her many decorations, and the way the sun caught in her kitchen window. "Maybe we can have lasagna?"

"That'd be nice," I nodded, and before I could say more, the lunch crowd began to pour in, grabbing their sandwiches and even a few more flower arrangements. By the end of the day, Liz's grand flower scheme had worked. We sold most of the flowers and doubled our typical sales. As we left, she tucked half the tips from the overflowing tip jar into my hand. Maybe, just maybe, I could make it all work.

When I got home, Ray was gone. He had been helping out one of his friends on a job in the next town over and had been staying late to help "clean up," which was nice since it meant we'd have extra money coming in, but I knew it also meant that half his paycheck would be spent at the local bar on the outskirts of town. It didn't bother me too much, though. I was happy to have the house to myself, and at least some money coming in was better than no money.

I made myself a sandwich and sat on the back porch and watched the sun go down over the tangled rose garden that had started to bloom a few weeks ago. I thought of Mama and her bedtime story about the princess.

As the years passed and the girl grew, the monster never left her side, and as they both got bigger, the girl's flowers were not enough for the monster. It roiled with pain, hunger, and greed. It wanted the girl. It slipped into the girl's shadow and grew as the sun passed its pinnacle in the sky.

The girl had lived with the shadow for so long that she didn't even notice — notice the lengthening, the widening, the darkening until it was too late.

One day, the girl looked around. She looked around and could not see anything except for her shadow. She would chase the lightning bugs to drive away the shadow, but as the year went on, the lightning bugs became less and less. The days grew shorter. The air turned cold.

The nights stretched as long as the darkness that followed her. With nothing to keep her warm, the monster wrapped its arms around her. It whispered to her in the dark and sang her lullabies until she went to sleep.

I could almost smell the princess's garden, the musk of blooms as I finished my last bite of dinner, and I heard a knock at the door. Puzzled, I made my way to the front of the house, wondering why I hadn't heard someone pull up the dirt drive.

I peered out of the front door's window but didn't see anyone in the dim light, so I switched on the porch light and opened the door. No one was there.

I stepped out onto the porch, craned my neck to peer down the driveway, looking for receding tail lights, something, but I found nothing but trees and darkness. Wondering if I was going crazy, I turned around to go inside and stopped short.

Flowers.

A beautiful bouquet of small white flowers, miniature stars, refracted at the ends. Did I step over those when I walked out? Was someone else there?

I looked around again, shivering, but the porch was empty. I scooped up the bouquet and went inside, scanning the ground floor for intruders, knowing full well that no one would have been able to come inside with me standing there on the porch. I would have seen them or heard them.

I smelled the flowers but only got the scent of the dying day. Strange. A flower with no smell.

I entered the library, my free hand searched the shelves until I found Mama's flower book. She had been obsessed at one point with flowers and their Victorian meanings. She had researched the roses in the backyard, convinced by an old family story that they had magically changed from white to pink and finally to a deep burgundy red the color of dried blood. I scanned the printed watercolor images of flowers until I found the one that matched the bouquet.

White Catchfly.

I read, my finger trailed the words across the page. Perennial, although some gardeners grow it as an annual. Typically flowers from May to June or in late summer. Bright full shade. The small white flowers traditionally symbolize young love and gentleness.

My brows furrowed. Young love? Who would send these? I shook my head and scanned the page until I found more.

The small flowers can also trap pollen and even small insects on their sticky calyces, which contributes to its other meaning: betrayal.

I felt goosebumps making their way up my arm and closed the book, returning it to the shelf and heard a sound above me on the upper floor. I checked both the front and back doors, making sure they were locked before heading upstairs, but it was empty, as usual.

White Catchfly, I thought again and pulled out Mama's journal. What are you trying to tell me, Mama?

Interview with Eddy Sparrow
5:06 p.m. April 27th, 2021
Case No. HI30823

Have you ever heard of Victorian flowers being used to tell messages?

I hadn't either before I read Mom's notes. Mom couldn't find an exact reference to the change in rose color, yet I did see in the original newspaper article about the Saunders estate that the roses were white.

A few decades later, the roses were referenced as yellow. Mom found that the yellow color could be from the end of the blooming season when the white flowers yellow, but she also found an article in the gossip column about it being the curse of the Saunders women.

I don't know how they got cursed. Maybe the land was cursed all along. Anyway, a few decades later, the roses were described in an article as red — this was at Helen's marriage announcement. I know, right?

But get this, in the newspaper announcement of her death, the red was described as burgundy.

I know, roses don't change color like that.

Yeah, it gives me the creeps, too.

May 8, 1999

Ray's gone again. He said he's working a job with a friend a few towns over, but I have my doubts. He's been staying out so much lately. Who is he with? Why doesn't he want to stay here? With me? What's wrong with me?

I think back to my grandma sitting at the kitchen table, this very table, and wish that I could do magic the way she did. I flip through old books, desperate to find a prayer, a spell, anything that could work to keep Ray.

I tried a few, actually. I prayed — no, begged — God to just give me this one thing. I promised that I wouldn't eat for a week. They used to fast all the time in the Bible. So, I stopped eating. I think I lost five pounds in a week. I barely touched water, just a few sips a day, fearful that water might break the deal, but I was so weak.

Needless to say, that didn't work.

Cat took me to the doctor who gave me an IV of fluid and vitamins. I told them it was just a stomach flu, but they wouldn't let me out of the hospital until I was eating solid foods again, so that was spoiled. Next, I tried a basic love spell — a honey jar spell to "sweeten" our love and a full moon spell to entice Ray to stay, but they all failed. How had Grandma done it? Why wasn't I as special?

So, I concentrated on my herbs to make some "Love Teas" with fresh rosehips, lemon balm, and meadowsweet. I figured that if I couldn't get Ray to love me more, then maybe it was the way that I loved him that was broken. If I could be more devoted, a better partner, show him that I couldn't live without him, that he would realize what we had. That's what all the advice books say, isn't it? Be vulnerable and open? Increase your communication to be a better partner? I even planted a Casa Blanca Orchid, a night-blooming flower to help cultivate our love, and ventured out to the garden maze to smell it every night. What was it that Mom used to say?

That the original Saunders woman would also roam the maze. I could feel her there next to me, walking with me through the maze. Was she as lonely as I am? Was her heart as broken without her love?

There was no way to know for sure, but it made me miss my mom. She was diagnosed with cancer right at the time I learned that I was pregnant with Cat. I remember being so afraid for her and so afraid to tell her about the pregnancy. She was given only a few months to live, so I knew I had to tell her. She was going to be a grandmother. Her legacy would live on, and maybe, just maybe, it would give her the motivation to keep living, at least for a few months more, to see the birth of her grandbaby.

But when I told her, she just looked sad. She said she hoped it wasn't a girl because all the women in our family were cursed to be alone, cursed just like the house.

I told her that a baby was just what the house needed to cure it of its shadows, a baby to light up every corner, but she grimaced again and said that was not possible. That she had just sold the house to Mr. Johns.

---

39 In the spring of 1856, the paper published a wedding announcement for Helen Saunders. She married Charles Richardson on June 15th at the Saunders's estate. Charles was said to have owned a business that made money just to buy more money (stocks, maybe?). That is to say, he made a living off of collecting things – and owning them. The only thing he couldn't buy was a son – something he desperately needed so that his life's patchwork of conglomerated companies wouldn't be in vain, as he often said to reporters (I can confirm these quotes in at least three separate articles in just 1857 alone).

Nellie (Eleanor Saunders was publicly going by her nickname starting in 1857) designed and constructed Olivia's dress and planned the entire affair. Nellie was described as being "good at all things feminine: the flowers, the dresses, the dinner. She was delicate – kind in a way you read about in books but never met in person – kind in a way we all aspire to be" (McClintock 278). She was also described as incredibly shy (264) while Olivia was described as "incredibly smart and could match wits with the best of men, and it is rumored to be the masked woman who would often outplay some of the most cunning men in town in secret poker games that took place in a juke joint on the outskirts of town" (279), although no one ever saw her face to confirm.

Olivia wore Nellie's custom-made white dress trimmed in Parisian lace. Olivia descended the wide staircase at the amazement of their family members, and a few select friends. Nellie, Olivia's only surviving relative in her immediate family, gave the bride away (The Daily Tribune 15 Jun 1856). Charles and Olivia were married in the vestibule in front of close family and hosted a gala in the gardens for the town to meet Charles. The gossip column for the paper (written anonymously, of course) gushed over Charles' "devilishly handsome looks" and "fine attire, a real gentleman."

I couldn't believe Marianne hadn't told me, and when I approached her about it, she acted like it was this great opportunity to start over and maybe get a place of our own, best friends with a fresh start.

Needless to say, I was so mad. That house had been my dream. It was where I wanted to raise a family and grow old. And they had taken that from me without even asking. He had taken it from me without even asking.

My mom lived a few more months but didn't get a chance to see Cat after she was born. I tried to visit her again, but she refused to let me in. How could she do that to her own daughter? Anyway, if it wasn't for Marianne, I wouldn't have met Ray, and I wouldn't know love like I do now. God, I just love him so much. Why can't he see that? Why won't he come back to me?

Transcript
Interview with Eddy Sparrow
5:21 p.m. April 27th, 2021
Case No. HI30823

No, I don't mind. My story always leads back to him somehow. What do you want to know?

Stephen started coming to all of Mom's parties that winter into spring. We'd both sneak a bottle of wine and meet in the library or in the pergola hidden behind the back patio when the weather warmed up. Mom used to say there were snakes back there, but it was where she used to sneak and hide when she wanted to smoke. Hosting her parties as the center of attention, I knew it would be unoccupied.

This one particular party had been just before Easter, and it was the first nice evening of the year — the kind of evening that smells green and warm. There was just this energy, ya know?

Anyway, the wind picked up all of a sudden, and it started to rain. Everyone ran inside, and I started to follow, when I felt a hand in mine, pulling me in the opposite direction — toward the pergola.

It was Stephen.

We squeezed in under the awning, but we were drenched and getting even more wet by the second, so we dashed inside and ran to my room, unnoticed as everyone laughed and tried to dry themselves by the fireplace that Mom was struggling to light.

I know what you're thinking, and I was not that kind of girl. Sure, I'd been kissed, and I'd had a boyfriend in college. I wasn't a virgin, but this was different.

Stephen was a man. He was twenty-five, while I was just eighteen. He'd already been to college, and I was just starting. I think he was even teaching at the time and was up for all these awards for his writing. He'd applied for a full-time position, and as my mom and everyone else said, he was a shoe-in for it.

Anyway, there we were, dripping all over the carpet, when he pulled off his shirt. I followed suit and pulled off my jacket, realizing too late that you could see right through my shirt.

I tried to cover myself, but he caught my hand and said,

I didn't know what to do, so I dropped my hands and let him look at me.

Then, he told me that I was beautiful, and I started to say something, but then he said,

I didn't know what else to say, so I nodded, and he brushed the hair out of my face. Of all the things he could have done, it was the softness he showed toward me that made me want to agree to anything he asked.

And then he asked if he could kiss me, and I said yes. It'd been so long since someone had taken interest in me, and Stephen made me feel like I was the only woman in the world who mattered. What more could I have asked for?

I closed the book, my eyes bleary with sleep and tears, and went upstairs. I took my nightly pills and made a warm cup of tea to help calm my nerves, but sitting in Mama's chair and not able to help it, I was thinking about Ray.

After Ray's drinking got more intense, so did his vicious fists. Anything could set him off: burned macaroni and cheese, a light being left on, a spoon left in the sink.

Mama took the brunt of his blows. She rode the disorienting corkscrew of teacups, terrified and exhilarated and lost in the world of Ray, until she forgot what it was like to have two feet on the ground and her stomach not in her throat. She forgot how to breathe and speak for herself. She forgot how to get off the ride or that there was even a ride, to begin with.

I was a late bloomer, and on my fourteenth birthday, I started my period. I had gone through a growth spurt that winter, my legs lengthened, and my baby fat melted away. On the morning of the spring solstice, I awoke with cramps.

As the weather warmed and heavy coats and sweaters were put away, I noticed a change in Ray. His eyes began to slide up my bare legs like he'd suddenly realized that I was, in fact, a girl becoming a woman. I'd feel him watching me out of the corner of his eye as I looked for a snack in the pantry. He'd try to talk to me using that charm that worked on other women, but I'd seen it too many times as a bystander to be pulled in, and I'd leave my food abandoned on the pantry shelf still in its wrapper.

Mama started to notice, too. She said something once, just once, when she thought I was asleep. Ray's fists became hammers. He punched her again and again, calling her all kinds of names. He had spit on her when he left and mumbled that he wasn't a "goddam pervert" before disappearing for days. Ray had hit Mama so hard in the stomach that the bruise lasted for a month. Mama said that she deserved it, that she shouldn't have said anything, to begin with, but the damage had already been done.

At the same time, Ray insisted on teaching me to drive. But he couldn't just teach me how to drive. No, not Ray. Ray resolved on starting with the basics.

Every Sunday morning, Ray woke me with the sun. He pulled me, very much unwillingly, to the driveway. Most of the time, I could smell liquor on his breath from the Saturday night bender. He started with the truck's motor, pointing things out and quizzing me, his chest swelled pompously with each wrong.

After a month, Ray moved on to engine maintenance. We changed the oil together, me mirroring his every move. Then, the next week, he had me change it by myself. He made me practice again and again each week with his dark eyes watching every twitch of my fingers until I could change the oil from memory.

Then, Ray announced that I could crank the truck. My hands shook as much from the engine roaring to life as from being so close to him without Mama.

"That's my girl," Ray's voice purred low, making me cringe. "That's my good girl." His fingers tucked a piece of hair behind my ear and I pulled back.

"What's with you?" He spat, not used to a woman resisting his "animal magnetism," as I heard him refer to it once.

I didn't respond. Instead, I sat rigid in the driver's seat, unable to move and afraid to breathe for fear that I'd let out all the awful things I thought about him. Thankfully, Mama came out then and announced breakfast.

That year, Ray taught me how to monitor all the truck's fluids and how to change them, how to work a stick shift, and how to hold my tongue and not tell him how much I hated him and blamed him for how weak Mama had become.

Then, Ray announced that it was time to work on the truck's brakes. He had been showing me how to change the brake pads and check the brake fluid. Ray noticed that brake fluid had started dotting the driveway, and when we looked, he pointed out the brake lines. They were old and worn with age, in desperate need of repair.

Ray ordered the parts and talked about finally taking me driving. He stared at me eagerly across the dinner table. I was his prodigy, something to mold into what he wanted, and it was best to let him think I was complying. As much as I wanted to learn how to drive, I knew that Ray could be dangerous alone, so I kept quiet and followed his directions exactly. I was the perfect student.

The next Saturday, Ray had everything set. We worked all morning, ignoring Mama's call that the food was ready, and worked until the heat of noon.

"Okay, now tighten these screws," Ray directed, pointing at the brake screws. "You'll need to tighten it all the way but be sure not to tighten it too tight. You don't want to strip them out."

"What would happen if it's stripped out?" I asked timidly.

"You wouldn't have pressure in the lines."

"So that would…"

Ray's face twisted with disappointment, and he turned his face to spit in the grass next to the driveway.

"You wouldn't have brakes, so you wouldn't be able to stop." Ray looked me up and down with smug malice and chuckled to himself. "And all this time, I thought you were learning something. I guess you're not so grown after all."

I felt my cheeks grow hot. Anger boiled in my stomach. *I'm old enough to know what a scumbag you are*, I thought.

"Just tighten the screws. Your mama says lunch is ready," Ray said, wiping his hands on a burgundy rag and tossing it my way. "And clean up when you're done."

I watched him open the front door and call for Mama. Her laugh rippled through the screen door. I leaned over and spit in the grass in the same spot that he had spat.

"I'm not stupid," I mumbled as I grabbed the wrench. Scooting under the truck, I tightened the brake screw, replaying Ray's words as I turned the wrench.

I thought of how he always treated me like a child.

Turn.

I thought of how he wanted to control everything he touched.

Turn.

I thought of how he drank and broke things.

Turn.

I thought of how he screamed and hurt Mama.

Turn.

But no more.

Turn.

I was done.

Turn.

Thoughts swirled around my head as I thought of all the horrible things that Ray had done to me and Mama, so I turned the screw, pressing with all my might until I finally heard the crack.

I stopped, shaking with shock and used up anger, and touched the screw. It looked normal enough. I replaced the wrench, and the screw spun freely without catching. It maintained a clean seal momentarily, keeping the brake oil in the lines and off of the driveway, but there was no doubt the screw was stripped.

"You almost done out there?" I heard Mama call from the parted screen door. I could see Ray's shadow behind her, stuffing a sandwich into his mouth. His free hand, grimy with work and with want, wrapped itself around Mama's waist. It was the same hand he'd hit her with the week before, and I felt anger build once again.

"A few more to go. Wanna come check?" I lied, hoping he would decline.

Ray shuffled down the driveway and leaned down to peer under the truck. My stomach tightened, and I felt my heart pound as his eyes inspected the brakes, but the concrete was spotless, and the brake lines were in place. Everything looked normal.

Ray smiled that stomach-twisting grin he had and said in a low voice so that only I could hear, "That's my good girl, doin' just what you're told." Ray lifted his eyebrows a fraction of an inch and laughed over his shoulder as he approached Mama at the screen door, wrapping his arms around her and daring me to say anything else as he pulled her back inside the house.

I turned back to the truck, scooting under the other side, and worked, tightening each screw until I felt it snap and spin freely. Each one looked normal, untouched, perfectly safe.

I wiped my hands and pulled myself off the ground, dusting off my jeans and hoping that Ray would finally get what was coming to him.

Interview with Eddy Sparrow
5:42 p.m. April 27th, 2021
Case No. HI30823

I know you want to know more about Cat and Ray. I mean, going back home after your mom has passed away is tough enough, but I can't even imagine Cat having to go back and live with that man. I've heard horror stories about child services after a child loses a parent, but it seems like there should be laws against someone like Ray ever getting custody of a minor, even for a year. The thought makes me sick.

Maybe by Cat. It seemed like she's the only person who doesn't immediately fawn over him, ya know? I bet he hated that, and he sure didn't know how to relate to women other than flirting or acting generally slimy, according to Cat's writing.

And Cat's mom? Don't get me started. I just don't know how she could have been okay with how he treated her. I mean, didn't she see how awful he was to Cat?

I know when my mom found out about Stephen, golden boy that he was, even she freaked out. That's why we had the falling out.

Well, she caught us one night after everyone had gone home. Stephen was trying to sneak down the stairs and out the front door. We were whispering and laughing, drunk and too star-struck with one another to notice her sitting there in the living room.

Yep, she was not pleased. She said that he was too old and that he was corrupting me. She said that I didn't know what I was doing, that I was throwing my life away — along with my credibility — on a man.

And then I said that no, that she was the one who threw her life away — she pushed Dad so hard that it killed him and ever since then she'd been pushing me so hard that I'd had enough. Poor Stephen, he just stood there, looking back and forth between the two of us saying the most awful things to each other. And that's when I said I was leaving. I packed my bag and marched out the front door. Stephen had still been standing there, not sure if he should help me with my bag, offer some reassuring words to Mom, or leave and never come back to that crazy house, and when I flew past him, he had no choice but to follow.

We rode in silence. We weren't technically girlfriend and boyfriend and neither of us had planned to live together, but there we were, a couple of young kids flung together, heading to his studio apartment in Birmingham that overlooked Vulcan to the south and Sloss to the east. I had no idea what I was getting into.

A few weeks into May, Liz grew restless. After closing at the cafe, we often walked to her house where she cooked dinner and made an extra plate for Ray in case he was there when I got home. Sometimes I stopped at the grocery store for ingredients, and other times, she would bring veggies home from the cafe so they wouldn't go to waste. And she was a good cook — a damn good cook — who wasn't afraid to experiment. I never knew what I was in store for.

But as the month went on, Liz started to neglect the food, burning it half the time. She'd grow quiet and glare out of the window at her art studio in the backyard until one day I asked, "Is everything okay?"

Liz startled as if I had interrupted a dream; her eyebrows relaxed and face eased into a polite smile, but she didn't respond.

"Seriously, what's going on?"

She exhaled and leaned against the kitchen counter. "It's nothing." She waved her hand as if that would make the issue go away, but worry persisted, and she exhaled, visibly deflated. "I can't paint," she said finally.

"Yes, you can," I said. "You're a great painter."

She shook her head. "It's not that. I know I can paint. I just can't paint right now." She gestured into the air.

"Like writer's block?"

She nodded. "And Josh keeps calling. He keeps asking what's next after my 'brilliant' blue phase." She ran her hand through her curly hair.

I was silent for a moment. I, myself, used to write — stupid stories, knockoff versions of Narnia-type adventures with secret worlds, amulets, and mythical creatures — but lately, all of my previous ideas seemed childish and uninspiring. And writing was a hobby anyway, not a part of how I made my living.

I could see the weight of it on Liz's shoulders and asked, "I remember you always painting or drawing, growing up. Remember that mural you did in, what was it, middle school?"

"Yeah," she smiled. "Some kind of Earth Day, save-the-planet theme?"

"What did you use on that again?"

"Trash from the lunchroom," she laughed. "The principal was horrified when she heard that I was digging out milk cartons and used plasticware."

"It was so cool, though. It was like 3-D."

"That's what I was going for — a beach scene that had something to say, you know? Only now, I have no idea what I have to say."

"Sounds familiar," I muttered, then looked at her. "How did you get into art, anyway?"

"I guess it started with nightmares," she exhaled.

"Nightmares?"

"Yep," she nodded. "I had these awful nightmares growing up. They're called Night Terrors."

"Sounds awful."

"It was." She nodded. "There was this man in my dreams. He always dressed in black, and he'd always be there, watching, waiting, and when I least expected it he'd come."

I shivered beside her as her eyes glazed over, remembering.

"I used to call him the Bad Hat because he wore this top hat. He was always chasing me, and sometimes, I'd wake up screaming. My mom was terrified. There was nothing she could do to prevent them and had no idea what to do when they happened — which was almost every night at the height of it all."

"But you don't have them anymore?"

"My mom took me to this preacher. He lived up in the mountains where my grandmother grew up. I guess she and Ray used to visit there in the summer. Anyway, she took me to see this man who prayed over me. I remember being so nervous and worried that it wouldn't work, that my mom would be disappointed, and that she'd have all this stress from not knowing what to do. She'd even had to call out of work a few times because I was so exhausted from missing sleep.

"But that night," she continued, "after the pastor, we got home, and I had this dream about this beautiful city. I was kind of like the Emerald City from The Wizard of Oz, all green and sparkly and breathtaking, not like something I'd seen before, and I sat there on this hill and watched the sunrise."

I nodded hesitantly, trying to picture it.

"And that was it," she finished.

"What do you mean?"

"I mean, that was it. I never saw the Bad Hat again."

"Really?" I asked, unable to hide my skepticism.

She nodded and repeated, "That was it."[40]

"Huh," I breathed.

"But you know," she said in a hushed voice, "sometimes I wonder about him. I mean, I know he's not real, but sometimes, I wonder where he went and why."

I must have raised my eyebrows at her, so she continued, "I just mean that I was so used to him being there. And I was used to my mom worrying over me. It was like life had a pull – a constant– you know? And then, suddenly, life moved on."

I nodded, thinking about Mama, how the worst had happened, and how the world seemed to go on spinning despite her not being there anymore. It felt like betrayal.

"I know what you mean," I whispered. "You know, though, you could use some of this."

"What do you mean?"

"This hat-person, it sounds like your shadow self."

---

40 Also known as, The Top Hat, this dream has been reported across the globe and is most common during sleep paralysis. The first instance of a clinical study of sleep paralysis was in 1664 but had been described in literature dating back centuries. Most instances were attributed to demons and the occult, but it wasn't until the 20th century that doctors understood the importance of sleep cycles to this sleep disorder. Sleep paralysis occurs during REM sleep when a chemical is typically released to stop motor functions and allow for deep, restful sleep. When sleep paralysis occurs, however, the body does not resume motor functions right away and can lead to a feeling of being awake while being paralyzed and not able to move. Many people report strange visions or noises during this paralyzed state, the most common being The Top Hat, a man dressed in black. He is described as being between six feet to ten feet tall. Sometimes he has red eyes or carries a golden pocket watch, but across cultures and countries, he is always described as a sort of shadow man. He does not hurt the sleeper. He doesn't attack them or hurt them or even touch them in any way. Instead, he just stands in the shadows, watching the person sleep, knowing they can't move or run away.

"My shadow self?"

"Yeah." I nodded. "Like Freud's iceberg? The subconscious? That deep down part inside of you that's scary."[41]

Liz raised her eyebrows, clearly not following me.

"Maybe, instead of trying to force your art, you can be vulnerable. Let that shadow self be seen. That part deserves a voice, too."

She thought for a moment, staring at me, and then leaned forward and kissed me on the forehead before darting outside toward the studio. She stayed there long past sunset, sketching like a madwoman. Over and over, she drew the same figure — a man hiding in the shadows, his face blurred slightly each time she drew him. Not wanting to disturb her, I cleaned up dinner and closed the door as I headed home.

The walk was easy, and a full moon lit my path. I wondered if I had my own Bad Hat. Could I be the one manifesting the strange flowers? The strange sounds? The visions? I shook my head and continued to walk, imagined that I could talk to my own shadow self. What would she have to say? And would she blame me for Mama?

---

41 Freud wrote and spoke at length about sleep disorders, including sleep paralysis. On one occasion, a woman reported being paralyzed but awake with her mother in the room. Freud concluded that the woman was aware of her desire to free herself, if not violently, from her mother, yet her conscious mind was paralyzing her from acting out, and even freeing herself, from her mother's control. Freud believed that people should dive into the id, or the unconscious aspect of their identity, to explore their core fears and motivations. By exploring these, the person can be freed from shame and fully deal with inner issues that develop. Freud is seen as the father of modern psychology, yet many of his ideas and treatments are disputed today, including his view of sleep paralysis.

So, I had nightmares after I left home. Stephen's place was nice, but it wasn't home, and I'd never been away from home before, not even for summer camp or sleepovers.

I was sheltered, I know. So, it was an adjustment living with Stephen. I started school at UAB to finish my degree, and Stephen started teaching full-time that fall and got me a job as his research assistant.

Don't look at me like that. I had references from Georgia State and was more than qualified to be a research assistant, thanks to Mom's insistence on "networking." It turned out her parties actually were useful in the long run.

And, I guess you're right about that. It didn't hurt that technically I was sleeping with my boss. But it was money, and it was in my discipline, and it was helping to pay for college.

No, I never called her. I was so mad at her.

Sure, she tried to call a few times, but then she stopped after a month or so. I remember being amazed that it took nineteen years to raise me and only a month to forget about me altogether.

I started wearing her locket, though. It seemed to ease the nightmares. It's silly, but it worked.

Excuse me, my throat is dry. Do you mind if we take a break for a minute?

JUNE 2001

I woke up the first Saturday in June to the sounds of Ray loading his truck out front. He was tying down his ladder and securing his toolbox in the thin light before sunrise. I made my way downstairs and started the coffee pot in the kitchen, peaking down the hall to check on him every few minutes. He came in after loading all his tools, and I pushed a thermos full of coffee his way.

"New job?" I asked.

Ray nodded, looking down at the coffee and back up at me. "It might be a late one. Don't wait up."

I nodded back to him and knew that meant he'd spend the day working and the night spending half of what he earned at the bar on the edge of town. Recently, I'd started selling some of Mama's things. Just bits and pieces. Things I didn't really need — some of her old albums, first-edition books, antique vases, and silver figurines. They didn't get much, but they filled the gap so we could make some extra house repairs.

Heading upstairs, I heard Ray pull out of the driveway. I got ready for work at the cafe and before I left, I noticed he had left his thermos untouched on the counter. I shook it off, poured the still-hot coffee down the drain, and rinsed the cup before heading down the mountain. As I walked, I couldn't help but think about our maintenance lesson with the brakes.

I didn't know much about how it would all work or how long it would take for something to happen, or more likely, for Ray to notice that I had done something. I sat with a stone in my stomach that weekend, but he spent most of his time with Mama, making up for his awfulness, and for the fresh bruises across Mama's left cheek and wrists, by cooking her dinner on Saturday and bringing her breakfast in bed, but when Monday came around, he pulled down the driveway with no issues. Maybe I couldn't even sabotage the brakes correctly.

With Ray out of sight and out of mind, I went to school and came home early, hoping that Mama would want to have dinner out back to watch the sunrise. I didn't expect Ray home until after sunset, so I was looking forward to eating and spending time with Mama.

She cooked pasta that night, and I made the salad. Clouds gathered on the horizon, and we had to move inside when the wind picked up. From the kitchen window, I watched lightning dance as I washed the dishes, and when I said that it was time for bed, Mama's eyes strayed to the front drive. Her thoughts were with Ray. Where was he? Who was he with? Would he be safe in the coming storm? I could almost hear the worry circling her head like hungry buzzards waiting for fresh flesh.

I had tea with Mama and went to bed, lulled to sleep by the low thunder in the distance and was awakened, not by thunder, but by a knock at the front door. The sky was a deep purple, projecting Mama's fresh bruises across the sky. A smear of red streaked across the eastern horizon.

That's the funny thing. I remember the sky but not the man's face — the men's faces. There were two of them.

Officers.

Police officers.

"Ma'am, is your mother home?" The officer said as he cleared his throat.

Mama pushed me aside, her eyes filled with knowing worry. Officers didn't show up out of the blue for minor issues. This was major.

"*Sorry, ma'am, can we come in?*" *He gestured over his shoulder to his partner who was standing at the foot of the stairs.* "*We have some unfortunate news…*" *I heard from over Mama's shoulder, but she didn't let them finish. She refused to let them in. She screamed at the police and spat at them through the thin sliver of the front door that framed her face in the warming light.*

"*Liars.*" *She spat.* "*Liars. Where is he?*"

Mama raged against them. She pounded the door frame, broke the lamp on the side table, sobbed until she melted to the floor, and finally let them in, having spent her energy. She let them take her in their arms.

"*Ma'am, I'm sorry,*" *the policeman pleaded as he led her to the sofa. He was just doing his job.*

"*It can't be. He was just here. How did this…*" *Mama's voice trailed off, and she gripped the officer's collar.*

"*He had too much to drink,*" *the officer said slowly.* "*He was rounding a corner and didn't slow down.*"

"*He can't leave me. I can't live without him,*" *she sobbed. She lowered her head and moaned, giving in to her grief. She let out a howl like a wild animal, still holding on desperately to the officer's collar.*

"*It's okay, ma'am,*" *the officer crooned and exchanged a glance with his partner.* "*It's going to be okay.*"

"*How can you say that? He's dead.*" *Mama breathed.*

"*He's not dead, ma'am.*" *He shook his head.* "*He's at the hospital. It doesn't look good, but he hasn't passed away.*"

Mama looked at the man, then at the other officer near the doorway. Desolate fire danced behind her eyes. "*Which corner?*"

"*The corner of Honeysuckle and Elm,*" *the man said as he pointed down the driveway.*

Mama's eyes filled with fresh tears. "*He was coming home,*" *she breathed, sinking to the floor.* "*He was coming home to me.*"

She gave a sad laugh and stood up, grabbing her coat. "*Take me to him,*" *she demanded and rushed toward their car. The policemen let her inside, and the driver waved to me.*

"You coming?" He asked.

I shook my head, my eyes on Mama, but she didn't look at me. Her eyes, her everything, were already miles away, down the mountain, across town, and at Ray's side as he laid in his hospital room. The officer nodded and started the car, leaving me in the doorway as I watched the receding police lights.

Somehow, Mama turned Ray's death into a tragic romance, and the miracle was that he had lived. But I knew it wasn't a miracle. It was the opposite of a miracle. A curse. A hex. Because I knew he would survive. I knew he was coming back home. And I knew that there would be consequences. But just how bad they would be, I had no idea.

The first Wednesday of the month, Liz didn't show up at the cafe, and after I waited for her for over an hour, I walked to her house. The door was unlocked, and I came in to see her leaning against her bathtub, head hung over the toilet.

"You okay?" I asked stupidly as I touched her forehead.

She moaned in reply, so I went to the kitchen and made some ginger tea to help her stomach. She was able to gulp down a few sips, and I got her into bed, but I could see that she needed rest, so I grabbed her keys and headed back to the cafe.

I ended up opening late, but at least I had muffins and breakfast sandwiches ready, most of which I had prepped the day before. Liz had developed a good number of regulars who stopped by the cafe on their way to work, so I knew it would be busy in the first few hours.

Working alone was much different than working with Liz. She seemed to zip around the kitchen with ease, refilling coffee in the dining room and prepping things in the bakery. Her fingers knew all the keys on the cash register by heart. I, on the other hand, felt like I was stuck in a hurricane of orders, tasks, and faces. Yet, I got through it, and many people smiled with sympathy when I answered their questions about Liz — yep, it's a bad one. Sure, I'll try some chamomile later. Same, I hope she's feeling better tomorrow — and everyone was uncharacteristically patient. I guess that's the kind of charm Liz had around people, although I remember Mama saying the same thing about me long ago.[42]

Just before lunch, a lady came in with a baby on her hip. The baby looked to be a little over a year old. I recognized the lady immediately. Sharon. [43]

"A coffee please?" The woman managed as she shifted the wiggling baby on her hip. The baby's nose dripped, and drool hung from the corner of its mouth. Dressed in a white onesie and jeans, I couldn't tell if it was a boy or a girl.

"Of course." I nodded and filled a fresh cup.

"I heard you were working here," Sharon started as I rang up her order. "It's nice to see you."

I nodded and she dug in her shorts pocket and produced a small wad of ones and a few coins. I sorted through the crumpled bills to find the exact change.

"Has Ray said anything lately? He's been coming around, but I just didn't know if..." She trailed off and wiped the baby's nose with the inside of its onesie. I pushed the coffee and change across the counter to her.

"I just didn't know if Ray said anything about me and little Rose here. You know, our lease is up at the end of the year, and I was hoping that —"

"It's hot," I interrupted, nodding at the coffee cup. "Be careful, and I hope you have a nice day."

Sharon squeezed out a smile, and the baby — Junior, as she called him — let out a wail that seemed to shake the mugs on the shelf behind me. Scurrying out of the cafe, Sharon took one last

---

42Common herbal remedies for digestion issues include chamomile, ginger, lemon or peppermint teas, acupuncture or acupressure, breathing exercises, certain spices (such as fennel, cumin, and cinnamon), vitamin B6 supplements, sitting upright, and getting fresh air. My mom always made me a warm, but not too hot, peppermint tea that she said she learned from her grandmother long ago.

43Cannot confirm Sharon's identity. Perhaps Cat has changed it here?

look at me over her shoulder before pushing open the front door and shushing the baby one-handed as she walked down the street.

I exhaled and rolled my eyes. Was she serious? Was she really asking about moving into Mama's house? I guess I knew where Ray had been spending most of his time lately. He wasn't at the bar across town. He was snuggled up with Sharon, and whoever else he kept in secret, playing house while I mourned Mama and struggled to keep the bills paid. But I knew she'd soon learn that Ray's promises were as shallow as a fall rain puddle and that she, too, would be left wanting and waiting; disappointed and alone.

June 21, 1999

Today was the longest day of the year, the summer solstice. Grandma used to say that it was a day to have a big adventure; stuff all the life you can into the day to make the most of the daylight, but I think this is one of the darkest days I've had in a long time.

Ray was in a terrible accident.

He was coming home, and it was raining, and they said his brakes went out. Just like that, that there wasn't any fluid in them. Ray said he put his foot on the brakes to take the turn, and his foot went straight to the floor. It bugged me because they were just working on the brakes. I remember going out to the driveway and seeing Ray teach Cat how to change them or something. They were working on them all morning. They were both so dirty and sweaty from being under his truck when I called them inside. What did I have? Lunch or tea or something?

I remember Ray coming inside and me calling Cat to join us, and I remember seeing her face through the screen. She looked so angry, like a wild animal. It made me frightened for a minute. I left her alone, but when she came in, she was all smiles. She even hugged me close.

Maybe Cat did something? I can't even believe I wrote that. I know Cat, and I know she's a good girl. She's so smart and so cunning, but... Her wild streak has only grown as she's gotten older. I used to love that streak. She never stood for a bully.

Anyway, when I got to the hospital after Ray's accident, I was so relieved. He was sitting up and talking. The doctor said it was a miracle that he was mostly unharmed. When they pulled him out of the truck, there was blood everywhere. They thought he was seriously hurt, but when they got him to the hospital, the doctors were amazed. A bloody nose was all that was wrong.

At home, I cooked him a special meal and pampered him as much as possible. I was just so thankful, but Cat was quiet. Too quiet.

I don't know, something didn't sit right with me. And then I remembered how I was at her age. I remembered that night, sneaking out to Marianne's birthday party. I remembered thinking I was so cunning, getting Marianne's present, agreeing to stay. I remembered

143

the party was a whirlwind of presents, cakes, candles, and games. I don't think I'd ever smiled so much. I didn't even realize the time until the sun started to disappear behind the trees.

As the party wound down and the other girls started to leave, I began to get nervous. I could feel my stomach start to sink as the sun disappeared behind the trees; my conscience finally weighing on me.

Marianne noticed, of course, she noticed, and she took my hand to show me where she had set up our beds together. Her enthusiasm was contagious; I couldn't help but smile and told her I'd stay until sunrise so I could sneak back upstairs before Grandmother woke up.

I remembered she had posters all over her walls and velvet curtains and a bedspread that could almost swallow you whole. A dollhouse that was taller than us both and a whole closet of dress-up clothes. Her new presents lined her dresser just waiting for us to come and play.

We played dolls in the dollhouse in between bites of cold pizza from the party. Although we were too old for that at twelve, neither of us cared. While her mom and dad were busy cleaning up and listening to music, and I saw them kiss across the kitchen counter. I had blushed before scurrying away with my piece of pizza. I remembered thinking, "Now, THAT's love."

Marianne and I talked and laughed about the party before they tucked us in, our heads barely peeked out from the giant comforter, and after giggling for what felt like hours, we finally fell asleep. Soon after, thunder woke me up.

Groggily, I sat up in bed and saw lightning flash, and it lit up the room in shades of white, blue, and black. I remembered shivering, thinking how different the room looked. I shook my head and wondered if I really was in a dream, and my head did that swimmy thing that it does when I'm sleepy but not quite awake yet. Lightning flashed again and again in pulses, highlighting the bed, the dresser, the dollhouse.

And then I saw it.

A faun in the doorway.

Or at least I thought it was a faun, a tall other-worldly being that watched us while we slept. I blinked, unable to make a noise, and waited, and when the lightning flashed again, I could see that the faun was still there, standing upright in the doorway leaning against the frame, but this time, he was smiling. He called to me, and his voice was soft and familiar, like wet moss.

The faun came over and lifted me out of bed. I inhaled soft moss and wet leaves, and the faun's arms felt like they were made of thick branches and straw, soft and scratchy at the same time, holding me close, and I could hear the strange beating of his heart like a clock stuck inside a tree. I swayed in his arms, back and forth. I fell back asleep, lost in the arms of the mysterious faun.

Anyway, lately, I've been plagued by nightmares, which brings me to today, the darkest day on the longest day of the year. How ironic. There was a knock on my door this morning. It was a woman, a mouse of a woman with beige-brown hair and a washed-out complexion, round eyes and squished nose staring back at me when I opened the door.

She was from the other side of town, down in the hollows where the river cut through, but I had seen her at the general store in ripped leggings and a stained white shirt, hair piled on the top of her head, pupils the size of saucers. Another sad addiction story like so many others from that side of town.

She didn't say anything at first, even when I asked her what she needed, and when I started to close the door, she pulled out a white stick and shoved it in my face, literally and figuratively, a white stick with two pink lines and mumbled something about being pregnant and she thought I should know.

When I asked her why I would want to know, she looked me in my eyes and told me the biggest lie I've ever heard. She said it was Ray's baby and that he planned to leave me and marry her. Can you believe her?

How dare she show up on my doorstep and accuse Ray of something like that, something so outrageous — an outright lie — especially when Ray wasn't home to defend himself.

Needless to say, I sent her away and told her never to come around here again, I mean, the audacity, and although I tried to push it from my mind, I kept thinking about all the nights that Ray wouldn't come home, about the span of days he'd disappear, but no, Ray wouldn't do that to me. He'd never — well, I can't even write it. I won't write it. He'd never leave me. It would kill me to even think it.

Transcript
Interview with Eddy Sparrow
6:24 p.m. April 27th, 2021
Case No. HI30823

Mom found a few more details about Helen's marriage to Charles but find't get a chance to include them. The gossip column published an article about marriage troubles. I guess Charles was seen with various women around town, and someone else wrote in about Helen's suspected infertility. I can't even imagine. I would have been too upset about the rumors alone to go outside. Maybe that's why Helen retreated from the town. Her sister Nellie was still staying there along with a cook and presumed companion named Abigail.

And then I found this. Helen and Charles were married for about two years before this birth announcement in the papers — a baby girl named Lorelai.

But the gossip column readers weren't satisfied.

Yeah, you're right. A gossip column wouldn't be a gossip column without the drama. They wrote in claiming that Charles was hoping for an heir, a son who could carry on his name. And then another article said he was relying on the Saunders' fortune and had only married Helen for her money, so —

I know it's just a gossip column. I'm just telling you what Mom found. Anway, Charles started traveling again, and he seemed to want nothing to do with the baby. I mean, he twenty years older than her, but some men are born with a desire for chase — for seeking out new experiences in spite of current circumstances.

Stephen was like that sometimes. He was magnetic, and it seemed like he could never be satisfied. We were inseparable when we first met, but sometimes, it was like a cloud came over him. He was there, but he wan't really you know?

Stephen always joked that it was fate that brought us together. It was the Red String of Fate —

It's an old Chinese folk tale that says that from the moment we're born, we're tied to everyone who will impact our life. No matter the twists and turns, the detours, the complicated tangles we take in life, we are destined to meet those people. The string can be stretched, lengthened, or knotted, but we will always meet the people in our life who will change it the most. It's destiny. Some people even say that's why we pinky swear because we're connected from the moment we're born.

I know, it sounds like a line, but I thought it was romantic.

Hey, I was young and didn't know any better. Stephen used the Red String of Fate for our the toast at our wedding.

I know. I know. He made a toast to us at our own wedding. I should have seen his narcissism then, but like I said, I was young.

Stephen's family came from old money. That was how he'd had the ability to attend classes while writing that "groundbreaking" book about the history of Alabama's mines. It seems that most people who achieve success early achieves it because of networking and opportunity, both of which are made a little bit easier with money.

Anyway, our wedding was this huge ceremony. You know the kind, a weekend wedding full of events and photoworthy moments.

It was at the Cornelius House — don't look at me like that.

Yes, it was for the entire weekend, and no, I don't know how expensive it was. Stephen's mom was the one who paid for everything. I was still a research assistant and a lowly adjunct professor at that point.

Yeah, it was beautiful. The house was old

but solid. Have you been there?

Exactly. It's the kind of house that just feels like it's seen so many things. We got there on a Thursday with friends and family arriving by Friday night.

We had a nice dinner —

I don't know. Chicken or steak? Anyway, all day Saturday was filled with games and events. Stephen's mother hosted a ladies' spa day while the men played golf. She made me feel so special. That afternoon, we went swimming as we watched the sun go down, and I almost didn't miss my mom. Almost...

Then, on Sunday, we had the ceremony, celebrating our reception with a few hundred of our closest friends, most of which were Stephen's relatives, but I invited a few close friends. Mom didn't come but a few of my friends did.

I don't know why she didn't come. We'd said some of the most terrible things to each other, and a few years had past. It just seemed like too many of the wrong words had been said and too much time had passed. That is to say, it felt like it was too late.

Anyway, we had fireworks at dinner, but sometime after the toast and before the first burst of the fireworks show, Stephen had disappeared.

I couldn't find him anywhere, but I remember Stephen's mom said something I still can't get out of my head. She'd had too much to drink. She said that she loved Stephen's speech about the Red String of Fate and then brought up the minotaur in the maze, half man and half bull, you know the one?

Well, this bull-man was trapped in the labyrinth, and he fed on human flesh. A red string was used to help lead the god Theseus to the bull and then to safety after he killed it. The string was a guide to get out of danger.

And I know it's been a long time, but I clearly remember her saying that these animal-like creatures were manifestations of us, of our animal side — the ugliness that can hide on the inside, ya know? They are the creepy bits that we don't allow anyone else to see because we're too afraid to see them ourselves.

Anyway, I'm getting ahead of myself.

After closing the shop, I checked on Liz, who was still in bed, and I cooked her some chicken broth for dinner. The air was warm on my walk home, and I took the long way home, zig-zagging past the park and around the town square.

The town was nice at night. The shadows offered anonymity, a chance to see others without having them see me.

Just as I was passing the library, I felt a truck pull up next to me, and expecting Ray, I was surprised to see Owen's white Jeep.

"Out for a walk?" He asked, and I let his stupid question die between us unanswered.

"Sure is a nice night," he continued as he kept pace with me.

"I hear they're having country-fried steak at the diner." I looked at him, and he raised his eyebrows.

"Come on. I didn't mean anything at the dance, and I'd love to make it up to you."

"Is that your form of an apology?"

Owen exhaled. "You never give anyone a break, do you?"

"Never have, and I'm not gonna start now."

"I'm sorry, Cat. I had too much to drink last time, and I just... I'm sorry."

I focused on the ground in front of me, fuming about the dance, his sweaty hands, his hungry mouth.

"I'm serious, Cat. I'm sorry. Let me make it up to you by buying dinner."

I thought about making dinner at home in the ghostly spot in the kitchen where I feel Mama the most, and I could almost see the dark, empty house.

"If you don't, you know my mom's gonna be worried. I'd hate to —"

"Okay," I burst. "Fine."

Owen celebrated by drumming on the steering wheel, his smile spread so wide that I couldn't help but smile too. "I'm getting dessert, okay?"

He raised his hands in a sign of truce and stopped the truck. I hopped inside, not knowing what the night would bring but knowing that it would be an adventure because, with Owen, it always was.

The diner wasn't busy. The usual dinner crowd was gone, so Owen took the opportunity to sweet-talk the waitress into free breadsticks. He made jokes about his brother, Davis, and complained about school. He proudly suffered from senioritis and couldn't wait to get out of town.

"Where would you go?" I asked.

"Anywhere but here. I have a scholarship to Alabama, so that should get me out of here for a little while." He sipped his Coke and nodded at me. "What about you?"

"I graduated early, but I have to stay the year, you know?"

"How'd you manage that?"

I shrugged. "I took a bunch of independent studies and courses through the community college."

"Nice. I always knew you were smart, but that sounds like a lot of work." He raised his eyebrows and stuffed more bread into his mouth. "What do you wanna do? Go to college?"

"Yeah. I always liked writing. Mama got me a typewriter for a graduation present, but I haven't touched it since I've been back."

"The blank page," he said in a spooky voice, wiggling his fingers.

"Exactly. I wouldn't know where to start or what to say."

"It'll come to you." He grabbed his drink again; cleared his mouth before the waitress came back. "Know what you want?" He gestured to my menu.

The waitress came by and he started to order. I studied his face, his friendly eyes that saw everything, even a girl afraid to tell her own story.

Do you do any writing?

Well, we're all storytellers.

is probably one of the best pieces of writing advice that I've ever heard. Pen to paper and the trust that "it" will come.

The most successful creatives aren't necessarily the most talented, you know, but they are usually the most consistent.

They have the consistency to write and finish a book, paint the work of art, compose the piece of music, etc. or they do not. No manner of talent can replace consistency.

Oh yeah, I never finished that, did I?

Well, like I said, Stephen disappeared after the fireworks and reappeared a few hours later, but he said he went up to the roof to see the view. He said it was so beautiful that he just stayed there until he remembered that he was supposed to be downstairs.

No, I didn't believe that at first, but you know what? He asked if I wanted to see it.

Yeah, he took my hand and pulled me through the house, past the wedding guests still dancing, up the stairs, and onto the widow's walk.

And it was just like he said.

The world was at our feet, the whole of the Birmingham skyline and the surrounding ridgelines, Vulcan pointing to Electra's spear, and we had it all to ourselves, and I remember looking at him and being so proud that this beautiful, observant man was mine. Mine forever, and no matter what, he would always come back. I though that that was what it was like to belong to someone.

Owen's Jeep rumbled up the mountain. I snuck a look at him in the dark cab. He was the same as before, yet different. Sure, I had seen him at his worst, a drunk jerk who was so full of himself that he thought I would be flattered at his parking lot advances, but I had also seen him as an observant boy coming into his own, not quite sure how to be a man but taking note of those around him. He was extremely intelligent underneath it all, making him capable, yet potentially dangerous. As Mama used to say, "A happy God created flowers, bunny rabbits, sunrises. A bored God created platypuses, pangolins, and leafy sea dragons. An angry God, though, an angry God invented death." As I'd grown, I learned the same is true about men. They could be loving and kind, but also cruel and dangerous, Owen notwithstanding.

"It looks like a party," Owen breathed as we pulled close to the house.

The windows were bright with light and music streamed from the open front windows. I knew it was no party inside.

"I'd better go," I said as I unbuckled my seatbelt. "Thanks for dinner."

"Of course." He nodded.

I paused and said, "And tell your mom I said hello."

"You should really come by sometime. She misses you, you know."

Before I could stop myself, I said, "Me, too."

"Really?" He raised his eyebrows. "I thought you hated her."

"I don't hate her. She was Mama's best friend."

"Then why do you avoid her so much?"

"I don't know. She just-" I looked at the bright windows and took a breath. "She just reminds me of Mama, you know? All the fun times we had, and then, in the end, well…"

I felt Owen squeeze my hand as he reached across the seat. "I know. We all miss her. I can't even imagine."

I nodded again and opened the door. "Thanks again for dinner."

"Any time," he replied. "Good night, Cat."

I took the front steps slowly, wondering what I would find

inside. The sounds of The Rolling Stones met my ears, and I was enveloped in light and sound as I pulled the front door open.

Ray was in the living room, flipping through records and doing an awkward shimmy that turned my stomach. His thin frame moved in time with the music. The beer belly he had developed protruded slightly over the top of his belt. His work boots and his socked feet whispered over the hardwood floor.

"What are you doing home?" I asked, leaning against the doorframe.

"You know," he said over his shoulder. "I gotta spend time with my daughter and all."

"I'm not your daughter, Ray," I muttered.

He shook his head and flashed a tight smile. "That's not what the court says."

I felt my jaw tighten.

"A little birdy told me that you ran into Sharon today."

"A little birdy or Sharon herself?"

"Clever," he returned. "So clever. Just like your Mama."

"Don't talk about her," I said.

"I can talk about whoever I want to talk about, little girl," he spat but continued to dance to the music. I watched him and felt my anger build.

"So, what's the plan?" I asked as I crossed my arms over my chest.

"Plan?"

"Yeah. Sharon moves in? Get a second chance at raising a perfect child? One who's actually yours?"

"That's none of your business." He turned to face me, his finger pointed in my direction. I must have hit a nerve.

"It is when she thinks she's moving in here at the end of the year."

Ray exhaled and ran a hand through his hair. "I never told her that." He shook his head.

"I don't care what you told her. This is my home. Besides, you're the reason that Mama-"

"Don't," he interrupted.

"Everyone knows that's the truth. Mama was fine until you-"

"I'm not the one who was there that night," he raised his voice and stepped towards me, his accusing finger closed the distance between us. "You were there, Cat. If anyone's to blame, it's you."

My mouth dropped open, and I took a step back. The music faded and was replaced by static, the needle receded as the record stopped. Ray laughed sadly.

"You have something to say about everyone else, but never yourself, Cat. Take a look in the mirror before you start coming for other people."

He flipped the record and placed the needle on the spinning vinyl, flooding the house with sound once more and drowning out any reply I might have had. I let out a breath, pushed off the door frame, and headed upstairs.

Still angry, I drew a bath and sank into the warm water, thinking about Mama's pages and Sharon showing up that night on the doorstep, with a double-pink wand in hand. Mama's insistence that she heal both Ray's injuries and the rift between them.

And her plan seemed to work at first. For a while at least. Mama cooked dinner and cleaned, but something was different about her. She started taking long walks through the rose maze after sundown. She said she could feel a presence there, like someone was walking alongside her, and I had to admit that sometimes I felt the same. But it looked like she was getting better. It really did.

And then came the morning of water.

About a month after Ray's accident, I woke up to strange echoes filling the house. Ray had already left as the doctor had cleared him for work — a miracle, truly a miracle that he was able to walk away, everyone said — so we had the house to ourselves.

I sat up and put my feet on the carpet, but it was wet. Water was everywhere. The carpet was soaked. It made a wet, sucking

noise every time I took a step. The slap-suck cadence of my feet
shattered the echoes of water down the hall. I called for Mama,
but she didn't answer.

Groggily, I followed the sounds of water. And that's where I
found her.

She was in the bathtub, fully submerged with her eyes open.
At first, I thought I was dreaming. Her brown hair fanned out
from her face. Her eyes were huge pearls. A stray bubble attached
itself to her cheek like a reverse tear.

I grabbed her, this strange mermaid who looked just like
Mama, and pulled her out of the water.

She burst out of the water, eyes wide with surprise, gasping
and coughing.

"What'd you go and do that for?" She asked me sideways, her
dripping hair obscured her face.

"I thought — I thought —" but I couldn't finish the sentence.

"You thought I was dead?" She asked, pushing her hair back
from her face. "Maybe I already am," she whispered. "I don't
know anymore."

After that, Mama stopped coming inside as much, and she
stopped showing up for her shifts at the diner. She turned her
attention to the garden, growing plants with strange names I
couldn't pronounce, cultivating a life that she couldn't even
summon for herself.

I started tutoring to support us both after school started.
Between advanced classes and working as a tutor at the library, I
didn't have much time to worry about her. As long as she stayed
outside, she was safe from the bits of Ray that clung to the edges
of things. Instead of teacups, we were stuck, frozen, survivors
with no purpose.

Drying off from the bath, I heard Ray head upstairs to bed.
After I was sure he was asleep, I crept downstairs and took out
the typewriter that Mama had given me. It was dusty, stuffed
under the desk with a few boxes of books that Mama had planned

to donate. I set it on top of the desk, my fingers touched the keys, but I couldn't bring myself to write. Instead, I tucked it back under the desk with the unwanted books and headed back upstairs. In the hallway, I stopped short.

Footprints.

There was a set of footprints, my own, trailing down the hall and descending the front steps. But there was another pair of footprints alongside my own. They followed my steps to the front stairs, wavered, and then disappeared into my room.

Holding my breath, I crept carefully to the door of my room and peered inside. It was dark and empty, but the front window was pulled open. A breeze came in through the wide crack and blew through the room, fluttering the curtains and shifting the haint-blue mobile I had hanging in the corner. And on my bed was Mama's diary, open and waiting, its pages fluttered and beckoned me to read. I shivered, closed the journal, and tucked it under my mattress.

I had had enough ghost stories for tonight.

Transcript
Interview with Eddy Sparrow
6:51 p.m. April 27th, 2021
Case No. HI30823

I know. I have the shivers, too.

No, I had no idea she was researching this. I mean, Mom was always researching things and writing in her notebooks, so I didn't think anything about it. And I was a little distracted at the time with the divorce.

Well, after the wedding, things were fine. I was teaching, still adjunct, but I was working on a project about the history and cultural significance of kudzu…

You keep giving me that look, but it was actually pretty interesting.

I swear. It was about —

Okay, okay. I'll get back to it.

So things were fine. I was teaching and writing, and Stephen secured a tenure spot, so it was like everything was looking up. We bought a house. Well, Stephen's parents helped a lot, but we had a great spot.

Oh, it was a place downtown. One of those old houses that was barely standing but had all the original hardware. Stephen's mom knew of a restoration company and an interior designer. She knew everybody.

Hey, I said not to look at me like that. I wasn't the one who was born rich. My mom worked for everything we had, and I always got the impression that she'd had a hard childhood, but I grew up happy enough. I think we all go through that "hating our moms" phase, right?

Anyway, things were good. We had a home and careers ahead of us. And Stephen was talking about how the department chair was set to retire soon, so we had these dinners to go to. It was like Mom's house all over again, except this time, Stephen wasn't there to run off with me. He was there to rub elbows instead.

I'm not complaining. Or at least not tryin to. I'm just saying that it was hard. Lonely,

159

ya know?

And I can't imagine how Cat felt that summer. That last chapter gave me the creeps so bad that I started seeing things.

Well, I mean that I started seeing things.

Look, I'm not one for ghost stories or silly superstitions, but when I was reading it, it was like I could feel someone watching me. I'd look around, but I'd be in the house alone. I'd go back to reading, and then I'd feel it again.

This one night, I accidentally read til after sundown, so I decided to take a bath to warm up. I checked for footprints like Cat'd seen, didn't see any, and locked tha bathroom door just in case.

I'm not being silly. Stop looking at me like that.

I know it sounds crazy, but Cat's last words had me on edge. I tried to relax in the bath, but I kept having this feelin, so I got out.

Again, I was in Mom's house with all her things, so that didn't help. But I also knew that I was the only one home. I used the blowdryer to clear the steam from the mirror, and as I did, I noticed how grown up I looked. Isn't that something. You wish you were older your whole life so you can finally be independent and do what you want only to look around and realize that you'd skipped over all the good parts. At least, that's what it felt like.

I'd been so bright-eyed and ambitious. I'd fallen in love and left home to go on these great adventures, but it didn't end up like that, and suddenly, I had wrinkles.

Anyway, it's about this point in my reading that I started hearing noises at night. Nothing that I could pinpoint, just knocks and creaks that could have been the house settling, but what about that feeling I kept having? The feeling of being watched?

I hoped that I wasn't so alone, but I also didn't want to be haunted, either.

I'm not pulling your leg, I swear. I felt it, kinda like what I'm feelin now. Like something's off. You feel that?

Okay, okay. I'll keep going, but it was this point that I started to wonder if a book could be haunted. But that's silly, right?

JULY 2001

It wasn't my idea to go to the Fourth of July parade. It was Owen's.

Liz said the shop would be closed since the town shut down, stopped, and held its breath while we celebrated Independence Day, and since I was planning to go down to help her set up, Owen convinced me to let him give me a ride into town that morning.

I dressed and made coffee, knowing full well that Ray would pour anything I touched immediately down the drain. He still didn't trust me. That whole week was hot and humid, soupy and thick as it was suspended at the height of summer. The air was so thick that it was hard to breathe, so Liz brewed fresh sweet tea to serve in her normal coffee air pots. We brewed the tea for days, knowing that everyone would want some refreshment, and our fingers were stained brown from brewing and mixing in way too much sugar.

As we came to the town, Owen slowed. The lamp posts were decorated with flowers, and a modest crowd was already gathered along the sidewalk. The local businesses had tables outside selling their merchandise before the parade began, and I caught sight of Liz.

"Come on," I whispered, taking Owen's arm before he could even lock the car. "I'm late helping out Liz."

Liz was setting up a table with muffins and coffee to go when I reached out and tapped her on the shoulder. She turned, and the early morning sun caught the waves of her hair. It matched her eyes.

Pure honey.

I shook my head to clear it and smiled. "It's great to see you."

"You, too," Liz returned, but her eyes were on Owen.

"I'm Owen," he said in his most charming voice.

He often did this.

I was afraid to look at Liz, knowing how all women act to his charm, but she surprised me.

"I know. We've met several times... at the cafe," she forced a smile. "And how convenient, I was just wondering how I was going to carry all the coffee air pots from the cafe to the table."

Instead of offering her hand, she picked up the coffee pot she propped near the cafe's front door and dropped it into his arms. Owen struggled to get his hands around the container in time, his face turning red with the anxiety of manual labor. "Over there." She gestured toward a table with stacks of paper cups and plastic lids. He skipped a beat, waiting for a punchline or a hidden camera, but none came. He cleared his throat and started walking to the table, puzzled, and I tried to hide my smile.

Liz was a feisty one.

"No problem," Owen said over his shoulder.

When he was out of earshot, she turned to me and asked, "You came with him?"

"Yeah." I blushed. "You know, he's an old family friend. We kind of made amends at dinner the other night."

"You went to dinner together?"

"Yeah, a few nights ago. It was no big —"

"Wait, when I was sick?" She eyed me, distaste hanging at the corners of her mouth.

"Yeah. I mean, no. You were feeling better, and I was walking home that night, and then Owen —"

"You know what? It doesn't even matter," she said and picked up a box of baked goods she had stacked in a cardboard box before calling over her shoulder. "Those air pots aren't gonna carry themselves."

I sighed and picked up the steel coffee pot. As summer had set in, so did the heat. It brought with it a feeling of child-like freedom that only summer holds, and the town came to life with the possibility of summer adventures that could stretch into eternity.

As soon as the table was set up, Owen left to do what Mama called schmooze everyone in sight while I was left wandering around the booths since Liz was busy and gace me the cold shoulder. It was nice to walk, though, and I enjoyed the summer breeze and the opportunity to see people gathered together and families holding hands. A few people nodded to me, smiled, and even spoke to me.

In the afternoon, the school hosted a sort of Olympics — a foot race, a three-legged race, a potato sack race, a limbo competition, an arm-wrestling contest, and a pie-eating contest. I sat in the shade across the street and watched families laughing together, wiping each other's foreheads. Men brought steaming pots of their wives' chili and dishes of potato salad to the tents along the street, and Marianne waved from her spot in front of an entire spread of goodies. I waved back and felt a tug at my stomach as I remembered the picnics she'd pack for Mama and me. I could almost taste her chocolate chip cookies.

I could hear the marching band before I could see it. Kids stood at attention and toddlers climbed atop their father's shoulders. Standing crowded together, the people lined up shoulder to shoulder and reminded me of a skyline, jagged and beautiful, imperfect yet tangible. I wondered if the buildings in big cities like New York got excited about parades or if their windows yawned at the same show played again and again for decades.

The sound of drums and the shouts of trumpets shook through the crowd while candy rained down as if shaken from the sky by the cymbal's crash. I snuck a few Reese's and handed some extra lollipops to the nearby kids before turning my attention back to a teenager in the procession, out of step and out of time, who looked like she was going to faint with fear. Her doe-like legs trembled, and her eyes were wide, but she marched along and out of sight before the next float that played a new song for a new cause.

Next were the church floats, packed with kids throwing candy to the ones in the crowd who could not have fit on the float. Then, the clowns and the Shriners. The police and fire departments showed off their best vehicles while those in uniform waved on foot.

Float after float passed. Groups of people smiled and waved. After a while, my head swam with songs and chatter in the afternoon heat above the pavement. I searched the crowd for Liz or for Owen but only saw strangers who I had known for years.

The sun sank quickly as the floats passed, and darkness swept down the western mountains and into the valley of town. And then I heard a familiar voice.

"Just wait," the deep voice thundered. I looked but could only see unfamiliar faces slide past.

"O, there's no way you're gonna tap that." Another voice taunted. I pushed through the crowd to get closer, but still couldn't see the voices.

"If I'm not tappin' it, then why's she been beggin' me to give her rides?"

"She came with you today?"

"Yeah, and just wait 'til u give her that ride tonight." The deep voice let out a cackle, and just before I could picture his face, the crowd slid apart, revealing Owen, smiling with a cocky smirk on his face, and I immediately knew that he was talking about me.

Was he serious? He was the one who kept showing up and offering me rides, playing the good guy. I felt shame paint my cheeks and turned to disappear back inside the crowd before anyone could see me.

The sounds of the parade pressed in on me, and I felt my chest tighten as panic climbed from the pit of my stomach.

Searching again for Liz or even Marianne, I felt trapped and alone. I tried to take a deep breath, but pain stabbed my chest, and I couldn't breathe. Instead, I felt the earth tilt. I reached out my hand, but only found the elbows of strangers.

"Liz?" I called out, making my way back toward the cafe, but I could already see the cafe's windows, dark and silent, the front door, locked and solid.

"Liz? Marianne?" I yelled, but the band had wound its way through the town and was bearing down on me again. I pressed myself against the brick of the cafe's front and sank slowly to the ground, holding my ears to try to block out the sound.

I've been to the hospital for the last few weeks. I started making teas that would dull the pain of Ray's disappearance. It's just easier if I don't remember Ray being gone, if I can sleep until he's back. Like Sleeping Beauty. Wouldn't that be wonderful?! To just shut my eyes and for all my problems to disappear just for a little while.

I found some recipes in Grandma's old books. Notes scratched in the margins about chamomile, mandrakes, and sleeping nightshades. I tried to call the pharmacy in town to see if they could give me something, and when they couldn't — or more importantly, wouldn't — I started making my own teas. I'd drink them when I couldn't sleep if Ray didn't come home.

That woman hasn't been back, but I feel her there, creeping just outside, waiting for the perfect moment for her to pounce and take Ray away from me. Sometimes it just gets to be too much. The maze outside called to me, and instead of wandering the rose's thorns in the dark, I started drinking tea.

I make a ritual out of it. Take a bath, sip my tea, then go to bed. She found me there once– my sweet Cat. I felt tired in the bath and wondered what it would feel like to just sink to the bottom, let the water cover me, protect me from the world, and slowly fill my lungs while I drifted off to sleep.

It would be like a return.

Just as I started to see spots, tiny explosions of fireworks behind my eyes, I felt hands on my shoulders, pulling me back to the world and inside my own skin. Worried eyes searched my own, and I realized that it was Cat.

My Cat.

You should have seen the desperate look on her face.

After that, I started to make my teas after dinner. I'd make a whole pot and serve Ray and Cat a tiny bit, just enough to make them sleepy, to slow things down, freeze them for the night, all of us suspended and together and momentarily permanent.

On the Fourth, the air felt different when I woke up. Ray was already awake, and I noticed that he took an extra pair of clothes with him as he packed up his truck for work. When I asked if he was really going to work on the holiday, he mumbled something about time and a half and that I should feel lucky, but it just didn't make sense, and I told him so.

But he just grabbed my wrist, and pain shot through my whole arm. I thought he'd broken it, but it was only bruised. Yet again. I asked him not to leave. I told him that if he really loved me, then he would stay. He couldn't keep running away like that. He looked at me then, and I did the only thing I could think to do. I lifted my dress, my hand on my thigh as if to say, look what you'd be missing.

He gave me a sly smile and carried me up to the bedroom, and we made love for an hour. Hot, sticky, and exhausted, I laid down and stared at the ceiling while he rinsed off in the shower, but when he got out, he kissed me on the forehead and jogged down the stairs, whistling as he went. And I was left with damp sheets, covered in sweat and disappointment.

A little while later, I went down to the kitchen. Cat sat there, moody as she always is these days. She said that we should go to town, get out of the house and see the parade, but the thought of all those people made my skin crawl.

Do you think they know about Ray and that woman? Do you think they all know? That they're all laughing at me?

I just couldn't bear it, so I made tea and served it to the both of us, my cup brimming with leaves while Cat's only had a touch and more honey than was necessary. My vision began to swim, and about an hour later, I felt Cat's body grow heavy and still beside me as we sat on the sofa and listened to the radio.

I asked her if she felt well, and she said that she felt drained and wanted to take a nap.[44] She slid her head onto my lap, and I stroked her hair as she went to sleep. She was so beautiful, a young woman already but also still my little girl, the one who fell on the curb outside the general store and cried before the store owner came out and gave her a sucker so that she might feel better. The same little girl who used to play dolls at my feet while I cooked stew. The same little girl who would crawl into my bed at the first sounds of thunder. She always hated loud noises.

We stayed there like that, with her sleeping on my lap and me in and out of sleep until the sun went down. Then I heard the car coming up the driveway. My vision was blurry and my arms and legs so heavy that I couldn't get off the sofa.

Who's there? I asked, but I couldn't hear an answer or recognize a face until it was right next to me.

Sarah, what have you done? The voice asked, and it took me a minute to place the voice.

Marianne.

What was Marianne doing here?

I must have passed out because the next thing I knew, I woke up in the hospital. Cat was fine when she woke up and was checked out by the doctors, but me? I had to stay until the tea's effects wore off and a psychiatrist was called in.

A crazy doctor.

Marianne thinks I'm crazy.

---

44 This seems to reference atropa belladonna, which can be a deadly nightshade, depending on the dose. It was originally used to heal wounds, cure gout, aid in pain relief, relax spasming muscles, ease inflammation, treat menstrual problems, stop histamic reactions, east motion sickness, cure peptic ulcer disease, and treat sleeplessness and was even used as a love potion. It was also used in cosmetic eye drops that would dilate the pupil, making the eyes appear more seductive. It was named after the goddess Atropos, the "unturning one", who was a member of the Three Fates. According to Greek mythology, one of the sisters spun the thread of a person's life and the other sister measured it. Atropos would cut the thread, ending the person's life, and Carl Linnaeus chose this name to describe the plant's toxic (and even deadly) properties. Belladonna is Italian for "beautiful woman" and references its cosmetic use. Although it is not regulated by the FDA in dietary supplements, belladonna can be found in some over the counter cough medicines and teething tablets. Additionally, it is being tested as an effective treatment for irritable bowel syndrome, including irritable colon, spastic colon, mucous colitis, and acute enterocolitis.

And the worst part is, they decided to keep me until they could be sure I wouldn't be a hazard to myself or my family. Had I done this before? No. How many times before? I don't know. Why have you been doing this? I don't know.

They kept me for a few weeks with these pointless counseling sessions about how I was feeling and what might have happened in the past to cause me to act and feel as I do. And the sad part was, they wouldn't let me see Ray.

They said it might be too triggering since it looked like he left me. But Ray would never leave. Not really.

And it was Marianne who gave me a ride home when I was discharged from the hospital. I was so angry at her. I still am. She keeps saying that her dad would pay for it all, that he'd want me to feel better, but I couldn't even look at her. I felt so betrayed.

They took my grandmother's books and either threw them away or hid them because they were nowhere to be found. I guess they thought her notes were the only place I could find exact measurements of plants and ingredients, and although there were other reference materials out there, I had to admit that it would be tricky to find something that powerful without hooking up with a Laudanum dealer. But I don't have to worry about that.

Last night, Ray came home again. It was late, and he smelled like dark liquor, but he came in and stood in the doorway. I could feel him looking at me, and when I asked him what he was looking at, he said the most beautiful woman in the world. He was back and that's all that mattered.[45]

---

45 I've been looking deeper into the Saunders' estate and found more details. Helen, the Saunders twin and daughter of Olivia and Saheter, is mentioned in The Daily Tribune. See clipping below.

The Saunders Curse Strikes Again

Early this morning, police were called to the Saunders estate in an apparent accident. Helen Saunders, age 30, was found at the bottom of the front stairwell. Although officers tried to revive her, they were not successful, and Saunders was pronounced dead at 9:53 am of an apparent accident.

Last night, guests were in attendance at the Saunders' estate for a small event to raise money for the church. Attendees were local families, and although many of them would not comment on the record, several reported that Helen Saunders was not in attendance, and her absence was explained by a sudden headache.

Charles Richardson, Saunders' husband, stated that he went to bed that night in his office on the top floor after all guests departed for the evening. Richardson was awakened the next morning by screams from downstairs. Frances Abigail Miller, a housekeeper, reportedly found Saunders's body while she was preparing the house for the day.

Although officers are treating the death as an accident, the house's nefarious past has resurfaced yet again. Strange tales of the mountaintop have always existed, dating back to the original settlers who fought a bloody battle, slaughtering an entire settlement of Indians while they slept. The Saunders estate's original builder, Samuel Saunders, died unexpectedly after he fell into a well on the estate's property. During the house's construction, however, rumors of accidents and even a few deaths were prevalent, although none were confirmed. Samuel Saunders's surviving wife, Olivia Saunders, was diagnosed with a rare lung disease a few years after her husband's death and passed away over a decade ago. The surviving daughters, Helen and Eleanor Saunders have lived in the house until Helen's death early this morning.

Helen Saunders is survived by her husband, Charles Richardson, and her twin sister, Eleanor Saunders. A small ceremony will be held at the ███████ Cemetery tomorrow at 10 am. The family is asking for privacy to heal from this tragedy, but rumors are swirling with everyone asking if the Saunders Curse has returned yet again.

Transcript
<u>Interview with Eddy Sparrow</u>
<u>7:26 p.m. April 27th, 2021</u>
<u>Case No. HI30823</u>
I know. This part always made my stomach ache. How could she still love him? He seems like such a sleeze ball.

You're right. Plenty of women are with men like that, and no matter how abusive they are, the women always came back.

No, Stephen was never abusive. He'd run from confrontation rather than actually address an issue.

Sorry, no, it's not you. I just get frustrated when thinking about him. After he got word that the chair position was opening up, he started staying after class and showing off with more research. He had a few research assistants that sung his praise everywhere they went.

He had this one assistant named Penny that used to come over with wine when she knew he'd be at events late. I just remember being so jealous of all the people that got to be around him all day. I had early morning classes and left campus before ten when he was just starting his day.

That last year, he said he'd take me to Birmingham's Sidewalk Film Festival, but it turned into a kind of PR campaign — shaking hands, kissing babies, that kinda thing.

No, I hated it. I just wanted him to spend some time with me, but I felt like such a small part of his life. We'd been married for seven years by that point, but I always felt like I was chasing after him and couldn't quite catch up.

In some ways, I can emphathize with Cat's mom. I was always the one left waiting, but I can't imagine doing that to my daughter. Anyway, want me to keep going?

I made my way to the alley next to the parade, I stopped and looked around me. I found a familiar red Thunderbird — Marianne's — and felt my knees go weak. I tried the door to escape the loud noises, but it wouldn't budge. I hugged myself, still sobbing, and slowly slid down the driver's side door, coming to rest on the cracked pavement of the old lot. Cheers and laughter poured down the street and spilled into the alley. I brought my knees to my chest and let out a howl that didn't even sound like me. It came from somewhere deep inside, from the place that Ray had hurt Mama, from the place where she had hurt me. Why wasn't I enough for the both of us?

I let myself go and sobbed until the music stopped, until the people dispersed, until I saw Liz's shoes come to a stop in front of me.

She didn't seem to need an explanation. She scooped me up and led me to her bike. I put my arms around her and stood on the back spokes while she peddled through town, past people and miniature supernovas captured at the ends of sparkler wands, past the smells of chili and the sounds of cheers and squeals of laughter.

She peddled in serpentine up the mountain until it became too tough and then stopped, lifting me onto her back. I felt the great nothingness that hid in my stomach at night crawl up my throat. I clung to her, so afraid that if I let go I would fly into a million pieces and be lost forever.

Liz carried me almost to the top before she set me down, and we walked together the rest of the way until we reached the front porch. She paused at the doorstep, but I pulled her inside.

"Please," I whispered and led her upstairs.

Instead of going to my room, I led her to the bathroom, to the tub where I had found Mama. We sat inside with our clothes still on, the hall light illuminated half our faces from the open door, and I could see that her eyes were kind, but they were worried.

"Cat, you're safe now," she said as she squeezed my hand reassuringly.

I nodded and didn't know how to answer. I didn't know how to tell her that I wasn't. I didn't know how to tell her that I'd never known what safety was or how to live without the shadow of shame.

After we sat there until our bones started to ache, I got up, finally done shaking and crying at being made a fool of, of thinking that I could move on without Mama, and said goodbye to Liz, promising her to come by the cafe in the morning.

I watched her disappear into the darkness and then did the only thing I could think to do. I took Mama's spot in the kitchen and made a fresh cup of tea.

You know, I'm really glad that Cat found Liz.

No. I don't really have a friend like that. I feel like I've had so much work to do compared to Stephen that I never had too much time for friends.

There's always been a new project or a new opportunity that I've been working toward, and it hasn't really been a priority for me. I mean, Stephen was my best friend from the moment I met him. While my classmates were out partying or going out, I was studying and then busy starting over. I learned that Stephen wasn't the smartest person in the world but he was very productive. I'd do most of his research, even when he had research assistants for that, and he'd put everything together. He had a way with words, ya know?

Anyway, that fall we had this one event downtown. I hadn't been going to events as much because they make me so nervous. I'm more of a book person.

Yeah, I'm not good at meeting people.

Well, it's different with you two. We all have a purpose here. I'm supposed to talk about what happened, and you're supposed to ask questions. There's no small talk.

So, Stephen was guest speaking about the importance of Birmingham as a cultural touchstone, not only of Civil Rights, but of

Yeah, major eyeroll. I know. It was hosted by Dr. Smith and his wife Mrs. Smith, a tiny lady who always seemed to have a lipsticked smile plastered to her rosy face. You know the kind, saccharine sweetness, very polite, but there's something about her that makes you want to accidentally spill your wine on her?

Yep, sounds like she was exactly like your cousin Heather.

Anyway, you should have seen the way she fawned over Stephen, just parading him along, and she introduced him around as if he was her personal guest.

I got so irritated because it seemed like every second I stepped away, she would whisk him off and whisper to him, touch his arm, share a laugh, and whenever I would come up, she would fall silent and say she needed to get herself some water or that she had to go to the ladies' or say hello to another guest.

It was always something different, but I could see right through her. She didn't like me. I tried to say something about her to Stephen, but he just shrugged me off.

Thank goodness Penny was there. It was a relief to see someone I knew, and we sat in the corner talking about Sloss and its many ghost stories until I couldn't stand it anymore, and I told Stephen I wanted to go home. He said he'd meet me there, that he was still having fun, and I was left to go home alone.

I just felt so lonely. That is to say, I felt absolutely abandoned and unimportant.

Yeah, that's how it started anyway: the end of me and Stephen.

You sure you don't want me to make a cup of tea?

Okay, well suit yourself. August is a doozy.

AUGUST 2001

The dog days of summer were so hot and so still you could barely breathe, much less sleep without air conditioning. I tossed and turned all night until one Saturday morning, I was rustled out of that half-asleep, half-bored state by the sounds of Ray banging around in the basement.

"The goddamn plumbing is falling apart," Ray spat as he threw a wrench across the room. It skidded across the tile and crashed against the far wall, leaving a small dent in the baseboard.

"And I go down there this morning to fix it and find a shitload mold." He threw his hands in the air. He was already in a mood.

"This stupid house is gonna be the death of me." He ran his hands through his hair and let out a breath while I finished the coffee and tucked a clean apron into my bag. Just as I grabbed my things, he looked up at me with that sad puppy dog face he used to give Mama.

"I can't have the house like this," he said as he held my gaze. "Your Mama would roll over in her grave if she could see the mold down there."

I pictured it, black spots growing into slimy patches lurking just beneath our feet.

"With some cash, I could probably remove it myself," he said.

"You can't remove that by yourself, Ray. That takes a

professional."

"They're a scam. All I need is a mask and those thick black trash bags, then I could burn it out back next to the tree line."

I sighed and dropped my bag. "How much?"

"It wouldn't be that much. I only need to —"

"How much, Ray?" I interrupted.

"A couple hundred. A thousand, at most."

"A thousand, Ray? Really?"

I took my wallet out of my bag and laid three hundreds on the kitchen table. "That's it. That's all got."

"Cat, I didn't mean it like that. I only want —"

"I know what you want, but this is all you're gettin'." I interrupted again. "I gotta go. I have a job to get to."

I made my way to the cafe. Liz smiled at me as I came inside. She never brought up my meltdown a few weeks ago at the parade, and since then, she started walking me home after dinner each night. Without Ray there when I got home, I showed her what was left of my mom's library, her records, and her dresses. I showed her the kitchen and Mama's recipe books. I showed her the back porch where we used to sit and eat, the maze where Mama would walk at night.

The morning went well with Liz singing and throwing prepped ingredients my way — washed blueberries for muffins, strawberries for the jams, round dough forms for the bagels — and I finished each task like someone finishing her sentence. It was a conversation made of hands, made of labor, of temperature and time.

Our regulars were satisfied, we told jokes over the counter and waited in the empty shop for the lunch crowd when Owen came in.

An involuntary groan escaped my chest, and Liz nodded to the door. "Want me to get rid of him?"

I shook my head once and steadied my face so that before he even approached the counter, I blurted out. "What do you want?"

Owen paused as confusion painted his face. "I just came in to see you." His voice rose into an almost question.

"Well, I'm not interested," I said flatly.

He looked around, still confused. "Sorry. Did I do something?"

I crossed my arms over my chest and tried to ignore Liz unashamedly eavesdropping as she wiped an already-clean table.

When I didn't answer, he continued, "I mean, the last time I saw you was the Fourth, and you just disappeared —"

That was the line I was waiting for, the line that would blame me for everything that happened, so I cut him off.

"I disappeared after I heard you bragging about giving me rides home."

Across the room, Liz dropped her rag and her jaw, and Owen sucked in a breath.

"What? No. I never said —"

"That you would really give me a ride on the way home? I'm sorry, was that a different Owen?"

"No, I — it wasn't like that, I didn't mean…"

I just raised my eyebrows at him.

"It was just the guys. I didn't mean that —" His voice cut off, trying to find the words but finding only his awfulness instead.

"It's not gonna happen, Owen. It was never going to happen. Especially now."

He looked at the floor, shame colored his cheeks, and he rocked on his heels, looking like a little boy being scolded by his mother.

"I understand," he mumbled, not meeting my eyes. "I didn't really mean…"

But his words trailed off and what he did or didn't mean remained unspoken. Instead, he turned and left, the door's exiting bell echoing through the shop's hush.

When she couldn't hold it in any longer, Liz burst, "Damn, Cat. That was cold-blooded."

Her face beamed and she giggled. I laughed in return,

replaying the conversation.

"This cat's got claws, baby!" She laughed again and threw her rag at me.

"Then you better watch it!" I caught it in the air and tossed it back to her, which made her cry out playfully as she dodged it and stuck her tongue out at me. I don't know what made me do it, but I picked up a croissant sandwich, a turkey melt with Dijon and cranberry sauce, and tossed it at her. With her attention on the rag, she didn't have time to see the croissant sailing toward her, and it landed squarely in the middle of her forehead.

I froze, surprised by my actions, but also tense at her reaction, her wide eyes, the O of her mouth, the Dijon, cranberry smear across her forehead. I opened my mouth to apologize or make a joke, but before I could say anything, her nostrils flared and she muttered, "Oh, now you're gonna get it."

She rounded the corner and dipped her hand in the fresh pot of cool strawberry jam and flung it at my chest, plastering it with a thick, sticky splatter of sugary crimson.

My jaw dropped. The jam smeared into my white apron. I grabbed a spreading knife full of mayonnaise, and threw the mayo at her hair, and she countered by throwing two eggs. I grabbed everything I could and threw them at her, and she did the same — muffins, raspberries, blueberries, sauces, sugar, flour all flew through the air — until we heard the doorbell's chime. The lunch crowd had arrived.

We stopped like two children caught stealing cookies from the jar and used our aprons to wipe our faces as if this was the most ordinary thing to do before lunch. Nothing to see here. Just a food fight before the crowd arrived. No big deal.

The regulars blinked at us. "Is this a bad time?" One lady asked as she gestured behind the others. "I can always come back if —"

"No. No. No." We said in unison, and Liz grabbed the extra bread from the cabinet while I took out a fresh pack of turkey meat from the fridge.

"It'll be ready," Liz breathed.

"In just a second," I finished, and the woman frowned and studied us over the top of her glasses. We worked in mirror movements, readying the woman's sandwich — the turkey that I threw at Liz earlier — as well as the other regulars who came in. They all stopped once they saw us, unsure of the food smears and mess behind the counter. We handed them their typical orders before they even got a chance to order them, so they shrugged to one another and set off with their lunches scratching their heads.

When the crowd had gone, Liz and I exchanged glances, and I looked at her with mayo matting her hair down, and various fruit smears across her apron. Was that chocolate across her chin? Hazelnut? I couldn't help it, I swiped my finger across her chin.

"Chocolate," I said and cracked up, and she joined me, laughing until we couldn't breathe.

There was a total eclipse in Europe today, and as Grandma always said, it marks the beginning of change, of a new era of evolution. And guess what? He came back to me. I knew he would. He said that he was trying to do the right thing. He was trying to be a man and take care of that woman and the baby, but he said that the whole time he was with her, all he could think about was me and how much she wasn't me and how much he just wanted to be here — with me.

Tonight, I slept the whole night through. No sleepless nightmares. No wandering the maze. Just sleep. Pure and dreamless sleep. It was delicious. I cooked breakfast this morning, a great big breakfast with French toast and hash browns and bacon and sausage and eggs. I had the energy to clean, so I started cleaning the house from the baseboards up, playing Simon and Garfunkel over and over again, singing and cleaning, and getting breakfast ready. You should have seen Cat when she came down the stairs. She was so surprised, and I found a new truck for sale for Ray and already called to see if it was still available, so I made an appointment for us to go and see it this afternoon and that I would cover the cost since it was so cheap.

Ray was so happy that he pulled me into him and danced with me, saying that he had missed me so much and that he can't live without me. God, my heart swelled.

Marianne tried to come over last weekend, but I still can't look at her. The doctors said something about a manic episode. They gave me papers and everything, said the teas could set off another episode, but it didn't make sense to me. I'm not crazy. I was just sad. I mean, I was heartbroken. [46]

I can't do this without Ray, but he's back now, and everything is

---

46 This sounds like bipolar disorder, periods of extreme focus, productivity, and energy followed by exhaustion and depression. People with bipolar often also struggle with addiction issues as they try to self-medicate with alcohol, drugs, and other vices. Bipolar episodes can last anywhere from a week to a few months and are categorized by manic high and depressive low phases. These phases reduce the quality of life and can inhibit the person from their everyday activities. Episodes can be triggered by stress, sleep issues, positive and negative events, substance abuse, trauma, changing seasons, and a change in medication. If left untreated, bipolar disorder can be deadly.

fine. I'm fine, but I just can't stand it when Marianne calls or comes by and has that tone of voice, that look in her eye like she's worried about me or like she's pitying me. That's the last thing I need. I mean, Cat's about to start school, and I've been working to get this house back on track. Ray had been in the middle of re-finishing the floors when he left, and he's already planning on tackling them this weekend. I can't wait. This all seems like a fresh start, like it was all meant to be.

We must have looked ridiculous on the way home, Liz pedaling, me standing on the rear wheel, flying through downtown on her bike, giggling, and still covered in food. The air was so hot and so still that it was like being swallowed by the sun, even though the sun was low in the sky. The bank sign flashed the temperature — the hottest day of the year so far — and we made it to my house in a sluggish walk-ride up the mountain.

I opened the front door, but the air was so hot and suffocating that I poured us some sweet tea, and we took turns rinsing off with the rusty garden hose out back. The water was cold but quickly warmed in the steamy summer air. We stripped off our aprons and pants and sat in our shirts and underwear, dripping on the back steps as we sipped tea.

"So, Owen —" Liz started.

I shook my head and took another sip. "Is an idiot." I finished her sentence, and I could feel her trying to gauge my emotions. "I heard him bragging about giving me rides, saying that he was... you know."

I touched my head and felt Liz's hand on my arm.

"I just feel like such an idiot. Nothing happened, of course, but that doesn't stop a guy like Owen from bragging about it."

"Well, like you said, Owen is an idiot. No one is going to listen to him, and if they do, they're as much of an idiot as he is."

"I don't know. It's just the principle. Why even say anything at all?"

She thought for a moment and took a breath.

"After Mom died, I went to live with my aunt," she broke the silence. "She used to sing at a club downtown."

"In Birmingham?"

She shook her head. "In LA. It was at this dingy club that smelled like stale cigar smoke and sticky drinks. Her voice was like velvet, like water, so thick and tangible. It was like a presence in the room, a separate person who sat down at the table with you while she sang."

I snuck a glance at her while she spoke. She pushed her hair back and leaned on an elbow. "There was this one guy, this regular who came into the club. He would always sit at the center table and order whiskey, every night, as he watched my aunt sing."

She smiled and swayed slightly from side to side as if she could still hear her aunt at the microphone. "Then, one day, he noticed me."

"How old were you?" I asked.

"I don't know, thirteen, fourteen maybe? Too young. You know what I mean?"

I nodded.

"Anyway, he was tall, dark, and handsome, like they all should be." She smiled at me. He was in his early twenties, but he had a look in his eyes that said he'd seen more than his fair share of tragedy. I used to wonder why someone like him would waste his time in a bar like that. I mean, where was his family? His friends? Surely a man like him would have somewhere better to be than the nightclub. But there he was, every night, drinking all by himself."

Liz took a breath and continued, "One night, he asked if he could walk me home. My aunt stayed after, networking and asking around for other gigs, so I said yes. I didn't see the harm in him walking me home.

"And then, when we got to my aunt's apartment, he asked if he could come up for a drink. I said yes because I didn't know what else to say. We had drinks. We talked. And then he started kissing me. So soft at first, as if he thought I might break if he wasn't gentle enough. Like he was afraid he would hurt me."

She rubbed her shoulder, looking self-conscious for the first time. "But I could see the look in his eyes, the same way he would look at me every night while my aunt sang, the way he would tip his drink my way every night, the way he stood looking at me in my aunt's apartment. So, I moved back and slipped off my dress.

"I remember I still had on my underwear, but his gaze changed from wanting to sadness. I didn't know what I had done wrong, so I stepped back. But then he took me in his arms and began to kiss me.

"That's when he started to speak. He leaned down, kissed my neck, and softly whispered, 'Angelica.' At first, I thought maybe he had gotten my name wrong or something but then he kept going, the next time whispering, 'Veronica. Michelle. Christina. Sophia. Rachel. In between every kiss, he would whisper a different woman's name.

"I didn't know what to do while he was kissing and whispering. I must have stiffened, frozen in place because his kisses became even more tender. He leaned back and asked me for my name. I told him, and he whispered it, adding it to the chorus of other women's names as he kissed me."

Liz's eyes searched the backyard, and she continued. "It's hard to explain. At the time, I felt like we needed each other. He wanted to feel good again, whole again maybe? He wanted to make someone feel good, perhaps he wanted to make the whole world feel good again, and I needed someone to make me feel okay too. But it turns out, I was just another name to add to his chorus."

Liz leaned back in the kitchen chair and ran her hand through her hair. "Afterwards, he clung to me as if he thought I would burst into a million pieces. And, in truth, that's exactly how I felt. I didn't feel healed at all. I just felt trapped by the weight of his arm and the expectation of being whole again, of making him whole again."

She took a breath and looked at the ceiling.

"What happened next?" I asked.

She shrugged. "The sun came up, a new day began, and we moved on."

"Did you ever see him again?"

She shook her head. "I couldn't go back in there after that. It just wasn't the same."

"Did you ever tell your aunt?"

"God, no," she laughed. "She would have killed me."

I smiled and touched her hand. "Men, can suck, sometimes,

you know?"

"You're right about that. But sometimes they're all right."

"Yeah, sometimes," I had to admit.

"It helped me dive into my art again. I hadn't really been painting after my mom died."

"I know what that's like," I muttered, thinking about my dusty typewriter.

Liz stirred beside me and stood up, stretched. She shifted from side to side on her long, tan legs and reached her hands above her head. "How hard is that maze?" She asked, gesturing to the wilting rose garden. She stood in front of me in only her underwear, I could see the water from the hose had quickly dried on her legs. Looking past her, I could see lightning bugs dart in between the bushes.

"There are sixty-four variations. It's pretty hard, but most of the hand gates are either rusted shut or rotting." I crinkled my nose, thinking about the sad state of the maze. "My mom planned to rehab the maze when she bought the house. It used to be manicured and even made the paper back in the day, but now…" My voice trailed off as I took in the overgrown mess of thorns, the bald spots where walls used to be, the tangled paths that followed no rhyme or reason.

Liz walked to the entrance, and I got up, feeling self-conscious in my underwear as I followed her between the wild roses as we entered the maze.

"My mom loved this place," I said as she looked over her shoulder at me. I caught up to her and led her to the right. "She would walk out here a lot when things got bad."

"Maybe this was her safe space," Liz offered.

I nodded in return and made the next left.

"Remember when Ray was in a car accident?" I asked.

"When was that?" She returned.

"The year Mama died," I clarified.

"I was in California. I hadn't heard."

"He was," I continued. "He was teaching me to do his brakes, and I guess I didn't do it right. I don't know why he didn't check before he —"

"You can't blame yourself."

I blushed, thinking about the spinning brake screw, my rage, and the feeling of the screw breaking free, and the relief spread up my arm at finally doing something. "He was fine, but after that, he came back different. He already had a foot out the door before, and then after —" I thought about Sharon and her double-pink stick. "He left us."

"Ray's an idiot," she interjected.

"Agreed, but Mama didn't take it well. She went to the hospital and after that…" I felt a lump in my throat tighten. "She wasn't the same."

"That's tough," she breathed, and I felt her hand in mine. "I bet it was hard for you. Was this last year?"

"The year before." I stopped and looked from side to side.

"Which way?"

"This is the part where I would always get lost," I admitted, looking for clues and trying to remember which way Mama would always go. Instead, Liz pulled me in the opposite direction from where I was about to step, and I followed her, thankful to have someone with me in case I got lost.

We followed a few more turns, and the courtyard at the center of the maze opened up to us. It was a smaller round space with a half-fallen stone bench and rough weeds that poked out between crooked boards. She dropped my hand and walked in a wide circle then crossed the overgrown courtyard before I called out.

"Watch it." I held out my arm, catching her before her foot met the crooked boards. "It's the old well. Who knows what lies down there and how far it goes."

She withdrew her foot and looked down, squatting to see if she could see the bottom. She dropped a few pebbles in the space between two rotting beams, but no sound returned. She raised her eyebrows and stood up, continuing her circle around the courtyard, careful to avoid the center.

"She used to take me out here for tea parties and picnics.[47] And her stories..." My voice caught as I thought about my mom, and I felt Liz's hand in mine.

"What was the one about the princess? What happened to her after the monster?"

I smiled. She always seemed to know how to get my mind off my worries. She sat on the edge of the bench that was barely standing, balancing as she stretched out her legs in front of her.

I looked at her curly hair, half dried and blowing in the warm evening wind. She was so beautiful, sitting there, and I felt a surge of happiness.

"For a long time, it was just the monster and the princess. It would cradle her in its arms, and the girl went into a sleep so deep that everyone in the town forgot about her."

I paused and looked at the purple bruise of the sunset. "One day, many years later, a young man came by. He was a prince, tall and handsome —"

"As all princes are," she interjected.

"Naturally," I smiled. "The prince had been riding through the forest, escaping his royal duties for a whole golden hour."

"A luxury," she exhaled and stretched out her legs, staring across the courtyard.

"The air was sweet, and he followed a delicious scent in the air to a wild garden. The prince wound his way through the sweet grasses and the purple flowers until he found the girl's tower. But she wasn't a girl anymore; she was a young woman."

"Beautiful?"

"Of course. And he was so overcome by her beauty that he

---

47 This could reference the Mad Hatter and his tea parties from Alice in Wonderland. The tea parties symbolize the inverse of civilized tea parties at the time where manners and polite conversation reinforced strict class and gender roles. The Mad Hatter's tea parties have no rules other than to break traditional rules of politeness. During the tea party, Alice finds out that Time is actually a person and that he has been stuck at six o'clock since getting angry, leaving them perpetually in the middle of teatime. Imagine being suspended at the height of strict rules that are so mad they drive all in attendance mad.

leaned down and gently touched the princess's cheek, and she opened her eyes."

"For in that sleep, what dreams may come," she quoted.

"Are you going to let me finish?" I asked, playing at frustration.

"Okay, okay," she said, making a face.

"Sun flooded the princess's eyes and blinded her. She tried to look around, but all she could see were blurry shapes the color of sunshine. No matter how much she blinked or rubbed her eyes, her sight would not come back.

"Seeing the princess's beauty and her blindness, the prince couldn't leave her in the woods alone. The prince bundled the woman up and rode off with her even further into the woods. The woman felt the trees graze her shoulders. It rustled her hair, and she forgot to be afraid.

"Instead, she allowed herself to laugh, and the prince laughed along with her. They laughed, and they kissed, and they fell in love. They were married and whisked off into what fairy tales call "happily-ever-after."

Liz nodded, looking genuinely happy to hear the princess's happy ending.

"Only," I continued and noticed a smile on Liz's face, "in the still moments when she would drift off into her imagination, she would ask herself if she had ever said yes," I continued. "And it made her wonder if he had ever really asked her to begin with.

"As the years passed, the woman's eyes began to adjust. Slowly, the prince's eyes came into focus. Their blue matched the sky on a spring morning. Then, the prince's hair became clear. It was the color of golden wheat fields ready for harvest in the fall. His rosy cheeks and lips were the color of apples ripe from neighboring orchards.

"But when he smiled, the woman stopped short. He had the same teeth as the monster.

And so, the woman knew what she had to do. She went out to her magic purple flowers, which by now were heavy with fruit.

She ground them up, made her tea, and served it to him every night. At first, she started with just two berries: two, the number of lovers. But that wasn't enough for him. He would down the drink and then ask for another. So, she made him one. And then he asked for another. And another. And another."

I paused.

"And she obliged."

I heard Liz let out a breath beside me in the dying light.

"The prince with his sharp teeth grew smaller and smaller. Sometimes, in his hunger, he would bite the princess, but he couldn't tell the difference between the berries and the princess' sweet blood.

"He kept eating and shrinking until all that was left was his teeth. And so, the princess gathered up his teeth, put them in her pocket, and set off on her own."

"Whew," she exhaled. "It's dark, but I'm glad the princess made it out. And speaking of," I heard the sounds of her rousing and dusting off her bottom, "I think it's about time we made our way out of here."

"Good idea," I hummed.

I found her hand quickly in the dark, and we made our way back, trying to retrace our steps while avoiding the sharp thorns of the wild roses. When we emerged from the maze, I could see bright lights coming from the windows of the house and heard music playing over loud fans propped up in the downstairs windows. Ray was home.

"I can go around," Liz said as she nodded to the windows. She grabbed her clothes and put them on. I mirrored her movements, shrugging on my shirt and pulling on my pants. "I'll see you tomorrow," she whispered as she slid on her sneakers and waved, disappearing around the corner of the house.

I hesitated at the rear door, wondering if it would be better if I came in the front door, but I took a breath and twisted the knob. Bright light flooded my eyes, framing Ray in the middle of the kitchen, a cigarette in one hand, a drink in the other, suspended mid-dance with a smirk on his face as his eyes found mine. My gaze dropped to the floor, and I pulled the door closed behind me.

"You eat?" He asked and gestured to the remnants of a pot of boxed mac and cheese.

"I'm okay," I answered, keenly aware of the food stains on my clothes.

"Looks like it," he muttered and took a drink then a long draw on his cigarette.

I watched him, smile on his face, offering me food, dancing in the kitchen. Something was up.

"Why're you in such a good mood?"

"Why shouldn't I be?" He asked. "I have a good-paying job, a roof over my head, and such a sweet stepdaughter to share it all with."

My eyes narrowed at him.

"What?" He laughed. "Can't I be grateful for all this?" He gestured around the kitchen. I still didn't answer, and he laughed again, continuing to dance to the music. Instead, I shook my head and moved past him to head upstairs.

Just as I passed, he cocked his head to the side.

"Nice bike." Ray gestured out front. "Does it belong to whoever left their clothes out back?"

I froze. He laughed.

I felt my face go red and then continued down the hall, swinging around the staircase and taking the steps two at a time before reaching my room and locking the door.

I stood at the window and looked down at the front lawn. I could see Liz's faint silhouette as she kicked one foot over the bike and pedaled off. I watched her disappear into the velvet dark. The trees swayed softly as lightning bugs flitted back and forth beneath the shadows of their branches.

My chest tightened, and I could hear my heart beating loud in my ears as I searched the lawn, but only shadows greeted my eyes as they inched their way across the grass and edged up the stairs, stretching toward my toes, itching to get inside.

So, I have to come clean.

No, not about the body, about this part of the story.

After reading this chapter, I started to have nightmares. And not just any nightmares. I started dreaming about the maze.

I'm not pulling your leg. I'm serious. I started to have these dreams that I was stuck in there and couldn't get out.

That is to say, it was dark like that velvety night Cat described. How did she put it?

Exactly. It was so dark I could hardly see my hand in front of my face, and I could hear Ray's music in the dark.

I'm not kidding. I could hear him singing, and I was tryna find my way through the roses, but the thorns were sharp, and I didn't know which way was up and which was down.

I don't know if there's a dream meaning or anything, but it freaked me out. I'd go to bed needing rest and would wander around that maze in my dreams all night and wake up exhausted.

And the farther down I got into the maze, the more dangerous it became. It was terrible.

I'd try to free myself and this panic climbed up into my chest so I couldn't breathe. And I didn't want to call out in case Ray heard me.

But one time — I was so desperate — I screamed and heard Ray's singing stop.

Yeah, he was coming for me, alright. I could hear him laughing and running through the bushes. It was like we were playing some sorta hide and seek, only I was trapped, and he was playin with his prey.

I'm not being dramatic. I could hear him creepin in among the rows and laughing like he was havin the time of his life.

He started whistling, really enjoying it,

playin it up, ya know? He did this half spoken-half sung thing, and the maze had me. There was no way out, and he was the only other person around, the only person who could hear me scream.

Well, I sat there trembling, tryna free myself, but the thorns just twisted tighter and cut into my skin. My heart was racing, and when I opened my mouth to call out again, I heard it. At first, I thought it was a grasshopper or the wind. A sound so small that it could easily be excused.

It stopped, and when I moved to free a piece of my hair from the thorns, I heard it again. It as this scratching noise. Rocks crunching, maybe. Footsteps?

My heart was racing, and I yanked my arm free, but I could feel the thorns tear my skin. It was awful.

Then, the crunching sound moved. It sounded like it was getting closer, and I yanked again, ripping my shirt and jeans.

The sound turned into a thump then a drag. Thump. Drag. And then, this scared animal sound came from my chest, and I twisted, ripping the skin on my free arm and both legs, but the thorns held fast, and I still couldn't get free.

Then, I felt hot breath on my shoulder.

Don't think I'm crazy. I could feel it bearing down in the soft space on my neck between my shoulder and my ear.

I stopped to listen again, and I heard the thing open its mouth and scream.

What do you mean, what did I do? I did the only thing I could think: I screamed back and tried to fight it off, but I was stuck. Then, I realized that I was in bed, twisted in my sheets, screaming myself out of my nightmare.

Yeah, it is something. Trying having one of those every day or two. It was awful.

And that's when I noticed Mom's herbs

outside. I started gardening at night to help with the nightmares. It made me feel not as alone, if that makes sense. It gave me a purpose, and it taught me how to make tea like Mom.

That's also about the time that I noticed pages missing from Mom's research. I'd read an article or passage and then not be able to find it later.

I could have sworn I found some letters between Nellie and her friend, Abigail. Nellie talking about Charles's temper while Abigail visited family in Atlanta. Nellie wrote about Charles throwing his dinner plate across the dining room wall and slapping Helen when she tried to defend the cook, Helen trying to reassure her that it was okay, that she could get them out of this mess, that they were planning to leave, but Nellie wasn't convinced.

It was in these letters — they were photocopied, so Mom got them from somewhere. Nellie went on to say that he knew it was Charles who killed Helen, said he pushed her from the top of the stairs.

Yeah, I know the newspaper said she fell, but it makes sense. If Charles really was low on money and Helen was planning to leave, he'd be desperate.

Well, that's the thing. He knew the house went to the first born. He assumed that was Helen. She was the bossy one, after all, but any twin knows that it's the second born that has to fight for everything, food, space, love.

Exactly. Helen was the second born. Nellie — the one who blended into the background — was the heir to the Saunders fortune.

Charles would never get the house, but he wouldn't let her go so easily. So, she came up with a plan.

No, I searched Mom's desk, her entire

office. I even checked to see if they had fallen behind the desk or between the drawers, but those pages are just gone.

One night, as I looked under the bookshelves, just in case, I heard a knock at the door.

I don't know. Eleven or there-abouts.

I looked out the side window, but no one was on the porch, so I opened the door an inch at a time.

Nothing.

The front porch was empty.

I stepped out and looked down the street but saw nothing out of place. As I went back inside, though, my foot hit something soft. I bent down to pick it up.

It was a bundle of flowers.

White flowers.

I couldn't believe it. My heart started thumpin real hard, and I felt like I couldn't breathe because I knew those flowers. I knew exactly what those were.

White catchfly.

SEPTEMBER 2001

Cooler weather ushered in a change in the house. Ray had transformed the kitchen into Mama's dream with new paint, new countertops, and fresh tile floors that he had swiped, no doubt, from one of his jobs, and he was starting to renovate the bathrooms. When I wasn't at the cafe or hanging out with Liz, I typed away on my typewriter. Fairy tales mostly, but sometimes I wrote about Mama, about how we used to dance before Ray, about our picnics and bedtime stories, about all the things she wanted to do. Where would I be if she were still here? In college? Would I be living here?

Business at the cafe had been light after the return of school with a mad rush of customers as school let out each day. The cafe was a popular hangout for chatty studying and socializing. Plus, we had snacks, and all teenagers loved to eat while they hung out with friends. Marianne still came in at least twice a week to pick up treats for the church, although Liz said it wasn't until I started working there that she started coming so often. I didn't mind. It started to feel good that I had someone who looked out for me. Owen mostly left me alone, although he'd come in and mumble another apology.

After work, Liz was consumed by her art. She moved into her Rose Period, as her agent called it, in late August when an unseasonable cold front moved through, breaking the dog days of summer, causing it to suddenly feel like fall. It was like a breath of fresh air, and so was this new art, all warm textures, and swirling colors, abstract sunsets in the shape of a lover's embrace. She bought me a notebook, and we sat in her art studio, her on the stool painting and me in the tattered chair in the corner writing until the sun went down. Then she'd walk me home.

One night, when the moon was nearly full, we decided to take the long way through town. We skirted the edge of downtown's brick buildings and followed the stream and train tracks until we came to the school. Then we turned and followed the two-lane road, often referred to as the "highway" — although it only serviced local traffic and was never busy — and led to the base of Blood Mountain and the start of my driveway.

Liz and I talked about anything and everything, and one night in particular, we argued over who was better: Backstreet Boys or *NSYNC? Britney or Christina? Coke or Pepsi? Anime or comics? Conversation was easy, just like the water babbling next to us, when Liz interrupted my explanation that Whitney Houston was the best vocalist in all of history because of her gospel background and raw talent.

"Why do they always build train tracks near streams?" she asked.

"What do you mean?"

"It's just that every train track I've ever seen has been right next to water. Doesn't that cause flooding? More erosion?"

I thought about all the train tracks I'd ever seen and shrugged. "No idea, but that is weird."

"Not as weird as —" Her voice cut short, and she pointed ahead of us at the school. "Wait, isn't that Ray?" she asked.

I looked across the parking lot, and silhouetted under the lamps of the school, sat Ray's truck. He was leaning against it, his hands stretched over the bed of the truck as he talked to someone leaning against the other side. They were short and hard to make out in the dark, but the way the figure held its head to one side made me think it was a girl. I stopped and saw that she had one foot kicked backward. The duchess pose, as Mama called it. A giggle echoed through the parking lot, and my stomach lurched. Thank God there was a truck between the two. Something needed to protect that girl. Was she a high schooler?

"Come on," I pulled Liz in the direction of the highway, but she resisted.

"Do you think she's... safe?" Liz asked, not taking her eyes off the girl.

On cue, the girl giggled again and tossed her hair. If I knew Ray, I knew he was interested in anyone who breathed. It was how he felt good about himself. He liked to have things — people — he liked to own them... at least, until he didn't need them anymore.

Liz let me lead her away from the parking lot, but she still glanced behind us every few steps to make sure the girl was okay.

"So, Ray's working at the school?" She ventured.

"No idea," I responded. "I used to go there, you know. Before."

She nodded.

"I only went there for my first two years. I took independent study courses so I could graduate early," I continued.

"You graduated early?"

"Yeah, after the fall of what should have been my junior year. I was sixteen."

"Then what?"

"I'd gotten into Brown."

"Brown?" She stopped walking and forced me to turn and face her.

I nodded in return. "Yep. My essay really helped."

"What'd you write about?"

"Survival rates among domestic abuse partnerships."

"Not good?"

I shrugged. "There's not a lot of accurate data. It's hard to admit and even recognize when you're in an abusive relationship, so many times, it goes unreported."

"I bet your mother had a field day when she read it."

"She never did."

"You didn't let her read it?"

"I couldn't. It would have killed her." I thought of her perfect face under the water. Her perfect pearl of breath suspended in time.

"So…" Liz pushed.

"So what?"

"What happened to Brown?"

"You know I couldn't go. Not after —" I thought about Mama and stopped short.

"Just because her life ended doesn't mean that yours had to also."

"I know that. It's just… I was in the hospital for so long, so I had to give up my spot."

"You're out now."

"Yeah," I nodded. "I know."

"I'm sure they'd love to have you."

I mulled over her words and felt the familiar tightness in my stomach that I always felt when I thought about the future.

"You should write to them again. What have you got to lose?" Liz nudged me, and I couldn't help but smile because she was right. What did I have to lose?

School started a few weeks ago. Cat has been taking independent study classes all summer and is almost done with her high school courses. I can't believe how smart that girl is. She blows me away every day. Marianne says that she takes after me, but I wouldn't call getting pregnant at fourteen smart. God, Cat's older than I was when I had her, so I guess she's doing pretty well.

I walked in last night, and she was busy filling in a stack of college applications. And they were from fancy places, too, like Yale and Harvard and places like that. I don't know anything about college, but it seems like Cat always has a plan. Ray calls her Maggie the Cat sometimes when she's being extra sneaky because he says she reminds him of the character from Cat on a Hot Tin Roof, always calculating, always a few steps ahead. He says she gets it from me, but again, my calculations haven't always worked for me, obviously.

After Cat went to bed, I tried to snoop, but she had sealed all the envelopes and stuffed them into the mailbox at the bottom of the driveway.

But I did find one.

A single application that I guess she'd been working on for weeks but hadn't quite gotten the confidence to mail.

It was an application to Brown, and they requested an essay to be admitted to their English program. I shuffled through the papers and found a handwritten essay. Cat's narrow letter danced before my eyes. "Domestic abuse... very common... don't even know it... My mom... and I don't know if... but I wish... my only chance... please." I felt my blood run cold.

An abusive relationship? I know my relationship with Ray isn't perfect, but it's hardly abusive. We're passionate, that's all. And all relationships have problems. Hell, my own mom never even got married, and she had two of us. And Cat's never been in a relationship, thank God, so what did she know about it?

My hands shook, but I did the only thing I could think to do. I slid it back inside the envelope and put the package back underneath her bed where I found it. I never said anything about it. I just didn't know Cat would lie about something like that; put our business out there like that. I never would have thought it. Did I make her like this?

And Ray's been so much better since he's been back. He's been home most nights, although I did smell perfume on him a few nights ago. He said they'd been working in some fancy lady's house remodeling her bathroom, so it must have come from that. I wasn't so sure, but I made myself a cup of tea — just plain tea, mind you — and felt better.

I've been doing well since I've been back home, I've had lots of time to think about all my decisions. I still regret not having told Mom the truth about what happened. I know she'd only blame herself. She was always like that. And after a while, it was hard to tell the truth.

I guess I was in denial for so long that I didn't know what was true anymore and what wasn't. After Mom died, I stayed with Marianne. She said she'd always wanted a sister, and her parents insisted, especially since Cat was so young. Marianne's mom was like that, just the picture of a southern belle. I guess that's where Marianne gets it from, all lipstick and smiles and sweet teas and thank yous. They both always made me feel so welcome, and I know they always meant the best. They set me up in the guest house out back so I could have my own space but still have family around.

Mr. Johns had bought Mom's house anyway, and he said he could never turn me out like that with nowhere to go. I told him that I had a sister in Atlanta, that I could always just go and stay with her, but he insisted that I stay with them, and then Mrs. Johns insisted, and then Marianne insisted, and I could never say no to Marianne.

And it wasn't like I was staying in the house with them. I had my own place. It was just on their property. Sure, I had dinner with the family each night, and I was invited to all their parties and things like that, but I had my own sort of independence. At first anyway. And then the nightmares started again. The faun returned.

Yeah, I noticed that too and so did Mom.
Sarah's diary entries keep referencing the
faun and spiral structures.
Can I see your pen?
Thanks.
If you look at a faun, the horns are also
spirals, ever-tightening into nothing. See?
And Mom found spirals in tons of great works
of literature: Yeats, Beckett, Duchamp, Joyce,
etc.
See, she wrote about spirals moving in dual
directions, moving both inward and in reverse,
left and then right, up then down. Spirals
produce a tight structure that provides both
security and mobility.
I wonder if that's how Cat's mom felt at the
end: if she headed into the crushing spiral
and nothingness while finally feeling free.
Yes, I'm gettin there. Look, Mom also found
out more about Charles next. About a year after
Helen died, Charles died.
They said he dropped down dead of a heart
attack. Only forty-two years old, and the town
started whispering about the Saunders house
being cursed. The gossip column had a field
day and wrote all these dramatic things about
death and destruction.
I know, a bunch of old biddies with nothin
to do, probably.
Anyway, that left Helen and her friend
Abigail, and you know there's nothin the South
hates more than independent women.
I'm not bein political. I'm just saying.
Let me see that stack again?
Oh yeah, look. Mom also found this. Ever
heard of Russel's Teapot?
Me, neither, but Mom found it and made some
notes on it. I guess it's about who's role it
is to question beliefs. That is to say, the

burden of proof lies with the challenger.
No, you're right. It usually has to do with
religion. Well, most people think the
challenger has the power. A person asking
questions is usually in a position of power
because the other person has to provide the
proof.
It's not just you, this is confusing all
around. So, let's say you go to a pastor and
tell him to prove that God exists. Well then,
he'd be the one who would have to explain why
he believes in God and why you should too.
I know, I know. I'm just saying.
Well, Russel's Teapot flips that model on
its head.
It all starts with a man named Bernand
Russel — no, sorry,   Russel — who wrote
an article titled "Is There a God?". He
proposed that there was a teapot revolving
around the sun between Earth and Mars. See
this drawing here?
Since they didn't have technology to either
prove or disprove this, Russell argued that
since there   be a teapot in space, the
burden of proof should be put upon the person
trying to disprove the teapot's existence.
Well, what I think he was trying to say is
that people shouldn't always have to defend
themselves.
When it comes to Cat's mom, it seems like
the proof of Ray's cheating was always there,
the late hours, the abuse, the woman at her
doorstep with the positive pregnancy test, but
she clung to the idea that she could disprove
it instead.
I mean, what does it mean to have proof
anyway? And even if she did have proof, what
then?
And I don't even know if she recognized the
signs. Hell, I didn't even recognize the signs
with Stephen even after he started staying out
late. I didn't see the phone calls coming in

or the whispers by people in the department.
It's harder than you think, especially when
you don't want to see the signs of your life
falling apart bit by bit.

I knew something was wrong the minute Marianne came in, wide-eyed and pale in the middle of the breakfast rush. "A plane," was all she could say, and she grabbed my hand and led me to the sidewalk outside of the electronics window.

We entered the store and packed in with a dozen other people to watch the twelve TVs tuned in to different channels that all displayed the same scene. Two towers silhouetted in the sky: one solid, the other smoking, red ticker tape scrolled across the bottom reading PLANE CRASHED INTO WORLD TRADE CENTER.

How could a plane crash into a building like that? Was it trying to land?

Marianne squeezed one hand, and I felt another hand squeeze my other. Without having to look, I knew it was Liz.

"Who's running the store?" I asked.

"I locked up. Everyone rushed out anyway." She gestured at the people around us and the people lined up on the sidewalk to watch the TV screens. That's when we heard screams, people pointing, a second plane, a second explosion.

Collectively, we gasped and watched debris fall to the ground on each of the screens.

And that's all we could do.

We held our breaths and waited. And watched. Bore witness and prayed. Even those who didn't believe in God bowed their heads when the towers fell one by one. Then we heard the TV anchor's voice announce that a third plane crashed into the Pentagon and then a fourth crashed into a field in Pennsylvania.

We walked home in silence, in the dark, stiff from standing so still and being packed so close to others watching the news coverage until the sun went down. Everyone filed down to the church, and there were so many people that they had to line up in the parking lot, unable to find a spot inside. Candles were passed out, and their glow circled the pastor who had no words and could only cling to his family and ask for a moment of silence. We saw the halo of their candles until we entered the dense tree line of the mountain.

Ray was home by the time I got there. He had dragged out an old television Mama bought a few years back. Ray had it propped on the dining room table and was fiddling with the antennas, causing the picture to waver between static and an abstract newsroom striped with primary colors and fuzz. He sighed and gave up, the screen oscillated between fuzz and inverted colors, but the audio came through clear and strong: George W. Bush promised that we would never forget, that we would seek vengeance, and that we would never let the innocent die in vain.

Ray drank out of a bottle as he stretched out his legs and rested his feet on an empty kitchen chair. "I can't believe it," he said between swallows, wincing and nodding at the TV. "I was at the school when the planes hit. We all sat there like zombies. Every TV in the school was tuned in."

"Same here. I watched it outside Waldo's with a bunch of people."

He nodded. "You eat anything?"

"I'm not in the mood for mac and cheese," I muttered, trying to make out the shapes on the screen.

"I got a plate from school. Almost no one ate lunch today, so they were handing out leftovers."

I looked over at the counter and saw three to-go boxes stacked one on top of the other. My stomach tightened.

"I wonder if school will be in session tomorrow," he said, taking another drink.

"You're working at the school?" I asked, looking at his face. He nodded, not taking his attention from the fuzzy screen.

"Making a shitload, too," he laughed.

"Don't they do background checks and stuff like that?"

"Sure, but they don't care about DUIs, just touching kids and stuff."

"You mean like fourteen-year-old girls?"

Ray whipped his head around to look at me, narrowing his eyes. "You trynna say somethin'?"

I shook my head.

"No. Go ahead, say it." His voice sounded like sandpaper, and I winced. "Just like your mama. A crazy bitch like your mama."

He took another drink then reached forward and turned up the volume on the static-filled TV, and taking the hint, I went upstairs and closed the door, trying to block out the confused babble of news anchors. I tried and failed to find the words to explain loss and helplessness as I idly types at the typewriter. As I sat back and listed to the slosh of Ray's bottle downstairs as he filled the silences between seconds with his seemingly endless supply of alcohol. The absence of Mama and her laughter that would never again ring up the stairs.

When Ray went to bed, I cautiously crept downstairs, my stomach pulled me guiltily toward the food he had stacked in the fridge. Ashamed that I could feel hunger amid so much sadness, I gulped down an entire plate, only realizing how hungry I was when I started eating.

I stood at the kitchen counter and looked out at the shadows of the maze. Lightning bugs streaked across the backyard, and a light caught my eye as it wove between the roses. I watched it sway from side to side and thought about Ray in the parking lot with the girl, her giggling and tossing her hair, his voice low and murmuring, like a wolf enticing its prey. What big teeth you have, my dear, and my blood started to boil because I knew exactly what those teeth could do, but did he know about mine?[48]

---

48 Reference to the fairy tale titled The Big, Bad Wolf. Wolves were often featured in fairy tales as dangerous and conniving beasts who would hungrily eat the innocent. Examples of wolves in fairy tales include "The Big, Bad Wolf," "The Three Little Pigs," "Peter and the Wolf," "The Boy Who Cried Wolf," and "The Wolf and the Seven Young Kids" (or "The Wolf and the Seven Young Goats"). Although these tales were generally written to warn children of the very real dangers of wolves and other beasts in the wilderness, they also contain warnings about the greediness of society and the dangers to innocence that result from growing up.

Dear Admissions Officer,[49]

My name is Cat, and I was accepted into your English program almost two years ago, but regrettably, I didn't get a chance to attend. As the daughter of a woman who had me at fourteen, I've had to fight for everything I have in life. I started working at thirteen and learned how to pay the bills at fourteen. I saw first-hand the effects of domestic violence and physical abuse. I worked hard, taking independent study courses so I could graduate early, and for years, I was driven by the desire to escape, but there's no escaping my story.

My first essay for the English department was about the survival rates of women in relationships with domestic violence. and I'm sad to say that my mother did not survive her own experiences of domestic violence.

Mama struggled with undiagnosed bipolar depression,[50] at least that's what I think it was. Again, it was never diagnosed, and that coupled with such an unhealthy relationship, led to her death. She used to tell me stories, so I'm going to take a note from her and tell you a story.

Once upon a time, there was a woman named Seleme. She was beautiful and kind and so loving that Zeus, the god of all gods, fell in love with her the moment he saw her. Zeus would send her gifts and visit her at night where they could meet in the cover of darkness. Little by little, Seleme fell in love with Zeus, and the two were the envy of all in the kingdom, especially Zeus's wife, Hera.

Hera disguised herself and visited Seleme one day as she worked to harvest crops in the field. Hera told Seleme that Zeus would often visit women at night and that she was nothing special. If she really was that special, then why had Zeus never shown himself to her?

---

49 Presumed to be to Brown's Admissions Office.

50 I knew it! I tried to contact both the UAB Medical System and Brown's Admissions office to confirm these, but each has said that information is confidential and can only be disclosed to immediate family members.

That night when Zeus came, Seleme refused to see him. When Zeus pleaded with her, Seleme demanded that he show himself to her, all of himself without holding back. It would be a symbol of his love for her. Zeus agreed, desperate to prove his love, but as Zeus revealed himself in his full power, Seleme was consumed by fire and lightning, Zeus' true form.[51]

You see, life can be terrifying. It can be filled with fire and lightning and trickery, with twists and turns and tragedy, but it is also full of love and beauty. Eventually, fire burns out and lightning moves on. I've been through it all — fire, lightning, tragedy — and I'm on the other side a little older and a lot wiser, hoping you'll still take a chance on me and reconsider me for acceptance to your university so that I might share my story with others.

Thank you for your time,
Cat

By Friday, we were all still numb, although everyone had gone back to work as usual. All the businesses in town were decorated in red, white, and blue, and most houses that we passed on our way home proudly displayed a fresh American flag on their front porch.

We took the long way through town again, passing the school, and we both noticed Ray's truck in the empty school parking lot, although neither I nor Liz said anything about it. I fumed all the way up the hill, but Liz remained silent.

"See ya tomorrow," she said over her shoulder as she hopped on her biker. "And call me if that idiot bothers you."

That idiot, meaning Ray. She knew she didn't have to call him

---

51 Story taken from Greek mythology. I love the way she uses it as a model for her own life. Cat really did have a way with stories. I would definitely accept her essay as admission-worthy for my own department. I wonder if she enjoyed Brown and what she did while she was there; what stories she was able to write and what she's done since then. I'd really love to meet her.

by name.

That idiot stayed out late again. Someone had taken to calling and hanging up when I answered, and tonight was no different. The phone rang, but when I answered, I heard the soft click of the receiver in its cradle as the line disconnected. I wondered if it was Sharon and if she knew about Ray working at the school.

I took a hot shower that night and stood with my pills in my hand. I counted them out, the magic beans that promised normality then tipped my hand over the toilet and watched them fall in one at a time, like a cauldron, swirling and transforming into nothing.

I padded down the stairs and paced around the empty kitchen before taking a breath and moving deliberately to the kitchen phone. With the phone in my hand, I paused and listened as a fresh dial tone sounded. Pressing the numbers by memory, I listened as the phone rang once then twice before a sugar-sweet voice answered. "Hello?"

"It's me," I said softly. "I was wondering if I could ask for a favor?"

"Oh, honey, of course," sang Marianne's familiar croon.

"It's about Ray. He's been working at the school and —" The words fell from my mouth in a flood of worry, filling the silence between our houses with all the things I had been imagining Ray do to that girl. I could hear the cut of his voice that knew just what tender parts to slice, his hands that could grab, push, and slap at a moment's notice, his smile as he knew that he could do whatever he wanted, and Mama would excuse it all.

"Don't you worry, baby," Marianne exhaled. "I know just what to do."

I hung up the phone and paced back and forth in the kitchen, trying to find that light through the maze, but all was dark and silent. I went to bed, feeling lighter than I had in weeks, and for the first time, I slept through the night knowing that Ray wouldn't be coming home that night. The sheriff would have a lot of questions for him, including what exactly he was doing after hours in the school parking lot with a teenage girl in his truck. I would have paid to hear him get out of that one. Instead, I slept soundly, dreaming of tea parties and the feeling of summer vacations and Liz's hand in mine.

Yeah, Cat was handling a lot. I don't know how she managed it all.

Well, you don't have to say that but thank you. I've been trying.

Sorry. My throat's giving out on me a little.

There. That's better. Where did I leave off?

Oh yeah, Stephen's late-night calls. I hated staying by myself, especially at night. I'd gotten so paranoid that Stephen bought me one of those retractable metal sticks and some bear spray — which I didn't trust myself with because I'd heard too many horror stories about those cans going off and flooding the place with gas, so I threw out the spray and put the metal stick in my purse.

I kept it next to my bed, so it made sense at the time. Plus, even though we'd redone our house, it still sounded like it was old as it was.

Oh, it creaked and popped even worse than this house.

Well one night, I was working so late that I didn't hear Stephen come in until he tapped me on the shoulder. I jumped so hard, you should have seen it.

But he made me dinner, and we had wine. We made love — sorry, I know that's a bit much, but it'd been awhile, and it suddenly felt like we were back to normal. God, I missed him.

Later that night, I woke up to whispers. I sat up and heard Stephen's voice real low, like he was murmuring to himself in the dark.

Then I saw him on the narrow balcony. He was pacing, a reverse image of a widow, a man instead of a woman, eyes looking down instead of searching the horizon, voice barely audible instead of calling someone home. The irony isn't lost on me.

Well, I heard him whispering that he couldn't get away that night but that he'd call back soon. And then he said I love you.

I couldn't believe it.

My Stephen telling someone else that he loved them.

Stephen got off the phone, and I pretended that I was still asleep. I mean, is it eavesdropping if it's in your own house? On your own balcony? With your own husband who is supposed to be asleep beside you?

Now, I'm not proud of it, but later, when I was sure he was asleep, I swiped his phone. He'd deleted his texts, but he had several voicemails fron an unsaved number.

It was local.

I tapped the first one.

That sorta thing.

My stomach dropped to the floor, and my heart broke.

I don't know how to explain it. It felt like I was out of my own body — like I was looking down at myself, and I could see all the lies, and it made me feel like I wasn't even me. Like, if I had this whole identity based on Stephen and all of that was a lie, then who even was I? You know?

Well, I'm sorry to hear about your ex-wife, and it's a shame about your best friend — well, ex-best friend. That's awful.

After I found out about Stephen, I stayed awake until late. It makes me wonder what Cat would have done. I know her mom would have stayed. That's what she did with Ray. But Cat's different, isn't she? She's not afraid, or if she is, then she knows how to deal with it.

Yeah, it does help to have a Marianne on your side, but I had no one.

Anyway, want me to keep goin?

Good. Then, I'll keep reading.

OCTOBER 2001

The first thing I saw was the light. The horrible light.

It spilled in from the window, interrupting my dreams, interrupting the silence and the peace. I heard Mama's voice in my head. A case of the Octobers.

Mama always said that everyone loved spring and summer. The warmth and the sunshine drove out any unhappy thoughts. That's why most books and movies ended with sunny, warm days — the happy ones anyway. Their stories seemed to wrap up at the end of a beautiful day with the hero or heroine enjoying their much sought-after happily ever after and so much sun.

There were a few stories that ended in the august of summer with their summer adventures coming to a close and their year returning to normal before the start of fall, but rarely, very rarely does a happy ending occur in October.

Mama declared it the cursed month. It was the month when everything became markedly different. Darkness slowly overcame light. Coldness tinged the wind as it bent from the north. Leaves turned, slowly dying on their branches, scraped away by an indifferent wind that knew nothing about heat or thunderstorms or adventure, only the cawing of colder days and seemingly endless nights.

And it was always when Mama felt her lowest. It's the Octobers, she would say as she sat in the cool night air of the garden as if that were explanation enough.

I didn't want to get out of bed, I didn't want to go to work, and after three days, Liz showed up at my doorstep, knocking incessantly and demanding Ray to let her inside. I heard them argue briefly then heard Liz's footsteps on the stairs.

Liz pulled the door open, and I winced at the blinding light once again. I put my hand to my face and shielded the sun, the white clouds, the blue sky to find the brilliant smile of Liz.

"Hey, sleepyhead," she called, and for the first time, my smile didn't instantly mirror hers. It fell heavy on my face, turned down in a grimace.

Without pause, Liz grabbed the hand that shielded my face and pulled me to sit. "Come on," she said as she pulled me down the hall toward the bathroom.

She pulled off my shirt and pajama bottoms, removing layer by layer, the shells grown thick by sweat and sleep and the October numbness. She leaned over and turned the knob of the shower, bundling my clothes into her arms. Finally, she turned to me with a look of exasperation before adding, "And use soap. You smell like shit, Cat."

I ran a hand through my hair, wincing as oil coated my fingers.

"In, you go," she muttered. "I'll be downstairs getting tea, then we're getting you some breakfast."

I opened my mouth to whine about the cold and the light, but she held up her hand. "No excuses. I'll see you in ten minutes, or I'll come back in here."

Liz closed the door, and I was left with my reflection in the mirror.

My hair was matted to the side of my head where I slept. Bags hung themselves in dark moons under my eyes, my face pale and gray. My ribs showed, and I could see that I had been losing weight for the past few weeks. I sighed, my eyes lingered on my stomach and the crooked scar on my abdomen.

I stepped into the shower and scrubbed my body until my skin turned red, carefully cleaning every inch of my skin, scrubbing my scalp, soaking my pores until the water turned clear once more.

Transcript
Interview with Eddy Sparrow
10:18 p.m. April 27th, 2021
Case No. HI30823
Sorry, I need a bit more water.

There, that's better. Now, where was I?

That's right. Cat's Octobers.

You ever had a case of the Octobers?

What a name for 'em.

You're right. That's exactly how I felt after I found out about Stephen. Now, he was never perfect.

We'd been together for so long, and lookin' back now, I can see all the red flags, but that's hindsight for ya, isn't it?

Well, first off, we'd get calls from time to time during dinner, but I just wrote that off as Stephen being an important person.

And there was the time that I discovered the hotel bill he'd run up at the Grand Bohemian even though we lived a few short minutes away. He said that he hadn't wanted to interrupt my research and needed a "staycation" because he couldn't afford to get away, and I felt like I had no choice but to believe him.

But he'd go through these phases. He'd be present and in love one minute, and the next, he'd be gone, pulled in the opposite direction. It's like he wanted to feel like a "man" sometimes. That's my best guess. And then he'd get his fix, and he'd come home. We'd be fine again, and it's like we were newly married, and everything would be perfect again, as if it never happened.

I should have known better. Mom sure would have known what to do, but I felt like I couldn't call her, so I called Penny, and we went out for drinks, and I ended up sobbing to her about it all night. I felt so bad. She was younger than me, and there she was, having to take care of me. I was pathetic.

And that made me think of the things my mom would say growin' up. That is to say, it made me think of the warnings she made: to stay away from men with who need healed. She's talk about boys born with holes inside 'em that couldn't be filled, that the only way they would ever be whole is in the end — when they were filled with dirt.

Morbid, I know, but my mom always had a dramatic flair. She never married after Dad died, so I think it was easier to project her insecurities on men than to be vulnerable with them.

My father died young — way before I could remember anything about him — and she had never dated since.

Nu-uh, not even once. She said that one great love was enough, but sometimes I wonder if she was afraid to try again, to really fall in love. But maybe I don't understand anything. That's life though, isn't it? You think you have everything figured out, and then the unthinkable happens.

I let the water run over me, but my thoughts were stuck on Mama. She was different toward me after Ray came back. She would hover over me, asking me where I was going when I left the house and who I was going with. She became obsessed with showing me things in the garden, the passing of hours, of time together with one hour ticking into another in the invisible metronome of time. She would hold my hand and caution me about letting things slip through my fingers and as the air turned cold once more in October, she would sit out in the garden and tell me stories on her grandmother's quilt.[52]

Mama spoke her stories under the stars, and I noticed that they began to turn dark. She caught me trying to write them down once. I sat at the kitchen table and scribbled down all the strange stories she would tell, trying to get the details just right, but I could never capture the feeling of her words, and my stories always fell flat.

Mama read them once. She sat there silent and said that I was much too good for this world, that people would try to steal my words and make them their own, but isn't that what everyone does with stories? We borrow and change things, make them our own, bend them to our will. Mama might have been wrong about Ray's love, but she was right about the cruelty of the world.

I turned the water off and dressed slowly, feeling the strain of every muscle as I pulled on my underwear, bra, pants, and sweater. Liz met me at the door, my old sheets in her arms. I reached down to pick up my discarded undergarments, and the sharp smell of body odor and sweat hit my nose. She added my clothes to the pile and headed downstairs.

"Tea's ready," she called over her shoulder. "Don't let it get cold."

---

52 Quilts are typically a staple of Southern culture that symbolize family ties and values. Typically, they represent connections, family, stability, a strong foundation that has passed down from one woman to another. It's a labor of love and shows creativity through labor, the binding together of separate pieces with thread to create something beautiful. My own mother has passed down several quilts that have grown soft with age, one of which still sits at the foot of my bed.

Ray sat at the kitchen table with a cigarette in hand, looking from me to Liz and back again. He watched as Liz fried a few eggs and made toast and fresh coffee, sliding the food onto clean plates and bringing them over to the table.

"How's work?" Liz asked as she sat down in front of her own plate. I joined them cautiously, this strange collection of family gathered at the worn table.

He let out a breath and took a bite of toast. "Should be another job out in Springville by the end of the month."

"Weren't you working down at the school last?"

He nodded as he chewed a mouthful of eggs. "Dumbasses don't know good work when they see it," he grumbled.

Liz raised her eyebrows and gave me a look as she took a sip of coffee. The truth was, Ray had been home for the past week, ranting about being let go at his latest job at the school and having to answer questions from everyone from the school board to the police, but the girl, whoever she was, wouldn't come forward to testify, so he was simply let go quietly and had been having trouble finding a job since.

"How's the cafe," he countered. "I hope this one's not scarin' off the customers." He nodded in my direction.

"She's actually my best employee," she smiled.

"I'm your only employee," I mumbled.

"Still," Liz shrugged. "She carries her own, and I bet her paychecks have helped. This place is starting to look nice."

I looked around the room and noticed the new light fixtures, the refinished wood floors in the hall. How had I missed all this? And when had he been working on it? At night? During the day when I wasn't home?

"Thanks," Ray nodded and looked around the room, admiring his work and then returning his attention to the newspaper on his lap. "They got this stupid Halloween carnival opening this week. You guys goin'?" He said with an unlit cigarette between his lips.

"Maybe," Liz said. "Is it just some stupid hayrides or do they have anything new?"

"Beats me." He scanned the page, his lips moved around his cigarette, causing it to seesaw up and down. "They got a hayride, maze, food, games... same old stuff as normal, but you never know."

Liz reached out and slid the paper out of his hands and read silently. "Fortune teller. That's pretty cool."

He rolled his eyes and relit his cigarette. "Pretty cool if you like that voodoo-type stuff." I glared at him. He knew Mama hated when he smoked in the house, but there he was, doing it anyway.

"It's not voodoo. It's divination," she muttered and tossed the paper back over to him.

"Divi-what? Sounds made up to me."[53]

Liz stood up and took our plates to the sink and began to wash them. Ray turned the page of the newspaper and glanced up at me. I had barely moved and hadn't spoken the whole time.

"What's wrong with you?" He sneered and turned another page. Then he paused and looked at me again. He seemed to recognize something in my eyes. "This isn't one of those depressive episodes or whatever that the doctor was talking about, is it?"

My skin crawled. The last thing I wanted to discuss with Ray was my health issues. I thought about my nightly ritual for the past month, collecting the pills from their orange containers, rolling each one between my fingers, and casting them one by one into the toilet as I made wish after wish. I wish Ray would leave me alone. Plunk. I wish I was beautiful. Plunk. I wish I

---

53 There is a correlation between extreme religious beliefs and strict adherence to superstitions in the South. "Old Wives Tales" are followed as closely as scripture, although anything considered to be "Wiccan" or associated with the occult is considered "the devil's work," which is interesting since Wiccans don't believe in the existence of a devil in the first place. A southern woman would possibly paint their front porch "haint blue" to ward off any evil spirits and would also praise Jesus every Sunday while "blessing the hearts" of those she doesn't approve of. In short, the South is full of contradictions.

could escape. Plunk. I wish I could hear back from Brown. Plunk. I wish Mama were still here. Plunk. Flush.

"She's just got a fall bug," Liz said over her shoulder. "You know how it is with the season changes."

Ray's eyes narrowed, and I looked down at the floor.

"But she's feeling much better. Isn't that right?" she said.

I looked up at Liz, and she nodded, causing me to mirror her movements. Ray rolled his eyes and resumed reading his paper as he said, "Whatever. Just don't do anything stupid."

Don't do anything stupid. His advice. The man who regularly cheated on his partner. The man who liked to play with underage girls or any girl who paid him attention. The man who had an illegitimate two-year-old boy. The man who couldn't hold down a job to save his life. The man who still held onto this house, onto me, like a cancer that laid in waiting. Hiding and metastasizing. Don't do anything stupid. *Sure. I'll get right on that, Ray,* I thought. *I'll be just like you.*

Interview with Eddy Sparrow
10:37 p.m. April 27th, 2021
Case No. HI30823
I guess it's time for a confession.

No, not that kind.

Look, I'm tellin this story, so just hold your horses.

Just listen, will ya? You know I enjoy research — especially being able to go back and see what Mom was workin on — but I immediately recognized the signs of bipolar disorder.

Well, if you must know, I also struggle with a mild form of it.

No, it's not like that. I mean, I know a lot of people think it's where you're happy one second and angry the next and there's never a midddleground, but there are millions of people with it, and most of the time, you'd never even know from the outside.

Mom was the one who recognized it first. I was such a perfectionist, and I'd go through these phases where I would obsess about my school work. Then, there'd be other times where I was so worn out that I wouldn't have the energy to get out of bed.

I always just thought it was me burning the candle at both ends, but Mom knew.

She took me to a doctor who started me on supplements, but then he referred me to a psychologist after those didn't work and Mom revealed that mental illness ran in our family.

On my first visit with the psychologist, he smiled at me and said that mental illnesses are more common than cancer, diabetes, and heart disease and that it was nothing to be ashamed of.

He gave me appropriate medication and taught me some skills to recognize episodes and how to manage symptoms.

Well, if I notice myself obsessing or having

low energy, I can keep communicating with friends, get outside, make sure I'm eating and taking care of myself.

I never told Stephen. Looking back, there were a lot of things we never told each other. Sure, he'd see weeks where I'd be more energetic than others, and he knew I took medicine daily, but he never asked about it and never seemed to be concerned.

I can't confirm what medications Cat was on, but I know that a handful of medications seemed excessive, even for someone with major bipolar disorder. And it seemed like she should have been monitored more closely.

I mean, she'd be taking a mood stabilizer, which is one of the most common ways to treat bipolar disorder, and an anxiety medication, which would be useful when managing the anxiety of living in a small town with an awful person like Ray. Maybe a sleep aid, but perhaps there were additional issues?

Sorry to go off on a tangent. Let's get back to Cat.

We went to the carnival later that week just at sundown. I was able to work, although I felt so exhausted that I could barely function. I just wanted to go to bed after work. But Liz knew how to convince me to go. She had that look in her eyes and that tone in her voice, so I reluctantly agreed.

The park was strung with lights, and booths offered face painting, games, crafts, and other activities. Liz paid for our faces to be painted. She was a skeleton, her painted bones solid and prominent. I was a ghost. Washed out and shapeless. We bought snacks, hot dogs and candy apples, Frito pies, and rock candy. Liz won a goldfish and a straw hat, and I won an oversized blue teddy bear and a carnival shirt. By the time we made it to the fortune teller, our bellies were full of food and our arms were full of prizes.

The tent was empty, lit only by candlelight that flickered in the soft wind. A small woman sat behind a wooden table with a deck of cards. She smiled when she saw us.

"Come in," she crooned. "I've been expecting you."

Liz gave me a sheepish look and shrugged. She took my hand and pulled me toward the tent's opening.

"I'm Madam Pythia,"[54] she continued. "Come in. Take a seat." She gestured to two chairs against the wall of the tent. We carried the chairs toward the table before taking a seat. "Now, what brings you here today?" She leaned forward, and I could see the thick liner on her eyes, her broad swath of lipstick that extended well past her lip line, the red circles on the apples of her cheeks, and her foundation that fell into the creases of her wrinkles, making her look young from afar and much older the closer we got. Her face was like an illusion poster that showed all the lines and creases in unidentifiable shapes until we stepped back and saw something else altogether, making it impossible to tell her age.

---

54 Madame Pythia, the chief priestess of the god Apollo and the oracle at Delphi in Greece. Although she was not simply one person, but a collection of oracles who would give prophecies and advice, she successfully made hundreds of predictions that have come true.

Liz spoke first. "We want to know the future," she said simply.

Madame Pythia nodded and shuffled her cards once, twice, three times before offering them to Liz to cut in two. Madame Pythia took a cleansing breath and leaned forward as she revealed the first card. A hand holding an upright stick.

"The Ace of Wands," Madame Pythia smiled. "A creative with ambition. It looks like your life has been filled with a desire to not appreciate art and beauty around you, but to produce it. And this has done you well in the past."

Liz raised her eyebrows at me and smiled as if to say, *See. I told you this would be fun.*

"Now for the present." Madame Pythia flipped over the next card. A man and woman stood beneath an angel. "The Lovers." She looked up at Liz. "You feel connected and can express yourself in a way you never have before. This connection goes beyond the physical realm and extends to the spiritual realm. You are being called to align your values and are called to embody your true self. All things are possible right now."

She paused as if she was listening to something we couldn't quite hear. "Although," she looks up at Liz. "It can also about a choice, which can also be hard. There's some sort of dilemma that you've been feeling lately, and it's clear that you are approaching a precipice. Soon, you'll need to make a change."

"I hate change," Liz said as she looked down at her own hands. "Doesn't it always turn into a bad thing?"

"It doesn't have to. Sure, change can be hard. That's because we don't know what to expect, but neither did the first explorers or the first man on the moon." She took Liz's hand and whispered, "Whatever you decide, listen to that inner voice and choose love. Never fear. Love is the only thing that will get you closer to your authentic self."

Liz nodded, looking serious and rapt. "Now," Madame Pythia continued. "Let's get to the good part: the future." She flipped over a third card. A woman on a throne. "Justice." She placed her fingers on the card, trying to find the words to convey its meaning. "It's a card of action and decisiveness, fairness and structure. You know in your heart what you need to do, what your values are, and what you want your life to look like."

"The Lovers," Liz murmured.

"Exactly. You can hear the voice of your higher self. It's inside of you, and soon, you'll need to act without wavering. It might be hard, but a cycle needs to be completed."

"How will I know when to act?"

"You'll know," Madame Pythia smiled. "You'll know."

"What if I'm wrong? What if I decide something, but it's not —"

"Your fears are completely normal, and look," she pushed the card toward Liz. "The queen sits upside down."

"What does that mean?"

"It means that you will soon make an unethical choice."

"I don't understand."

"Sometimes, we're not meant to, but for now, you have that inner voice to listen to. Get to know how it sounds because you may have never been this close to it before, and when this cycle closes, when you make that difficult choice, it may not be the 'correct' decision, but it will teach you something in the process."

Liz opened her mouth to ask more but closed it. She looked at Madame Pythia and nodded. I felt a strange sense of peace radiate from her.

"Now," she said as she turned to me, "let's see what your friend has in her cards."

"No, thanks," I said, shifting my weight in my seat.

"Oh, come on," Liz pleaded. Her eyebrows drew together, and she stuck out her bottom lip in a pout.

"I don't know," I said, looking at Madame Pythia's hands. She shuffled the cards once more. I noticed her lips move slowly with each shuffle.

"It will be fun." Liz looked at Madame Pythia.

"Tell you what," the fortune teller said. "I'll do two for one. How about that?"

I sighed, knowing that I could never say no to Liz. Not really. Madame Pythia continued to shuffle her cards. When she was satisfied, she pushed the cards toward me, and I cut the deck in half. She leaned forward and I could feel my heart thumping in my chest.

"Death," Madame Pythia said in a low voice. I shivered. "Don't worry, dear. Death doesn't always mean hope is lost. It just means an end to something." I looked down at the crooked smile of the Grim Reaper's skeleton.

"There's been an abrupt ending in your past, as a sudden, unexpected change." I felt my throat tighten and tears threaten behind my eyes. "Resisting this ending can be unhealthy and can lead to catastrophic results. It might be something that you're still struggling with." She reached out and took my hand. I felt Liz studying my face.

Madame Pythia turned over a second card — a man lying face down with swords in his back — and paused. "Pain," she said simply. Hot tears spilled from my eyes. "Oh, honey, it's okay. It all right to feel these feelings, especially with everything you've been through." My shoulders shook, and Liz tried to pull me close to her, but I resisted. Panic flooded my throat, and my head spun. The sounds intensified around me, and the air felt like it was pressing down on me.

I stood up, knocking down my chair. I tried to catch my breath, but everything was moving too fast, and I couldn't quite grasp onto anything. I ran out of the tent and moved faster, running between kids squealing as they played carnival games, mothers pushing their strollers and tending to their squirming babies, fathers making jokes as they ate burgers in thick clusters. Everywhere I turned, it seemed like there were more and more people until I finally broke through the crowd as it thinned near the school.

"Cat, wait," Liz called, and she caught up to me as I dropped to my knees in the grass. "Cat...." She dropped to her knees next to me and took my hands. We knelt on the empty lawn, the busy carnival moving as usual across the street.

I tried to catch my breath, but pain stabbed my lungs with every breath. She put her face in front of mine and said, "It's okay, Cat. Just breathe. Breathe with me."

She took my hand and put it on her chest and took a deep breath and let it out steadily. I felt the rise and fall of her chest as she inhaled and exhaled again. I tried to breathe with her, but panic still filled my chest with each breath. After several tries, my breathing got closer to hers. "That's it. Just keep breathing."

I kept kneeling with her in front of me, matching her breath, mirroring her movements until my heart stopped racing and my normal breathing returned. With the urgent panic gone, sadness set in. I felt the heaviness, the exhaustion pull me to the ground, and I sat back on my heels.

"It just hurts so bad," I sobbed. Tears burned as they slid down my cheeks. "I just miss her so much."

"I know," she said as she wrapped her arms around me. "I've got you, Cat. I've got you." She whispered over and over until I calmed down and was able to wipe my eyes.

"I'm sorry," I sniffled and pulled back, putting my hands to my lips, taking a breath. "I feel like I've been trying to hold it together for so long. I just miss her so much, and now it feels like everything is on me — the house, the bills, my schooling, my entire future — and I'm doing it all alone because she's not here anymore."

Liz shook her head. "It looks like you're doing more than okay. And you're not alone. I'm right here. I'm not going anywhere."

I nodded, but I knew that she could see the doubt on my face.

"I just don't think I can do this anymore. People keep saying that time makes it easier, but it doesn't. It still hurts just as bad and now, I feel like I'm forgetting Mama, like she's slipping through my fingers." I looked into Liz's eyes and she squeezed my hands.

"I don't have a solution for that, Cat. Life sucks sometimes. It hurts, and it feels like too much, but you have some amazing things right here in front of you."

"What do you mean? I am barely getting by, and I think Ray is trying to weasel his way into getting the house — no, I know that's what he's trying to do. And I have no idea if I'm able to go to Brown like I've always wanted, and if I do, I have no idea how I'll be able to write again and —"

I opened my mouth to say more, but Liz leaned forward and put her lips to mine. They were warm and soft and fit so perfectly. Her fingers found my cheeks and pulled my hair away from my face. Her mouth moved against mine hungrily, and my heart began to race again. Instead of panic, however, I was pulled by desire, and I kissed her back.

Her hands moved to my shoulders, down my spine, and up my arms, and she pulled me to her. I could feel her breasts against mine, and a moan escaped my throat. It had been so long since I felt loved, since I felt safe.

"Hey," a male voice called, "this is a kid's carnival, not a freak show."

I pulled back, eyes wide as I realized what we were doing. What was I doing? Why was I thinking about sex when there were so many other things that needed my attention? I jumped to my feet, mouth open as I tried to make an excuse, but all I could say was, "Sorry," as I stumbled down the road toward my house.

Liz scrambled after me. "Cat, wait," she pleaded, but I was already running, taking the turns through town, desperate for home, for somewhere truly safe.

I ran faster and faster until Liz's footsteps receded, and the sounds of crickets overtook the chorus of children laughing at the carnival. As I rounded the next corner, headlights flooded my vision, and I jumped onto the curb to avoid being hit.

The car screeched and veered to the other side of the road, bumping to a stop on the shoulder. I turned around and looked at the car and recognized Marianne, looking stricken, hands tight on the wheel.

"Cat," she exclaimed as she rolled down her window. "You all right, baby?"

I nodded and walked to her car. "Sorry, Ms. Marianne," I breathed.

She shook her head and smiled. "Just like your mama," she laughed. "At first, I could have sworn you were her… You know, she loved walking at night."

I nodded again, trying to keep my tears away. Talking about Mama was the last thing I wanted to do at that moment.

"You need a ride home?" she asked, and I knew that she'd never let me say no.

I walked to the passenger's side. Slipping inside, I was immediately transported to times of summer car rides. Squeezed in between Mama and Marianne with Marianne on my left and Mama on my right. All of us sang along to the radio with the windows down. Marianne used to take us to the lake where we would spend the day on the boat. I could smell coconut sunscreen and taste red, white, and blue rocket ice pops. But the quiet of the car and the emptiness between us reminded me that I was alone, that summers on the lake were gone, that Mama would never again sit beside me. I longed for her laugh. I remembered she used to laugh with her mouth open, a smile spread across her cheeks and into her eyes. But I couldn't remember the sound, only the feeling I got when she would giggle and put her arms around me.

Of course, no one believed me about the faun.

The faun began to creep into my dreams more and more often, when I was at Marianne's and also when I was at home. I would sit at the breakfast table and tell my mom about him. His furry legs and velvet ears as he stood watch in the doorway. She thought it was "such a nice little dream," but I knew she didn't really believe me.

When I would tell Marianne or her mom or her dad, they all smiled and said the same thing — what a nice dream — until Marianne jumped in and told us all about her dream, that they had a new swimming pool filled with mermaids or that they went to a thick jungle and rode elephants to a lost city, but when I asked if she ever dreamed about the faun, she shook her head no.

I didn't understand.

He had been so real standing there in the door that first night, and I knew he had come other nights. I would see him in the dark, through the veil of dreams, in the hazy thickness of sleep. Night after night, he would come, and when he didn't come, I wished he would.

Finally, when I turned thirteen, he visited my dreams the next time I visited Marianne's. There was no storm that night, no lightning or thunder, but from the moment I woke up I knew he was there. It was like I could sense him standing there, and when I blinked, there he was, standing near the door.

I must have said something "You came back" or "It's you" and he put his hoof to his lips in a hush gesture. He took three large strides toward me and picked me up, his strong arms thick like vines. The moss on his chest soothed me, and I inhaled the familiar smell of leaves, of dirt, of Scotch.

Groggy, my eyes drooped as I swayed back and forth in his arms. He whispered in my ear that he had me, that I saw safe. I willed myself to stay awake as he took me down the hall. Shadows hugged us, and I clung to him, my head swimming, not knowing which way was up. He was taking me to his forest. I tried to focus on the blue shapes around me, but my eyes found his face. It was blue like lightning, blue like a corpse deprived of air, or else someone who refused to breathe.

When we arrived at the house, Marianne put the car in park and drummed her fingers on the steering wheel as she gathered her thoughts.

"You know, I can help if you ever need anything," she started and turned to look at me. "I know you were planning to go to college."

She paused as if she were waiting for me to confirm this, so I nodded and said, "I'd gotten into Brown before..." My voice trailed off, and she put her hand on mine.

"Cat, it was important to your mama that you get out of this town and have all the opportunities possible." I swallowed but couldn't respond.

"And at the end..." she paused and chose her words carefully. "I know that she was afraid."

I looked down at my hands, at her hand squeezing my own.

"I also know that you have to move on, Cat. You can't let the past trap you here." She reached up and lifted my chin so that she looked me directly in the eye. "Otherwise, you really will become a ghost," she said, referring to my specter face paint.

I felt sadness bubble up again. "I don't know if I can," I admitted.

"No one does until they try. Now, I'll call Brown and let them know that you're ready to come back. I think it would be the best thing for you. Just pick back up where you left off, you know?"

I gave a hollow nod. "It's what my daddy would have wanted, too. He would have given you the world. Before he died, he..." Her breath caught in her throat before she continued. "He loved you. I just want you to know that, okay? He really did love you."

I nodded but didn't see what that had to do with anything. Mr. Johns died when I was a baby, but I knew he'd meant a lot to Marianne. He was the anchor for their family, and I knew that after his death, Marianne shouldered most of the responsibility for the Johnss.

I nodded again and whispered, "thank you," not knowing what else to say. I stepped out of the car and watched her taillights fade down the mountain.

Transcript
Interview with Eddy Sparrow
10:51 p.m. April 27th, 2021
Case No. HI30823

You sure you don't want some tea?

I have fresh honey.

Okay, I have water too, so just let me know.

No, we didn't get divorced after I found the voicemail. I should have said something, should have confronted him, but I think I was afraid. I mean, I had this nice house and a good teaching position and really smart colleagues and a whole   established there, ya know?

Anyway, it did spur a depressive episode. I withdrew and didn't follow my usual self-care.

And I slept so much and just binge watched reality TV. I was just so tired, and Stephen wasn't really around to notice. He made some chicken noodle soup one night, but he was gone again before it was even ready to eat.

Penny stopped by a few times. The first time, she was dropping off some notes for Stephen, but then she showed up with dinner and some wine.

Yeah, it was sweet.

And I can see why Cat's mom sunk under all the mess, just let herself fall to the bottom of that bathtub until she felt that beautiful ache, forgotten underwater while life went on above.

Yeah, I can keep reading.

NOVEMBER 2001

We hadn't really spoken since the Halloween carnival, but slowly, my energy returned and so did my mood. Liz and I worked together and ate together. I caught her looking at me when she thought I wouldn't notice, but she never said anything. She busied herself with work and cooked dinner for us and walked me home, but she kept the conversation light until the week of Thanksgiving.

The whole week before Thanksgiving, Liz was at the cafe well before it opened. She frantically baked and cooked side dishes and breads before I got there. I wiped my feet and hung up my coat in the back before heading behind the counter. She nodded to me when I came in and slid a container of dough my way to start kneading.

We were busy with students meeting as they wrapped up projects due before the break and families picking up special orders. On Thanksgiving Day, Liz planned to open the first part of the day to help sell the remainder of her pies and planned to drop a few off on her way home. We helped the last customer and then packed up some of the pies she had baked that morning. She checked her list and started to prepare a side dish of sprouts, sweet potatoes, and kale that needed to be roasted for a delivery.

"It looks like it might rain again tomorrow," I offered in an attempt to make conversation. She nodded in response. "And it might rain the day after," I continued, but she only wiped her forehead and continued to chop sprouts before tossing them in olive oil.

"Our roof is getting replaced next week," I said and didn't wait for her to respond, realizing that she was in one of her rare bad moods, but I also wanted to talk to her. "I've been saving up for it and sold a few of Mama's old books to that book collector to afford it. I just hope they don't find anything else while they're working. When he was repairing that leak, Ray found the roof problems and he found out that the heat and air conditioning needs to be replaced... it's just a little overwhelming..."

Still, silence.

"Liz, did I do something? I mean, I know what happened at Halloween was —" My voice cut off, not knowing how to finish my sentence, but when I turned to look at her, I lost my train of thought. She stopped chopping, put down the knife, and leaned against the counter, wiping her forehead again. I saw circles under her eyes, and her mouth was stretched thin against her tight jaw, but her eyes — they looked exhausted.

"Are you okay?" I asked, immediately regretting my question because I knew how it felt to barely hold things together and have someone ask me if I was okay. Before I could say anything else, Liz's face crumpled, and tears filled her eyes. I stepped forward, surprised because I had never seen her cry.

"I'm sorry, Liz. I didn't mean to —"

"No, it's not you," she shook her head. "I just hate this time of year. Thanksgiving through the New Year is... hard. You know?"

I nodded. "Yeah, I know exactly what you mean."

"My mom used to cook these huge spreads. Even with cooking all the time, I still can't touch her Thanksgiving dinners. They were so good." She smiled with tears still falling down her cheeks. "I just miss her."

I moved closer to her and put my hand on hers, squeezing it lightly, but I knew that words couldn't make it better.

"Do you remember the last thing you said to your mom?" She asked, and her lips trembled, eyebrows pinched together in a pained expression. And then, I saw Mama in the garden smiling, her hand in mine, and I jerked my hand back involuntarily, jarring Liz out of her own head.

"I do," she gave a sad laugh. "I was so stupid back then. So selfish."

"You were young, Liz. You were, what? Eleven?"

"Twelve." Her gaze held mine.

"Exactly. You were a child."

"I just remember being so mad at her. She had gotten so sick, and all I wanted was to go to this stupid summer camp, but we couldn't afford it."

"Liz —"

"You should have seen her face. I yelled at her. I asked her why she had to be so sick, why couldn't we be like other families. I remembered the look in her eyes. Shock, you know? Pure shock. Her eyes were so wide and so yellow, and she tried to sit up on her elbows. She tried to comfort me, and you know what I did?"

She choked between her words, her voice grew high and thin, panicked as if she was afraid the words would get stuck in her throat and stay there forever. "I said that I hated her. I told that to my mom as she laid on her deathbed."

"Oh." The sound escaped my throat. I took her face in my hands and wiped away her tears. "Liz, you can't let that haunt you. You were a child, and she knew that. Grief makes people do some of the most terrible things, but she knew you loved her. Otherwise, you wouldn't have been there, and I remember that you never left her side."

"She died later that night. She'd wanted to be at home, and when I went in to see her before bed, she was gone."

"You found her?"

She nodded, took a breath, and lifted her hands to mine. "It was a blur after she died. I remembered my aunt came, and shortly after the funeral, I went to live with her." She looked up at me again. "Was it like that with your mom? Just a blur after she died?"

I dropped my hands and inhaled, steadying myself. No one had come right out and asked how I felt after Mama died.

"Yeah," I said. "It was."

"You were in the hospital, though, right?" Her voice was timid as if she was afraid that her question might scare me away. I could feel the distance between us.

"Yeah. I was there for a few weeks and then in and out for surgeries and my treatment program. They called my aunt, but she wouldn't come."

"Why not?" Liz's forehead wrinkled with concern.

"She and my mom had some kind of disagreement after I was born. They met once, to put flowers on their mom's grave, but Ray was an idiot, and I guess Mama took his side." I shrugged and continued. "Anyway, I think my aunt had her hands full with her daughter. Mama said she struggled to get pregnant and had lots of problems before she had her. Since then, Mama said they couldn't be bothered."

"Sounds familiar. When I went to live with my aunt, even she couldn't be bothered half the time." Liz smiled sadly and nudged me with her elbow before turning back to the boxes. "It helps, you know?"

"What?"

"Talking about," she responded. "Especially to someone who knew her, someone who's also felt loss. You get it, you know?"

"Yeah," I said and smiled, helping her with the to-go boxes. "I do."

Just as we finished up the orders, we heard the front door clang open, and Ray walked in. At first, he seemed so out of place that it took me a minute to recognize him. He was wearing his button-up flannel shirt tucked in and had even combed his hair. But that wasn't the strangest thing about him. The strangest thing was his mouth. He was smiling.

And not just the type of smile you flash someone to be polite.

His smile reached from ear to ear and into his eyes. It brightened his cheeks and made him stand a little taller, and I knew that anything that made him smile like that would be bad news.

"How's my favorite stepdaughter?" He asked as he approached the counter.

"I'm not your stepdaughter, Ray. You and Mama were never married," I muttered and slid a few boxes into a paper bag, double-checking the receipt.

"Now, don't be so pessimistic," he replied, and he ran his fingers over the counter. He noticed a stray crumb, grabbed it with his fingers, and dropped it on the floor with distaste. "Ever heard of a common-law marriage?" He asked, not taking his eyes off the counter.

"A what?" His smugness made my skin crawl. I hated when he pretended to know more than me.

"Yeah, neither did I," he said as his smile seemed to grow even more, "but Sharon has an uncle who runs a law office in Birmingham, a real professional place with hot shots running around, real rich men, you know what I mean?"

I raised my eyebrows at him, he clearly enjoyed drawing this out.

"I mean, this is the kind of place where the richest people go to have their expenses looked at. You know, deeds and estates and that kind of thing. He even said they have a fountain out front and free coffee and muffins inside."

"Does he have a drug problem like Sharon?" I jab, and I can feel Liz try to hold in her laughter.

"Now, don't you go makin' accusations like that. It's not funny, Cat. Sharon's a nice wo–"

"What are you getting at?" I interrupted.

"I'm gettin' to it if you'd let me. Well, we all sat down to dinner, and we got to talkin' about my work and Junior and the house —"

"Mama's house."

"Yeah, your mama's house, and do you know something? He

said that when folks live together for more than ten years, they enter into what's called a common law marriage. You see, sometimes folks just don't get around to gettin' married, they don't have the money or the time to take off work, or they can't find a preacher, but it's all the same according to the law."

I felt my cheeks grow hot, and I gripped the edge of the counter, trying to steady myself.

"Yep. Sharon's uncle sure does love Junior. Said they'd just about do anything for him. Even make sure he has somewhere nice he can live. And that house is almost perfect. Especially once we get the roof done. Hell, it'll be almost like new."

"But it isn't your house, Ray. It's never been your house," I interjected.

"Aw, come on. No hard feelin's, Cat. You and I both knew you'd never get that house anyway. How about you get your proud step-daddy a nice treat, sweet daughter? I'm sure Sharon'd love a little dessert, don't you?"[55]

He flashed that stupid smile my way one more time before Liz stepped forward, wiping the counter in front of him so that he had to take a step back.

"I'm real sorry, Uncle Ray, but we're closed." Her voice was high and cheery. "Maybe you could try us tomorrow morning? Before work?"

His smile faltered, clearly having been thrown off his stride.

"You still workin' at the school, right? I bet that's a real cushy job."

He gave a cruel laugh but didn't respond. Instead, he turned to leave, but as he pulled the door open, he turned back to call over his shoulder, "It should go through by the first week of January, holidays and all. Just in time for the end of that court

---

55 Common Law marriages were established nationally during colonial times when access to clergymen were not available in remote settlements. Often seen as unnecessary and unlawful in modern times, Alabama abolished Common Law marriages in 2017, six years after Cat's manuscript was presumably written, making Ray's argument plausible.

order. Just in time for your birthday."

The door clanged closed, letting in a draft of cold air from the darkening day. I shivered, less about the cold and more about Ray. I felt my veins pulse with ice, and my stomach felt like a giant fist squeezed inside me so hard that it was difficult to breathe.

"Cat," Liz started, but I was already pulling off my apron, grabbing a pie, and heading for the door. "Cat, wait."

"I have to go," I said over my shoulder as I grabbed my coat.

"Cat, where are you —"

"I'll see you tomorrow." I pulled on my coat as I headed out the door, headed to the only place I could think to go, headed for the only person who would know how to fix all this.

Okay, I'll get it over with. I was just taking
a breath, but I know that look. It's part of
why you're here, isn't it?

I confronted Stephen shortly after I'd
started to feel more like myself. One night,
he stayed out late, and he wasn't answering
his phone. I tried some of his friends, even
Penny, but they were all unreachable.

Anyway, I waited up for him until he
stumbled in at two in the morning where I was
sitting there waiting for him in the dark.

Yeah, I almost gave him a heart attack. He
turned on the lights and found me sitting in
the living room, a glass of wine in my hand.

How many? I don't know. I wasn't counting.

Well, he jumped, of course, his face filled
with surprise, and he tried to smile, tried to
make a joke about traffic — traffic! — but I
didn't laugh.

I asked just as
sweet as you please. And then I added,

Then, he realized that I   . He tried to
tell me that it wasn't what I thought, and the
excuses started. He said that he hadn't meant
for this to happen, that things had been so
hard for him, and that he hadn't meant to fall
in love with Penny —

Yep, you heard that right. Penny, as in his
research assistant, as in the one nice person
I thought I could confide in. Yeah. He had a
type, though, didn't he? I mean, hadn't   been
his research assistant at one time?

And I know what you're thinking. You're
surprised about Penny, but I was surprised by
the fact that he said love. He said that he
was in   with Penny.

Even after all those times — the missed
calls and the hotel bills — he always came

back. He'd never   anyone before. He'd
always   me.
  Yeah, it felt terrible.
  I really am sorry to hear about your wife,
and that friend of your goin' behind your back
—
  No, I guess not. Sorry.
  Okay, enough about cheaters. Let's dive back
in.

My hand shook as I rang the doorbell. I shifted, readjusting the pie in my hands in an attempt to steady them. I could hear the sounds of a family dinner in progress, excited talking, gentle laughter, the clink of silverware on fine China. I waited and listened to the hush fall over the room as the doorbell sound rippled through the house, the quiet questions of who it could be, the clink of high heels on polished wood as they made their way to the door, the sliver of light that hit my toes and grew, making its way up my legs, torso, then face. My cheeks blushed, embarrassed by my rash appearance on the doorstep. I looked up and smiled sheepishly.

"Cat," Marianne said as she smiled. She snuck a look behind her, concern painted her forehead before she turned back to me and searched my face. "What's wrong, baby?"

I opened my mouth, but nothing came out. I felt my throat tighten in panic.

"Come inside," Marianne said softly as she took my arm and led me into the vestibule.

I looked around as she closed the door. The entryway was decorated in gold and florals. Vintage oil paintings of various family members hung in the hallway, their eyes judging my presence. I looked down, studying the swirls of the oriental rug that ran the length of the floor to protect the wood. I could smell food from the kitchen and could hear conversation resume in the dining room across the hall.

"Let's get you settled in," Marianne said as she took my coat. "Wanna bite to eat?" Her voice was pleasant and seemed genuinely happy that I was there.

"No, thank you. I just came because…" Again, my throat tightened, and I felt so small. It seemed like everything I tried just ended up falling apart.

"Listen, baby," Marianne smiled, taking the pie from my hands. "You don't have to explain yourself. Why don't you come help me in the kitchen and help me get this ready?"

I nodded and followed her, aware that the conversation in the dining room came to a lull as we passed it, but I kept my eyes straight ahead so I wouldn't have to make eye contact with Marianne's family at the dinner table.

Walking further down the hall, we entered the kitchen, a sterile room that mimicked a serene modern farmhouse devoid of any personality aside from the copper pots and PYREX dishes, still steaming with the remnants of Thanksgiving dinner.

She set the pie on the counter and opened it, lifting it out of the box and transferring it onto a round baking sheet that I could tell had never been used.

"Now, how long should it go in?" She asked as she moved to the oven, her finger already working the temperature controls.

"Uh, ten minutes should be good. You don't want to dry it out when you warm it up."

She nodded and hit the start button before turning back to me. She didn't say anything, just stood there with a smile. Again, she seemed genuinely happy to see me, and she gave a little laugh before opening her mouth. "You know, I remember the first Thanksgiving we had after you were born."

Her eyes sparkled, and she spread her hands on the marble countertop in front of her. "Your mama wasn't so sure about being here. Your grandma wanted nothing to do with her in the end, and when she died, she had to give up the house. Daddy bought it for them and said he would save it until she got on her feet until you got older.

"Daddy had his annual Thanksgiving dinner planned, and we were expecting people from all over — friends, relatives, business partners, enemies. In other words, it was an intimate affair." She smiled and tapped her red fingernails on the marble, making a percussive tinkling sound.

"But that year, he cancelled, and it was just us. Me, Mom, Daddy, your mama, and you." She smiled, her eyes hazing over.

"It just felt right to make it a tradition. Even after Mom and Daddy died and your mama started dating Ray."

"He always hated it over here," I admitted.

"Yeah, well, the feeling was mutual. Believe me. Daddy wasn't the only one who disowned him. He burned every bridge he had over here." She raised her eyebrows. "The last Thanksgiving, we were all together was when you were two. Daddy made this huge toast to us after dinner, and I thought it was going to be this perfect night. Did your mama ever tell you about it? Staying here? Thanksgivings?"

I shook my head, and she studied me, measuring her words before she continued.

"That's just as well. Just as well." Sadness sat just behind her eyes, and she sniffed. "Anyway, enough about me. What's bothering you, baby?"

I took a breath, gathering my words. "It's... it's Ray," I started. "He said he's taking the house, something about a common law marriage and Mama's assets, and I'm barely getting by, and now he's just gonna take the whole thing, and I don't wanna lose the house, and I don't wanna lose her —" My voice cut off, my words choked in my throat, and hot tears welled in my eyes.

"How's he even planning on getting it? He doesn't know anything about a common law marriage."

"Sharon's brother. I guess he's a lawyer."

"I know exactly who he is, and no," she shook her head. "Over my dead body. He's not gettin' that house." Her face grew red, and she took a breath to steady herself. "You just wait here. I'll be right back."

Marianne's lips were pressed thin in determined thought as she left the kitchen. She whispered something to the people in the dining room, and I followed her footsteps as they clicked upstairs.

I looked around the sterile kitchen and moved into the hallway, careful not to move in front of the dining room door and interrupt dinner. I looked at the pictures on the walls, family portraits of Marianne and her parents smiling in front of various locations. Her father was broad-shouldered and had a smile that could charm anyone. Marianne often said it was how he made so many business deals. He would give them that one look, and it would be a done deal. Ray tried to replicate his father's charm but fell flat. He stood in several of the early family portraits, aloof as if he already had one foot out the door. He and Marianne were never close, and I could imagine Ray's anger over perfect Marianne — the overachiever, the perfect one, the favorite. He was only a half member of the family, afterall — the remnants of Mr. Johns' first failed marriage.

Marianne's mother was tall and slender with shoulder-length brown hair. Beside her, Marianne aged with each picture, and on the last one, I saw Marianne, her mom, and her dad gathered on one side of a Christmas tree, their faces painted in the same expressions as all the others, and on the other side of the tree, Mama was there with me in her arms. A knot twisted in my stomach.

You know, my mom has a picture wall like Marianne's. It's out there on the stairs. I can show you in a bit.

I was like most kids turned teenagers — I didn't pay attention to it much, and I remember being so annoyed that my mom displayed some of my worst phases. Seventh grade braces. Tenth grade self-cut bangs. She framed them and put 'em up there for everyone to see.

She never really talked about her family, though. She'd say that me and dad were all the family I needed, and that's how I'd built my life with Stephen.

Kids? No, I was never pregnant. Some women don't want kids, ya know? That's not what some of us are "born to do," regardless of what society says.

Sorry, I just got those kinds of questions all the time.

It's just a tender spot for me.

Yes, Stephen's the one who filed for divorce. He served me papers a week or two after he told me he was in love.

Yeah, and with Penny, of all people.

Anyway, he told me that it didn't have to be a messy divorce. He would give me more than my fair share but that he'd like to keep the house. His mom was the one who restored it, afterall.

And I felt so blindsided. I didn't want to leave. I just wanted everything to go back to normal. But things couldn't go back to normal after that.

Yeah.

Oh, it looks like this next part is from Cat's mom. Want me to keep reading?

After the faun dreams turned dark, my mom would hold me in her arms as I cried. She couldn't understand why it kept showing up. She'd wipe my hair from my face and whisper some of the spells that Grandma used to say over her kitchen table when women would show up with their worst nightmares nipping at their heels — unfaithful husbands, dead children, unfulfilled lives — but it never helped.

I even had those dreams over at Marianne's, and her mom would call Mama to tell her I needed her, but I never quite knew when I would dream of the faun.

One night he whispered into my ear that his name was Pan[56] and that I was his. His words rang in my ears for days. My mom, worried about this string of nightmares, had me visit the doctor, who reported that sometimes kids go through phases of nightmares, that it was just a phase, that it would pass as I grew older. Maybe I just needed to get my mind off of it, he suggested, and that weekend, I spent the night with Marianne.

Even when things were bad, she always knew how to make me laugh, and we could talk for hours without me thinking about the faun once. I didn't have to worry about Pan or concerned parents and doctors. I could just be myself.

And it was that night that I had the worst dream.

It was the night I learned the truth.

It started like all the others. We all fell asleep, and the house grew quiet when I woke up in the night. Pan stood there in the doorway, a sly smile on his face, as if he knew I needed him. He lifted me in his rough wooden arms and took me to his forest of blue. I shook with fear but there was something about him that made me think that I

---

56 This is a reference to Pan from Greek mythology. He was a god who was half man, half beast and represented nature and the wild. He was lustful with an animal-like sexuality. He haunted the hillsides and terrorized cattle in the pasture, causing stampedes and herds to stray from their home pastures. It's interesting how Sarah's stories are influenced by the oral tradition. She takes snippets from mythology and fairy tales and fixes her own meaning to them. It seems that she even passed this down to some degree to Cat. That is to say, story and identity are tied together, influencing one another as they are expressed either through written or verbal storytelling.

deserved these dreams, these nightmares, something that made me want him to take me away. There was something in the way he grinned with teeth like razors, a voice that whispered like a forgotten cigar sizzling in an ashtray, hands that tightened around me growing in knotted vines, his black eyes that pierced the dim blue of the room. I told him that I was thirsty, and he took me to the kitchen and gave me a cool glass of water. I gulped it down greedily and wanted more, so he filled the glass for a second time and put the cold cylinder to my lips when a flash of blue caught my eye, cool blue light spilled into the hallway from the den.

Pan took my hand and led me to a worn plaid couch, a drink in his hand, and I was so groggy that I didn't even question what a faun was doing with scotch in his cup. A baseball game flickered on the television, and he let out a groan and glanced over at me. He said that he often couldn't sleep either — that fauns can also be nocturnal — and he took the glass from me and set it on the table next to his glass half-filled with brown then felt my head, asking me if I was feeling okay. He pulled me in and set me on his lap that smelled like wet leaves.

I relaxed on his rough chest and watched the camera zoom in on the pitcher's sweaty face, and I must have said something like "You smell funny," because Pan laughed. He smelled like the forest, sure, but he also smelled like Scotch. Then he put his hand on my leg, and I saw it, the moss of his hairy arm, his razor smile, the blue light of the TV on his terrible face, and I froze.

And the truth was that I wanted to be held. I want to be loved and needed. But not like this. This was something different. I shivered in his arms, and he wrapped them around me even tighter and said that it was our little secret and took another sip of Scotch. He said that magic let him visit me at night, that it was a sacred sort of ritual that allowed him to come, and that it could easily be broken.

He said that I should be quiet and that I should have some of his Scotch. He called it medicine, then, but now I know what it really was. I remembered that it burned going down, but I did it because he told me to. I was too afraid that he would go and never come back.

All I could do was sit there, voiceless and torn to shreds, ripped apart like Echo and thrown to the four corners of the earth.

I felt the fragments of myself separating, and the floor dropped out from under me. I was nothing and nowhere as his hands were all over me, tears dripped down my cheeks as I tried to whisper stop, don't, no.

But I couldn't.

I felt the medicine make me sleepy, pull at my eyelids, but it didn't work like before. I didn't drift off to sleep or pass out. I felt everything that happened, and it stayed with me ever since. After all the months of wondering what would happen once he consumed me, I felt ripped open and relieved. I just wanted to feel it, all of it, so I could finally be at peace. And then he opened his mouth and swallowed me whole.

"Here we are," Marianne said at the top of the steps, jerking me out of my thoughts. "I knew I had it somewhere." She approached me with a small rectangular card in her hands.

I reached out and took the card, examining the gold scrawl on the front.

"He's an estate lawyer in Birmingham. He owed Daddy a favor. Call him on Monday, and I'll follow up." She paused and looked me in the eye. "Don't worry, Cat. We'll take care of this together."

I forced a smile, still unsure. "Thanks."

"There's also this," Marianne produced an envelope from her other hand. "I know that lawyers can be expensive."

I took the envelope and opened it, seeing bank records. At the top, Mama's name and address were printed.

"Daddy set up this account for your mama before he died. He wanted to make sure she was taken care of and that you were taken care of. Your mama planned to pay for school and incidentals with it."

I thought of Brown, the acceptance letter, and Mama's grim face. I'd never considered how much it would cost.

"It's helped to cover all your medical expenses so far." I thought back and realized that I'd never gotten a bill from the hospital. Almost a year later and nothing. I couldn't believe how stupid I had been to not ask about it. I really had no idea what it was like to be an adult.

"There's enough there if you need help with a lawyer or anything and still have enough for Brown."

I followed the line of numbers down the page and flipped it over. My mouth dropped. There was over a million dollars in the account.

"Wait, Mama had this the whole time?" I ask, looking up. Marianne nodded.

"I thought she always saw it as a handout, so she barely touched it. She was saving it all for you."

"Jesus," I breathed, looking at the total again, and I felt my eyebrows raise. "I don't know what to say."

Marianne squeezed my arm and smiled.

Then, I felt my stomach lurch. "Does Ray know about this?" Marianne shook her head, and I let out a relieved breath.

"Thank you, Marianne," I whispered. "Thank you for checking up on me and being there whenever I've needed you. This money changes everything."

"Of course, baby." She smiled again, and it warmed her face. "You're family to me."

I snuck a glance at the picture in the hall, the one with Marianne and her parents on one side of the Christmas tree and me and Mama on the other. I took another breath as I noticed Mr. Johns' hand, raised in a toast, wrapped around a glass of Scotch.

I feel so ashamed that I didn't say anything. For years, I didn't say anything because a part of me had wanted to be loved, had wanted to be a part of Marianne's family, but I was a child and didn't know what that really meant.

For years, he took advantage of me. All I wanted was for it all to be over and for it to have never happened at all. I wanted it to disappear like my voice that night. I wanted it all to go away.

After Cat was born, everything changed. I remembered being so angry at my mom for selling the house. How could she do that, especially to him? I was so mad that I remembered coming straight to their door and demanding to see him. You should have seen the look on Mrs. Johns' face. I think she knew even then that something was going on. Marianne's dad said that he was just looking out for me, that he had bought the house because my mom was in financial trouble, and that he would hold it for me until I got back on my feet. He told me that I could stay with them, but I told him that I wouldn't be caught dead in that house at night, so he offered me the guest house. He said I could put my own locks on it — which I did — and I told him that he could have nothing to do with Cat's upbringing.

He said that was just as well, that no one could know — especially not Marianne, seeing as how that was his precious little girl, and he'd never want to let her down. And it was fine for a few years, but that last Thanksgiving changed everything.

You see, the thing about an echo is that it still has a voice. It might be small, so tiny you can barely hear it, but it's there, hiding in caves, in canyons, in dark corners just waiting to be found.

Echo was not silenced when Pan sliced her up, shattered her forever, and sent those shards out into the world. Instead, it magnified Echo, repeating its chorus of no over and over, through neighborhood streets, between houses, over family dinner tables filled with the hardest confession I'd ever had to make, in between arms that held love and devastation, through phone cables to tell the horror of what he'd done.

Even gods fall. Their time comes to an end. Their magic hour is over. Their throne grows cold. Echo was never able to put herself back together. She was never quite whole ever again.

But she was alive and so am I. When I told Marianne's dad that I had to tell everyone the truth, he threatened me. He said that he would take the house and sell it. He would change his will, and I wouldn't get a penny. I knew I had to do something. I knew that if I wanted the house and if I wanted to get out from under his control, I would have to act that night.

I made a beautiful pecan pie, nutty and sweet, for dessert, and prepared the after-dinner coffee. I knew he loved his coffee with three sugars, but I didn't have time to dry Grandma's herbs, so I did the next next thing when you're in a pinch. I grabbed the anti-freeze from the garage and sweetened his coffee. I was desperate, and that was the only thing I could think to do. The thing I didn't know was that Marianne's mom also liked her coffee with sugar and a splash of cream. It was an honest mistake. Do I regret it? No, because the great Pan is dead.[57]

---

57 *The Daily Tribune* article dated the day after Thanksgiving 1985.

The Daily Trib

Iss. 872   Friday, the 29th of No

Johns Tragedy

Jonathan Macon

After Thanksgiving, a holiday often celebrated with
family and friends, the entire greater Birmingham area is
shocked after a pair of heart attacks claim the lives of
Kenneth Johns, 42, and Monica Johns, 38. Police were
called to the house the morning after Thanksgiving after
the Johns housekeeper found both Mr. and Mrs. Johns
deceased in their beds. Police have said they found
sleeping pills that were lawfully prescribed to Mrs.
Johns as well as alcohol on the bedside table, which can
be a deadly cocktail, but police also said they are
awaiting toxicology results.

Kenneth and Monica Johns are survived by their eighteen-
year-old daughter, Marianne Johns, who could not be
reached for comment. Funeral services will be announced
as soon as the date is released. If you or anyone you
know struggles with addiction or thoughts of self-harm,
please contact your local healthcare provider.

I didn't know where to go after I left Marianne's house, so I walked through town, winding the streets until I came to a painted door. I knocked timidly, well aware of the late hour. The door opened, and Liz smiled at me from the sliver of light from inside.

"I was wondering when you'd show up," she smirked and opened the door wider in a sign of welcome. She was playing music and had sketch paper pulled out on the living room floor. I walked to the kitchen and peered into her pantry.

"You sell all the pies tonight?"

She nodded.

"Let me bake for you, then," I said and started pulling out ingredients from the pantry.

"You know how to bake?" She said.

"It's a special recipe."

Liz looked impressed. She reached down and took her sketchbook from the living room and pulled up a seat across from me. I worked steadily, mixing flour and eggs and spices, chopping nuts, combining everything in the pie crust that Liz kept in her freezer. We listened, and she drew as I worked.

We talked as the pie baked in the oven, and I told her everything I had learned about Mama. She listened. I told her about Mr. Breelove and the nightmares. I told her about how Mama suffered from his abuse for years, believing it was her fault. I told her about how Mr. Johns bought the house and said that he was holding it for Mama when all the while he was using it as insurance for her silence. I told her about the Thanksgiving she wanted to come clean and the threats to remove her from the will. I told her about Mama's pecan pie and both Mr. and Mrs. Johns dying of heart failure that night.

We sat and ate in silence, savoring the pie and thinking about what I'd said. Then, Liz squeezed my hand and made us a cup of coffee, which we both drank black — no sugar.[58]

---

[58] Sweetened coffee could be linked to the kidney-damaging compound ethylene glycol, and is commonly found in commercial coolants and antifreeze. Initially, the compound causes lethargy, slurred speech, and blurry vision, similar to alcohol, but the body isn't able to metabilize it properly, leading to a rise in oxalic acid in the bloodstream, which crystalize and cause damage to organs, especially to the kidneys since they help filter the blood. If left untreated, organ failure can occur, resulting in permanent organ damage and even death. That's why I always drink my teas and coffees black, especially if I don't know the person. Call me crazy, but I'm not taking any chances.

Transcript
Interview with Eddy Sparrow
11:53 p.m. April 27th, 2021
Case No. HI30823

I know. It was Mr. Johns all along.

I can't imagine how Sarah felt. She was such a young girl, and he was supposed to protect her.

He seemed to care about Cat, though?

No, I know. It's no reason to poison someone. I get that. I'm just sayin that I've experienced the death of two parents and such a messy divorce, but I can't imagine what she was going through.

Sure, we can talk about it some more. After the divorce papers, I acted… yeah, irrationally.

I should have just packed my bags and left. I should have been long gone, but I just wanted my old life back, and I felt so claustrophobic and out of control, like everything around me was spinning uncontrollably.

Yep, that's when I went to the party. You heard about that?

I knew Stephen would be there, and probably Penny, and I don't know, I just wanted to something, ya know?

Well, I went. Stephen was there, of course, and so was the whole department.

Yeah, she was there too.

Everyone avoided me like the plague. It's funny how people act once your business is out in the open like that.

Mrs. Smith was there.

Yeah, that sugar-sweet woman who was obsessed with Stephen. She had her arm wrapped around his and was introducing him to everyone like he was her pet yet again.

I tried to hide in the corner with some wine. Tried to blend into the background, ya know?

I wasn't tryin to eavesdrop, but they came over to the drink table, and I was just on the other side behind this fern thing.

Anyway, I was so mad. I mean, she was old enough to be his   , for godsake. Shouldn't she be ashamed?

So, there I was, hiding behind that fern with my drink to my face when Dr. Smith, her husband, came up to her. He pulled her into a hug and said,

Yep, you heard me right. Marianne. Marianne Johns, married name Marianne Smith.

Yep, she was Ray's sister — well, half-sister. Said she felt like she always had to look after him. Him and his baby, Junior, who everyone called by his middle name — Stephen.

I didn't know what they were all talkin bout, not havin read Cat's story. All I knew was that Marianne was Stephen's aunt somehow. An aunt I'd never known about. It made me start to wonder what else I didn't know.

And then she gave me this look, and I could almost see something behind her eyes, some secret, murky, hard to see, but still there, lurkin beneath the surface. She looked at me like she knew who I was, like she'd always known who I was.

I excused myself and went home — well, to Stephen's house. I was in the process of packing. Or thinking about packing. I hadn't actually started yet because that would mean it was real. My life was over.

No. Stephen wasn't home that night and neither was his car.

Well, he came by about a week later. He'd been staying at Penny's. I still hadn't touched my stuff and had all these pages spread out on the desk.

I admit I was going through a sort of mania at the time, and it probably looked crazy. I looked up the Johnss and made a sort of family tree. Marianne was Mr. Johns' only daughter with his wife, but he had a baby from his first marriage. The baby was named Ray and was disowned at some point. Anyway, he had a baby with this lady who OD'ed, and his name was Ray Jr., and that's where my research ran out. I couldn't understand what that all had to do with Stephen. I mean, his name wasn't Ray Jr. or RJ, and he had parents — parents who were alive, who I met.

Anyway, Stephen came in to see if I'd left yet or where I was in the packing process when he stopped short.

He picked up some of the papers on my desk and asked what I thought I was doing.

I told him that I'd been doing some research on the wealthy families in Birmingham, which was true, but didn't say that it mostly concerned him.

He asked what I was doin' looking at his family, so I told him it was for a book.

I don't know why I said that. Maybe I was embarrassed. Maybe I'd already started writing things in my head.

Then, I asked him what he meant about it being his family. I couldn't find any ties to him, and he said he'd grown up in Mountain Brook.

Then, get this, he said that he was adopted. Said his mom overdosed and his dad took off or something and hadn't been seen for years. His mom's brother — yep, the lawyer who wanted to help Ray get the house — took him in and raised him as his own.

Well, I couldn't wrap my head around it at first. I mean, his mom was always hovering and his father made sure he had everything he needed and didn't have to worry about school or publishin' contacts. He had all that covered. And if I think back, it always seemed like they were too nice, ya know? Like they were compensating for something.

Then, he said he didn't want to talk about it because who wants to talk about dead and missing people that were never really in his life anyway and how I needed to move on and how it was his house and he'd given me all this money already — it was already in my bank account — so what was I waiting for?

I guess I don't know what I was waiting for either.

Yes, he drove there.

I don't know. He probably went upstairs, took a shower, got some more of his things.

Yeah, why are you asking me about his car?

Suit yourself. Don't tell me then.

No, the last time I saw the day I finally left. I crept down the stairs, and there he was, making sandwiches in the kitchen like old times.

He told me I looked good but couldn't meet my eyes.

I took a bite and measured my words.

—

He said it wasn't about that, and I told him that he didn't even give me a chance. He just announced that he was leaving. He said he hadn't handled it perfectly, but it was the best he could do. And that he'd always been honest — discrete, yes — but he never lied.

I just thought it was like the others. He was bored but he'd come back. He always came back.

But he said this time was different. He was in love. And then he started with the platitudes,

He said we were so young when we got married — that we didn't know what we wanted at the time.

I didn't want to hear it. I couldn't even look at him, but he kept talking and saying that it was hard. That it was hard always being so good. It was like a cancer. The expectations were driving him insane, and he felt like he couldn't even be himself.

He said it was different with her. There was no expectation. There was no pressure to be good, to be the protector, to live up to all the expectations. With her, it was just easy. I watched Stephen pack up the rest of his things and head to the door where he stopped. For a second, I thought he would turn around and come back but he took a breath and kept walking.

I got terribly drunk that night, I must admit, and I cried myself to sleep. I got up the next morning, showered, packed my bags, and headed out the front door to see my mom whom I hadn't seen since I was eighteen.

Look, I'm about to make some more tea whether you want some or not.

You do?

Sure. I'll make a pot. Just give me a minute.

DECEMBER 2001

The house was quiet. We had just finished dinner and were about to open the presents. Liz kneeled in front of the Christmas tree, and I moved to get my bag from the front door. Opening my backpack, my fingers brushed a worn envelope that I'd opened and read over a dozen times, even though I had gotten it in the mail less than a week ago. Instead, I grabbed a small package wrapped in gold, and when I turned around, Liz held out a red present in her hands.

She smiled, and we exchanged gifts. She unwrapped hers without waiting, eager to see what was inside, and let out a squeal of surprise. "A watercolor set," she said as she opened it.

"It's a travel set," I explained.

"I love it." Her finger brushed the powdery ovals filled with a rainbow of colors. "Now, open yours," she said with a gleam in her eyes.

I carefully opened the present, not knowing what to expect, but as I pulled the red wrapping paper away from the rectangle, I could see that it was a journal. "For your stories," she explained.

I turned the book over in my hands. It was green and made of cloth with vines embossed in the woven cotton. It looked like a real book, and my heart squeezed in on itself. I could see my stories ending up in a book like this, a book that fit perfectly in my hands, could be opened with whole worlds inside, and could be closed, put on a shelf, and read for years to come. I had been so afraid of letting people in since I'd moved back, but sometime in the past few months, I had fallen irrationally and completely in love with Liz. I hugged her after we exchanged presents, smelling vanilla in her hair, and as the side of our faces touched, I remembered how her lips felt against mine, soft, expectant, warm, and my heart thumped in my chest. She moved a piece of scarlet hair from my face, and I looked into her eyes. Something broke loose inside me; all of my fears faded, all of my doubles crumbled, and I leaned forward and kissed her.

Liz stiffened at first, not expecting me to be the first one to lean in, but she softened and put her hands on either side of my face, touching my cheeks lightly as she kissed me back. My mind went soft as hunger took over, hunger for her fingers, for her lips, for her whole body against mine.

I lifted off her shirt, and her fingers found the hem of my own and pulled it gently over my head. Her lips moved down my neck, between my breasts, and down my stomach, stopping at my belly button before she pulled back. Her fingers traced the pink scar on my abdomen.

"Is this from that night?" I felt her breath against my skin, and I recoiled.

"It's nothing," I said, wrapping my arms around myself and sitting back on the sofa.

"Cat," she said, tucking my hair behind my ear, "you can tell me. I promise I won't…" but her words died on her lips.

I shook my head and pulled on my shirt, but when I looked at her again, I didn't see pity. I only saw a genuine desire to know me, the real me.

"She'd had a hard time that fall, you know? She went into a major depression after Ray left, and it seemed like she was getting better. I'd just graduated, and we wanted to celebrate. She packed up this picnic in the garden, and not just regular picnic stuff. She had a five-course meal: quiche, soup, salad, turkey melts, and her specialty, pecan pie. It was a special night."

I tried to smile, but when I pictured Mama's face in the twilight as she spread out the food on our family quilt, my stomach tightened, and I felt that phantom pain in my stomach.

"I'm sorry," I said, standing up. "I need a minute."

I headed for the bathroom, and I could hear Liz stand up., I reached the bathroom and she called out, "Take all the time you need."

I shut the door and leaned against it, closing my eyes, and rubbing my temples. My chest tightened, and I swallowed hard to push back the tears. I leaned over the sink and splashed water on my face and felt the pain in my chest release. My throat relaxed, and I took a deep breath to steady myself. I reminded myself that I wasn't in danger. Liz was safe. She was home.

I dried my face, resolved to sit down and tell her, tell her all of it, even the ugly parts. I opened the door.

"Okay, I think I'm ready to..." I started, but when I stepped into the living room, I froze.

Liz stood by the door. Her eyebrows were drawn together in a pained expression, and her eyes filled with tears.

"Liz, what's —" I started, but then I saw it. The worn envelope was in her hands.

"You weren't going to tell me?" Her lips trembled.

"I was, I swear."

"What, when you left?" She held up the letter. "Brown starts in a little over a week."

"I know. I was just waiting for the right —"

"Save it, Cat, and just be honest. You were never going to tell me, just like you were never going to tell me about your mom." She put up her hands and sighed. "I've heard the rumors, Cat."

I opened my mouth to say something, and when I did, my voice came out small and thin. "You said you didn't believe the rumors."

"I'm not saying that I did, or at least not all of them. But there has to be some truth to it."

"Like what?" I asked, feeling the sting of her words and taking a step back.

"That something was wrong with her, that what she did was wrong, but you keep hiding it all. You keep defending her."

"I'm not defending her," I said, feeling my cheeks burn in anger.

"Maybe not intentionally, but what she did was wrong. What she did made you like this."

"Like what?" I asked, stepping forward. I felt anger pulse through my arms and legs, and I glared back at Liz's judging gaze. I don't know how I'd never seen it before.

"You're sad, Cat. I get that. But she pushed you into a corner. She isolated you and told you that she was the only person there for you for so long. And you believed it. And you've punished yourself for it every day since she died. You're not to blame, Cat. She is."

"You don't know anything, Liz," I spat and grabbed my coat.

"Then tell me," she pleaded. Instead, I picked up my bag, looked her in the eyes, and snatched the letter from her grasp.

"Why waste my breath? It seems like you've already made up your mind."

I pulled the door open and walked out into the night, shivering in the darkness. The sharp wind cut to my bones and hot tears quickly froze on my cheeks. I half-jogged up Blood Mountain as I sobbed into the wind and let myself into the equally cold and dark house, knowing that I was alone and that no one was coming to check on me.[59]

---

[59] I'm not sure I can finish this. I don't have the heart or the time, but I am thankful that I have my daughter back.

I've missed her so much, and it's so nice to have her home.

Transcript
Interview with Eddy Sparrow
12:16 a.m. April 28th, 2021
Case No. HI30823
How's the tea?

Good. Mom used to make it sometimes. Like I said, it's an old family recipe. Camomille, Lavender, and a few special ingredients.

Yep, that's the honey, and it does have a bit of spice to it, doesn't it? Nutmeg and a sprinkle of cinnamon.

Okay, so what were you asking me last?

Yeah, I packed up after Stephen's visit and headed home.

It was last year. End of April, early May, maybe? I'd left with a suitcase and came back just about the same, only a decade older.

The house still looked the same — small, a little older too, but still the same place.

I remember being so nervous before I rang the doorbell.

No, I didn't call first. I didn't know what I'd say, so I just showed up.

It took a while for her to get to the door, and when she opened it, I could see that she was older too. She had wrinkles. My mom — the lady who wouldn't settle for anything, who was so independent that she didn't need anyone, not even me — had gotten old.

But to my surprise, she didn't even hesitate. She wrapped me in her arms and she smelled like peppermints — she always kept peppermints in her pockets in case her mouth got dry.

It was fine. Different. We'd both gone through so much since we'd last seen each other. Mom made dinner — baked chicken, green beans, and mashed potatoes. It was nice.

I told her about Stephen and about how he was leaving me and how I'd never felt so lonely. And she was great. She sat with me and held my hand, just like she did when I was young. I told her I was sorry for leaving, sorry for saying all the terrible things that I said to her, and she said none of that mattered anymore.

Instead, she told me all about how she had wanted me since she was a child and how hard it was to get pregnant. She talked about how she and Dad found out that she was expecting and described her hard pregnancy. She said she even lost a tooth when she was pregnant with me, just like the saying goes — gain a baby, lose a tooth.

And then, she did the strangest thing. She leaned back and said,

I had no idea it was connected to Cat or that she'd soon be working on this project. It's funny how things all come together isn't it?

She told me the story of the princess and her monster, the bloodthirsty prince, the return of the monster… Needless to say, I had nightmares that night.

No, I had no idea that Sarah, Cat's mom, was my mom's sister. I'd always had a feeling that I was missing a piece of me. I knew she kept things from me, things about who she was and where she came from, but I never imagined.

That's what I thought. How's a person supposed to know who they are if they don't know their roots? No wonder I latched on to Stephen so easily and accepted the little bits he gave. I was used to doing that with Mama all my life, collecting the scraps and tryna make it all work. I didn't know who I was, and sometimes I still don't.

Um, let me see. It had to be July when the manuscript came. Didn't I say that already?

Yeah, she worked on it all fall and got really sick that winter. If you notice, her annotations stop after this. She was in the hospital for Christmas and passed away on New Years.

It was   fast. We had her funeral the first Sunday in January.

I found the manuscript… a month or two ago maybe?

I don't know the date exactly. I know it was freezing. I'd lit a fire in the fireplace and started going through all the papers in her desk. She had so many notes about all these different projects, but this one was buried under a stack of her hospital bills.

It was cancer. Kidney cancer. Yeah, pretty terrible. I remember that she didn't eat much that summer, and she had trouble keeping food down at all that fall. It got so bad that we went to the ER and that's when I found out it was cancer, but I suspect she already knew.

No, she hadn't told me. She looked embarrassed when the doctor came in, and I remember being so mad at her that she didn't tell me. I felt like I had wasted so much time.

Anyway, it was freezing, and I was curled up in her chair, and here was this crazy story about this girl who I'm related to. And her step-father who Stephen's related to. It was all so surreal, and then I started having those nightmares and hearing noises, feeling like someone was watching me.

And then, I started feeling so bad about Cat, and the house was creepin' me out, so I decided to head out there.

Yeah, to Cat's house.

I don't know why I went out there, either. It just seemed like the right thing to do at the time.

Well, you'll see. Let me keep reading.

I always thought the end of the new year was like the closing of a book, the old year passing, and a new one opened fresh and clean, like the crisp pages of a new book just waiting to be written in.

Cat has been accepted by Brown and leaves in two days. All of her things are packed, but I can't imagine her not being here. I don't know how I'm going to survive without her.

I've lost Ray. He's pretty much moved in with Sharon and the baby at this point, but he keeps hanging on, which is worse. It reminds me of everything we used to have and everything that has been lost.

I know Cat had something to do with his accident — I can see it in her eyes. She blames herself, but everyone knew that Ray was a drunk, even the doctors. They just assumed that his drinking slowed his reactions and that the slick roads caused him to lose control of his truck, but anyone who's paying attention can see — the blurriness of his vision, the slowness of his speech after the accident, the haziness of his memory — there must have been more in his system than alcohol and more to his failed brakes than the slick roads.

I mean, what was I supposed to do? I'd seen the way he'd started to treat Cat, the driving lessons, the controlling behavior. Men can't be trusted.

And I couldn't let him do that to Cat.

But now, the house is so quiet, and I feel like I'm losing Cat. I'm losing her to that great big world that could just swallow her up, and I'll never see her again. I can't bare that. How can anyone expect a mother to endure that?

So, I won't allow it. I know what I have to do. I've planned out our last night together — a picnic, like old times. Something special. Something to remember. I just know that I must save her and myself. I hope I'm not too late.

Transcript
<u>Interview with Eddy Sparrow</u>
<u>12:20 a.m. April 28th, 2021</u>
<u>Case No. HI30823</u>
It sure is sweet. Here, let me top you off again.

Where was I?

Right, so I headed out to Cat's house.

The roads were pretty much deserted. Everyone was headed to family dinners or parties with friends and not on the road.

Well, after their mother passed away, Mom and Aunt Sarah — it feels weird calling her that — they argued about their mom's will, how everything went to my mom, and nothing went to Sarah. Not even the house — now I know it was sold to Mr. Johns — and Mom used the money to set up a new life in Atlanta far away from the town and her sister and everything in her past.

I don't know. I guess she was sort of ashamed of it all. I mean, her mom was kind of mean, and her grandmother was this sort of crazy witch lady. She had nothing in common with her sister. I think she just wanted a fresh start. It makes me understand why she was so dedicated to getting ahead. Looking back, she probably felt like she constantly had to prove herself.

The house?

Yes. Olivia Saunders owned it originally, and after her daughters Helen and Eleanor died, the house went to Helen's daughter, Lorelai. Lorelai became a sort of naturalist and published books on the wildlife of northern Alabama — everything from wetlands to mountaintops and everything in between. She even made a series of watercolor guides and was an expert on conservation.

She married the sheriff — the gossip column joked that it must have been because he was always at the estate for some death or another. I know, not funny at all.

Anyway, she had a baby — my grandmother — who had two little girls of her own, also twins. Mom never mentioned her sister or her mother, and I never really thought to ask.

But after Mom died, with Stephen gone, with no job — yep, I wasn't hired back in the spring — I didn't know what else to do. Suddenly, no one was telling me who to be or what to do next. All I had was Cat and her story, these tiny pieces of Mom. Where would that take me? I had no idea, but I had to see.

Want me to pour you another cup?

Ray was out most nights, especially on the nights after Christmas, and I'd taken to watching the sunset from the kitchen window, just like Mama used to do. I watched the tall pines behind the garden eat the sun inch by inch until it disappeared. Mama used to say sunsets were both comforting and terrible: comforting because they were always on time and terrible because they reminded her of all the seconds that had passed by idly, without notice, never to come again. They were something she could always count on, but they couldn't be controlled. No matter how much she wanted to hang onto those moments a little longer.

A cold front left storm clouds from earlier lingering on the horizon. They painted the sky in smears of golds and oranges and dark pinks. A streak of red sliced its way across the sky, setting the whole sky on fire.

After a few moments, the light changed. The sky changed. The brightness from the clouds faded, and a blue quality took over the light, almost like sadness. Instead of that glorious magic from before, it was a solitary light that hurt the soul. The one that reminded me of how alone I truly was. How could light change so fast?

Then I heard a truck door slam, and I knew Ray was home.

He stumbled inside, clearly intoxicated, and he smirked when he saw me. "Big New Year's plans?" He asked in mock interest.

I didn't answer, and he threw his coat across the back of one of the kitchen chairs. "I'm headed up to change."

"Want dinner? I was thinkin' of making a casserole or something?" He made a face, but I continued, "Liz has this great recipe that uses winter squash, so it'll be fresh —"

"Honey, I wouldn't eat anything you touched if you paid me. I don't know what when on in that garden, but count me out. Anyway, I won't be long."

I didn't respond and listened to his heavy feet move upstairs to the main bathroom upstairs. After a few minutes, I could hear water running through the pipes, and I turned to walk down the hall when I saw a figure appear through the frosted glass of the front door.

I stopped, heart in my throat, and crept down the hall as the dark figure wavered on the doorstep. Was it Mama? The creeping woman?

I tiptoed closer and wrenched open the door, determined to reveal whoever was creeping about when I stepped back in surprise. It was Liz.

She stood there, shifting from foot to foot, looking embarrassed.

"Sorry to show up like this," she started, but when she opened her mouth again, she couldn't find the words.

"Come in." I motioned, and she smiled.

We sat in the kitchen as we waited for the water in the kettle to boil.

"I've missed you at the cafe," she said. "It hasn't been the same without you. Even Owen was asking about you."

I gave a sad smile.

"I've been worried about you." She paused and added, "We all have." She leaned closer and took my hand. "I know it's been hard, and I know that none of us have any idea of exactly how hard it's been, but I'm always here," she said as she squeezed my hand. "I'm not going anywhere."

Liz leaned forward and brought her face closer, gently pressing her nose to mine.

"You promise?" I asked.

She nodded, and her lips pulled me forward like a magnet.

"And you won't leave me?" I asked, our lips almost touching.

She shook her head, and I closed the distance between us, our foreheads touching.

"I love you, Cat," she whispered.

"I love you, too," I returned, but before either of us could move, the tea kettle whistled. When we drew back, Ray was standing squarely in the doorway.

We separated, and I picked up the kettle and poured the steaming water over the tea bags as Ray sauntered into the kitchen, toweling his hair as he walked.

"Well, well, well," he laughed. "My little niece." He turned around to look at us both. "I had no idea."

Liz blushed and cleared her throat but didn't respond.

"I'd always had my suspicions about Cat, don't get me wrong, but I never suspected you." He gave a cruel laugh.

"Leave her alone, Ray," I shot.

He put his hands up in defense. "I'm not judging." He looked out at the bare gardens in the backyard. "But if your mother knew, she'd be rollin' over in her grave."

"Don't talk about my mom," Liz warned.

"Testy. Testy," he called out. "I'm just bein' honest." He continued to look out the window at the backyard, pulled a cigarette from his pocket and lit it, "Oh, I saw that man downtown..."

Neither of us responded.

He blew a stream of white smoke that ran up the window and disappeared near the ceiling, "you know, that agent guy or whatever." He waved his fingers through the air, and his cigarette dropped ash to the floor. "He said the strangest thing to me. He said he'd been workin' on something with you, some art inspired by some cursed girl... a haunted girl. Isn't that somethin'?"

I let the words settle around me and looked over at Liz who turned an even deeper shade of red. "Cat, it's not like that, I —"

"That's not what that agent man said. Said you talked about a woman who died under strange circumstances and the cursed girl she left behind. Said you wanted her to be your... muse, is it?"

"No," Liz shook her head, panic filled her eyes from the bottom up, like a flooded room gulping water.

"That's not what —" She started to say, but I interrupted.

"Is true?" I whispered, and she took a step back, mouth open, searching for words that wouldn't come. "I was just your muse?"

"No." She tried to step forward, but she still wasn't able to find the words.

"I was some art project?" I asked. "This whole time."

Her mouth moved, but again no words came out. Ray chuckled. "Looks like it, sweet daughter of mine." He leaned in on the word daughter, and I cringed.

"Cat, I —" She started. "I moved back because my art wasn't working out. And then when I saw you in the cafe, I thought about your mom and everything that you'd been through, and that night I started painting, real painting about real things, you know?"

My heart started to break, slicing into a million tiny fragments.

"I'd been experimenting with blue dyes, and after I saw you, it was like something clicked. I sent my art to my agent, and it sold the next day. That's how he found me. That's why he showed up at the cafe. He wanted more."

"Your contract," I said deliberately.

She nodded. "I had to pay back the advances, and then I started to turn a profit. A profit," she gushed, and I couldn't even look at her. "Do you know how hard it had been? And then suddenly, when you come in, I felt this spark —"

"Spark," I repeated.

"Art was flowing out of me, and business picked up at the cafe." She must have seen my face because her voice softened. "But then I got to know you."

I let out a sad laugh and rolled my eyes. So that's how Josh knew me. He'd asked if I was that girl, and I thought he meant the girl with the dead mama, but that wasn't quite right. I was the girl with the dead mama who was being used by Liz.

"It's true, Cat. I got to know you, and you were so wonderful."

"Please don't," I started, but she stepped forward, and I couldn't stand it. I couldn't stand being touched by her, being pitied by her, so I stepped back.

"I mean it," she said, and I looked at her, really looked at her, and I saw the desperation in her eyes. She needed me to believe her. But why? To make more art? This whole time, she really had me fooled... I couldn't be a fool anymore.

"I think you should leave," I said, lowering my gaze. I heard her take a breath and step back. Then she did the thing that hurt the most. She turned around and left.

So, it was true. She'd been using me the whole time.

From the kitchen door, I looked down the hall and watched her walk to her bike and disappear down the mountain.

Transcript
Interview with Eddy Sparrow
12:23 a.m. April 28th, 2021
Case No. HI30823

Sure.

Did I stop by my old house?

Well, I was in the area, so I might have driven by.

It looked different, ya know? I didn't know if Penny was there or not, but Stephen had painted and redone the front garden beds. It looked horrible.

I didn't stay long. Like I said, it was more of a drive-by.

No, I didn't see him.

Let's see, I made it to the Marathon gas station that Cat must have stopped at that first night she came back to town. Maybe it was five or so. The sun was gettin kinda low.

I went inside, eager to see that snaggle-toothed woman, but a young man was there. He was pale and bored, and he took my money with a frown.

It was cold, and the town was totally different than I'd imagined. It was completely redone. The sloping houses that Cat described were replaced by gated subdivisions and manicured hedges, a new Target and Starbucks had gone up, a few micro-breweries, a Mexican restaurant, a wine bar, an ice cream shop, even an axe-throwing place.

Yeah, I know.

Everything looked new and polished, but I knew it was hiding a town with so many stories from the past — not just the Saunders' history, but hundreds of other histories all stacked on one another. I wasn't worried about all the other stories. I was worried about Cat, and I had to get to her.

I don't know what that means. I just felt like something was calling me there, like there was this clock ticking.

I mean, maybe it had to do with the fact

that I'd gone through so much and time seemed extra short after Mom passed away, but I just had this feeling that I had to get there.

And that's not the crazy part. I took this manuscript with me. It sat on the front seat, and it was like it was whispering

, the entire time.

Well, I made it to Blood Mountain right at sundown. I followed the driveway all the way to the top, and when I got out, a gust of wind blew through the car and sent pages flying so that this page was on top.

I read it — the part about it bein' just Cat and Ray in the house — and I had this bad feeling.

I didn't know what I could do. I mean, Cat's story happened years before, and the house had since been torn down. I grabbed the manuscript, my bag, and my phone and had to step over some of the brick from the foundation but stopped short.

Roses.

They were still there.

I know. I picked through the rows. They were overgrown and tangled in places, bald in others, and I tried to make out a path, but the light was growing dim, and in all my wildest dreams, I never thought about the house as real, but there it was, right in front of me.

What happened next? Well, I had that feeling of being watched again like I had at home. Tryna get away, I stepped into the maze, desperate to find any clue to what happened to Cat and where she might have gone.

The dark crept in faster than I expected — you know how it is on the mountain —

Yeah, spooky, especially at night, and I had to feel my way through the maze. Even with my flashlight, it was hard to see.

I tried to orient myself, but I didn't see anything that I could recognize. Instead, I

looked down at Cat's manuscript again. I
thought maybe she'd give me a clue about what
to do next.

You'll see. Let me top off your cup again,
and I'll keep reading.

I went into the kitchen and picked up my tea, but it was still too hot to drink. "What'd you have to go and do that for, Ray?"

He shrugged and moved into the formal dining room, opening the China cabinet and thumbing through the plates. "Anything in here worth money?" He asked, and my skin crawled.

"It's not yours, Ray," I answered. "And you don't have to be such an asshole."

"I just thought you should know," he shrugged. "Anyway, this stuff is just sittin' in here rottin' so we might as well —"

The kitchen phone rang, interrupting him. I turned and picked it up with a grunt. "Hello?"

"Cat?" The voice sang.

"Hey, Marianne," I returned, and Ray made a noise from the dining room.

"Well, I was just calling to check on you. I haven't seen you down at the cafe this week, and I wanted to make sure you were okay."

She paused.

"I'm fine, Marianne. I was just... under the weather."

As soon as I said it, I knew it was a mistake. I heard her sharp intake of breath, her worry wormed its way through the phone.

"Under the weather?" She repeated, and I realized that that's what Mama used to call it when she got a case of the Octobers. Under the weather didn't mean the same thing it did with other people. Under the weather meant depression. Under the weather meant something serious. Under the weather meant trouble.

"No, nothing like that," I tried to explain. "It was a little cold, that's all. I'm feeling much better, though."

"Oh," she said, but I still heard the worry in her voice. "You know, if you need anything, I'm always here. I could send over some soup or somethin', if you need."

"Marianne, I'm fine." I paused, pictured the concern on her face, and smiled. "Thanks for calling, though. It means a lot."

"Of course," she sang in her normal voice.

"As you always say, we're like family, and family's the most important thing there is."

I felt my words travel through the receiver, across town on black static-filled wires, and to her ear pressed to the phone. She paused, and I could tell she was trying to figure out how much I knew before I added, "I know it would have meant a lot to Mama, too."

"Yes," her voice wavered slightly, and I could tell that she missed Mama almost as much as I did. "I sure hope so."

"Hey, I'm leaving for Brown in a few days, and I'd like to see you before I leave."

"That sounds great," she said. "And remember, I'm always here if you need me. You sure you don't need some soup because I could —"

"I'm okay, Marianne," I laughed.

"All right, just checkin'. I'll see you soon for that coffee."

I hung up the phone and smiled. It would be nice to catch up with her, to tell her everything I knew, and Liz would be there the whole time if I needed anything. I knew she would.

Ray sauntered into the room, not giving up on the stump of his cigarette. "That Marianne's dumber'n a bag a rocks," he said out of the corner of his mouth.

"She's not so dumb," I said, finally able to pick up my tea and take a sip. "She's the one who told me about the lawyer."

"What lawyer?"

"That estate lawyer."

"Sharon's brother?" He asked, leaning in to inspect the silver.

"No. My lawyer."

"Your —" He chuckled and stepped back, enjoying a laugh.

"It turns out that you can't exactly have a girlfriend — much less a child — if you're in a common law marriage. Funny, isn't it?"

Ray stopped and peered into the kitchen, his eyes searched, and I saw a hint of desperation behind them.

"Whadduyamean?" He asked in one word.

"It's just that common law marriages are almost exactly like traditional marriages, and judges look down on infidelity, especially when the cheating party is making a claim to assets."

"You wouldn't," he started, but stopped short, and I couldn't help the smile that hinted at the corners of my mouth.

"You little bitch," he snarled and took a step toward me. Everything seemed to move in slow motion in his cigarette smoke.

His hands reached toward me as he lurched into the room, and I sidestepped him and stretched myself towards the door. The knob turned easily; thank goodness Ray had replaced the handle not more than a month ago. I wrenched the door open, sending a breath of cold air into the room, and I took the back steps two at a time, feeling Ray's fingers graze the back of my sweater as I reached the grass.

I heard Ray call out and snuck a glance behind me to see that he had missed the top step and fallen headfirst onto a patch of bald dirt in the grass, smearing brown on his right cheek. He winced and shot a glare at me with his left eye.

"You aren't taking this house, Cat. It's mine!" He bellowed and tried to scramble to his feet but winced when he tried to put weight on his right ankle.

I turned and ran. I followed the jagged skeleton of rose stems snaking through one another. Above me, the disappearing light that had turned the sky into a rich chocolate, and I was thankful for the coming darkness, for the coming night that could conceal things; hide them from greedy hands.

I made another turn and tried to put distance between myself and Ray. I could hear his labored breath a few rows over and turned right to make my way to the other side of the maze. As long as the rose's thorns protected me, I could hide. I could stay safe.

"I can hear you, Cat." Ray sang in a cruel voice. "You can't hide forever."

I turned right again and was met by a tangle of roses with a narrow sliver just big enough to squeeze through. I steadied myself and pushed through the thick thorns. I could feel the ends break off under my skin as I slid through the small space and emerged on the other side.

I made a few more turns but was met by another dead end. Turning around, I found another solid wall of stinging roses, and I realized that I was lost.

Blindly, I put my arms out in front of me and walked with one hand catching at thorns to my right.

"Please," I breathed. "Please, help me."

I heard the wind to my right and didn't hesitate. I moved as silently as I could and followed the noises further into the maze. I followed the creeping footsteps for a few more turns and then burst into the center of the maze.

I'd made it.

I tried to slow my breath as I looked for someplace to hide. I had been so eager to make it to the center — what I thought of as safety — only to discover that there was nowhere to hide.

"Here, Kitty-Kitty," Ray sang, and my chest tightened in panic.

I stepped over the half-fallen bench and gave a wide berth to where I knew the sunken well must be. "Where are you hiding, Kitty Cat," Ray continued.

With nowhere else to go, I backed into the far corner of the courtyard and held my breath.

Ray didn't need to announce himself. I knew he was there, just inside the courtyard, trying to be as quiet as I was. I could feel him there in the dark.

"Aw, come on out, Cat. I saw your light on, silly girl," he sang in a tight, rough whisper that sounded like sandpaper. "Come, now. Your daddy's not gonna hurt you. He would never," I moved to my left, but that was just what he was waiting for: for me to move and give away my position.

He lunged at me, grabbing me by the shoulders, and I fell to the ground. He followed me downward and sat on top of me, pinning me against the dirt. Then, his hands found my throat.

"No," I struggled, gasping as his fingers tightened. "I —" but I couldn't speak, couldn't breathe. He squeezed with all his might, and I heard the choking sound come from my mouth; the cotton sounds of my heartbeat in my ears.

I scratched at his hands, desperate to get them off, but he squeezed even tighter. My hands dropped to my sides, and I searched the ground for something, anything, to defend myself.

The fingers of my right hand hit something hard and flat. I grabbed at the stone, but it wouldn't budge. It was a part of the well. My fingers flew over the other stones, but they too were cemented into place by decades of wear. Spots shown in the dark. Great big fireworks of light danced in my eyes, and I knew it wouldn't be long. I was running out of air.

My hands found his again, still wrapped around my throat, and they followed his arms to his face, his nose, the tip of his chin, but that's all I could reach. I felt my hands go numb and closed my eyes to try to block out the pain when I heard a loud crack, and his fingers relaxed against my throat.

The sparkling lights faded, and I gasped for breath, drinking it in and sitting up, still focused on escape when I saw Ray on the ground.

I scrambled up to stand and gasped for breath. I coughed, trying to get my breath to return to normal. The moon had risen over the trees, and I could see Ray in the dim light already moving, a hand to his head as he gripped a tar-like wet spot. He brought his hand down, wincing at the tacky liquid on his fingers, and looked up at me with fiery hate. His lips curled, and when he tried to get to his feet, I exploded.

I raced forward, plowed into him and hit him squarely in the side. He stumbled over the uneven ground and looked back at the black hole of the well. His arms flailed as he tried to regain his balance when I reached out again and pushed him.

I pushed him as hard as I could. I pushed him for hitting Mama. I pushed him for making me feel so uncomfortable for so long, for being afraid to be in my own body and have my own voice, for being terrified to live in my own house. His eyes grew wide, haloed in the moonlight, and his mouth formed a perfect O, silent with an intake of breath when the well swallowed him whole.

Transcript
Interview with Eddy Sparrow
12:40 a.m. April 28th, 2021
Case No. HI30823

Yes, I made it.

The both of us did.

That's what I told myself.

We'd made it to the center of the maze.

My hand found a large opening, and I knew it had to be the center of the maze, so I called out to Cat. I know, it's stupid and doesn't make any sense, but she heard me somehow, didn't she?

The center of the maze was just as Cat had described — a small courtyard with statues and a falling down bench. Vines and winter weeds ran wild, and I could almost feel Cat there.

I'm not makin' it up. I could feel her, like her spirit. She felt scared. I just wanted to protect her.

That's when I remembered the well.

I shined my light at the center of the courtyard, and there it was — the well.

It looked like this huge mouth that drank in the darkness.

I don't know how to describe it. It was just creepy.

Well, I picked my way toward it, careful to not get too close so I wouldn't lose my footing. It made a gasping sound as the wind blew across its top, and it belched this dank smell from its belly. Thinking about it still gives me the shivers.

And I swear to God I'm not making this up. I heard something else.

Something from deep inside the well. It sounded like a whisper, so I leaned in and held my breath.

Here, Kitty-Kitty, it hissed, and I jumped back. Cat's manuscript was still in my hands, and I looked from it to the well.

It couldn't be. It was a story — a novel or memoir or whatever you'd call it — but it

290

wasn't real. It couldn't be. Again, if it was real, it had happened years before.

At this point, the whispers got louder. I shone my phone's flashlight at the well, and you'll never believe it.

I heard this scraping sound.

Yeah, first the whispers and then the scraping sounds. I thought I was losin' my mind.

Then, I saw movement.

Sorry if this is scarin' ya, Bob, but you shoulda been me.

What looked like fat worms emerged from the well, wriggling in the air before curling around the lip. They inched forward and merged into two white masses.

Hands.

I lurched backward and fell on my butt just as Ray's head lunged out of the well. His arms, now reaching out of the well, pulled his body from the hole, and it felt like I was moving in slow motion. Like a dream where I was under water.

He kicked one leg over the side of the well and pulled himself the rest of the way up. In the dim light, I could see his face, haggard and gray, skin hanging like melted wax, eyes bulging and running with the remnants of the acrid well water below.

I tried to scramble to get up, but it was too late. His hands pulled me toward him and his fingers found their way to my throat, and I tried to choke out a scream, only no sound came out, and my locket musta come off because I was tryna get out from under him. I was trapped and scared and all alone.

With Ray's hands around my throat, I searched the ground for a weapon. My hands found the edge of the well but nothing I could use to defend myself. Instead, I found my bag. Rummaging through it, my hand closed around the metal stick Stephen had gotten me months back. For protection, he'd said, and if I'd ever needed protection in my life, it was at that moment.

I flicked out the metal stick, extending it to full reach, and swung with all my might until I heard a sickening smack.

I felt Ray's fingers relax and him slump over me. I pushed him off of me and scrambled to my feet, shinin' my flashlight on him before I stood up and felt my head swim. I clutched at the empty air around me, desperate to grab onto reality before my world disappeared. The last thing I saw before everything went black was Ray's eyes, menacing and dangerous.

I sank to the ground, listening for noises of Ray at the bottom of the well, but all was silent. I let my tears go and hugged myself, still shaking and afraid that he might come back.

And then I felt a hand on my shoulder. I jumped but stopped short.

"Mama?" I asked, squinting in the dim light.

My heart beat in my chest, I tried to slow my breathing, slow my thinking. I had dreamed about this moment for two years. I had dreamed about what I would do, what I would say if I were ever to see her again. I'd run to her. I'd wrap my arms around her. I'd tell her that I missed her and that I was sorry, that I was so, so sorry for what I had done to her. For all the things I'd done that had made that light go out behind her eyes because I'd never do anything to hurt her. Never.

"Mama," I burst, kneeling beside her and throwing my arms around her.

"Baby," she crooned, stroking my hair. "I'm here, baby." She smelled just the way I remembered.

"Mama, I'm so sorry," I said, looking into her eyes. "Please, Mama, I never meant to-"

"Shhh, baby," she hushed me. "All that is past now."

Mama put her arms around me. She pulled me close, and I felt myself relax in her arms. I put my head to her chest and listened for her heartbeat, steady and true.

"Mama, I messed it up. I messed it all up," I sobbed.

"Hush, baby. It doesn't matter anymore," Mama called, again stroking my hair. "You're here now, and that's all past. Just a dream."

I felt hot tears pour down my cheeks.

"Just a dream," Mama sang. "You were always so bright," she continued. "The smartest one in your classes. I still remember the letter you brought home. A full scholarship to college. I was so happy, so proud of you, baby girl. But that year was hard."

I nodded and felt her hand in my hair, stroking my head like she used to do when I was little. "Ray was leaving me. He'd moved on and was having a baby. My mother left me —"

"She had cancer," I started, but Mama continued.

"I had no one for so long. Except for you. I always had you." She smiled down at me, "But when you brought home that letter, I knew that you would end up leaving me, too."

"But Mama, I wouldn't —"

"It's okay, baby. I know. That's the way it is, being a parent. You raise your children to be the best they can be, and then you send them out into the world, into that great, big world where there are monsters, awful monsters that will lie to you, hurt you, even kill you. And I couldn't let that happen."

I wiped my tears and pulled back, looking at her.

"I knew that if you left me, too, I couldn't survive. And I couldn't let the world destroy you, not my baby."

"Mama?" I said, but she kept going.

"So, I turned to my garden, to my herbs. I spent months caring for my plants, tilling the soil, planting the seeds, watering the ground, and fertilizing the roots until they grew. Leaves burst forth, berries grew plump and weighed down each branch until it was time for harvest. And the year you planned to leave, harvest came early."

"I don't–" I started, but Mama interrupted me.

"It was our last night together. Remember that? I made dinner —"

"The five-course meal."

"Exactly," she nodded. "A dinner fit for a princess. We ate together, just the two of us, a big celebration meant for a big night. We even had seconds," she giggled softly, but her laughter was cut short. "And do you remember the tea?"

I nodded, wordlessly.

"It was such a lovely tea. Dark and slightly bitter. Perfect for an after-dinner cup out in the garden."

She paused and moved my hair out of my face so that she could look at me.

"But you didn't drink it, did you? Not like you were supposed to.

I did, but you didn't."

"I was scared," I admitted. "I poured it out when you weren't —"

"You don't have to explain, baby. You were always so smart," she patted my hand. "And I knew you might do just that."

As Mama continued, I wanted to pull away. I wanted to plug my ears and make it all stop, but I couldn't separate myself from her, not after I had waited so long to see her again.

"Do you know what was in that tea?"

"Belladonna Atropa," I said, lowering my gaze. How long had I known? Since before the dinner. Well before when the cup was in my hands.

"That's right, baby. Legend has it that Atropa holds your fate in her hands, and once you ingest the plant, you have taken your fate and irrevocably ended it. Your thread has been cut."

"You mean death?"

"If you ingest enough." Mama must have seen the horror creep into my face because she paused. "I told you. I knew you'd suspect the tea."

"I didn't like it," I admitted. "And then you..." my voice trailed off. Memories floated to the surface of the dinner, of the tea, of what came after in the garden. "You didn't feel well. You were out of breath. You said you were dizzy —"

"The teacups."

"The teacups," I repeated. "You said you were dizzy, and then you went pale." I felt fresh tears sting my eyes. "You said you could see her."

"The woman. The creeping woman," Mama breathed, smiling sweetly at the thought of her face. "She had one green eye and one blue, just like me. And we were all so happy together."

"No," I shook my head. "No, Mama. We weren't happy, and we weren't all together. We were alone in the garden, with me holding your hand, watching you slowly die."

"Oh, baby. I never meant for that to happen. I thought you would drink the tea and —"

"And what — join you? Die, too? There were plenty of other options, Mama." I felt sobs creep into my chest. Tears spilled down my face.

I shivered, and I could see the warmth from my breath mixing with the cold outside in wisps of white. "I just didn't see a way," Mama said slowly, measuring her words like she measured her tea that night. "I knew that you'd hate the tea anyway. I told you I know my girl."

Mama hugged me close and kissed my forehead, then she exhaled and whispered into the part in my hair. "That's why I put it in the soup, too."

"What?" I asked, sitting up and pushing away from her.

"The soup, baby. I had to be sure."

"No," I said, not wanting to hear her. "No."

"Yes, baby. I had to be sure. I couldn't let you get hurt."

"Get hurt?" I asked, finally seeing Mama as she was: scared, desperate, selfish, and completely mad. "I held you in my arms. I watched you gasp for breath as you seized in my lap. And it wasn't until after you stopped breathing that I felt funny. I thought I had just drunk some on accident."

I remembered how the earth tilted, laying back in the dirt, the smell of soil thick in my nose, looking up at the stars, and it was like VanGogh. It was so beautiful, swirling and spinning.

"I spent months in that hospital. I missed school. I had to have surgery. They had to remove a piece of my intestines because of the poison. Do you know how cold I was? How long it took me to crawl out of the maze to get to the phone?" I asked, not meeting her gaze. The thought of looking at her at that moment was too much. As much as I missed her, I was finally able to see her for what she was: a murderer.

Mama shook her head. "I'm sorry. Don't be angry, baby. I tried to fix it," Mama said. "Things always have a way of working out. That's why you ended up in the hospital and not with me. You were supposed to be with me, but it didn't quite work out that way."

"Mama, I had no one after you died," I confessed. "I spent the rest of the year in therapy and in rehab. Aunt Beatrix was too busy with Edith and didn't have time to take me, and Ray was the only one to step forward."

"Oh, baby. Don't cry," she crooned. "Shhh. Things are all messed up. It's teacups again."

"It's always teacups," I whimpered. "There's no stopping. No getting off, no catching your breath, no laughing once the world comes into focus, no asking to ride one more time."

"But you're wrong," Mama said evenly. "I am so proud of you," Her eyes shone with pride. "My beautiful girl. The writer. And what beautiful stories you wrote, too."

"You read them?" I asked, somehow still hoping that I had made her proud.

"You have such a way of telling stories, of writing down these incredible tales. How heartache must run through your veins and out your fingers. The way you wrote my words was so beautiful. It was like you could read my mind."

I shook my head, hot tears fell down my cheeks. "Sometimes I don't know what to do with it all." I licked my lips and felt Mama's warm hand on mine.

"All of what?" She whispered.

"All of it. The sadness. The hurt. The beauty of it all." I wiped my eyes with the back of my hand. "That's why I started writing this story. Those things were just so heavy. It was impossible to carry around all by myself, my real father, Ray's abuse, your death, so I took them and wrote them down. I edited them and changed the words around, shaping them into something whole. And then I printed them out onto a page, closed the book, and put it on a shelf. And if someone else read my words, then it meant that I wasn't alone."

"It's beautiful, baby. Just like you," Mama smiled sadly, and I was reminded of her face suspended in water all those years ago, a mermaid with a pearl of air on her cheek, how sad, how still, how lonely.

"And sometimes, yes, it gets to be too much, and I just want it all to stop. The teacups —"

"You can make it stop," Mama squeezed my hand, her face suddenly serious. "You don't have to keep riding the teacups. You can get off any time you want."

"What? Like you did?" I scoffed.

"Like so many people do," she responded.

"Are you —"

"I'm just giving you options. People get off all the time. No questions asked."

"But —"

"Quiet now, baby," Mama hummed and put her hands out to me.

Silhouetted in the moonlight, she sat with a steaming cup of tea.

"Mama, what —"

"Shhh, baby. Come here," Mama held out her arms, and I settled my head in her lap. She gently stroked my hair and hummed softly as I looked up at the stars. "What do you say," I could hear the smile on her lips. "What do you say I tell you a story?"

"Any story?" I asked.

"Any one you want."

I heard my heart thunder in my ears, my chest began to tighten. I licked my lips and said, "Tell me the one you told me that night. That last night. The one about the princess. The princess who finally escaped the evil prince."

"Okay," Mama squeezed my shoulder and smiled. "So, the princess was free of the prince, but she was never able to escape her tower. Instead, she spent her days staring down at the town below, at the normal lives beneath her while she carried the prince's teeth in her pocket. But in her haste to get away and start anew, the princess didn't notice her shadow.

"It trailed after her as she fled during the day and grew taller than the trees at night. It bled into her dreams and seeped into her pores in the murkiness of midnight. The shadow refused to eat. It refused to bend or fold or shrink.

"The woman brewed her sweet tea with fresh honey and lavender, but still, the shadow would not drink. The nightmares whispered in her ear while she tried to dream, and the next time she made her tea, instead of offering the tea to her shadow, she drank the tea herself. It was the first time the woman was able to sleep peacefully all night without the shadow's constant whispers.

"When the woman woke up, she noticed that the shadow was much smaller. It sat sulking in the corner but still followed her at a distance. And so, the woman brewed her tea and drank it every night, and the shadow shrank even more. She brewed and drank, night after night, until the shadow shrank so much that it finally disappeared."

Mama licked her lips. "But so did the woman," she said, her voice faltering. "After a while, she would look down at her hands and realize that she didn't have any. She would try to speak, but she'd only hear the wind. Until one day she forgot who she was. She even forgot her own name. After many years, brave men from the town were able to breach the tower. They crept inside and were astonished. After all, they had heard tales of the beautiful princess locked in her tower. But all that was left was the woman's tattered dress and her pocket full of teeth."

I exhaled and watched the slow melting of stars in the sky. "Mama?" I asked softly, not sure if she could hear me.

"Yes, baby?" She answered.

I tried to turn my head to look at her, but all I found was darkness and dirt. I thought about the princess and her dark monster that would never leave her side, the prince who was supposed to rescue her but didn't, his teeth that knew how to cut, to eat. How sharp his teeth must have been before they found their place in her pocket, only for the monster to return, hungry and half-starved, swallowing her, leaving nothing. My stomach made a noise that sounded like a wounded animal, that sounded like the princess's monster, and it was hard to focus on anything around me except for the cool, dark earth.

"Is that what's going to happen to me?" The question was out before I even had a chance to think about it. "Am I just going to disappear?"

"Oh, baby," Mama's voice sounded like the wind. "No. You won't disappear."

"Then what will happen to me?" My heart raced, and my mouth felt like cotton.

"You'll become what you were always meant to be." I could hear her smile through the cold night. "You'll become a star."

"Promise?" I asked.

"Promise," she responded. Behind her eyes, I saw the darkness. I saw the monster, the one that she had been fighting her entire life, the one I had been fighting, too. The one who held me every night when Mama was busy with Ray. The one who held my hand when I was in the hospital, my heartbeat mixing with the beeping of machines. The one who hid anyway until life's teeth emerged. Teeth were the price for love.

Deep down, I knew the monster never really left in the first place. It just hid, hid in the last place I'd ever look. Inside. In that deep, dark place beneath my lungs where emptiness and despair sat and chewed and waited until a night like this with stars so big and beautiful and important hung over me in the velvet above that could swallow me whole.

Mama stroked my hair. "I'm so proud of you," she sang softly. "And look, I've made you another lovely drink."

Before I knew what I was doing, my hands were reaching forward. Accepting the warm mug into my ice-cold hands, and I felt my scalp prickle with indecision.

I sighed and relaxed into the earth, feeling the soil cradle me. I thought back to all the terrible Liz using me. My rage. My inescapable grief. My shame.

And then I thought about all of the wonderful things. Playing games with Mama. Working in her garden. Going to school. Falling in love. Writing down my stories. I smiled and looked to the east. Purple clouds colored the horizon. Even on this night. The longest night of the year. The night would not win. Not quite.

I took another breath before the sun began to rise.

It was then that I felt the monster turn, lick its lips, and bite, continuing to eat, to consume me from the inside. Chewing a hole inside myself, a hole so deep that it felt impossible to escape. From the bottom, all I could see was a narrow circle highlighting the distance between me and the rest of the world. And the burden wasn't on me, it's on the hole, on the pocket that became a pit that seemed inescapable. In the quiet and the dark. And the truth is, some people can't escape it while others can.

I heard it again, the one I've called the woman in the walls, only it wasn't a ghost from the past. But she, held me like the soil, the floor, the sofa, the chair beneath her. I've heard her whisper, turn the pages and murmur into the words, into the walls of this story as I wrote ever word until the book closed, I'd hold our story in my heart forever, just as she held me. And maybe I'd come and hold her hand in the dark, give her a shovel and help her dig herself out of the monster's pocket, the monster's pit. I'd be there with her every step of the way. Because she was not alone. She was me. I was her. And I love her. Come and find me.

Transcript
Interview with Eddy Sparrow
12:52 a.m. April 28th, 2021
Case No. HI30823

Yeah, I know.

Look, I know this is all hard to believe, but how else can you explain…

Yes, that's what I'm tellin' ya.

I woke up in the maze just as the sun was coming up. Ray wasn't there, and nothing seemed out of place, so I left.

All I know is that I have been loved by someone and have truly loved them in return. I've had my heart broken and lost someone, like   lost them.

And I sat here with this book in my hands, in my heart for hours, days, weeks, month in hopes that we wouldn't be forgotten: me, Cat, our mamas, Olivia, Helen, Nellie, and now you're a part of the story, whether you like it or not.

We're all a part of something bigger that might not be remembered forever but will never truly be forgotten. It's the cycle: the tragedy and the comedy, the love and the loss, the passage of time, the spinning of the teacups, and the constant reminder of the time we have left.

Wait, he's not asleep is he?

I knew my story was boring, but I didn't know it'd spur unconsciousness.

I'm just joking.

There was no sign of Cat. I've looked for her since. She never started school at Brown that spring, and I found another funny thing. According to the owner of the general store, the cafe never reopened on the new year, and shortly after, the cafe was shuttered. Liz had disappeared, too.

Sometimes, I wish I could be as bold as Cat and say that I exacted revenge on Stephen, that I came up with a
kind of plot where I designed a genius and

untraceable act of revenge, but the truth is, I'm not like that.

And this is real life where people get hurt and things are messy. Instead, I've been searching for traces of Cat and Liz throughout the South.

I guess I wanna see that they're safe and happy, but everything leads nowhere.

Until late last week.

I read a news story about an artist in Northern Alabama. She lived in a small house tucked away in the mountains. In the article's interview, she said that she was inspired by dreams she had had as a child. She said they were often scary, but a friend of hers had pushed her to embrace those fears, and she eventually put those into her art.

I know, right?

So, I thought about Cat's words.

Come find me.

And I decided to follow the lead from the news story and visit the artist. I visited the town's story first, a closet-sized buildin' that looked more like a roadside stand tucked away in a deep valley. The owner gave me directions to her house on a paper napkin that I had tucked away in the glovebox.

I followed it, and as I pulled into the driveway, I saw a woman out front. A small woman with red hair about ten years older than me.

I asked for Liz initially, and the woman squinted her eyes at me and told me that no one lived there by that name. I asked for the artist instead, and in turn, she asked me if I was from the papers.

When I said I was from UAB — a small lie really, I'd stopped teachin' there only the year before — she told me that Ginny wasn't interested in selling her art.

I nodded and asked for her name, and do you know what she told me?

Maggie.

As in, Maggie the Cat from
  . It had to be Cat. My cousin Cat with her
red hair and her skepticism. She was just as
I had imagined, fiery hair, ruddy cheeks,
older, but just as spunky. I told her I would
wait for Ginny to come home, and Maggie invited
me inside.

Ginny arrived as the sun sank below the
treetops, and Maggie made dinner. We sat
outside and talked about art and cooking and
herbs and southern tales. Maggie was an
amazing storyteller.

She told me about how they used to have these
grand adventures, the both of 'em. She said
that Ginny even saved her once. She was lost,
and Ginny had come and picked her up and saved
her. Was that what happened in the maze? Had
Ginny shown up just in time?

I sat with my questions, unable to do
anything but listen to them recount their
travels.

When the conversation quieted, Maggie asked
me if I'd like to hear a story. A story about
a princess. A princess and a monster. Ginny
rolled her eyes and said,

And here's what Cat — or Maggie — said:

—

—

—

Ginny went to bed first, and after she left, Maggie talked about how she wouldn't have survived without her — said that in her darkest moment she had shown back up even though they'd been arguing at the time. She said Ginny saved her life. Isn't that something?

Then, Maggie said she was tired and sore from pruning earlier that day. I asked what she was pruning, and she said it was roses.

Yep, she was startin' another maze, this time, without the haunted well.

Before I left, though, she turned to me and said that she loved my eyes. She said that her own mother had two different colored eyes too.

That's when I said it's genetic. I said I musta got it from my aunt.

Do I know for sure that this was Cat? No.

But stranger stories have been told, after all.

Could it have been my imagination? Certainly.

Maggie never woulda confirmed it. And for all you know, I could be making this up. I could be inventing a happy ending just to make sure they didn't suffer, that Cat survived and found happiness.

But we do that all the time, don't we? We hold stories in our hands, and we have hope, even when we feel that all is lost. We long for the happy ending where everything is okay because it gives us hope that all could be okay with us as well, that someone might hold our stories in their hands and hope that everything will turn out okay for us too.

I'd like to think we all deserve a happy ending, and if it doesn't turn out that way, then maybe this one will do.

Look, it's been over a month since I last touched this manuscript, and I'm still not sure what happened. What was Cat's experience and what was mine, but I do know that it changed me forever.

I'm the one who called the town mayor and had the well dredged, ya know.

Yep. And I'm guessing they found the body — Ray's body — at the bottom.

Wait, what do you mean?

That can't be right. You're saying it wasn't Ray's body?

Stephen's?

But that's impossible. He wasn't there that night.

You're sure?

I still don't understand. You don't think I had anything to do with —

No, it was Ray on that mountain, not Stephen.

And you think that I —

Sure, I understand my rights, but I didn't —

Look, I'm no danger. I've sat with you and talked to you all night. I'm not a dangerous person. You should know that by now —

Oh, let me help you. You stood up too fast, probably.

You feelin' okay?

Here, sit down. I've got you. Just take a

seat in this chair.
There. You're all right, now. Just lay back
for a second, Bob.
Sure. Just take your time.
Want some more tea?
It's really no problem. Now, how do ya turn
this thing off? Oh, there it is. You sure you
don't want another cup of tea? It's a family
recipe, ya know.

ACKNOWLEDGMENTS

To be honest, this book came out of my own Case of the Octobers. I was stressed out and unhappy and felt like I was at a crossroads in my life but had no idea how to proceed or which direction to go. And then Cat showed up. Just like that. It was like she sat down and took my hand and told me that I didn't have to feel so alone and that I didn't have to carry it all by myself. I didn't know who she was or where she came from, but I got to work that next month getting to know her and writing out her story in an almost fever state.

When the manuscript made its way to Lisa Kastner, she left a single comment: Who is Cat writing to? I wrote Cat's story in order to get to know her and for people to know her story. She'd been there for me, and I was just returning the favor, but Lisa was right — there was someone else hiding in that manuscript, creeping around just beneath the surface. And then, one day, there she was: Eddy. Icy Eddy who was smart and charming and so slippery that I'm still not sure she let me see all of her.

But stories are like that, aren't they? They're messy and tangled and frustrating and liberating in ways that keep us coming back for more. They're nourishing and sometimes poisonous. They bring us together and divide us. And they can refuse to let us go, haunting us long after the book is finished.

All that being said, I would like to express my deepest gratitude to everyone who played a role in bringing this book to life. This novel really would not have been the same without Lisa Kaster's prodding questions that made me think and her encouragement to embrace all the weird and strange things that came out of these questions.

To my faithful beta-readers Maranda Bell and Dianna Minor, all my friends, mentors, and well-wishers who have stood by my side on this incredible journey, thank you for your encouragement, inspiration, and guidance.

I'd like to thank my family. Thank you to Cindy Milam and

Ellen Jones for being my dedicated beta readers and cheerleaders on all my new projects. Thank you to Alice Hardy and Fred Hardy Sr. for helping with the kids and managing hectic schedules while I was writing. And thank you to Adrienne and Ezra for showing me how to look at things with fresh eyes and allowing me to play. I am eternally grateful for your unwavering belief in me. Your constant encouragement, understanding, and sacrifices have sustained me throughout this journey. You have been my pillars of strength, and I couldn't have asked for a more loving and supportive family.

Last but not least, to my husband, Fred, your boundless love and encouragement in my dreams have been the driving force behind my accomplishments. You are my biggest cheerleader and always push me to follow my dreams. Your sacrifices and endless patience during late nights and weekends spent writing have not gone unnoticed, and I am forever grateful for your support.

This book is the culmination of the collective efforts of these remarkable individuals and so many others. I am deeply appreciative of each one of you for being a part of my life and for helping me turn my dreams into reality.

With heartfelt gratitude,

- Aimee Hardy

ABOUT RUNNING WILD PRESS

Running Wild Press publishes stories that cross genres with great stories and writing. RIZE publishes great genre stories written by people of color and by authors who identify with other marginalized groups. Our team consists of:

Lisa Diane Kastner, Founder and Executive Editor
Cody Sisco, Acquisitions Editor, RIZE
Benjamin White, Acquisition Editor, Running Wild
Peter A. Wright, Acquisition Editor, Running Wild
Resa Alboher, Editor
Angela Andrews, Editor
Sandra Bush, Editor
Ashley Crantas, Editor
Rebecca Dimyan, Editor
Abigail Efird, Editor
Aimee Hardy, Editor
Henry L. Herz, Editor
Cecilia Kennedy, Editor
Barbara Lockwood, Editor
Scott Schultz, Editor

Evangeline Estropia, Product Manager
Kimberly Ligutan, Product Manager
Lara Macaione, Marketing Director
Joelle Mitchell, Licensing and Strategy Lead
Pulp Art Studios, Cover Design
Standout Books, Interior Design
Polgarus Studios, Interior Design

Learn more about us and our stories at www.runningwildpress.com

Loved this story and want more? Follow us at www.runningwildpress.com, www.facebook/runningwildpress, on Twitter @lisadkastner @RunWildBooks